CROSSING INTO DARKNESS

Howard Giordano

International Standard Book Number 13: 978-1-60452-165-8
International Standard Book Number 10: 1-60452-165-1
Library of Congress Control Number: 2020939190

BluewaterPress LLC
2922 Bella Flore Ter
New Smyrna Beach FL 32168

This book may be purchased online at -
https://www.bluewaterpress.com/crossing-into-darkness

Also by Howard Giordano

The Second Target

Tracking Terror

Chapter One

Father Don José spent several moments replaying the bad dream that disturbed his restless sleep the previous night. A bad dream, or was it an evil omen? The nagging ache of foreboding refused to disappear.

Once he passed the *Ciudad Juárez* border checkpoint, Don José joined the long line of slow-moving vehicles crossing the Bridge of the Americas to the US side. The priest gazed through the Ford Expedition's windshield and saw the round moon hanging in the clear black sky. It appeared like a white balloon whose string had slipped a child's grasp. His eyes traveled over one shoulder to the SUV's cargo area, to the shadowed forms hidden under the tarp. His mind, a jumble of discordant thoughts, taunted him with those flashing, restless images bullying his priesthood life these many dark days. He couldn't do this anymore, he decided.

Don José slowed the Expedition and stopped at a US vehicle inspection booth. An American border guard familiar with him called out. *"Hola, padre. Adónde vas esta noche?"*

"Diego, *mi hijo*. I'm picking up the bishop. He needed to cut short his meeting in El Paso. A touch of the stomach flu, he claimed, but maybe too much wine at dinner with the Cardinal."

Diego tossed him a friendly chuckle. The guard flashed a green light, raised his arm, and waved Don José through.

With a sigh of relief, Don José relaxed and pulled away. Monthly crossings on church business with the bishop over the past two years made him a familiar face to many US border guards. They recognized the priest as the assigned driver to *Ciudad Juarez's* wheelchair-bound bishop. On three other crossings during this period while the bishop was absent, he'd smuggled an illegal hidden under a cover in the cargo area.

These unlawful trips stretched his nerves. He anguished over the off-chance of arriving at a checkpoint booth where the guard did not know him. Were he not recognized, he'd pray to God his priest's attire and passport would allay any suspicion, and the guard would wave him through without incident. At this point in his life, Don José doubted any of his prayers touched God.

Long before Don José reached sixty-two, the priest had questioned his faith in the Lord. After the diocese passed over him several times for a parish assignment of his own, and after the diocese relegated him to the position of chauffeur for the invalid bishop, his bitterness toward the Catholic Church intensified.

The indignation Don José suffered made him a willing participant in a scheme to transport desperate illegals across the border. That, and the sizable cash payment he received for each delivery. Tonight, the guilt that usually bothered him was redeemed. The two teenage girls, hidden under a tarpaulin in the back of his SUV, were on their way to well-paying employment in Florida where they would send money home to help support their parents. That's what he believed—that's what the teens believed—so what harm could come of it?

Keeping to the speed limit, Don José drove in the slow lane. The dashboard clock told him he had twenty-five minutes to get to the transfer spot. It was important not to arrive too early. Ever vigilant for vehicles passing on his left, the priest was conscious the US border agents maintained a presence on this stretch of highway. *Ciudad Juarez,* a city with one of the highest numbers of drug-related homicides in the northern state of *Chihuahua,* kept border agents busy and on alert around the clock. He couldn't afford to attract their attention.

After several miles, Don José switched to a lightly used road and traveled east until he pulled the SUV to the curb beneath an overpass of Interstate 10 and shut down the engine to await the van's arrival. His gaze traveled to the rearview mirror, into the darkness of his future, then at his watch. While early by two minutes, he'd been warned this isolated area represented a danger for any unsuspecting vehicle parked too long in one spot.

"Perdón, padre. Are we there yet?" The question came from the rear cargo area. The voice sounded anxious and tired.

"Rosita, shush!"

"But we're—"

"Silencio!" Don José hissed.

The priest wiped a trickle of sweat from his brow with the back of his hand. He leaned into his seat. Beneath his white cassock, the tight knot in his stomach begged for release. The pressure was more than he wanted, more than he bargained for. The money wasn't worth it. This trip would be his last. He told that to his contact in *Morelos* two days ago when he received the call to make this crossing. The teenagers had already been instructed where to find him.

"We are paying you well, *padre.* I would not be so hasty," the contact cautioned.

"Lo siento, but I am not made to play these games, to smuggle illegals."

"You knew that going in," the man shouted before he hung up.

Don José saw the van go by once, U-turn a hundred yards up the road and pass his SUV again. The van stopped. Its taillights visible in the priest's mirror, he watched it back over to his side of the road, then cozy up to the rear of the Expedition. According to instructions, Don José remained behind his wheel.

Perspiration ran down into his eyes, burning them for several moments. A banging fist on the rear window signaled him to lift the power gate. The teens' excited whispers rose from under the tarp. Don José turned and watched the two girls climb out from beneath their cover. Before the rising gate reached full extension, the man gave his command.

"*Vámanos.*"

Backpacks clutched in their arms, the anxious teens scrambled to the edge of the SUV's deck. They dropped to the road and disappeared through the waiting open doors of the van. The priest caught sight of several young girls already inside, sitting on benches lining the vehicle. Good, he thought. They will have company during their journey.

The van's doors closed, and Don José lowered the SUV's tailgate. He leaned into the headrest until he sensed the man at his driver-side window. The priest didn't look at him. That was forbidden. Eyes straight ahead, glued to his windshield, he waited as something rolled in his throat down to his stomach. A hand would reach through his open window and drop an envelope containing the delivery payment into his lap. A voice would dismiss him with, "*Vete, ahora!*"

Instead, Don José felt the cold, hard tip of a gun barrel pressed against his temple. Then nothing.

Chapter Two

L uke Rizzo ran his fingers through his hair while a surge of uneasiness churned in his gut. Why did his former snitch, known to him as Rabbit, call and leave that message? In a voice resonating with urgency, Rabbit insisted on meeting in Grand Central at six-fifteen, like in the old days when Rizzo was on the job and the snitch got hold of a hot lead about a drug deal ready to go down. This time Rizzo had no idea what was on Rabbit's mind.

In keeping with the old routine, Rizzo positioned himself at the Vanderbilt Avenue end of the terminal and waited on the top step of the marble staircase leading up to the mezzanine level. High above the massive concourse, a replica of the celestial universe blinked at him from the majestic arched canopy. Rizzo rested his elbow on the wide banister. Out of habit, he raised his eyes toward the blue ceiling, trying to spot the lighted constellations of Orion the Hunter and the winged steed, Pegasus, within sixty seconds. He would play the game in the station's concourse with his son Matt after they arrived on the number 7 train from Queens on their way to Madison Square Garden to watch their Rangers face off with a rival NHL team.

That was long ago, before his divorce, before Matt transformed into a teenager, and before Rizzo took the bullet that found the fatty muscle of his ass. The bullet fractured his hip bone and forced him into a three-quarters disability pension after a dozen productive years as a narcotics detective with the NYPD. His slight limp and the embedded bullet fragment, both leftover memories of his brush with death, didn't interfere with his ability to build a private investigation business.

Now he stood in the familiar arena of his past contests searching, not for a constellation of stars, but for the face of his old informant, to find him between zigzagging rivers of quick-paced commuters.

Rizzo spotted him coming into the concourse from the Forty-second Street entrance, shuffling across the marble surface toward the down staircase. A four-sided clock atop the information booth in the center of the crowded terminal approached six-fifteen. The public address blared announcements of train departures and track assignments, producing a cacophony like an orchestra tuning up before a concert.

In the past, Rabbit was always prompt and always sported a laundered Mexican *Guayabera* shirt. Rizzo grinned. Nothing changed. Rabbit wore a dark brown faux leather jacket, unzipped, with the tails of his *guayabera* visible below.

The procedure they planned to follow today would be the same as in the past. Rabbit would take the staircase at the Vanderbilt end down to the food court beneath the length of the terminal, find a two-seater at one of the many fast-food restaurants lining the lower level and occupy the spot until Rizzo joined him.

Before Rabbit reached the stairs, a tall, reed-like man in a black hooded parka elbowed his way through the crowd of home-bound commuters. His head bowed, the man hurried toward Rabbit. Twenty yards beyond the information booth, he pulled up in front of him.

The two confronted each other for several seconds. Rizzo followed Rabbit's head rocking in an angry interchange. They stood face-to-face in a pocket of travelers who were busy studying the timetable boards above the rows of ticket windows. In a flash, people scattered in all directions, screaming.

* * *

The last time Rizzo entered the Seventeenth Precinct on East Fifty-first Street, he had arrived to retrieve his Mustang. The car was delivered there as a courtesy by the Forty-eighth Precinct in the Bronx after they found the Mustang abandoned in an underpass of the Cross Bronx Expressway. Kids, looking for a joy ride, stole the vehicle off a Bronx street a short distance from Yankee Stadium while Rizzo witnessed his Bombers' loss to the Twins—a bad night all around. Once he retired from the NYPD, he gave up owning cars and instead rented when he needed one.

This was another bad night. Rizzo arrived at the Seventeenth's door for a different purpose: to give his statement on the stabbing of Rabbit in the concourse of Grand Central. Detective First Grade Frank Duggan of the Precinct Detective Squad conducted the questioning.

Duggan tended toward beefy, with a big flat face, high forehead, curly, premature gray hair, and the fixed expression of a man endlessly pissed off at the world. Rizzo met him a few times over the years on the job. A drug investigation that crossed over into the Seventeenth's jurisdiction brought them together. Duggan struck him as an uptight, not too bright law officer who stuck close to the book. On this night, Rizzo noticed the detective had stepped out of character. He'd unbuttoned his shirt collar and loosened his tie.

After sitting at Duggan's side for an hour answering questions, Rizzo reached the end of his patience.

"Where did you say you stood?" Duggan asked for the second time.

"Top of the stairs, Vanderbilt Avenue end, where I always waited for him when we had a meet." Rizzo took a breath while his fingers pawed over his trouser legs. "Jesus, Frank, write it down, will you?"

Duggan raised an eyebrow but offered no response. He clicked the ballpoint twice, scribbled on his pad and asked, "You see the perp move toward the victim?"

"Yeah. I got a glimpse of him pushing through the crowd. Never gave it a second thought until the guy stops right in front of Rabbit. Seems they knew one another—they were arguing. Then, the guy pulls a knife from under his parka, and the next minute, people around them are flying in all directions like scared pigeons. That's when I see the guy plunge the knife into Rabbit's stomach. Rips it up toward his heart. I fuckin' froze. Rabbit staggers forward, grabbing at the hilt of the knife, and the guy disappears through the crowd before Rabbit even hits the floor."

"So which end of the terminal did the attacker enter?"

"If I made a guess, I'd say he was already there, hidden in the crowd."

"Uh-huh," Duggan mumbled, still making notes. He raised up and asked, "And you don't know why he wanted the meet?"

"That's what I said. Rabbit was my best informant for a couple of years before I retired. Always had good stuff. The fact is, his info saved my ass once. Kept me from walking into a phony drug buy in the projects—a setup that would have exploded in my face."

"You keep in contact with him?"

"No. Hadn't heard from him in a long while. Rabbit knew I retired. That's why I couldn't figure out why he wanted to see me."

"You aware he has family here?"

"Christ, I don't even remember his real name. Rabbit went by his street name. You know how it goes with informants. As long as his info was on the mark, I never pushed the issue."

Rizzo bent forward trying to stretch the tense muscles of his shoulders and neck. He hated giving statements, sitting for long periods, always so damn repetitious and never-ending.

"The driver's license we found on him says he's Rodrigo Vega," Duggan volunteered.

"Oh, yeah. Now I remember."

"Lived in the South Bronx," Duggan said. "We're checking for relatives."

"You gonna put a man on it right away?"

Duggan shot him a steely glare. "Yeah, soon as we can. Got a bunch of other cases on our plate right now." He lowered his head and scribbled several lines on his yellow pad.

"Come on, Frank. We both know where this will end up. These cases fall to the bottom of Homicide's priority list. Rabbit was an indigent Mexican with a rap sheet for selling pot and a small amount of heroin. How much heat is his murder gonna generate with you guys?"

Duggan's gaze remained on his pad, his thumb mindlessly clicking the ballpoint. Rizzo knew he had annoyed him, but he continued talking.

"And if a murder isn't solved in the first forty-eight hours, odds are large the case will end up in your inactive file drawer."

The detective narrowed his eyes and slowly raised his head. "Thanks for your input. Now, you through with your street-lawyer rap?"

"Yeah, sorry, Frank. It's just..."

Duggan continued making notes.

Rizzo pictured the first encounter with his former snitch. He busted Rabbit one night in Spanish Harlem, but the man avoided prosecution when he agreed to sign on as Rizzo's informant. Rabbit proved to be a reliable source for information on a number of drug activities in the Chicano neighborhood. The alliance was a fruitful one, and Rizzo grew to like the man. On occasion, he would slip him a fifty or a hundred. Rabbit claimed the money always went down to Mexico to help his family.

"Okay, I got everything I need for now," Duggan said after he looked up. "You think of anything else I can use, you call me. Right?"

"Right, Frank. You come up with the names of any relatives, I get them from you, okay?" Without waiting for a reply, Rizzo got to his feet.

Before Rizzo could disappear from the squad room, Duggan pushed back his chair, stood, and called out. "Wait!"

Rizzo stopped and turned, his expression a blank. "Yeah?"

"You damn well better remember, you're no longer on the job. So stay the fuck out of this investigation, or I'll haul your ass in for interfering."

"I hear ya."

* * *

At ten-fifteen, the taxi drew to the curb at Rizzo's Manhattan brownstone on West Forty-eighth Street. He stepped out of the cab, happy to be home. After living in the middle-class borough of Queens during those fifteen years married to Terri, coming back to this noisy, bustling West Side neighborhood, to this apartment—at any hour—produced a sense of pure contentment. Rizzo was like a twenty-year-old who recently moved out of his parents' house and into his first apartment in the Big Apple. Except he was forty-six. A little late, but for the first time in his adult life, he felt like a real New Yorker.

His building was the last of the many brownstones that once lined West Forty-eighth Street. All the others faced the wrecking ball years ago, replaced by uglier, more modern structures. A brief subway ride to his office, close to local shopping, and a short walk or taxi ride to the many restaurants he liked, the location couldn't be more convenient to Rizzo's lifestyle.

Rizzo hopped up the brownstone's four steps to the front door and stepped through into the building's original white, hexagon tiled foyer. He unlocked the inner door, pushed it open and let it close under its own weight. He hesitated a moment, listened for the latching sound, then walked past his former studio unit on the ground floor and took the stairs to the second level.

At the top step, Rizzo paused and bent over the dark oak railing. He glanced down, remembering the lucky day three years ago when he moved into the building. He was separated from Terri and on hold waiting for the finalization of their divorce. After a few weeks living out of a suitcase in a West Side motel, he found the downstairs studio in this coveted Manhattan neighborhood listed in the Sunday Times real estate section.

Rizzo neared his apartment door and the sound of the TV from within greeted him—no surprise. He entered and found Flo curled up on the sofa, her frosted blond hair splayed across a throw pillow, her usual position for watching the ten o'clock news.

Florence Mae Oliver, a salty, funny southern girl from Bowling Green, Kentucky, entered into Rizzo's life the same year he found the downstairs studio. He had arrived at the Greater Pittsburgh International Airport on assignment for a London client. Flo was behind the Avis counter, and after completing the car rental formalities, he coaxed her into having dinner with him. Over the next two nights, they fell into bed and into love. The experience astonished him with the best sex he'd enjoyed in years and a flood of new feelings. Like so many one-night stands of the past, he assumed it was likely he would never see her again.

Three months later, Avis offered Flo a promotion to supervisor and reassignment to their office at La Guardia Airport. Flo called to tell Rizzo, and he responded with a surge of enthusiasm that surprised him. Their renewed relationship heated quickly, and he slipped into it like a comfortable old shoe. After months of commuting between Flo's apartment in Elmhurst, Queens and his Manhattan studio, a two-bedroom unit on the second floor of his brownstone became available. Rizzo leaped on it. That's when he asked Flo to marry him.

Flo rose from the sofa and walked to him with outstretched arms. "Darlin', I'm glad you called. I worried, you being gone this long. That was so sad, what happened to your friend."

Rizzo's mouth swooped down to capture hers. Her lips tasted like strawberry. When he pulled back, his grin telegraphed his reaction. "Man, I do love kissing you."

His hands slid down Flo's waist and onto her buttocks, pulling her in. Middle age made no impact on her firm, sexy body.

A smile tugged at the edges of Flo's mouth. "Well, I'm glad, hon. I'd hate to think my pucker would go sour this soon. Did you get something to eat on your way home?"

Before he could answer, a voice from the television intruded. "The stabbing took place in the concourse of Grand Central Station during the height of the evening commute when. . . ."

Rizzo moved to the TV, turned up the volume, and watched the network's sketchy report of Rabbit's stabbing in the middle of the crowded terminal. A chill ran through him. The image of his former snitch taking the plunging knife into his abdomen floated back into his memory.

"How awful. You saw him get killed?" Flo's drawl made the last word sound like *keeled*.

"Still can't believe it," Rizzo said. "The guy was on his way to meet me. Whatever he needed to see me about got him killed. I'm sure of it."

"Hon, why don't you rest while I rustle you a quick bite? You must be starved." Flo took his arm and directed him toward the sofa.

"I am, but times like this I wish I never gave up drinking." Rizzo laughed when Flo's eyebrows bounced. "Don't worry. I'll settle for a root beer."

She trailed him into the kitchen to the refrigerator. Rizzo leaned in to take a can of Hires from the lower shelf, and Flo reached over his shoulder to remove the wrapped roasted turkey breast from the upper shelf. "How about a Kentucky Hot Brown? You up for that? It's light."

"Sounds good." He popped the tab on the Hires can and kissed Flo's cheek.

Back in the living room, Rizzo paused in front of the antique Barcelona mirror hanging behind the sofa. The mirror, framed with carved open scrollwork, was Flo's gleeful find this past summer in a thrift shop down in SoHo.

He examined his reflected tired image and finger-combed his hair. His thoughts revisited the wild adventures of his past when the women he took to bed were always turned on by his thick, black hair and his sparkling white teeth. Not Flo. Oh, no. His Avis angel never acknowledged either of these qualities, although she often told him that having an *Eye-talian lover* made her so proud. Her Kentucky articulation always made him laugh.

Rizzo flopped down on the sofa, kicked off his loafers, and stretched his legs to the top of the coffee table. He raised the root beer to his mouth, letting the cold, creamy liquid with a hint of spice run over his tongue, pausing before swallowing, allowing the fizz to tease his taste buds, pretending the drink was a Bud Light. Prior to joining AA, Rizzo always considered the first beer of the day the best. Now, the best was the first root beer of the day.

It wasn't long ago during his midlife crisis, when Rizzo would bounce off walls from one quickie to another, wrecking his life and his first marriage to Terri. Alcohol, his dreaded demon, aided this wild period and provided his conscience with the easy excuse for his adulterous behavior. With Flo in his life, he found it easy to stay faithful and on the wagon. Even his private investigation business showed improvement.

He closed his eyes and leaned back into the soft-pillowed sofa. Yet again, he replayed in his mind the stabbing scene in Grand Central. How the hell did the killer know Rabbit was meeting with him?

Rabbit must have taken someone into his confidence, a person he shouldn't have trusted. In Rabbit's circle of drug dealing contacts, that would include many untrustworthy lowlifes. Perhaps a trip up to Spanish Harlem was in order; find a few of those dirtbags Rabbit called his *compadres*. A little conversation with them might shed light on why his old snitch asked for the meet. That is if he could find the names in his old NYPD records. Then figure a way to question them without setting the dogs loose on himself. Whoever killed Rabbit is not going to like him sniffing around.

Chapter Three

At eight o'clock on Monday morning, Rizzo entered his office on the fourth floor of the Flatiron Building. The twelve-by-fourteen workplace with Spartan furnishings contained a file cabinet, a small sofa, his desk, and two armchairs at each side. The lone wall decoration hung over the sofa: a framed poster-sized blowup of his son, Matt, standing next to his high school graduation present—a shiny new black VW bug.

Behind the desk to one side, a small table hosted a Keurig one-cup coffee maker. Rizzo paused to brew a cup, his second of the day, before approaching the file cabinet to hunt for the names of Rabbit's old associates.

When Rizzo retired from the job, the NYPD required he clean out his desk and surrender all his records. Instead, he violated department policy by making copies of the contents of his casebooks, including those involving Rabbit's inside information. He made a guess that one day the files would come in handy to him as a private investigator. This was one of those days. A quick search turned up a folder marked *The Rabbit Warren*.

Flipping through the folder became a time-travel experience. Drug busts and close calls detailed in his file notes came alive in the temporal lobe of his brain. Rizzo could visualize the events like they were fresh happenings, all those life or death situations when he drew his service weapon before a cornered drug dealer reached for the gun hidden under his shirt.

The names related to the arrests made possible by Rabbit's information were there in the folders. Many of them were doing time—a few skated serious prosecution as first-time offenders.

One name jumped out at him: Eduardo Soto, a close friend of Rabbit's. Back then, Rizzo busted him twice; the last time Soto did eighteen months. After that he stayed clean, or, at least, avoided getting caught again. If Rabbit continued sharing confidences with him, Soto might have a clue why Rabbit asked for the meeting in Grand Central. Perhaps Rizzo could ferret out the man for questioning.

Soto's whereabouts were anyone's guess. Rizzo remembered Soto and Rabbit had one constant. The two friends did their drinking in a dive on 110th and Lexington Avenue called *La Amistad.* Translated: the friendship tavern. The name was a joke to any thinking person of that neighborhood and in particular to the cops of the Twenty-fifth Precinct. Over the years, the name belied the bar's personality as a shooting gallery.

Rizzo would begin there because walking the streets of Spanish Harlem asking questions wouldn't work. His chance of finding a person in that neighborhood willing to speak with a stranger was a long shot. At least not while the sun shone, and, for certain, not to anyone with the aura of a cop. That left the risk-filled nighttime hours to do his exploration. If Soto was around, perhaps someone at *La Amistad* could tell him where he might find him. He would have to be careful not to set off alarms. On the job, he'd have a backup. Now, he would go in alone, unless—

He glanced at his watch. Too late to call Jabba Saint James. Jabba, a large-sized Rastafarian with a heart to match, was on a bus on his way to work. Three years ago, when they'd first met, Jabba would be in bed at this hour. Back then, the big Jamaican worked a janitorial job at a downtown Brooklyn courthouse, midnight to four in the morning.

Days after their first meeting, Jabba put his life on the line for Rizzo when Rizzo involved the Rastafarian in a case he was working. The caper landed the guy in the hospital with a bullet in his chest. After he recovered, Flo hired him as a vehicle detailer for Avis at their La Guardia location. Now Jabba rolled out of bed at the ungodly hour of seven in the morning. Rizzo was sure if he asked the moose to come with him up to Spanish Harlem, Jabba would jump on it. But he wasn't anxious to put his friend at risk again.

Rizzo picked up the desk phone and punched in the number on Frank Duggan's card at the Seventeenth Squad.

"Hold on," the voice responded when he asked for the detective. "I'll see if he's in."

Rizzo drew a few doodles on his notepad until the detective came on the line.

"Duggan."

"Hey, yeah, Frank. Luke Rizzo. Hope I haven't caught you at a bad time."

"No. What's up?" His clipped tone signaled he had no interest in a long conversation.

Rizzo rolled the pencil between his fingers. "You have a chance to check for any relatives of the guy who got stabbed in Grand Central the other night?"

"Rodrigo Vega?"

"Yeah. You turn up any Vega relatives?"

"Hey, Rizzo, you're not on the job no more. I'm not supposed to let this info out. It's an ongoing case. We haven't even—"

"Jesus, Frank, I want to express condolences to his family. Something wrong with that?"

"That's it?"

"Yeah."

Duggan paused. "You know and I know that's bullshit."

Rizzo didn't respond.

The lieutenant blew an exasperated sigh into the phone. "What the hell you think you gonna do? Solve the murder yourself?"

"No. Do a little digging, that's all. Christ, considering Rabbit saved my ass that night in the projects, I owe him. I promise if I come up with anything worthwhile, I'll call you."

"Stay there. I'll be right back." The phone went silent.

Rizzo resumed doodling on his notepad. How much Rabbit's family knew about the man's drug-dealing friends was a question. Probably little, but worth a try.

"Rizzo?"

"Yeah, I'm here."

"He has a sister, Carmen. Lives in the Bronx. Married name, Fuentes."

"Got a number? An address?"

Silence again.

"Okay, but remember bro. I didn't give it to you." Duggan recited the telephone number.

"Right, Frank. Thanks."

After opening the morning mail—mostly bills—Rizzo turned toward the storage closet in the corner, fixing his attention on the pint-size safe resting on the floor against the back wall. The SentrySafe held three weapons, a 9mm Glock, a 9mm Sig Sauer, and a .38 Colt Cobra. He kept the weapons locked away unless an assignment presented an element of danger. This trip to *La Amistad* would be one of those times.

Rizzo needed to be cautious. He would leave the two 9mm weapons and take the small, easy-to-conceal .38 snubbie. The

Colt Cobra, with a three-inch barrel, was sturdy, lightweight, and had a smooth trigger action. It became a collector's piece after Jack Ruby used this same model to kill Lee Harvey Oswald.

Rizzo thought again about asking Jabba to go with him to *La Amistad*. It was hard to dismiss the fact Spanish Harlem could be a dangerous place. Puerto Ricans, the largest of the Latino communities in New York City, made up most of the population. In recent years, a rising number of Salvadoran, Mexican, and Dominican immigrants also made this area their home. Jabba's Jamaican appearance might fit in, draw scant notice. Then again, Spanish Harlem also claimed the highest violent crime rate in Manhattan. He decided to leave Jabba out of this adventure and go it alone.

Rizzo punched in the number Frank Duggan gave him for Rabbit's sister. After several rings, someone picked up. No one spoke.

"Carmen?"

A voice filled with suspicion answered. "*Sí*, who's this?"

"Carmen, this is Luke Rizzo. I'm a private investigator, a friend of your brother."

After a stretch of wheezy breathing into the phone, Carmen responded. "My brother, he's gone . . . killed. Wachu want?"

Not the reaction Rizzo expected. The woman was clearly angry. He doubted the conversation would prove productive.

"I know that, but—"

"I already told the police. I know nothin' . . . nothin'. Why you callin' me, harassin' me?"

Rizzo sucked in a swallow of air and let it out slowly through his nose. He expected her to hang up. Before she could end the call, he spoke with deliberate slowness. "Carmen, I swear I was your brother's friend. You understand? I'm not the police. I want to find out who killed him and why."

She muffled the phone, creating dead air until she removed her hand. "Why you want to help Rodrigo? My brother did bad things . . . drugs . . . working for bad people. *Mi esposo* always say, 'Rodrigo, stay away. We not that kind.'"

He kept his tone friendly and said, "Listen, Carmen. Your brother was not so bad. In fact, he—"

"Then why he was killed? He did bad things with those people sell drugs, no?"

Rizzo squeezed his eyelids and pushed back into the chair. This was a waste of time. Rabbit's sister had nothing that could prove useful. He decided to give it one more shot.

"Carmen, your brother . . . I mean, don't you want to help me find out who killed him?"

"What's your name?"

The intruding voice was male.

"Who's this?" Rizzo said.

"No. First you. What's your name?" The voice had an edge to it, gruff, and demanding.

"Luke Rizzo."

Silence, then "Aha, oh yeah. You that former narc, now a P.I."

"You know me?"

"About you."

"And you? What's your name?"

"Fuentes. Luis Fuentes. Carmen's husband."

"Okay. And how is it you know me—or about me?"

No reply. Instead, Fuentes spoke in Spanish to his wife. Rizzo waited while the chatter continued. It had the sound of a disagreement.

Fuentes came back on the line, his voice softened. "Talking on this phone, it ain't smart. You get what I mean? You wanna meet in a safe place?"

The suggestion made Rizzo think set up. Did the man have a role in Rabbit's death? And if not, what did Fuentes know about it? How forthcoming would he be? Any information he had about Rabbit's murder, he'd be guarded about sharing it.

Rizzo pressed him. "What happened with your brother-in-law? He get in trouble?"

"I'm not saying nothin' on the phone. You wanna meet or no?"

"Can you get me a few answers?"

"Would I suggest a meet if I didn't think so?"

"You talked to the police?"

"Hell no. Carmen did. They never talked to me. Besides, I ain't saying what I got to the police. Don't trust them."

"But you trust me?"

"Rabbit trusted you, so I will."

Fuentes referred to his brother-in-law by his street name. That confirmed for Rizzo the man knew Rabbit was into drug-dealing.

"Okay. When and where?"

"Tomorrow night . . . six-fifteen . . . Edison Hotel. Forty-seventh and Broadway. Wait for me in the lounge."

"You know what I look like?"

"I'll spot you. Cops are easy to spot."

Chapter Four

R izzo entered the Hotel Edison from the Forty-seventh Street entrance. He pushed through one of two revolving doors as the second door spun out a couple of German-looking tourists carrying their obligatory knapsacks and wearing hiking shorts. Rizzo laughed. *Does anyone in Europe own long pants?*

He crossed the hotel's Art Déco lobby toward the lounge, passed a security man in a blue suit screening guests entering and exiting the bank of elevators. The man looked up and nodded at Rizzo. He nodded. There was something about cops that always allowed them to spot another cop. Even ex-cops. Nearby, two uniformed bellmen stacked luggage on a cart opposite the check-in desk.

Before he reached the lounge, Rizzo pulled up in front of a framed photograph hanging over the concierge's podium and studied the circa 1957 photo. The sepia image showed two New York Yankee veterans, Billy Martin and Mickey Mantle, posed outside the hotel's entrance. Mantle sported a light tan windbreaker and a ridiculous-looking porkpie hat on his blond head. The feisty Martin wore a light-weight sports jacket, unzipped, his shirt collar opened. The two men appeared ordinary, not like the famous eccentric personalities the public came to love.

Rizzo remembered the off-the-field antics of the two iconic baseball figures who thrilled Yankee fans during their long playing careers. The Edison Hotel, located in the heart of the theater district, was the favorite choice of Yankee players during that period; thus the photo's presence.

Settled on a sofa in the lounge area, Rizzo unzipped his nylon flight jacket. He scanned the murals on the walls, taking in the stylized Art Déco city scenes of the early thirties and forties. His scrutiny landed on the image across from him, the great swing of Joe DiMaggio at the plate. With eyes glued to the mural, he failed to notice the figure standing to his left until the short man wearing a bellman's uniform spoke.

"Mr. Rizzo?"

"You got me."

"This is for you, sir." The bellman handed him a standard letter-size envelope with the Hotel Edison's logo on the flap. The man nodded, did an about-face, and moved off toward the front desk.

Rizzo examined the unsealed envelope. Had the bellman given him a guest's room statement in error? He flipped open the flap, pulled out a sheet of hotel stationery and read the words written with a felt-tip scrawl: *Turning Point Tavern, across from Chelsea Piers. 11:30.*

* * *

The buzz of late-night traffic on the West Side Highway filled the humid air like a swarm of bees. Rizzo stepped out of the taxi at the corner of Twenty-second Street in front of the Turning Point Tavern. On the river side of the highway, darkness enveloped the Chelsea Piers. The popular daytime multi-sports complex and its famous four-tiered golf driving range stretched out over the Hudson River like a ghostly appendage to Manhattan Island, dark and no signs of life.

The odor rising from the Hudson's oil-slick waters filled his nostrils. Rizzo checked his watch before he yanked down on his jacket and squeezed his left arm against the holstered Colt Cobra strapped under his armpit—a hangover habit from years on the job. He pulled open the heavy oak door to this century-old establishment and stepped through.

Long favored by dockworkers of every ethnic group, the Turning Point Tavern played host to a number of lethal confrontations over the years. The recent rush toward an urban renewal of the Chelsea area significantly eased these problems for the local police precinct.

Once inside, the Hudson's oily scent disappeared, replaced by the odor of stale beer. Several fluorescent tubes hummed and flickered in their overhead fixtures, and the red and white glow from the Budweiser sign in the window gave the tavern a flash of color. A long, polished mahogany bar hosted a handful of locals while an overweight, attentive barman paced behind, keeping glasses filled.

Rizzo recalled a featured story in *The New Yorker* about this historic watering hole. The colorful word-painting of the tavern in the thirties had described the sawdust-covered wood-planked flooring and the Wurlitzer jukebox spinning out Rudy Vallée favorites. The wood-planked floor? Still there, but no sawdust—or Rudy.

Before he could climb on a bar stool, a meaty hand landed on his left shoulder. Rizzo reached back, closed his fingers around the wrist of the invasive hand and yanked it away. He slipped his .38 snubbie from within his jacket, whirled and shoved the weapon under the chin of the unexpected greeter.

The man backed away, raising his palms. "*Cuidado, amigo,* someone could get hurt with that thing. I'm Luis Fuentes. *Lo siento.* Didn't mean to scare you."

"Not too smart introducing yourself that way. God damn risky." Rizzo returned the .38 to the holster. He extended his hand and said, "I'm Luke Rizzo, but you knew that."

Luis Fuentes, a bear-sized man, took Rizzo's hand into both of his and shook it. "I apologize again, my friend."

Fuentes, in his early fifties, possessed penetrating, deep-set dark eyes. Short gray fuzz covered his enormous head, and a long beak-like nose stretched toward his chin. The face reminded Rizzo of a barn owl. Dressed in black slacks and open field jacket, Fuentes wore a purple long sleeve shirt with the Edison Hotel monogram stitched across the shirt pocket. Rizzo remembered seeing him earlier at the Edison's bag-check counter on his way to the lounge.

The barn owl-like man gestured toward the rear of the tavern. "We can have our meeting back there. Nobody's gonna bother us. That okay?"

"Lead on."

The tables in the back were empty except for one man at a four-top near the far wall. The man sat with his elbows balanced on the table, his chin resting on his finger-clasped hands. He didn't look up while they moved toward him.

Fuentes pulled out a chair and gestured. "Sit," he said. "Glad you came, detective. Maybe something good comes of it."

Rizzo sat and cut his eyes to the lone man who had not yet lifted his head. Fuentes dropped into a chair next to Rizzo.

"I am no longer a detective, Luis," Rizzo said. "I'm retired. Remember?"

"Oh yeah, you're a P.I. now. Hey, sorry about all this cloak and dagger bullshit. You'll understand when I tell you what I have. First, what do you want to drink?"

"Nothing for me, thanks."

"No? Nothing at all?"

"I'm AA," Rizzo said, keeping his tone firm. "I'll have a Coke, though." He almost said root beer, but he thought it sounded silly. Besides, no bar he knew stocked Hires Root Beer.

Fuentes summoned the bartender and gave him the Coke order. "And two more Coronas, Clancy, while you're at it."

They remained silent until the barman returned with the beer bottles and soft drink. Rizzo continued to stare at the unidentified man, a short Hispanic in his late fifties with a thin mustache lining his upper lip. He wore an ill-fitting denim jacket with black leather arms. The Mets ball cap sitting backward on his head amplified his ordinary appearance.

Fuentes laughed. "You don't remember him, do you?"

The man fixed his eyes on Rizzo. "Been a long time. Nice to see you again . . . I think."

The sound of his voice rang familiar. In an instant, it registered. "Eduardo Soto. Damn! You saved me a trip up to *La Amistad* to look for you. Figured I would find you there. I thought you might know why Rabbit wanted to meet with me."

"Don't go to *La Amistad* no more. I show up, I end up like Rabbit."

"Why? You run a tab and stiff them?"

A smirk creased Soto's mouth. "Shit, if that's all I needed to worry about, I'd light a church full of candles."

"But you're clean, are you? No more arrests since I busted you?"

The man's chin jutted upward. "Betcha ass. Eighteen months upstate in Dannemora? That was enough."

"Glad to hear that. What are you doing now?"

Soto shrugged and puffed out his cheeks. "Drive a gypsy cab, mostly."

Fuentes jumped in. "Hey, you ever come across the name, Umberto Salazar?"

"You mean the sleazebag behind half the prostitution in New York State?" Rizzo said.

"Yeah. And Florida, and Jersey, and the whole east coast. Yeah, that's the guy."

The high wail of a fire truck broke in. The emergency vehicle flew past the tavern, heading north on the West Side Highway. They waited for the noise to fade.

Rizzo worked in drug enforcement, but he was well aware of Umberto Salazar and his organization. He was on Vice's hit list, but Homicide also had their eye on him. A ruthless murderer, he was not shy about retiring his working girls once their production value slowed down, often by dumping their bodies into the river.

The fire truck's noise drifted off, and Rizzo looked back to Fuentes. "I had a pretty good read on Rabbit. He never got involved with anything to do with that slimy business. So what's the connection to Salazar, assuming there is one?"

"You tell him," Fuentes said, turning to Soto. He folded his arms and tipped back in his chair.

Soto picked up his beer. He took a long pull, stalling, trying to organize his thoughts. He set the bottle down with a shaky hand, and his reptilian eyes closed for a moment. When he opened them, his head panned the tavern.

"About a month or two ago," he began, "me and Rabbit, we was drinkin' at a bar in the South Bronx. We got to talkin' with a guy, somebody Rabbit met once or twice before. A real wise guy, horseshit artist. The place was his hangout. He knew everybody." Soto paused and looked at Rizzo, as though checking for a reaction.

Rizzo had difficulty hearing Soto's low voice. He moved his chair closer to the table and leaned in on his arms.

Soto continued. "This guy, he was sayin' about this house in Queens he goes to and gets laid. One of the two pimps Salazar assigned to the house is this guy's brother-in-law. He lets him have a freebie hump every once in a while. Claimed the two *putas* they kept in the house were like young, in their teens."

"I've heard about those places. Kids young as twelve, thirteen. Mostly victims of kidnapping."

Soto raised the Corona bottle. "Right," he said and took a swallow.

"Any other women in the house?" Rizzo asked.

"No. Just the two young ones. The guy claims Salazar added the house to his string a few months back." Soto raised the Corona again and took a mouthful. "So we're sittin' sucking up our beers and this guy, he brags to Rabbit about this young one he always fucks. That's when Rabbit wants to know what she looks like."

"Why? Why would he ask that?"

Fuentes cut in, taking over the narrative. "Let's go back to somethin' before he tells you. You know Rabbit was my wife's brother?"

"Yeah."

"Okay. So three months ago I receive a call from my younger brother in Mexico." Fuentes took a breath. "He says Rosita, his sixteen-year-old, and her girlfriend disappeared. A man in her village, a friend of the family, told her about these waitress jobs in Florida. He says he'll put her in touch with a priest who'll smuggle her across the border at *Ciudad Juárez*. A contact would meet her and drive her to Florida. Get her a waitress job. That's what the man told her. Rosita convinces her friend to come along. The two girls hitchhiked to *Juárez* to meet this priest, and nobody's heard from them since."

"Kidnapped, you think?"

Fuentes clasped his hands behind his head. "We were in the dark until Rabbit met this guy," he said and signaled to Soto to continue.

Soto picked up the narrative. "So he describes the girl, and Rabbit's convinced it's Rosita, his sister's niece. He goes fuckin' bananas. Tries to force the guy to tell him where the house is. Threatens to kick his ass if he doesn't. The guy wouldn't say. Makes it damn straight Rabbit knows who owns the house. Yeah, Umberto Salazar. He tells him he'd be in serious shit if he makes trouble. Two heavies who run the bar toss us out. 'Don't come back,' they tell us. Outside, Rabbit is goin' bonkers. The next day he says he's gonna call you, ask you to help."

"You remember the guy's name, the name of the bar?"

"Yeah. Frankie Cusack. The bar is called Ruby's. On Hunts Point Avenue."

That was the NYPD's busy Forty-first Precinct in the South Bronx on Longwood Avenue. It was known as an "A" house because of its location in an area full of crime and heavy prostitution. They labeled the neighborhood a Red-Light District.

"And Rabbit never called the police?"

"No chance. Frankie must have squealed to his whorehouse boss, and the boss tells him to get rid of Rabbit. So Frankie follows Rabbit to where he's meetin' you and does him."

"You ever talk to the guy, tell him about Rabbit coming to see me?"

Soto's back straightened. "Fuck, no."

"Well, Rabbit must have said something to somebody."

"Maybe they were watching him," Soto said.

"And you think it was dumb luck they hit him on his way to meeting me?"

Soto shrugged. "Shit, man, I don't know. It coulda happened."

Rizzo looked past Soto toward the front door of the tavern. Umberto Salazar was a dangerous man and smart enough to have Rabbit watched for a few days. It was that or Rabbit talked with someone other than Soto. Then again, maybe Soto was lying.

The NYPD Vice Squad thus far had little success in shutting down Salazar's operation, but peddling underage girls was a federal offense and should grab the attention of the FBI. The lead agent in the New York City field office, Jack Fields, came to mind. Rizzo pissed him off a few years back when he ignored the agent's warning to stay out of one of their investigations. But if the agent was past it, he might be willing to help find this Frankie Cusack.

Fuentes and Soto sat watching Rizzo, shooting glances at each other. "So what do you think?" Fuentes asked. "Can you help?"

Rizzo threw a wary look at Fuentes. "I have a few ideas—if they don't get me killed."

Chapter Five

*W*hat the hell am I doing here? Fields hates me. *He would sooner hang me by my nuts than become involved with me again.*

The elevator doors parted on the twenty-third floor of 26 Federal Plaza, the FBI's New York City Field Office. Before Rizzo could change his mind, the receptionist with a pretty face and long blonde hair that fell to her shoulders, raised her eyes and peered out at him from behind the glass enclosure.

Rizzo stepped off and into the reception area and hesitated, questioning again if his phoning the man was smart of him to do.

"Yes, may I help you?"

"Huh? Oh, sorry. Agent Jack Fields, please. He's expecting me. Lucas Rizzo."

"One moment, Mr. Rizzo. I'll tell him you're here. Have a seat, won't you?"

Rizzo eased himself into a club chair in the reception area. He unbuttoned his Harris Tweed, trying to lower his edginess. The white knit turtleneck under his jacket itched across his shoulders.

He picked up a copy of *Time* from the side table and thumbed the pages while he thought about the last time he came to 26 Federal Plaza. An English client, born out of wedlock, had hired him to find her American biological father. He located him in a town outside Pittsburgh. After that, a former German Stasi agent following him murdered the client's father out of revenge for something that happened on the eve of WWII. Within days, the case went Federal. That's when Rizzo got into hot water. He ignored the Feds' warning to butt out.

In addition to bringing the killing to a resolution, he did so to the embarrassment of Agents Jack Fields and Tony Condon. He'd located the killer on his own, chased him onto a Brooklyn rooftop, and watched him take a flyer over the ledge, down three stories to his death. Since then, Rizzo was *persona non grata* with the Feds. And yet, Fields took his call yesterday and agreed to meet with him today.

His eyes on the magazine page and his mind floating in a cloud of memories, Rizzo sensed a presence close to him. Coming out of his thoughts, he raised his head. Jack Fields smiled down at him. Rizzo dropped the magazine on the table and stood.

The agent reached out. "Luke, how are you?" The smile lingered as he gave Rizzo's hand a firm shake.

"Hey, Jack. Thanks for seeing me."

"Come on back," Fields said. He nodded to the receptionist and stepped toward the interior door.

The lock released with a click and Fields held the door open. Rizzo slipped by, leading the way down the hall. He remembered from his last visit the location of the agent's office and stopped at the doorway. Fields entered first and motioned Rizzo to the sofa against the wall.

Rizzo sat at one end and laid his arm across the top of the cushions. He never took his eyes from the man's face, studying him with curiosity. Rizzo felt like a high school sophomore called to the principal's office. Except in this situation, Rizzo did the calling.

Fields walked to his desk. "Been a few years," he said while bending over the phone console. "How's the P.I. business going?"

"Fine, Jack. Fine. Steady, with a growing client list, I'm happy to say."

"I'm going to have a coffee. Can I get you one?" Fields pressed the intercom button.

"Yes, thank you. Black."

"Rachel, two coffees, please. Mr. Rizzo takes his black."

"No sugar."

"And no sugar. Thanks."

Fields sat at the opposite end of the sofa, squaring around to face Rizzo. The agent built with a tall, fit frame, was attired in the standard FBI uniform: a dark suit, white shirt, and patterned tie. His youthful appearance contradicted the man's twenty-five years with the bureau. After an extraordinary early career, he became lead agent of the New York office in record time.

Rizzo opened the conversation. "How's Condon?" he asked, recalling Fields' second was never far from his side. He remembered Tony Condon as an agent with a personality profile of arrogance, efficiency, and antagonism.

"Tony is no longer in this office. He transferred to L.A. He's lead agent out there and doing well. Likes the southern California climate and laid-back lifestyle."

"Nice."

Rachel entered with the coffee tray and set it on the table.

When the secretary departed, Rizzo said, "I appreciate you seeing me like this, Jack, considering we—"

"Water under the bridge, Luke. Don't give it another thought. Anyway, you said the magic words when you called. Got my interest."

Rizzo laughed. "Umberto Salazar?"

"On the money. Been chasing the son of a bitch for a long time, waiting for the right opportunity to nail him."

"I figured that."

"Yeah, well, we know all about Salazar's string of whorehouses. We believe he's now involved in running drugs from Puerto Rico, through the Keys, and Mexico."

Smiling, Rizzo said, "That makes him a much bigger fish. He's been a major pain in the ass to NYPD Vice for years. Seems the locals can't make a dent in his operation. They'll be pleased to know he's moved up to the bigs, into the scope of the Feds."

"So what's your involvement with Salazar?" Fields took a sip of coffee and placed the mug back on the tray. "What brings you here?"

Rizzo paused a moment before taking it head-on. "The man is responsible for the murder of a guy, an informant I had in my pocket for several years on the job. I hadn't seen him since my retirement. He phoned me out of the blue a week ago."

"And Salazar had him removed? Could be he crossed someone in the organization? Maybe shot his mouth off when he shouldn't?"

"Nothing like that. Rabbit was never involved in Salazar's business. Drugs at the street level, yes. Not the sex trade." Rizzo uncrossed his legs and adjusted himself on the sofa.

Fields eyeballed him and waited.

"He called, frantic to set up a meeting. I agreed to meet at the same location we used back when he caught a hot lead for me—the food court in Grand Central. The problem was a guy stuck a knife in him before he got to me. I was standing on the top step at the Vanderbilt Avenue end waiting, and I watched the assailant move on him, hit him, and then disappear into the crowd."

"The middle of the concourse, right? I read about it. That's the Seventeenth Precinct."

"Yeah. That house doesn't catch too many murder cases. They're usually handled by Midtown South, so I'm not betting on their expertise on this one. The lead is a Detective Frank Duggan. Gave him my statement right after it happened. Not the most aggressive lawman."

"What makes you think Salazar's behind it?"

"Here's why," and holding the agent's attention without interruption, Rizzo replayed details of his meeting with Eduardo Soto and Luis Fuentes, at the Turning Point Tavern.

"Is it possible," Fields asked, "the girl wasn't the sixteen-year-old niece of your informant's brother-in-law?"

"I questioned that too. But if not, why would they bother to take out Rabbit?"

"It sounds like they were worried he might become a nuisance to them."

"They could've taken care of it without killing him. Doesn't make sense. No, my guess is they were afraid of getting caught using underage girls."

"You have contacts on Vice, don't you? Ask them to check it out?"

"I go to them without knowing where to investigate, they'd laugh. Salazar's got houses in all five boroughs. I need to find this guy, Frankie Cusack. When I do, I'll squeeze him for the location of the one he told Rabbit about. I have to move fast before they switch her to another spot, or even out of the state. Or worse, kill her."

"Who's the client on this? The uncle?"

"Hell, no. Fuentes can't afford to pay me. I'm doing this for personal reasons. Jesus, the kid is sixteen years old. I got a son not much older. Besides, I owe it to Rabbit, big time."

"What do you want from me?"

"Look to see if you have a file on this Frankie Cusack. The little info I have on him is Soto's description of the guy, and he hangs out in a bar in the South Bronx. I'll check that out, but what I need from you is anything you have on him, his rap sheet, where he lives, where he works, whatever you got."

Fields chuckled. "Then we see about a favor you can do for the bureau down the line. Yes?"

"An offer I can't refuse?"

"Something like that."

* * *

Umberto Salazar rose from his chair, unbuttoned the jacket to his tailored, fifteen-hundred-dollar suit, and walked to the picture window with a regal air to his step. Along the shore of the Miami skyline, Biscayne Bay broke through the morning haze. The scene filled the glass like a seascape painting. He loved the view, the feeling it created, the sensation that he, Umberto Salazar, soared above all the dirt and trash wallowing in the streets below. A product of a Mexican family struggling for existence in the poorest US border town of *Colonia Muñiz*, Salazar always thought of himself as untouchable.

He examined his reflected image. It was of a man with a pockmarked face, the result of a childhood disease that left him with severe scarring. This disfigurement, coupled with his dead eyes, imposed a frightening impression on people meeting him for the first time. They tended to shrink away from his glassy stare. He considered this menacing feature his most effective weapon against someone trying to con him.

Salazar was not unhappy with his physical appearance in spite of his short stature and thickening middle. His conspicuous girth was not a condition anyone dared to mention. Chasing fifty years, he was proud he could hold his own on a tennis court or in bed.

Married once to a Vegas showgirl during his early years, he had no trouble finding willing bed partners whenever the mood struck him. He stayed away from the pool of his sex slave business, leaving that repugnant behavior to his pack of lowlife underlings.

He turned to study his associate sitting on the shiny black leather sofa, quietly flipping through the current swimsuit issue of *Sports Illustrated* like someone without a care in the world.

Ilya Bodrov was clean-shaven, with a light coating of straw-colored hair on a head tending toward baldness. Salazar saw a resemblance to Vladimir Putin.

Bodrov wore a blue blazer, steel-gray slacks, blue broadcloth dress shirt, and a traditional rep tie, an appearance that would put him at ease at the bar of the Ocean Reef Club in Key Largo. The Russian always dressed up when Salazar called a meeting in his office. He wouldn't get beyond the secretary otherwise.

Salazar guessed Bodrov was on the north side of middle age, but closer to fifty than forty. He saw him as a handsome man—if one didn't mind the perpetual scowl on his angry mouth.

"So, Ilya, the matter up in New York. You took care of it?"

Bodrov, a former FSB secret service operative, raised his chin from the photo of the bikini-clad beauty. "Done. Frankie Cusack called after he removed him." His eyes returned to the tanned blonde on the page.

The sex slaver shook his head. He prided himself that people regarded him as ruthless. But the man on the sofa, reported to be responsible for hundreds of political murders in the USSR under Putin, went about his business in such a blasé fashion even Salazar found him unsettling. He couldn't decide whether Bodrov annoyed him or frightened him.

"Who's this cop the guy was meeting? He a Fed?"

Bodrov lifted his head. His eyes settled on Salazar's face. "No, not Fed. Ex-cop. He used dead guy as spy when he worked for New York police narcotics. That's all Frankie Cusack find out."

"Spy? You mean an informant, don't you?"

"Whatever." Bodrov's eyes returned to the magazine.

Salazar turned back to the picture-window view. His gaze carried down fifteen stories, settling on the boat basin to the left. The Swan, his one hundred and seventy-six-foot luxury mega yacht was berthed there. He could see several crew members scurrying about the deck, readying the Benetti-designed vessel for departure within the hour.

"Do you think the ex-cop knew why the guy wanted to meet him?"

"Who?" the Russian asked without lifting his head.

Salazar twisted around and zeroed in on Bodrov, his lips set in a hard line. "The ex-cop, you asshole. Put the damn magazine down and listen to me. That too much to ask?"

The Russian lowered the magazine. "You worry much, Umberto. You know? Already I ask. The guy who tells Cusack about meeting gives cop no reason. So relax. Everything under control. Is why you employ me, yes?"

Salazar returned to his window view. Bodrov's smugness annoyed him, although he couldn't deny his competence in disposing of enemies. After Ilya Bodrov defected from Russia into Mexico two years ago, he came to Salazar's attention through a well-placed politician in the Mexican government. Salazar immediately hired him for the role of enforcer. He proved to be a capable and lethal arm, dealing with gnarly problems of the organization. To date, the Russian was flawless in carrying out every assignment.

Salazar rolled over in his mind a credo he lived by for a long time. *To survive in this business, one needed to be thorough and careful.* He continued to stare out the window while he issued his directive.

"Ilya, I want you to keep an eye on this cop. Make certain he doesn't cause trouble about burning his informant. We don't want him nosing around, talking to friends of the dead guy. Maybe you see it doesn't happen. You understand what I'm saying?"

"Uh-huh."

Salazar spun around. "Hey, Ilya. Try speaking in full sentences. You get away with that shit when you were in the KGB?"

"FSB, Umberto. KGB died in 1991. Is FSB now."

"I don't give a fuck what initials they're using, you work for me now, so don't pull that deaf-ear bullshit. You hear what I asked you to do?"

Bodrov rose to his feet and dropped the magazine. The rapid blinking of his eyelids appeared as if they were transmitting in Morse code. His lean face wore a worried frown. "Yes, Umberto," he said with deadpan politeness. "I am sorry. Yes, I heard you. I will make arrangements."

"Okay, then," Salazar snapped.

It pleased him when he spotted Bodrov's eyes perform his nervous tic, an impulsive reaction Bodrov did whenever the man detected pressure. *Good, keep the arrogant prick on his toes.*

"Let's get down to the Swan. She should be ready to shove off for our meeting in the Keys. The cartel's shipment from Fajardo is scheduled to leave in a couple of weeks. We need to work out the details of the transfer."

Chapter Six

Sam Hoya considered turning back. Instead, he pulled the Range Rover into the shopping center and found a vacant space across from Starbucks. Towering cumulus clouds formed smoky-gray mountains in the sky, while lightning flickered through the clouds like a faulty fluorescent tube.

He parked the Rover, and the South Florida sky opened with a thunderous greeting. The angry rain pelted the autos scattered about the parking lot. He waited while the Rover's wiper blades battled the torrent of water cascading over the windshield. Out of patience, Hoya killed the engine and reached back for the golf umbrella lying across the rear seat. He stepped out onto the rain-soaked concrete, popped open the umbrella, and hurried to the coffee shop.

He carried his café mocha to a two-seater table, the top sticky from the previous occupant's sloppiness. Except for a few laptop users taking advantage of the free Wi-Fi, the handful of tables around him were unoccupied. He pressed back into his chair, the wetness of his golf shirt sending shivers down his spine.

Hoya faced the shop's front window with his coffee gripped with both hands like they needed the warmth. The wind's ferocity now carried sheets of rain horizontally across the parking lot, bending tree limbs with its force. It appeared as though the weather gods flipped Starbucks on its side.

True to Florida's inconstant weather pattern, the rain stopped as fast as it started. Hoya drained the last of the chocolaty liquid, stood to deposit the empty container in the trash, and turned for the door. That was when he spotted her.

She'd been sitting at the table behind him. Now on her feet, she paused, head elevated, shoulders pulled back in a military-like pose, and gazed out the window. The extraordinary resemblance surprised him. Eight years passed since his painful divorce, but the image of his ex-wife remained a fresh memory. He was shocked when she admitted she was in love with another man. It was the Titanic of all his life's disappointments.

The woman standing before him was a remarkable copy of Anita. Skin that glowed, dark chestnut hair curled behind her ears, the same sharp, jutting chin—she possessed all the features that gave Anita her haughty appearance.

Hoya reached the door ahead of her, holding it open while she slipped by.

"Thank you," she whispered.

They emerged together when a white flash and a loud rumble announced the storm's return. Once again, big droplets splashed on the parking lot surface. The wind picked up and raced at a frantic pace through the trees. Hoya thought nothing would satisfy the tempest until it tore one of the oaks from its roots.

He hesitated under the protection of the shopping center's overhang, while the woman edged toward the crosswalk. She carried no umbrella.

Calling to her, he said, "Where you parked?"

She stared back.

"Where you parked?" he repeated. "I'll walk you to your car." He waggled the umbrella to emphasize his intention.

She considered the stormy condition, frowned, and replied, "I better wait inside."

"In that case, how about I treat you to another coffee while we both wait?"

Before she could respond, a black pickup truck pulled up at the entrance. A screaming voice came from within the cab. *"Bella, consiga su culo a casa."*

The woman took a step back, spun on her heels, and raced past him into Starbucks.

Hoya remained under the overhang. He understood what the driver shouted. "Get your ass home" was not exactly a friendly order. He glared at the man, at his rain-soaked arm hanging out the cab's window, the arm dense with tattoos. The sinister-looking goatee under his lip and a pair of wraparound sunglasses covering half his face completed the bad-boy appearance.

He was uncertain what he would do if the bad boy followed the woman inside. He hated meddling in matters that didn't concern him. The last time he did, five years ago, the outcome produced a broken jaw. Not his, the other guy's.

A redneck football fan in a sports bar couldn't refrain from shouting obscenities at the images on the TV screen. The clown ignored the female bartender's frequent pleas to quiet down. His response to her last request was, "Why don't ya fuck off." That was when Hoya reached over, grabbed him by the back of his shirt collar and escorted him out to the parking lot. He let go, and the loudmouth rushed him, running straight into Hoya's right fist. The man hit the pavement like a felled tree.

At six-two, 225 pounds and thirty-five years old, Hoya possessed the linebacker physique of his playing days at Florida State. Now a general contractor for a major developer in southwest Florida, his size and fitness came in handy when dealing with the rough types in his work crew. A product of a

Mexican father and an American mother, he learned enough Spanish growing up in Texas to deliver understandable orders to those of his crew recently arrived from Mexico and Central America. The ability to communicate in their language also enhanced his position of authority.

Hoya watched the driver glower through the window into Starbucks. He bit off his instinct to say something. It might be a marital dispute. If so, he needed to butt out.

The man cast a wary glance in Hoya's direction before he threw the pickup into drive and fishtailed on the wet pavement toward the parking lot's exit. The truck disappeared in the downpour.

Hoya entered the coffee shop and spotted her seated at a rear table near the order pick-up area. He hesitated, waiting for a sign of recognition that would tell him it was okay to approach. She sat bent over the table, shivering, arms folded, and chin buried in her forearms. Her body language said, leave me alone.

At the counter, Hoya ordered another café mocha. He glanced at the woman and asked, "Hey, how about I treat you to a coffee while you're waiting out the rain?"

Her head remained tucked in her arms, and her trembling continued. Had she heard him? Hoya repeated his offer. She rolled her head to one side. Watery, dark eyes scrutinized him. With a squeezed out half-smile, she said in a quivering voice, "A latte would help."

"You got it."

He carried the two coffees to the table, sat and pushed the latte across to her. She raised her head and looked toward the door.

As Hoya sipped his coffee, his attention locked on her face. Quiet moments passed before he asked, "You okay?"

She failed to answer. Her empty expression gave him no clue.

Searching her features, she appeared to be in her late twenties. Her dark brown eyes and the contours of her lips conveyed the same sensual invitation of his ex-wife's mouth. He imagined their softness and taste.

Her long eyelids fluttered to a state of awareness, sensing Hoya's scrutiny. She raised the warm liquid to her pursed mouth and swallowed. "Thank you for the coffee."

Hoya noticed she wore no wedding ring. He waited for several beats. "I'm Sam Hoya." He explored her face waiting for a response. When none came, he said, "Bella, isn't it? Your name, I mean."

The corners of her eyes pinched, and the ends of her mouth tightened. "You heard?"

"I'm sorry. Standing right there . . . hard to miss." He reached for his café mocha and stopped when he saw her expression softening.

"I'm Isabella Fuentes. But I'm called Bella."

He nodded. "Bella. Beautiful. Suits you."

"Thank you, that's sweet."

His attention refocused on Bella's face, her dark eyes glistening like wet stars. His pulse quickened. The reaction surprised him. He wanted to question her further. Could he without appearing like he was meddling? Who was that idiot in the truck? Were they married? Living together? What?

"That was Manny, my brother," she said as if she read his thoughts.

Hoya squinted. "Angry fellow. What's his problem?" *There, I did it again. Will I ever learn to mind my own business?*

Bella gazed past him, over his shoulder toward the door. Her troubled expression made him think she didn't want to answer.

"Sorry," he said. "You don't need to—"

"No, it's all right. He's worried about me, because of what happened to my sister, Rosita." She lowered her chin and became quiet again.

More tears welled up and trickled down her cheeks. Hoya waited. He wanted to press her further.

A reply came suddenly as if the pressure in her heart was greater than any need for secrecy. "She turned sixteen a month before she disappeared."

"Oh, wow. What happened to her?"

Bella swallowed. "Three months ago, Rosita disappeared off the face of the earth."

Hoya tilted back from the table. "And you've never heard from her?"

"A family acquaintance came into the small cantina in our village, Morelos, where she waitressed. 'Go up to Florida.' he told her. He said she could make ten times more money waiting tables in the States. He offered help to get there if she wanted. It sounded wonderful to her."

Hoya's eyes never left her face.

"Four years ago, Manny received his green card. He got a job here in golf course maintenance at a country club. My card came two years later with a job offer of my own. I moved up here to join him. We both send money home."

"And Rosita wanted to help, too?"

"Yes. My father is a day laborer and doesn't earn much. Rosita suffered from guilt. She believed if she made enough, she could contribute to the family's expenses. The man told her if she got homesick, he'd help her get back home. My parents were afraid. Rosita ignored their warnings. She didn't want to wait until she reached eighteen to apply for a green card." Bella paused. "I'm sorry, I shouldn't be bothering you with all this. I'll stop—"

"No, no. Tell me. I want to know what happened. Finish."

She fixed on his face before going on. "Well, the man put her in touch with a priest in Juárez. Rosita foolishly persuaded her best friend to go with her. The two of them hitchhiked to Juárez. From there, the priest was supposed to take them across the border and deliver them to someone else."

"Why to another person? Did they know who he was?"

"No. She told my parents this other person would take them the rest of the way to Florida, get them jobs. That's the last we knew of her. No contact since. Nothing. My mother and father have been sick with worry. Manny is ready to kill, he's so angry."

Hoya remembered the newspaper stories of young women coming from impoverished backgrounds in Mexico, kidnapped, and forced into sex slavery. They ended up in many states across the US It left him with a bad feeling about Rosita's fate.

The few times he overheard the men in his crew bragging about their sexual exploits with underage girls pissed him off. On one of those occasions, he came close to saying something, but he knew it would provoke an argument. He wasn't clear whether they paid for these encounters or were merely taking advantage of gullible kids. He couldn't condone messing with underage kids under any circumstance.

"Where in Florida was she supposed to be going?"

"We have no idea. I don't think Rosita did either. That's why Manny's so protective of me. He gets crazy whenever I take off by myself."

"Hey, I can relate to that. I'd be the same if you were my sister."

Hoya reflected again on the boasters in his crew. Maybe one of them knows something about the sex slavery epidemic in southwest Florida. He decided to ask around on Monday at the worksite.

Bella stood. "I have to leave."

"Wait!" Hoya put his hand on her arm. "I may be able to help find Rosita." The words were out before he could stop himself.

She stiffened. "How? Do you know something?"

The hopefulness steeped in her expression stopped him. Hoya's neck warmed. What an ass. I'm raising her expectations, and the one idea I come up with is asking around the bozos in my crew. An impossible long shot, at that.

"No, no, nothing concrete. Only that . . . ah, I know a person who went through a similar thing. They found her later," he lied.

Her face beamed. She pulled a ballpoint pen from her purse, reached to pick up a napkin and scribbled on it. "My cell number," she said handing it to him. "Call me if you find something that might help us. Please! Please!"

Chapter Seven

As was his habit, Hoya arrived before any of his crew. He peered out the construction trailer window to the section of the development they needed to complete over the next three months. Nothing stirred and nothing would for another half hour. The rising sun laced the eastern Florida skyline with bright yellow and orange, promising a rain-free day.

Hoya stood at the desk unscrewing the top of his coffee thermos when Carlos Perez, his site supervisor, swung open the door. Hoya greeted him with a smile. The man's dependability made Hoya's job easier, always arriving early and forever the last to leave. Perez was a consistent Swiss watch.

"Morning, Sam. Looks like a good one." Perez shot him a warm grin. "Forecast for this week shows no rain. Maybe we make up for those days we lost a week ago."

"I hope so," Hoya said, raising the thermos. "You want coffee?"

Perez flicked the bag in his hand. "No, thanks. I picked up a container at Mickey D's on the way over."

Hoya moved from his desk to the blueprint-covered table and opened the manila folder that lay on top. "Tony Diaz, he working today?"

"He better be, the lazy ass *maricón*. He missed four days this month. I told him, no more or he's gone."

"He was the one you heard, you know, bragging about a teenage *puta* he had? About a whorehouse out in the Everglades supposed to have all this young pussy?"

Perez removed the coffee container and placed it on the edge of the table. He faced Hoya. "Yeah, but I believe the *pendejo* is fulla shit. Likes to run his mouth a lot." Perez made no attempt to disguise his disdain.

Hoya closed the folder and walked to the trailer's open door. Before stepping out, he told Perez, "Send him to me when he gets here. Okay? I'll be over in the new section."

The twisted expression on Perez's face held Hoya in place. "What?"

"Hey, Sam, you're not looking to score some—"

"Christ, no. You kidding me? I want to ask him a question about—well, shit. I'm hoping he can give me a lead on a teenage girl I know about gone missing. Nothing more."

Perez nodded.

Hoya took off across the construction site, toward the last building phase óf the project. Later, Tony Diaz approached while Hoya chatted with one of his equipment operators.

The laces of Diaz's work boots were untied, the sleeves of his blue denim shirt rolled up, his arms displaying his well-developed biceps. His slow stride was that of someone not eager to get to where he was going.

Hoya figured Perez gave him an earful, let him wonder if his job was in jeopardy. The truth was Hoya couldn't afford to fire the man. The number of skilled workers and the available labor pool around southwest Florida dwindled drastically during the past year when the housing market slumped to a level the state hadn't seen in the prior ten years.

Diaz stopped beside a backhoe loader. He leaned against the Caterpillar, wearing a face of concern. "Yeah, boss? You wanna talk to me?"

Hoya motioned for him to stay put. "I'll be right with you." When he finished speaking with the backhoe operator, he beckoned to Diaz and took him by the elbow. "Over here," Hoya said and steered him away from the Caterpillar to a spot twenty yards from the other worker.

He wondered if he was being smart taking the young man into his confidence, but if anyone in his gang of workers had any information about whorehouses in the local area, Diaz was the man.

Antonio Diaz, twenty-three, with an athletic body, a full head of tangled black hair, and a handsome face that reminded many of his co-workers of the Cuban actor, Andy Garcia. Diaz gloated whenever someone made the comparison, even when they tossed it at him as sarcasm.

His good looks worked well for him with the ladies. Not so with a few of his crew who believed he was gay. If anyone dared to say that to his face, the Andy Garcia look-alike's fists would fly. Diaz might be lazy, according to Perez, but he was anything but a *maricón*.

"Tony, verify something for me," Hoya began. "Let's say it came through the grapevine. Yes? No questions, no denials."

Diaz squeezed his eyes and tilted his head, his examination of Hoya filled with skepticism. Shifting from one foot to the other, he pushed his hands into his pockets. "Depends on what ya talkin' about. The job here?"

"Calm down," Hoya said, flipping up his palms. "Nothing to do with work."

Tony Diaz stayed silent, waiting.

"I need your help on a personal matter." He used a relaxed tone to dispel the man's growing suspicion.

The young man released his stiff shoulders. "Yeah, sure, I'll help if I can."

"Alright, then. It concerns a whorehouse I heard you might know something about, in the Everglades." He took care not to sound accusatory. Diaz tensed anyway.

"Hey, who the hell told you that? I ain't never—"

"Hold on, Tony. I said no denials." For a moment, Hoya thought he would storm off. "I'm not going to fire you. I need information, that's all. No judgments."

The young stud placed his hands on his hips and wagged his head. "Yeah, well, suppose I do go out there—I mean, once in a while. No harm. It's clean, nobody gets hurt." He kicked at a cement fragment and sent it bouncing away.

His defensive voice amused Hoya. It sounded like, *So I get laid, but I also go to church*. Hoya reached out and put his hand on Diaz's shoulder. "Tony, I don't give a damn if you go there. What I want to find out is whether they use underage girls to service their clients?"

Diaz's eyes traveled off into the distance.

"Let me explain why I'm asking. I promise nothing will come back on you."

"Yeah?"

"I give you my word."

No reply. Diaz remained immobile, his dark eyes trained straight ahead. "Okay, man," he said. "Tell me."

"The sister of a friend of mine went missing about three months ago." Hoya spoke using a tone a father would use to explain a family secret to his coming-of-age son. "Young, sixteen years old. From this small Mexican village called *Morelos* in the state of *Chiapas*. A priest smuggled her across the border with another teen."

Hoya stopped. He lowered his eyes and scrutinized his employee's face. "You see where this is going, don't you?"

"I can guess."

"The priest delivered the girls to a man in the States. Supposed to drive them here to Florida. You know the drill. Well-paying restaurant jobs, a better life, and all that other bullshit."

"You think they became *putas* here in Florida?"

"Yeah, or maybe somewhere else. But if they did, you can bet your ass it wasn't voluntary. You hear what I'm saying?"

Diaz flinched. "Hey, man. I don't know nothin' about that."

"Tony, don't con me. You know damn well a lot of those young *chicas* are kidnapped under false pretenses, then forced into turning tricks by a scummy pimp or the organization that runs these whorehouses."

His composure shaken by Hoya's challenge, Diaz rocked again from one foot to the other. He nodded without speaking.

"Not long ago, someone overheard you mouthing off to a couple of guys on the job about this great pussy you had at a house in the Everglades. Am I wrong?"

"No. So what?"

"Well, here's what I want from you. Where's this place located, and how do I get inside to have a look around—at the women?"

The Andy Garcia look-alike smirked. "Easy. Become a customer. You want, I'll take you."

Chapter Eight

Sam Hoya steered the Range Rover over the rutted, sandy road. His eyes panned the surrounding terrain. He left the paved section a mile back and found it surprising people actually lived out here. Despite having spent almost ten years in southwest Florida, he'd never been this deep into the Everglades wilderness.

"What did you tell them?" Hoya asked.

"That you wanted to have a look at the place before you decided. Told him you'd never been to a whorehouse, and you were skittish." Tony Diaz laughed. "He called you a cherry."

Hoya ignored the comment.

Moonlight snaked through the dense canopy of hardwood hammock and cypress trees. Hoya probed the night through his windshield. The road would bend left or right without warning. The Range Rover's bright halogen headlamps kept him from veering off-course, crashing through the sharp saw palmetto lining both sides and into a waiting slough. He realized he could never find the place alone. Diaz offered to drive, but he declined, reluctant to surrender complete control. Hoya suspected Diaz enjoyed his disorientation.

"How much farther?"

"Up ahead, another hundred yards."

Within reach of the Rover's high beams, the road looked like it would dead-end. Instead, it hooked to the right and blossomed into thirty yards of open space. Hoya followed the turn while the gravel surface pelted the undercarriage of the vehicle.

Ahead, two double-wide trailers parked end to end appeared in his headlights. One trailer was dark. A faint glow seeped through two high windows of the second trailer. A covered fixture above the door splashed a pool of light onto the steps leading up to the entrance.

Hoya pulled the Rover in front and killed the engine. Several floodlights mounted on trees dotted the parking area and produced an eerie atmosphere. Two SUV's appeared at one end of the darkened trailer.

Hoya pointed. "Customers?"

"No. They belong to the brothers."

"You tell them who I was?"

"Said you were my boss."

"What's their names again?" Hoya asked, thinking about how he would play this.

"Marco Espinosa. His brother is Andres."

"The cops know about this place?"

Diaz snapped his head around. "Christ, man—I mean, you're not thinkin' of rattin' them out, are you? Because—"

"Relax, Tony. I'm interested in one thing. To make sure Rosita Fuentes isn't one of the girls in their stable."

Diaz reached over and gripped Hoya's arm. His voice rose in pitch. "Hey, these guys, both of them, they're dangerous. They don't mess around. You know what I mean?"

Hoya pulled away. "Nothing's gonna happen, Tony. I look. I ask a few questions—that's all. So cool it."

"Ah, Christ, I don't know. Shit. I don't know. Maybe we shouldn't have—"

"Let's go in," Hoya said and pushed opened the Rover's door.

Diaz exited the vehicle, climbed the two steps ahead of Hoya and hesitated at the trailer door. He spread his hands and ironed them along his thighs. Before he could turn the handle, Hoya came up behind and touched his shoulder. "You alright?"

"Yeah. I suppose."

Diaz pushed open the door and stepped through with Hoya following. For a split-second, Hoya fought back the urge to laugh. He couldn't believe he was about to enter a whorehouse.

Two men seated at a reception desk glanced up from their game of dominoes. One was a square-jawed man with eyes close together, wearing a white tee shirt, his face covered with a light beard, his bare, oval skull sitting on a neck that disappeared into his broad shoulders.

The second man in a sports shirt produced an uncertain stare directed toward Diaz. He pushed back from the board of dominoes and waited. A lock of black hair fell over his brow, and his round face played host to a thin beard line running from one ear, down under his chin, and up to his other ear. A black mustache completed the picture of a *hombre* you didn't want to go *mano a mano* with.

The first man stepped toward them. Diaz reached out his hand. "Marco, *cómo estás*? I want you should meet my head honcho, Sam Hoya. You know, the one I told you about?"

Marco squinted at Hoya with a curious expression. The brother, a six-foot hulk weighing easily two hundred and fifty pounds, wore a long-sleeve, black, button-down shirt. The shirt hung loosely over stone-washed jeans tucked into a pair of Tony Lama cowboy boots. He took Hoya's hand into his and shook it. Hoya winced at the man's vise-like grip.

"*Mucho gusto*," Marco said, his tone tinged with insincerity.

Andres, the shorter brother, remained sitting, said nothing, and scooped the domino tiles into one neat pile on the board. A holstered .38 strapped to his hip caught Hoya's attention.

"Tony, here, tells me you wanna check out the place before you buy. Yes?" Marco smirked.

"If it's okay with you," Hoya said, flicking his thumb and forefinger in a nervous tic. "I've never been to a—"

"Brothel," Marco finished. "So Tony says."

Hoya's shoulders rose. "Well, you know what I mean."

Marco stood in one spot, facing the door, regarding Hoya with an amused expression.

Hoya's eyes traveled around his surroundings. He guessed the trailer measured around a thousand square feet of total space. The walls were paneled with dark mahogany wood. A cluster of loveseats in rich, red leather occupied three corners, each setting flanked by large plants. Thick wall-to-wall carpeting covered the trailer floor, and the low lighting set around the room gave the place a homey feeling. Hoya assumed the two doorways at either end of the interior led to bedrooms.

On one side of the trailer at a free-standing bar, a woman stood sipping champagne from a fluted glass. Dressed as though she'd just stepped out of a Frederick's of Hollywood catalog—wearing a lace push-up bra and lace panties—Hoya struggled to keep from smiling.

On cue, three of the four bedroom doors opened. From each door, a woman paraded out, wearing the same scanty attire, and sat on one of the three sofas. It looked to Hoya like a standard ceremonial presentation of the establishment's goods.

Marco made a sweeping gesture. "So then, wadda ya say we take a tour? Come," he said, taking Hoya by the forearm. "I show you the bedrooms. Then we'll have a beer."

The four rooms were identical in size, measuring twelve by twelve. The aromas of Lysol and cheap perfume battled each other. The rooms were furnished the same: a white duvet covering a double bed with an antique brass headboard. A tall, six-drawer lingerie chest hugged one corner of the room. Hoya imagined the chest held an assortment of sex toys. A reclining contoured, black armless leather chair, positioned next to a small table with a porcelain basin, caught Hoya's eye. He remembered the brochure of the Tantra Sex Chair he once flipped through. He bit his cheek to keep from smiling.

Each room had a bathroom, which Marco explained he added in such a way their walls extended beyond the original trailer exterior.

"Satisfied?" Marco said.

"Beats a lot of hotels I've been in."

"Okay, let's go meet the ladies."

Diaz stood between two women at the bar chatting away like old friends. Andres took a position behind the bar when Hoya and Marco came out of the last bedroom. The two other women remained seated on the red leather loveseats, holding their fluted glasses of champagne on their laps, their thighs and knees pinned together, posing like debutantes at their coming out party.

Marco approached the two standing at the side of Diaz. "This here is Linda," he said, sliding his hand behind the woman's neck and flipping up a swath of her brunette hair from her shoulders. Her dark eyes, accented by a fair amount of eyeshadow, made her appear spooky.

The second woman was a blonde on the plump side with rouged cheeks and an overbite, but with a prettier face. Her round breasts bubbled up from beneath her tiny, see-thru brassiere.

"Say hello, Zena. This is Mr. Hoya. I got a notion he likes blondes."

Zena flaunted her pearly whites and stuck out her hand. Hoya took it into his fingers for a second, then let it drop.

Before introducing the remaining two women, Marco said to Andres behind the bar. "How about a beer for our guests?"

While he waited for Andres to pop the last cap on the bottles of Heineken, Hoya scrutinized the faces of the two ladies at the bar. Despite attempts to appear youthful, sexy, and alluring, both had passed twenty-five a while ago.

Marco completed his introduction of the two seated women: a teased-out redhead and a frosted blonde with a pixie cut. Hoya guessed the pixie cut placed somewhere in her late twenties and the redhead would never see thirty again. Unless Marco had Diaz's so-called young pussy stashed away in the other trailer, nothing he saw so far revealed his visit here was anything but a waste of time.

Hoya found Marco staring at him. Uncomfortable being studied, he set his bottle on the bar. Was the brother expecting him to select one of the ladies tonight?

"Another?" Marco asked.

"No, thanks."

"You know, I have a hunch I seen you before," Marco said, wagging a finger at him.

Hoya shrugged. "Possibly. I've lived in this part of Florida close to ten years."

"No, no," Marco said. "Not around here." Suddenly his eyes opened wide. "Damn! Now I remember. Number forty-four, linebacker, Florida State. Right? Am I right?" Marco's expression looked like a winning contestant on "Jeopardy."

"Jesus, that was fifteen years ago. How the hell could you recall?"

"Hey, I lived up in Tallahassee those years. Not in this business. A jumping bar on the west side of the city. Made it to all the Seminoles' home games. Watched you kick ass lotta times. Man, do I miss that."

Marco's body became animated, and Hoya worried the big man was about to bear hug him.

"How come you never went pro?" Marco asked.

"Long story. I'll save it for the next time."

A grin slowly formed as Marco said, "You know, I don't believe there'll be a next time. My guess is you didn't come here to sample the merchandise. So what's the real story?"

Andres walked to the front of the bar and stood next to his brother. His right hand rested on the holstered .38. Hoya's eyes followed him. He glanced at the two women and then over to the pair seated. He flicked his thumb and forefinger again. Time to open up.

"I'm doing a favor for a friend, trying to find two sixteen-year-old girls. They were smuggled in from Mexico by a priest. The priest turned them over to a guy who drove them to South Florida. He was supposed to help them find waitressing jobs." His eyes returned to the two women in front of him. "Instead, we believe they forced them into—"

"What!" Marco's scream made Linda and Zena jump. "You fuckin' outta your mind. You aware here in Florida, you get a heavy hit for that? Where did you get the idea we use underage girls? Is that why this dickhead brought you here?" Marco scowled at Diaz. "Hey, dickhead. You tell the man we have young pussy here?"

Diaz dropped his Heineken bottle on the bar as though he'd been caught drinking illegally. "Man, I never . . . I never told him that."

Marco glared over his nose at him.

Shaken, Diaz sputtered, "What it was . . . I mean . . . I said somethin' to a couple of guys on the crew, you know, like bullshittin'. Yeah, like braggin'."

Hoya spoke up. "He's right, he never said it to me. My foreman told me he overheard one of my crew talking to his buddies. That's why I asked Tony to set me up. I wanted to come out here, see for myself."

Marco shook his head and faced the women. "Girls, it's late. We got nobody else booked. Let's call it a night. Get some sleep.

Sorry for the screw up here. Don't forget to double-lock the trailer door." He sounded like a concerned father.

The four ladies-of-the-night filed out as Hoya's eyes followed them. "Christ, Marco. I'm sorry. I never—"

"Not to worry, Hoya." He nodded toward Diaz and said, "I should have never trusted this dickhead. Hey, dickhead, you ever tell anyone we sell teenage pussy, I'm goin' cut your dick off. You hear what I'm sayin'? And your business ain't welcome here no more."

Diaz bent his head, acknowledging his fate. Tony Diaz would never face his pals again with the same testosterone-driven bravado, Hoya thought. Tonight's experience was certain to take a toll on the young stud's psyche.

Marco returned to the back of the bar and pulled out two more Heineken. "Have another," he said, and he popped their caps.

Reluctant to worsen an already inflamed situation, Hoya took the bottle without comment.

"Sit down," Marco said, pointing to one of the two barstools. "Let me see if I can enlighten you, make your trip here worthwhile." Without pausing, Marco went into an apologetic-sounding speech. "I run a quality operation here. My girls, all first class. I treat them good. So good, in fact, I got a waitlist of ladies who want to come work for me. Their cut is better than any operation in Florida. The place—you saw yourself—clean, furnishings upscale. It's a comfortable place to work. You know what I mean? The sheriff of this county leaves me alone. So when dickhead here shoots off his big mouth that could bring my business down around my ears, I get pissed. You know?"

Diaz stood behind him, shuffling his feet.

"Your missing kid?" Marco said, switching subjects. "This priest? I heard about him months ago. He gets paid by the Salazar syndicate. I'm sure the padre has no idea where the kids he smuggles end up. He thinks they're gonna get jobs up north, make good money to send back home. Instead, they're forced into the sex slave business by that dirtbag."

Hoya took a long pull on his Heineken and set down the bottle. "He operate here in South Florida?"

"Uh-uh. Above Tampa."

"You think she might be up there?"

"No chance. He's no fool. Ships the underage ones to New York, where he's less likely to face serious time if he gets caught. He competes with all those imported Oriental skags other groups sneak into the country."

After another swallow of beer, Hoya asked, "Are the cops in New York aware of him?"

"Oh, yeah. Salazar's been operating there a lotta years." Marco furrowed his brow. "You sure you wanna go that route?"

"It's a start."

"Right, but I gotta tell you, bro. You know the needle in the haystack saying? Well, your needle's in a dangerous haystack. So, watch your ass."

Hoya emptied his bottle and set it down. "Thanks, my friend." He shook Marco's hand and signaled to Diaz it was time to go. After giving Andres a quick head bob, he and Diaz exited the trailer and climbed into the Range Rover.

"Well, that was an amusing experience," Hoya said. He glanced at the young stud's face. The stud wasn't smiling.

Chapter Nine

Fields pressed the intercom. "Yes, Rachel?"

"Jack, Police Superintendent Emilio Sanchez is on line one."

"Thanks, Rach." Fields switched to the speakerphone to enable Carter Brooke to listen in on the conversation. *"Hola, Emilio, qué pasa?"*

"Hold on a minute, Jack," Sanchez said. "Let me shut my door."

Brooke, the recently appointed head of the New York City field office, was seated on the sofa. He looked up from the bulletin he was reading and put the document aside. "Doesn't he always keep his office door closed?" he whispered.

Fields chuckled. The tone Brooke used sounded like he asked: "Didn't the man always zip up his fly?"

"No. Unless Emilio has a meeting going on, or if he's involved in a confidential conversation. He always keeps his door open. He likes to see out to the reception area. The heavy crime situation in San Juan makes him feeling skittish these days."

The speaker leaped alive. "Sorry about that."

"No problem, Emilio. So, what's happening?"

"We have a red alert, my friend, concerning our undercover. One of the cartel's grunts reported seeing our man with a federal agent in a restaurant out in Bayamon. Of course, it's bogus. The guy produced a photo of the two men taken on his cell phone. The agent was someone known to the cartel, and the man with him looked similar to our undercover. But the grunt finally conceded his mistake."

Fields grimaced, and his fingers formed a teepee under his mouth. He worried about the fallout. The undercover was his man. He recruited him, trained him, and therefore was responsible for him.

Brooke stood and walked to the desk. Leaning over the speaker, he said, "Superintendent, this is Carter Brooke. Wouldn't the retraction remove any suspicion from our undercover?"

Sanchez released a deep sigh. "It should, Mr. Brooke, but the cartel is paranoid when it comes to any suspected security breach. Regardless of the recanting, they'll keep a close watch on our guy. It might be a while before they relax their surveillance."

"How long, Emilio? A week . . . a month . . . How long?"

"Hard to say, Jack. It complicates things. He told me he's not comfortable communicating the usual way. He says he can't take the chance, so he's going dark."

"Well, how the hell will we know when the fast boats are loaded and set to launch from Fajardo?" Fields said. "Good God, the timing of this whole operation is critical."

They heard Sanchez's chair squeaking as he moved around in it. There was a pause before he spoke. "I'm aware of that problem. When I last talked with him, he suggested we use the visual signal we employed a few years ago. You remember it, don't you, Jack?"

"I do, but it requires a conduit to receive the sign and convey it to me. I can't rely on an agent from our field office in San Juan. The cartel knows them all."

Sanchez snickered. "And surer than hell, I wouldn't trust anyone from law enforcement in Puerto Rico, local or state. Half of them are in the cartel's pocket."

Brooke turned to Fields. "How about someone from our office?"

"That wouldn't be a certainty either," Fields said. "The cartel has accumulated an extensive file of names and photos of agents. It would be hard to find one unknown to them. No, we need someone completely anonymous."

"I have an idea," Brooke said. "How about I go? I've been in Washington so long, I can't imagine anyone on the island would recognize me."

"Don't bet on it," he said. "Besides, I don't believe Headquarters would approve. You're not a field agent."

The room remained quiet for a moment before Fields got to his feet. He walked to his window that overlooked downtown Manhattan. With a population of over eight and a half million people in an area of about 302 square miles, surely in the city of New York, there had to be a person who would be a complete blank to the Ortega cartel. A thought jumped out at him.

"Emilio, I might have someone who could be our man. He's a private investigator who owes the bureau a small favor, and he thrives on action. Why don't I talk to him? See if he's willing to go down to San Juan for a week. Be our conduit?"

"Is he savvy enough to protect himself if things go south?"

"Oh, yeah. He's tough and he's smart, and he might be exactly what we need. My guess is he'd have no trouble riding under the cartel's radar. Let me knock the idea around with the boss here. Then I'll float it by this guy. Worse comes to worst, we'll send down one of our own agents and hope for the best.

I'll get back to you once we make a decision. We can hammer out the details then."

"Right, Jack, but we move quickly. The undercover is at risk every day he's there."

"I agree," Fields said. "And once the drug shipment leaves Fajardo, we pull him out."

* * *

After a quick lunch of a burger and two glasses of iced tea at a local coffee shop on West Twenty-third Street, Rizzo reentered the Flatiron Building through the Fifth Avenue side revolving doors. He waited at the elevator bank and followed the floor indicator moving at a snail's pace. The landmark building, built in 1902, suffered through several renovations over the decades. The updating of the Flatiron failed to bring the elevators into the twenty-first century.

The triangle-shaped structure with the limestone and glazed terra-cotta facade was one of the oldest commercial buildings in the city still in use. It was Rizzo's place of business for the last several years. He liked the convenient location—close to all public transportation. The building's proximity to subway lines made it a cinch for him to navigate the five boroughs with swiftness and ease.

Unfortunately, Rizzo's office lease had only six months left. Despite his pleading, the building management would not renew it. A major publishing conglomerate, already occupying several floors, contracted to take over the entire building within the next year or two. Therefore, the building management would not consider new or renewal leases.

Since Rizzo wanted to stay in the Chelsea neighborhood, he became proactive. He scoped-out a four-story office building across Fifth opposite the Flatiron. He put in his application after the management told him his prospects were good for office space within six months.

Two men he didn't recognize came into the lobby and paused at the elevators. The man standing closest to him had the body frame of an athlete. He was tall, broad-chested, with wide shoulders, and large hands. Rizzo pictured him shagging fly balls in the outfield of a professional baseball team. He wore a light tan windbreaker and a checked sports shirt opened at the neck. His shoe size, around a size twelve, balanced his sizeable physique. No hat.

The second man, Hispanic looking, had a thickset body and the weather-beaten face of a person who'd spent too much time in the hot sun. His wiry black hair leaked out from under a Tampa Bay Rays baseball cap, and a Charlie Chan goatee sprouted beneath his full lips. He wore a black faux-leather jacket zippered to the throat, baggy jeans, and a pair of white Nike sneakers.

The elevator arrived and the door slid open. Rizzo entered the empty car first, followed by the athlete, then the goatee. He pressed four. The athlete and the goatee watched his floor selection and failed to push a different number.

At the fourth floor, the car bounced to a stop. Both strangers exited ahead of him. They hesitated in the narrow corridor to examine the directory.

Rizzo slipped around them and headed down the corridor. He stopped in front of his office door and inserted his key. When he turned his head, he saw the two men continued to study the directory.

"Who you trying to find?"

They swapped glances until the athlete answered. "We're looking for Luke Rizzo, a private investigator. Number 402."

Rizzo pulled the key from the lock. "I'm Luke Rizzo, but I don't recall having made any appointments today. What's this about?"

The goatee took a step toward him. "My uncle, Luis Fuentes, he gave me your name. I'm Manny Fuentes. He said you might be able to help us locate my sister."

A sudden jolt of suspicion made Rizzo ask, "Who's your sister?"

"Rosita Fuentes. She went missing about three months ago."

Rizzo cut his eyes to the second man. The athlete didn't wait to be asked.

"I'm Sam Hoya, a friend of Manny's older sister. I'm along to lend a hand. We drove up from Florida. Got here last night."

"Then let's go inside, see what's what." He unlocked the door, pushed it open, and allowed his two visitors to enter first.

Rizzo followed and motioned them to the chairs at the sides of his desk. The door to the storage closet stood ajar exposing the safe holding his three firearms. If his two visitors posed a threat, Rizzo realized his weapons would be useless.

Rizzo dropped into his desk chair and leaned back, his elbows resting on the padded arms. He remembered what Luis Fuentes told him about the disappearance of his niece, Rosita, and her friend. Glaring at Manny Fuentes, Rizzo said, "How the hell does anyone let two sixteen-year-old girls take off alone the way they did? And into the hands of a total stranger?"

Manny's chin pointed down at his feet. When it came up, he found Rizzo's penetrating eyes. "My sister, Bella, and me, we had no God-damn idea what was goin' down. Not 'til we heard from my papa in Mexico. By that time, Rosita was long gone."

"But your parents let her go?"

"They tried to stop her. Rosita, she could be stubborn somethin' fierce. She was set on helping out the family. She believed if she came up to Florida and got a waitress job, she could send money back."

"How do you know she's here in New York and not in another city?"

Hoya jumped into the exchange. He related his visit to the Everglades and the information he received from the Espinosa brothers. "Then when Manny heard from his uncle about what happened to Rodrigo Vega—"

"Who?"

"Rodrigo Vega. You know, Manny's other uncle. The guy who got stabbed."

"Oh, you mean Rabbit."

Hoya blinked, then continued. "That's why we're here. To find Rosita and her friend. You think you can help us? We'll pay you whatever we can."

Rizzo rolled his eyes toward the ceiling and glared at a line of cracked plaster. "Do you know how incredibly risky it is, what you're trying to do?"

"So they've warned me," Hoya said with an uneasy grin. "By the Espinosa brothers and Luis Fuentes."

"You guys really want to do this?"

After a moment of trading eyeballs, both voices spoke as one. "Yeah."

Rizzo turned to Manny. "Where you guys staying? With your uncle?"

"No. A Holiday Inn Express on the West Side, near the Hudson River."

"Fiftieth between Tenth and Eleventh?"

"That's the one."

"I know it. I live in the neighborhood. Did you travel armed?"

"I did," Hoya said. "A .38. I'm licensed to carry. Not to worry."

Rizzo flashed him a troubled look. "In Florida, maybe. Not here. This state doesn't recognize Florida concealed-carry licenses. You'd have to register it here, and that takes time."

Hoya eyed Manny, then Rizzo. "Well, we're ready to take the risk."

"How long you planning to stay?"

"Long as necessary," Manny said, answering first. "I work in golf course maintenance in a gated community. I got a leave from my job when I told the course superintendent why I needed to come up here."

Rizzo looked at Hoya.

"Two weeks. Vacation time from my construction company. More if I need it."

Rizzo scrutinized the athletic one, visualizing him in pinstripes. He remembered his son Matt was having a try-out this spring for the Fordham University freshman squad. Unable to resist, he asked, "You play baseball in school?"

Hoya fidgeted before answering. "Football. FSU."

"No shit? What position?"

"Linebacker."

Rizzo looked at Manny. The solidly built Mexican cocked his head and released a snicker. "Running." He waited a beat, then added, "From the *Federales*."

The man's self-deprecating humor made Rizzo laugh. In a tone of concern, he said, "You got a record?"

"Hell, no. Kids' stuff, that's all. Would've never gotten my green card if I had one."

Rabbit's murder replayed in Rizzo's head like a movie. Angry at how helpless he was to stop it, he wanted to avenge his old friend's death, find the knife-wielding punk. Manny and Hoya also had a serious stake. Find Rosita and her friend soon before they too became victims.

Rizzo reflected on ways to use the two men. He needed to be cautious, avoid placing them in danger. Not so easy considering who they'd be going against. If Jack Fields knew, he would probably have a shit-fit.

"What do you say, *amigo?*" Manny asked. "You willing to help us out?"

Shutting down his thoughts, Rizzo said, "Okay, guys. We got our work cut out. I'm ready if you are. We'll worry about my compensation later."

The slap of high fives rang out.

Rizzo rolled back his chair and stood. "Our jumping-off point is to locate a guy called Frankie Cusack."

"Who's he?" Manny said.

"The one who stabbed Rabbit. Didn't your uncle tell you?"

"No. He told me about the stabbing but never said the guy's name."

"Cusack's the one who told Rabbit about your sister about—ah, having . . . ." Rizzo paused, unsure of how to phrase it.

Manny was ahead of him. "You mean the prick who shot his mouth off about screwing Rosita?"

Silence enveloped the room like a wake. Apparently, Luis Fuentes gave them the details of Rabbit's encounter with Cusack but nothing more. Manny's eyes flared with rage, fingers of both his hands curled into tight fists, the fists rested on his knees.

"Same guy. We gotta locate him to have a chance at finding the girls."

Hoya got to his feet. "How do we do that?"

"I already have the engine started. I'm guessing Cusack has a record, so I talked to a friend at the FBI. My contact there is looking into it. I'm hoping he can get me Cusack's last address. The problem is the agent will now own me. He expects me to return the favor. You know how that goes. *Quid pro quo.* Nothing is for nothing with the Feds. My worry is the favor could be a risky one."

Hoya gawked back at him through curious eyes.

"When do we move on this guy?" Manny said.

"A couple of days. First, I have to check out a place where he hangs out in the Bronx."

Manny laughed. "We catch him there, and after that, maybe I kill him?"

Rizzo made a face. "You're not coming along. And killing him wouldn't be too smart. No chance I'd let you do that." He waited a beat and then added, "After I track him down, it's possible you two could put a hurt on him. How would that be?"

"Works for me," Manny said, bobbing his head.

Chapter Ten

An inebriated, powerful looking man fell through Ruby's doorway. He stumbled to the curb after several unsure steps, regained his balance, and then supported his thick body against the lamppost that towered over the tavern entrance. He peered up and down Hunt's Point Avenue, looking like someone trying to remember where he parked his car. The pool of light from the streetlamp above made him visible.

Rizzo squinted across the span. "Not our guy."

"Good thing, mon," Jabba said, giving Rizzo a playful elbow. "From the size of him, it would take a few more than the two of us to pin his ass down. Besides, aren't we checkin' for a tall, skinny dude, a stretched-out bag of bones with fire in his eyes?"

"And a vicious killer," Rizzo said. "Let's remember that." He turned to face Jabba and saw a look of impatience. "You sure you want to do this? I can go in alone."

"Yes, mon, I'm with you. You need backup. Told me that yourself."

"What I said was, on the job I'd have another detective with me during a search like this. I wasn't asking you—"

"Bro, I be your backup man, and I ain't gonna change my mind. This don't worry me none."

"Yeah, but if you get hurt again, Flo will divorce me."

"No, mon, ain't gonna happen, so stop worryin'."

Rizzo watched the unsteady drunk pick his way up the avenue, using the roofs of parked vehicles for support. When he was out of sight, Rizzo reached for the Ford's door handle. "Then, let's go. Let me do the talking."

A handful of Ruby's patrons sat around the circular bar. Most of them were lone drinkers. A few groups occupied the tables and booths off to one side. No females in view. The place appeared to be a local male-only hangout, everyone familiar with one another.

Wall fixtures scattered about the room provided dim lighting, making it a challenge to recognize anyone. Ceiling speakers pumped out a song from Gloria Estefan and The Miami Sound Machine.

An anxious feeling crept over Rizzo as he and Jabba moved toward the circular bar. The husky voice of the barman greeted them when they climbed on the two stools closest to the door.

"What's your pleasure?" he asked, then dropped two Bud coasters in front of them. His angular face hosted a pair of dark set eyes that narrowed as they examined Jabba.

"Corona," Rizzo said and tossed a ten-dollar bill on the bar's surface.

Jabba nodded. "Same."

Both men sat eyeing the bottles lining the shelves dividing the round bar, careful to avoid any movement that would invite attention. The barman returned with the two Coronas. Rizzo smiled, trying to appear friendly. "Thanks."

"You want a glass?"

Rizzo shook his head. The man walked away without asking Jabba.

His voice kept to a whisper, the Rasta spoke first. "Too damn dark in here."

"Stay put. Let me look around."

Rizzo edged a half turn on his stool and lifted the Corona to his mouth. He scanned the tavern like a curious first-time visitor. His attention landed on the pair of men sitting at a nearby table huddled in conversation. From there, he checked out the three loners seated across from them. No one fit Eduardo Soto's description of Frankie Cusack.

Before Rizzo could examine the cluster of occupied tables on the left, he caught sight of the barman watching him. He spun back around.

The bartender approached them. "You lookin' for someone?"

Rizzo hesitated, then decided to take it head-on. "Yeah. A buddy of mine. Came here a lot. Said it was a nice place."

The barman leaned across. His head was inches from Rizzo's face. In a low voice, he asked, "You guys cops? 'Cause if you are, you ain't welcome here unless you got official business."

At that moment, the music switched off, and the Lionel Richie song playing went silent. The bar became deathly quiet.

"No, man," Rizzo replied. "We ain't cops. Shit, no. We came by to check out the place, see if my buddy was here. Nothing more."

"Who's your buddy?"

Again, Rizzo hesitated, then looked into the barman's eyes He thought, *In for a penny, in for a pound.* "Frankie—Frankie Cusack," he said. "You know him, right?"

From behind, arms the thickness and strength of a boa constrictor, wrapped themselves around Rizzo's shoulders. The steely voice that went with the arms said, "Yeah, Tommy knows him. I know him. We don't think you know him."

Jabba slid down from his stool. Before he could take a step, a second dry voice spoke. "Don't fuckin' think about it." The speaker placed the tip of a gun muzzle against Jabba's ear.

Rizzo saw fear ignite in the Rasta's eyes. These guys are crazy, he thought. I don't need for Jabba to end up in the hospital again. His mouth dried up. "Hey! Christ, we're not here to cause trouble. You want us to leave, we'll leave."

The man lowered the gun, and the boa constrictor arms holding Rizzo released him. "Why you lookin' for Cusack?"

Rizzo rolled his shoulders trying to relax them. "Like I said, I'm thinking this was Frankie's hangout. We were drivin' up to the Bronx. On the way, I remember him telling me about this place. So we stop. See if we can buy him a drink."

"What's your name?" the boa constrictor said.

"Perez . . . Angel Perez."

"How come you know him?"

"Ah, well, how it is, we shared a space once at the Downstate Correctional Facility."

The man glared at Jabba.

The Rasta shook his head. "Grady Judd. I just be along for the ride."

No one spoke while the man with the arms and the bartender exchanged glances in coded conversation. The barman shrugged his shoulders.

"Okay. You guys beat it," the man said, "And don't come back unless you walk through the door with Frankie Cusack. I make myself clear?"

Relieved the situation hadn't escalated, and no one got hurt, Rizzo said, "Got it, pal."

Jabba and Rizzo reached the door at the same time the music came back on.

* * *

Rizzo dropped off Jabba at his apartment in Queens. It was close to one in the morning when he arrived home. He turned his key in the lock and pushed open the door. The locking mechanism captured Rizzo's attention. It was a standard type installed fifty years ago when they built the original three-story brownstones. Not much was needed to defeat it. Over the years on the job, he'd done so many times. Any amateur housebreaker could sail right past them.

Worried about putting Flo at risk of a home invasion, Rizzo decided to call his friend at AAA Locksmith and change out the lock to a Medeco Deadbolt. He remembered reading an article in *Popular Mechanics* touting the Medeco as one of the best against the use of a pick, a bump or a drill. The article called it one of the most durable bolts on the market. That's what he wanted.

Rizzo closed the door behind him and locked it. He latched the security chain across the frame and thought, *What an entirely useless safety device. A pair of snips and bang! The door flies open, and the intruder shoves a gun in the face of the resident.*

He slipped off his shoes and left them under the night light by the door. A wave of worry followed him as he tiptoed into the kitchen. The snap and fizz from opening a can of root beer sounded like a minor explosion in the quiet of the apartment. He swallowed half of the soda standing in the kitchen and walked into the living room to finish the rest. Before he could fall into the club chair, Flo's sleepy voice greeted him from the bedroom doorway.

"That you, Rocky? We better hurry. He'll be home in about an hour."

Rizzo muffled a laugh. No matter how many times Flo played this game, he always went along with it. They would invent silly dialogue and a lascivious scenario that would end with them crawling into bed and giggling like teens at a drive-in. Their lovemaking always left them exhausted and euphoric.

He took Flo into his arms and planted a hungry kiss on her lips. In the short time they'd been a couple, she became his *raison d'être*. He could think of no other woman in his life that made him happier and more fulfilled.

"Do I have time for a shower?" he said, tossing his trousers and shirt on the floor.

"Okay, hon. You better hurry, you hear. I'll wait for you in bed. I put new batteries in the Big Bertha so it won't die on us like it did the last time. Wasn't that awful?"

Rizzo threw back his head and burst out laughing. His boxer shorts slipped to his ankles. With an exaggerated gesture of delicacy, he used his toe to flip up the shorts, caught it in mid-air with one hand and dropped it on the pile of discarded clothing.

"Oh, and it's your turn to be tied up," he said as he headed to the bathroom.

"No, no darlin'. We'll have none of that, you devil. Don't you remember what happened last week? It took me so long to untie you, my husband almost caught us."

"Oh, right. So keep the window to the fire escape open," Rizzo called out from the bathroom. He stepped into the tub and pulled closed the shower curtain. "Damn! That last time was a cliffhanger," he added from under the pulsing showerhead.

Chapter Eleven

Jabba Saint James slammed shut the trunk of the Ford Focus, wiped his hands down the sides of his green coveralls, and walked to the opened driver's side door. With an effort, he squeezed his bulk under the steering column of the compact. The Rastafarian glanced around, giving the auto's interior a final once-over before he ran the vehicle into the Avis parking garage.

Jabba rubbed his fingers over the surface of the console to test for dust or dirt he missed. With two more vehicles to detail until he got off duty in an hour, he'd have to work fast. Finished, he would clock out, catch the Q47 bus back to his apartment in Jackson Heights, and pick up a couple of burgers at Mickey D's. Then relax and watch the current episode of "CSI" on his new flat-screen TV.

He adjusted the rearview mirror on the Ford and caught a glimpse of Flo Rizzo emerging from the rear door of the Avis building. The waning afternoon sun back-lit her on her way to her auto in the employee's parking area. Unless a customer detained her with a gnawing problem, Flo always left an hour before Jabba's eight-hour-shift ended.

Jabba rolled down the Ford's window and stuck out his head. "Yo, Flo Mae," he called. "You have a good night."

Flo waved and continued on her path to her car without breaking stride. Jabba reached to turn on the Ford's ignition. He hesitated when he spotted a shadowy figure step from the corner of the Avis building. Squinting through the fading sunlight, he made a guess it was one of the agents heading for his car. On closer scrutiny, he realized the tall, gangly, dark-haired man was a stranger.

The man wore a quilted, long-sleeve, hooded jacket, his head encased in the hood, and his baggy trousers cascaded over the tops of his shoes. Jabba remained in the Ford, his wary eyes glued to the quick-stepping stranger. Something about him rang a bell. The man closed in on Flo before she reached her car.

A worried feeling churned in Jabba's gut. He pushed open the door and stood to keep watch on the man. Head and shoulders above the mid-size Focus, Jabba stared across the car's roofline. He was uncertain what to make of the stranger. Was it a disgruntled customer wanting to continue his bitching about a bad rental experience? Should he go over there? Would Flo resent his interference? The man stopped a few feet from her, with his back to Jabba.

"Mrs. Rizzo."

Jabba heard him. So did Flo. Startled by his voice, she spun around. The stranger said something to her that Jabba missed. A Delta flight passing overhead absorbed the words into the roar of its engines. But he didn't miss seeing Flo's eyes widen.

The stranger thrust the heel of his hand into Flo's chest and forced her against the car door. In the next instant, Jabba heard a click, then he saw a switch-blade spring to life in the man's free hand. The man raised the tip of the blade to below Flo's chin. She opened her mouth to scream, but she could barely manage a choking sound.

Jabba broke across the twenty yards separating them, charging like a linebacker with the ball carrier in his sights. From five feet away, he launched his body into the air, blindsiding the man waist-high with the full force of his two hundred and ninety-five pounds. Both men flew like projectiles. The released knife sailed overhead, and the man's hood fell away from his face. Before Jabba got to his feet, the attacker climbed to his knees. This time he held a pistol and had it leveled at Jabba.

"Stay down, ganja-head, or I'll blow the fucking dreadlocks off your skull."

Jabba ignored him. He raised to one knee in an attempt to stand. When the man swung the gun barrel toward Flo, he stayed on his knee.

"I said stay down," the attacker ordered. "You want me to put the first bullet in her?"

Suspended in place, Jabba glared at the man while his heart raced.

"I'm not here to do anyone. Not this time." The man looked back at Flo. "You need to deliver the message, Mrs. Rizzo. You know what I'm sayin'?" He got to his feet. "Make sure your boy gets the word and nobody's gonna be hurt."

The man edged away toward the Lincoln Town Car parked at the gate. He kept the gun trained on Jabba. On one knee, Jabba waited until the man slipped behind the wheel before he pushed himself to his feet. The car peeled away onto the service road leading from the airport, but not before Jabba made a mental note of the license number.

Flo remained motionless against the car door. Jabba moved toward the frightened woman. He reached out and took her into his arms, gently patting her back with his huge palms. "Flo Mae, you okay?" Her body shook while she pressed her temple to his chest. She pushed air out her mouth and nostrils, panting, trying to catch her breath.

"It's okay, Flo Mae, he gone. It's okay . . . okay. He not gonna hurt you. Don't you worry none. Jabba's here."

The Rasta could sense his anger rising. A stab of guilt ran through him. He allowed Flo to come close to serious harm by not moving soon enough on the attacker.

Flo meant more to him than any woman in his life. He treasured the kindness and caring she showed him while he recovered from taking a bullet protecting her husband. *Looked after me 'til I be better, then getting me this job and all. Changed my life, she did.*

Flo's body shakes slowed. When she calmed down, Jabba released her and stepped back. A shiny object on the ground caught his eye. The knife jarred from the man's hand lay on the gravel at the spot where Jabba tackled him.

"Flo Mae," he said, inspecting her. "You feel better now?"

"Oh my lord, that was so awful."

Jabba paused. "Flo Mae, you know those gift bags behind the counter?"

Her breathing slowed and her eyes looked intently at Jabba, then blinked. "Oh, you mean the ones we use for maps?"

"They the ones I need. For this," Jabba said and pointed to the knife. "Don't want to touch it, mess up his fingerprints. They be important to the cops when they try to find out who the dude was." Jabba figured he already knew, but he said nothing to her.

Flo nodded and disappeared through the door into the office. The Rastafarian snorted, raised his eyes to the sky, set his back teeth and hissed, "I gonna kill the motherfucker when we find him."

* * *

Rizzo opened the refrigerator door and reached in for a can of Hires Root Beer. His thoughts drifted back to the unexpected visit from Manny Fuentes and Sam Hoya. He worried he acted too quick when he co-opted them into his effort to search for Rabbit's killer and locate the two girls. He was sure they had zero experience with this level of danger. Oh, maybe a punch-out or two in a Florida bar but nothing like what faced them now. Hoya had a weapon and a license to carry limited to Florida. Rizzo would have to keep him on a short leash, the .38 out of sight.

He closed the refrigerator door, and the wet can slipped from his fingers. The Hires bounced on the floor, rolled toward the sink, and came to rest at the baseboard. He bent to retrieve it, his head working on his Manny-Hoya problem.

Rizzo didn't hear Flo enter the apartment. She stood in the kitchen doorway, and he almost dropped the root beer can a second time. Behind her, the figure of Jabba St. James loomed over her shoulder like a mini high-rise.

"Jeez, guys, make a little noise," Rizzo said. "Like, give me a clue someone came in." A smile formed, but it disappeared when a grave expression appeared on Flo's face. Concern washed over him. He set the can on the counter and came forward. "What's wrong?"

Flo rushed to him, tears coating her cheeks. Rizzo received her body into his arms and held her pressed against his chest. He glanced over to Jabba standing in the doorway, his face a blank page. As a rule, when the big Rasta showed up at their apartment, it meant Flo extended an invite to dine with them. These invitations lessened once Jabba made a full recovery from his bullet wound. Tonight, however, it was evident the Rasta was not there for dinner.

While Rizzo listened, Jabba described the attack in the Avis parking lot, stringing out every detail of the incident the way he liked to do when he told stories of his family in Jamaica.

Frequently, he would pause to inject an element of humor into his telling. Not this time. He wisely refrained from making light of Flo's frightening experience.

"And so, mon," Jabba finished, "I figured it be best I drive her home. You know, keep an eye on her, see the dude don't bother her again."

"Bro, I'm grateful," Rizzo said. He glanced at his wife stretched out on the sofa, her eyes closed and a wet cloth covering her forehead. Flo quieted down after he insisted she sip from a tumbler of Jack Daniels he kept on hand for her. She would not have managed the drive from La Guardia by herself. Not in her distressed condition. He was grateful Jabba took over and got her home safely.

Rizzo visualized the scene in the Avis lot, the man pressing Flo against her car, the tip of his knife under her chin, the terrified expression on her face. A hot bolt of rage rose from his toes. *Frankie Cusack. I'm going to find that bastard and . . . .*

Turning toward Jabba, he said, "Would you recognize him if you see him again?"

"Oh, mon, you know I would. 'Specially the shit-eatin' grin, him pointin' the gun at me. Yes, mon. I be pickin' the fucker out in the middle of Yankee Stadium."

"Describe him."

Jabba pushed back into the soft cushion of the club chair and crossed one leg over the other. He did that when preparing to give forth with one of his many Jamaican fairy tales, stories he told to entertain Flo. "He be 'round six-three, 'bout my height, skinny like a straw man, so he looks taller. I tackled him, and I think maybe he break in half. But the dude is rubbery. He bounces up right away. His voice soft, like a girl's. No accent, so I make him American. Oh, and black hair, long, and stringy."

"What kind of car did he drive?"

"Old Lincoln Town Car. Like the gypsy cab drivers use."

Eduardo Soto came to mind. That night at the Turning Point Tavern, Soto mentioned he drove a gypsy cab. Jabba's description didn't fit Soto, but there might be a connection.

Rizzo mulled over the words the man used while threatening Flo: "Tell your husband to back off. Rabbit is dead, and he will be too if he don't stop nosing around. This is his last warning." For certain, Rizzo thought, his trip to Ruby's set off alarms.

He glanced again at Flo. She removed the wet cloth and sat up. His mind raced with worry. They knew who she was, where she worked, the car she drove, and God knows what else about her. Unless he provided enough protection, she'd always be in danger. He could back off, he thought, heed their warning.

"Jabba, what do you think? Should I let it drop?"

The Jamaican closed his eyes and rocked his head from side to side, his usual routine when confronted with a heavy decision. The next moment, Jabba issued a firm, "No!" He gave a quick look at Flo and then back to Rizzo. "Mon, I want to find the dude. Hurt him bad. If you wanna pass on it, then fine. You don't, I'm with you a hundred percent."

"And perhaps this time get you finished off permanently."

"Hey, mon, don't worry me none." Again, his eyes landed on Flo. "I don't want the guy be walking 'round free."

"I'm with you on that," Rizzo said. He wasn't concerned about himself. He could be a match for them. Plus, he now spiked the interest of the FBI, although he couldn't play that card with any degree of confidence.

Jabba held out the plastic bag containing the switchblade. "Nobody else touched this, so any prints got to be his. Then the police tell us who he is. Right?" He pulled a piece of scrap paper from his pocket and handed it to Rizzo. "His license plate number."

"Your instincts were good, bro," Rizzo said, looking at the knife. "Unfortunately, you can't get prints from a serrated grip. It won't give up anything readable. The license? Well, that's another thing. I got an idea who owns the Lincoln, and it isn't the guy who attacked Flo."

Rizzo took the knife and the scrap of paper and laid them on the coffee table. He would drop them off with Detective Frank Duggan, anyway. The knife might match the type used on Rabbit. Not hard evidence, and without a positive ID other than Jabba's description, it would be difficult to get an indictment. Rizzo was certain the person who stabbed Rabbit and attacked Flo was the same. If Jack Fields came up with a concrete lead to Frankie Cusack, it might be all he needed to get at the truth.

Standing in front of the seated Flo, he reached down. "How you feel now, sweetheart?" Flo took hold of his hands, and Rizzo pulled her to her feet. Taking her into his arms, he kissed her cheek and rubbed her shoulders.

Flo straightened. Her composure returned, she lifted her eyes and found Rizzo's face. With a giggle, she said, "My Lord, darlin', I know New York is a rough city, but this little ol' southern gal never expected anything like this."

He squeezed her to him. "I'm sorry to say my snooping around caused it. I mean, had I thought . . . well, it'll never happen again."

"Amen to that," Jabba said.

"I'm not afraid. I just have to learn to be more aware."

"Alright, sweetheart, no cooking tonight. Let's hop over to Pat and Mike's for dinner." He turned to Jabba. "What do you say, bro? You like steak, don't you?"

"Yes, mon, you be buying."

Chapter Twelve

"That's what Jabba said, Luis. The sleazebag got into a Lincoln Town Car. Jabba's description of the guy doesn't fit Soto. Maybe he loaned Cusack the car. I give you the plate number, can you check it out without tipping off Soto?"

"I can do that. I'm meeting him tomorrow night at the Turning Point. He usually gives me a ride home afterward. What is it?"

Rizzo switched the phone to his left hand, picked up the scrap of paper Jabba gave him and read the number.

"Got it."

"Okay. Thanks, Luis."

"Bye, *amigo*."

He sorted through the pile of mail on his desk, pulled out the few bills from among the overwhelming direct mail solicitations, and tossed the commercial flyers into the trash. He was certain he landed on the mailing list of every company dealing with all aspects of the security world.

At least now, when the pile included his current bank statement or credit card bill, he didn't break into a sweat. The twenty-five thousand dollar bonus from his former English client served to cushion his expenses when business slowed down. He invested the money in the market with a smart stockbroker, and his portfolio continued to grow in value.

Rizzo pushed back into his leather desk chair, closed his eyes, and in wizard-like fashion, called up his English client's lovely face. The image did a slow dissolve into a bruised and frightened Amy Chatsworth he found facedown, lashed across the workbench in the converted schoolhouse woodshop, her jeans yanked down below her hips.

Rizzo left her alone that morning with no protection. His timely return short-circuited the crazy Stasi's intent on sexually assaulting her, sending Werner Schmitt fleeing. If Rizzo had caught the man, he would have killed him—if not out of guilt, then out of rage.

On the job with the NYPD, Rizzo traveled many times to the fiery edge of rage-filled explosions. If one of his drug busts dealt with the mistreatment of a woman, he would arrive home in an ugly mood. His behavior puzzled his ex-wife, Terri, and she would always nag him, "Why do you let it drive you bonkers?" He knew why but never told her. A twelve-year-old watching an alcoholic father abuse his mother became traumatic. Rizzo's inability to stop the damage scorched his heart. It marked him forever.

The light tap on the office door brought him back to the present. He glanced at his watch. Eight-thirty. No appointments scheduled.

"Open. Come in," he called out.

Jack Fields entered, a briefcase under his arm. The man's appearance surprised Rizzo. The last visit to his office by anyone from the FBI brought with it the purpose of a slap down. Agent Tony Condon had arrived to issue the reprimand: "Stay the hell out of the bureau's investigation of Werner Schmitt." Their confrontation became a heated exchange. Rizzo came close to taking a swing at the agent. He didn't. He did, however, ignore Condon and the bureau's warning. And for that, he landed on the FBI's shit list.

Rizzo stood. "Hey, Jack. What's going on?" and waved him toward the sofa.

"You asked me to see what we have in the files on Frankie Cusack, the guy you believe stabbed your friend."

"Oh, right. That was quick." Rizzo rolled his chair to the seated Fields.

"First, are you willing to help us out with a job?"

Christ, right to the point. "Yeah. So long as I don't get killed in the process."

Fields laughed. "I don't think we had that in mind. There's a bit of danger involved. I would be less than candid if I didn't tell you that. We'll have the bureau's resources behind you."

"Why does that not give me a comfy feeling?"

"We'd expect you to follow our directions. Not go off on your own, no improvising or shooting from the hip. You interested?"

Rizzo's fingers massaged his chin. When he surrendered Cusack's knife and the license number of the Lincoln to Duggan, he knew the NYPD would be all over the man. Rizzo wanted to find Cusack first. Fields could make that happen, but he needed to cut a Faust-like deal. The trade-off in the offering would be significant. The bureau didn't waste time on unimportant matters.

What the hell, I owe him. "Okay, hit me."

"Not yet. When we're ready to move, we'll go over the plan with you. Here's what we got on Frankie Cusack."

Fields opened his briefcase and pulled out a folder containing a printout of Cusack's rap sheet and three photos of the man. Another page provided resumes of Umberto Salazar and the Russian, Ilya Bodrov, with pictures of both men. A third page listed the names and headshots of other known hit men in the Salazar syndicate. Fields handed Rizzo the folder with an address written on the cover.

"As far as our records show, that's the last place Cusack lived. The South Bronx. "Enough to start you moving?"

"Sure is."

Fields got to his feet. "What do you plan to do when you find him?"

Rizzo rolled the chair back to his desk and placed the folder in the middle drawer. "You mean, before turning him over to Frank Duggan for the murder of my snitch? Get him to give up the location where they're holding the two girls."

"And you expect him to do that willingly?"

"The answer is obvious, so no point in lying. No, not without a bit of coaxing."

"You mean, by force?"

"Might come to that."

"My guess is it will." A knowing smile crept to the corners of his mouth. "You have something in mind, don't you?"

"You don't want to know."

* * *

Rizzo dialed the number he found in his files. A gravelly voice answered on the fourth ring. "Haallo, Clyde's bait shop. We got everythin' what fishes love."

Rizzo laughed. He spun around in his chair and looked out the window across Fifth Avenue. "Clyde, this is Luke Rizzo. You still in the bait business these days, you old fraud?"

Silence on the line.

"Who is this?"

"Com' on my man, you remember me, don't you? Detective Luke Rizzo, Narcotics Unit, Forty-Fifth Precinct."

"Holy shit, Rizzo. You still around? I figured you vested out."

"I did. I'm in private business now." Rizzo laughed, picturing a face straight out of an old cowboy movie, scored and polished like an old block of wood. He grew to like the old curmudgeon over years of arresting him. "You're not slinging pharmaceuticals anymore, are you?"

"Aw, gimme a break, will ya? I reformed after the last time you busted me."

"Just bait, now?"

"Yeah, just bait."

Rizzo snickered. Clyde Stuckey, a retired Coastguardsman and small-time pusher, had worked a busy marijuana trade on City Island for several years. He operated behind the façade of his charter fishing business. He was notorious for selling grass—a dime bag at a time—mostly to college kids from around the Bronx, Westchester, and Queens counties. Rizzo racked him up with three arrests within the last two years on the job. Over the time Clyde sold grass, he cobbled together a poor man's fortune.

"Clyde, my man, I need a favor."

"Uh-oh. Red flag alert."

"Not to worry," Rizzo said. "Nothing illegal. You still own the boathouse on the canal up your way?"

"Yeah. Don't use the place no more. Why? You wanna buy it?"

Rizzo laughed again. "No, Clyde. I want to rent it for a day or two."

"What for? You ain't got no boat, do you?"

"No I don't. I need a place to conduct an interview, a private interview."

"Aah, Rizzo, I don't need your money. Be my guest. When you gonna need it?"

"Don't have a date certain, yet. Sometime within the next week. Depends on the availability of the interviewee."

"Well, it's yours whenever and for as long as you want. No questions. Don't say nothin'. Call me ahead and I'll leave the door unlocked."

"One more thing."

"What?"

"I call you, can you go there, drop off two hand towels and two bath towels, a fifteen-quart pail, and a roll of duct tape?"

"Rizzo, you're a piece of work. Yeah, I'll get 'em for you."

"You're a prince, Clyde. Thanks. Bye, my man."

Chapter Thirteen

By eight-thirty, Saturday morning Willie, the young locksmith, held the locking mechanism in his hand. He examined it and shook his head. "This is a piece of garbage. I'm surprised to find it in use."

Rizzo stood a few feet away, watching. "Well, you gotta figure, at the time they put up this building, it was the most popular door lock on the market. Or at least the cheapest. I should have changed it out when I first moved in."

With the new Medeco Maxum deadbolt installed, Rizzo doubled the security level. He still needed to have a local alarm company come in and wire the apartment. He would arrange for that next week.

In the past, he'd never given much consideration to these precautions. The house in Forest Hills was on a safe street in a safe neighborhood. Not a security concern. While living alone in the studio downstairs, he never gave a thought to any personal danger. All that changed with Flo in his life and him wearing a Salazar target on his back.

Flo peered out in her nightie from behind the bedroom door. "He gone yet?"

"Yes, my angel. All done. You no longer have to sleep with my Glock under the pillow. It would take a battering ram to breach that lock."

She giggled. "Well, I won't miss your Glock so long as there's the rest of you next to me."

"How about a ham and cheese omelet? I'll get on it if you're ready."

"Give me a chance to shower. You made me work up a sweat last night."

"What do you expect when you marry a world-class sex object? Hurry, I'm hungry."

Flo's hair was wrapped in a towel when she took her seat at the café table in the kitchen. Rizzo whipped up a breakfast of her favorite avocado, cheese, and ham omelet, bacon done to a turn, and four slices of rye toast—the latter being her preference over English Muffins—and a mixed fruit plate.

Her eyes flickered across the top of her raised orange juice glass. She laughed. "You're going to make a good wife for someone one of these days. You know that, hon?"

They savored breakfast quietly, consuming their omelets and bacon while limiting their conversation to "You ready for more coffee?" Rizzo suspected their lack of communication foretold something was up with her.

Nearing the finish, Flo gazed across at him with a screwed up face like she always did when she wrestled with a problem. Rizzo set down his cup. "What's going on? Why the face?"

Flo bit her lip. "I've been thinking," she began. "After the man attacked me at the airport, I assumed that would be the end of it."

"Yeah, it damn well should be. I'm gonna make sure it never happens again."

"That's why the new door lock? You think he might try to break in while I'm here, alone?"

Rizzo saw Flo's expression darken. It angered him Cusack succeeded in generating this cloud of worry—a realistic worry, he conceded. It wasn't going away soon, at least not until the police took the bastard into custody. For now, he needed to relieve her of her concern. Should he tell her half-truths? Resort to lying about the potential threat? He hated being anything but open and honest with her.

"Sweetheart, I'm working on a way to nail this guy and bring him to justice. The FBI is helping me find him. And I will find him. After I do, you'll have nothing to worry about because he'll be in jail."

"Is it dangerous, what you're doing?"

"Not very. No need to be concerned. I'll be fine."

Flo puffed her cheeks and squeezed out air. "You promise?"

"Yes, I promise."

She wasn't buying it. Rizzo knew that by the way she bobbed her head.

* * *

It was late morning. Rizzo tossed aside the Sunday Times when Flo announced she was ready to leave. Before he could grab his iPhone and pocket it, the cellular sounded with his new ringtone—the opening bars to Dave Brubeck's classic, "Take Five." He'd grown tired of the old doorbell sound. He discovered the app featuring a significant selection of musical options, and he jumped on the one offering his favorite jazz pianist. Rizzo pressed the telephone icon on the screen.

"*Hola,* Luke," the voice said.

Rizzo hadn't noticed the caller I.D., but he did recognize Fuentes' voice. "*Amigo, qué pasó?*"

"I had drinks with Eduardo last night at the Turning Point."

"Yeah, and . . . .?"

"I checked out his plate number. Same one you gave me."

Rizzo paused. "Shit! I forgot. Yeah, so he lent Cusack the Lincoln to use when he threatened Flo?"

"Appears that way. The numbers matched."

He sent a quick glance at Flo primping in front of the Barcelona mirror over the couch and lowered his voice. "That deceiving bastard. Thanks, Luis. I gotta run. We're on the way out for a Sunday brunch. Let's talk again in a couple of days. We'll figure out how we want to handle Soto."

"Okay, *amigo*. I have a few questions to ask the son of a bitch. I'm sure he had a hand in getting Rabbit killed."

"I am too."

"Enjoy yourselves," Fuentes said and disconnected the call.

"Ready?" Flo asked and walked toward the door.

"Right behind you."

They strolled up the street to Eighth Avenue, and Rizzo flagged down the first taxi he spotted barreling north. "13 Doyers Street," he told the driver when they got in.

The cabbie took off and made a left at Forty-ninth, then headed west to Ninth Avenue for the ride downtown. Rizzo planned this to be a discovery trip for Flo. Their destination was a classic dim sum restaurant in the heart of New York's Chinatown, one of the many locations in the city Flo had yet to experience. They would spend a lazy Sunday afternoon sipping tea and feasting on a countless assortment of delicacies.

"Who was that?" Flo asked during their taxi ride.

"Who was what?"

"The person on the phone with you before we left."

Suddenly, another taxi cut in front, crossing over to make a right turn at the next intersection. The cab driver hit his brakes and swerved to the left. "Damn camel jockey," he shouted out his window. The driver looked into the rearview mirror and mumbled an apology out the side of his mouth.

Flo turned to Rizzo. "So who was it on the phone?"

"Huh? Oh, Luis Fuentes. I asked him to check out the plate number of the Lincoln Town Car, the one the guy drove when he visited you at work."

The day was cloudless, and the sun felt good despite a slight chill in the air. The taxi moved downtown along Ninth Avenue, maneuvering through the lighter Sunday vehicle traffic. At Twenty-third Street, the driver made a left, going east.

The mild weather invited heavier than usual foot traffic for this time of year. Slow responding vehicles, failing to get through pedestrian-crowded intersections when the light turned green, often became trapped between impatient walkers who stepped out into the crosswalk. The blare of the taxi and car horns made no impact on the speed at which those pedestrians moved.

"You know now who he was?"

His mind off in a cloud, Rizzo said, "I'm sorry, hon, what did you say?"

Flo repeated the question.

"We're not sure. We do know the car didn't belong to him. He borrowed it to drive to LaGuardia and to your office."

Her troubled expression remained.

* * *

At Broadway, the driver turned south and found clear sailing until he pulled up at the entrance of the Nom Wah Tea Parlor. The restaurant was the oldest Cantonese dim sum parlor in New York's Chinatown, opening its doors in 1920. They exited the taxi and Rizzo remembered the one-block-length of Doyers Street was notorious for the grisly Tong gang wars in the early twentieth century. He chose not to share that piece of the city's history with Flo.

The street-level restaurant, centered in a series of connected three-story buildings, displayed a multi-colored awning over its entrance. Inside the unpretentious eatery, a Chinese hostess in a tight-fitting satin dress with slits up to her hips, showed them to a six-top in the middle of the dining room. A colorful pot of Chinese tea shared the center of the table with an arrangement of fresh lilacs in a tall crystal vase. They were alone at the table, but the remaining four chairs would not be vacant long. The Chinese dim sum dining concept, meaning "to touch your heart," consisted of a variety of dumplings, steamed dishes, and other goodies served one at a time in small portions. He was certain Flo would love it.

Carts, each filled with specific dim sum selections, wheeled by the tables, paused to allow diners to choose from the offering or wave it off and wait for the next cart. Rizzo saw Flo's mystified expression and resisted a laugh.

"Okay, here's how this works. The servers wheel around those carts. Each cart offers different dishes, and you pick out whatever looks good to you. The hot ones are served in a steamer basket. The cart-pusher marks down what you took, then along comes another cart with other goodies, and you make another selection. You do that until you're stuffed. No hurry. It's the Chinese version of brunch, and it goes on all afternoon."

An expression of delight lit her face. "Oh, my. Like filling up on *hors d'oeuvres*. Sounds like great fun."

Over the next hour, along with many cups of tea, Flo consumed a sesame seed puff, two deep-fried vegetable spring rolls, two baked BBQ pork buns, and a dish called chicken feet. Initially put off by the name, she tried it anyway and loved it. She ended with a shrimp stuffed eggplant delight.

Rizzo stuck with the more traditional delicacies: shrimp noodle rolls, steamed pork spareribs, three shrimp dumplings, a taro croquette, and a custard tart.

Filled with a variety of dim sum selections that more than satisfied their appetites, they sat back and lazily sipped Chinese tea. Rizzo spied a young girl pushing a cart toward them, bussing tables. His eyes moved with her, watching her flit from one vacated table to another, picking up empty dishes. She appeared to be about fourteen or fifteen.

Flo put down her teacup. "What are you staring at, hon?"

"That kid over there, the one clearing tables. Her youth reminded me of the two kidnapped Mexican teenagers."

Flo lowered her eyes. "You're going to find them, aren't you?"

"Oh, yeah. I hope so. I was thinking of all those missing kids from so many Asian countries, kidnapped and shipped over here by the traffickers."

"And brought to New York City?"

"Many of them, not all. A number of them end up in California, Texas, Michigan, and Virginia. Even Tennessee."

The young bus girl rolled her cart by their table. She wore a man's white dress shirt hung over her denim jeans, and she sported a new pair of white Adidas tennis sneakers. Her ebony hair, pulled back in a ponytail, and tied neatly with a lipstick-red ribbon, glistened when she passed under the overhead fluorescent light fixtures. She possessed a clear, almond complexion, and bright, intelligent eyes that darted in every direction while she searched for tables to bus.

Rizzo guessed her to be either the daughter of the parlor owner or from a local family working to earn pin money. He reflected again on those kidnapped kids forced to turn out in the sex trade or slave long hours at a menial low wage job by an employer taking advantage of their illegal status.

"Are they all from Asia and Mexico?"

"A lot of them from third world countries, too. Many are from families who sold them to sex traders to survive their poverty."

Flo's eyes widened and her brow wrinkled. "They do that?"

"Oh, yeah, in the poorer countries. Listen, trafficking underage girls is a common blight around the world. This country has all but ignored the problem for too many years. The mainstream media doesn't even know it exists."

His attention landed again on the bus girl. Thinking out loud, he said, "I can't wait until the Feds come down on Salazar and his organization."

"Who?"

Rizzo looked up. "Never mind," he said, brushing off his unintended reference to the sex trader.

Flo pushed back her chair and folded her arms. "I want to ask you something."

"Shoot."

"Why did you decide to become a policeman—a detective?"

"I got too old for the boy scouts."

Flo failed to smile. "Not an entirely mindless answer, is it?"

Rizzo reasoned with the question's validity. "No," he finally said.

"You want to help people. Right?"

"A lot of folks need help."

She flashed him a warm smile.

He got out of his chair and walked around behind her. Flo twisted her head to see what he was up to. Rizzo ignored the other couple at their table, and without an overture, planted a kiss on Flo's mouth before she could open it to speak.

Flustered, she said, "What was that for?"

Rizzo laughed. "Because I love you. And hey, this was supposed to be a fun afternoon full of delicious edibles, not spent talking about depressing subjects." He pointed to the empty plates on their table. "Did you enjoy all the goodies?"

"Oh, you know I did. Look at all I ate."

He signaled to the hostess for the check. "Let's go home. See what goodies we can find there."

"Wonderful. It'll be my dessert. I'm positive I have room."

Chapter Fourteen

Rizzo leaned his elbow on the desk, the phone to his ear, while he related to a laughing Jack Fields the experience he and Jabba had at Ruby's. During his narration, Rizzo's eyes followed Sam Hoya pacing the floor in front of him like a sentry walking guard duty. Listening to the description of Rizzo and Jabba's life-threatening encounter at Ruby's had put Hoya on edge. Rizzo glanced over at Manny. The Mexican bad boy lounged with his arm slung over the back of the sofa, impassively taking in Hoya's pacing.

"Tough group at Ruby's?" Fields said.

"Oh, yeah. The goons gave me and Jabba quite a scare, South Bronx style. We went in being too obvious, but I managed to bullshit our way out with our skins intact."

"By the way, I might have an assignment for you," Fields announced with a tinge of mischievousness in his voice. "Something for the bureau that may interest you. I can't talk about the details yet. If you want to hear how it would work administratively, we can go over it this morning."

"Yeah, I can be there in twenty."

"You. No one else."

"Right," Rizzo said and ended the call. Looking at Hoya and Manny, he laughed. "Now aren't you glad you didn't go with us to Ruby's?"

Hoya shook his head. Manny shrugged.

"Guys, this is what I tried to tell you. There's a level of danger I am sure neither of you ever faced. You want out, this is your chance."

Hoya stopped in the middle of his last circuit. "No, not me. Is the FBI going to help?"

"I don't know. Depends if my guy has any more information that'll make it easier our grabbing Cusack."

Manny stood and stretched his arms like someone just rolling out of bed. "Well, I'm in."

"Okay. I have to leave, go to the agent's office and see what he has to say."

"You want us to wait here?" Manny asked.

"No. Why don't you shoot up to the Bronx? Pay a visit to your uncle before he goes to work. Fill him in. Maybe he's got an idea how we can grab Cusack. Tell him, once we do, I can think of a few ways to make him talk."

"Beat his fuckin' head in," Manny said.

"That's one way but not the most effective. Let's see what my FBI friend has in mind. I'll call you later."

* * *

Rizzo's chin shot up. "You mean I'd be on your payroll?"

Jack Fields leaned back on his elbows. Behind him, the morning sun filtered through the vertical blinds, creating a dappled pattern of lines across the surface of the agent's desk.

"Right. Well, not exactly on the bureau's payroll. The job would be off the books, so to speak. We subcontract our subversive business every so often to the private sector, to investigators we trust. There are things—necessary things—Federal law prohibits us from doing. So we look to friends like you to run interference when a situation gets sticky."

Rizzo laughed. "What my department brass used to refer to as black-bag stuff. Right? You can't pull off that shit anymore. Today, they slice off your balls if they catch you."

"Well, the bureau is a shade more tolerant of that type of operation, especially if it produces the desired results. We can't afford to get caught either, so we contract out the help we need. It's like the network of Jewish volunteers that Israeli Intelligence maintains worldwide, what they call their *sayanim*."

"Never heard of it."

"The network is made up of bankers who provide money in an emergency, doctors to treat injured agents, hotel owners who make available rooms under false names, rental-car companies who supply untraceable junk vehicles. Those kinds of things."

"And if it blows up, the Mossad is clean. They know *bupkis*."

Fields cocked his head and beamed a smile at Rizzo. "So, Moishe, you interested?"

Rizzo did a slow walk to the window, spread the slats of the blind with two fingers and gazed off into the distance like he was on the job and sitting on a plant—a term the NYPD used for a surveillance assignment. He caught his share of those tedious shit assignments after he made detective. The object of his interest this time wasn't out there amid acres of glass and steel. It was two things: the man who killed Rabbit and finding Rosita Fuentes and her friend.

Rizzo spun around. "Yeah, I'm with you. But I gotta find Cusack first. Force him to tell me where they have the kids. If I don't find them soon, I'm afraid they'll turn up in a dumpster."

"Was Cusack's rap sheet a help to you?"

"Oh, yeah. More than a help. I used the info on Cusack's jail time to convince the two gorillas I was once a cell buddy with the guy at the Downstate Correctional Facility. If they hadn't bought that yarn, Jabba and I might have left Ruby's in body bags."

Fields stood and came around to Rizzo's side. "The address I gave you in the South Bronx is the most recent one on Cusack. The man moves around a lot." Fields placed a hand on Rizzo's shoulder. "You think you should be using those two guys from Florida? You're taking a big risk involving them."

Rizzo looked back at Fields. "Jesus, don't you think I'm aware? The problem is, Manny Fuentes is off the rails to find his sister. He thinks he's a Mexican Rambo. I gotta take Cusack fast, and I can't do it alone. I'm gonna need their help. Don't worry. I'll keep both of them close. If I don't, Manny will get himself killed."

"First things first," Fields said. The agent walked back to his desk. "We'll talk about your contract service for the bureau after you rescue the kids. Agreed?"

"Yeah. And after we grab Cusack, we turn him over to Duggan at the One-Seven. See if the boys in the D.A.'s office can convict him for killing my snitch. If they can't, maybe I can arrange something like him falling from a roof." Rizzo rolled his eyes at Fields and laughed. "Nah. I couldn't be that lucky twice in my life."

"Alright, how do you plan to handle this?"

Rizzo laced his fingers behind his head. "First, I need to stash Cusack somewhere while I question him, then convince him to give up where they are holding the girls."

"You told me already you didn't think he'd cooperate."

"Well, then, I gotta squeeze him because I can't go around storming every cathouse in the five boroughs, searching for them."

"You said you had something in mind?"

Rizzo raised his eyes to the ceiling, then panned around the room, casting a furtive search to the corners. He paused and gave Fields a searching and slightly amused glance. "You want I should turn off the lights, close the blinds?"

With a grin, Fields said, "That bad, eh?"

"I'm gonna need a safe place to put him." Rizzo sat up. He tipped forward to assume a more confiding pose and raised his head. He glanced at Fields. "I thought I had one lined up. I checked it out Saturday afternoon, a boathouse up on City Island. It was a wreck, falling apart. So now I need to find something else to use for a couple of days." Rizzo saw the agent's brow wrinkle. *Shit. The bureau isn't going anywhere near that.*

"Would a motel room outside the city, someplace remote, work for you?"

Rizzo's mouth parted. "You mean you would—"

"Yeah, we would. Remember what I said about the bureau's friends. They often accommodate our needs, make lots of things available, including a safe house at times. Like the Israeli *sayanim* I mentioned. How would you transport Cusack there?"

"Not a problem. I could rent a van or use Hoya's Range Rover. But I need to overpower the guy first, and there's no way I can pull it off alone."

"You got your Jamaican buddy, don't you?"

"I don't want to put him in jeopardy. The last time he almost bought the farm."

"We can't help you there. It would be a hands-on involvement. Too risky for the bureau." Fields lowered his voice. "How about the brother and the friend?"

"Christ, first you tell me I'm taking a big risk having those guys around. Now you're—"

"You want Cusack, don't you?"

"Okay, okay, and after I have him, there are three different ways to make him talk. One is beat the shit out of him. Manny would like that. Number two, put him through a form of torture. That wouldn't be my first choice even though I'd probably enjoy it."

"And dangerous, filled with risk. Cusack could croak in the process. What's the third?"

"You could provide me with a supply of Pentothal."

Fields' right eyebrow jerked up. "Hmm. Truth serum. Ever seen it used?"

"Yeah, twice. I know it doesn't always work. In most cases, it loosens the tongue. Makes the subject more responsive to pressure."

"It requires an intravenous administration. You ever do that?"

"No, never. Christ, I watched lots of junkies shooting up. How hard can it be?"

The agent pushed back into his chair and closed his eyes. Rizzo stayed silent, hesitant to break the spell. Moments later Fields looked at him and shook his head. "I know I'm out of my mind to do this. If you can get control of Cusack without killing him, move him to a motel fast, I'll allow the man to get shot up with Pentothal. See what happens. You aren't going to be the one to administer the injection."

"You?"

"Of course not, wise ass. I'll arrange for one of the bureau's friends, an obstetrician, to be there. He'll give the injection and oversee the procedure. He's done it before for the bureau. That way, the administration of the drug will be done right."

"An obstetrician? Cusack's not pregnant. He takes humans out of this world. He doesn't bring them into it. He's a hired killer."

Fields ignored him and continued with his instructions.

"Obstetricians often use these psychoactive medications on their patients, to ease delivery. So, before anything happens, I want you to meet this doctor and let him brief you on what you can expect."

"How about today?"

The agent hit the intercom again. "Rachel, I need to speak with Dr. Haus, please. Then call Jackson Bell out on Long

Island." He turned to Rizzo. "Bell runs a motel in Bay Shore on the edge of the Great South Bay. The motel is empty this time of year. Use it for your interrogation. Go back to your office. I'll call you after I set up the doctor and Jackson Bell. And Rizzo. I'm going out on a limb with this. Don't screw up."

* * *

Rizzo found the office of Dr. Richard Haus on Gay Street in the East Village. A quaint, three-story brownstone, it sat on a narrow one-way street with similar buildings lining both sides. The road was wide enough to allow the passage of one vehicle, provided no one parked illegally—as rare in Manhattan as an August without humidity.

The doctor greeted Rizzo at the door. The man projected the image of an old-fashioned physician who made house calls. He wore brown and green tweed trousers, a matching vest over a white dress shirt, and a red bow tie.

After a warm handshake, Dr. Haus escorted Rizzo into his office on the first floor of the building. No receptionist, but the clean, empty waiting room the size of a postage stamp struck Rizzo as the office of a medical man's practice on the south side of a long career.

Haus was a short, balding man in his early seventies, with droopy cheeks. Half eyeglasses rested on the bridge of his nose. He possessed a soothing, soft voice that would have engendered the confidence of any woman in her third-trimester, suffering shortness of breath. Haus swept around his old, scarred maple desk and pointed Rizzo to the side chair.

"Come, sit, Mr. Rizzo. Agent Fields asked me to help you with your project. Do I have it correct, you need to elicit certain critical information from your subject under the influence of the barbiturate, Thiopental, commonly called Pentothal? Two teenage girls' lives are at stake?"

"That's it, in a nutshell, Doc. Here's the full story," and Rizzo explained the situation with Rosita Fuentes and her friend, and that Frankie Cusack held the key to their whereabouts. Rizzo told him he came up with the idea to use truth serum because it was the only way he could think of to get the information without having to resort to physical coercion. "How often does Pentothal work?"

"Well, it varies," Dr. Haus said. The red bowtie bounced under his chin. "If a subject is set against telling you their secrets, it might make them so disoriented they'll spill something. To effect success, you have to be aware of what you're looking for in advance."

Rizzo nodded. "That's so easy. I want to know where they have the kids."

"Because if they tell you, they'll tell you many other things."

"Like if he killed my informant? Can we tape him?"

"We can; however, the evidence is inadmissible unless the person agrees to take the drug and consents to be taped. Even then, you couldn't present it as stand-alone evidence. Any information given under the influence of a truth serum needs to be corroborated by other evidence to weigh whether it is true."

Rizzo remembered the knife used to kill Rabbit and the blade Jabba picked up at the Avis location. Too bad they couldn't lift prints from them. It would be all the corroborating evidence they'd need.

Haus continued. "Because a subject under the influence of any of the truth drugs will most likely tell you what you want to hear. The drugs make people more obliging. Mostly, however, they suppress the parts of the brain that have to kick into gear to assess what's wrong with a question, then articulate a lie, and assert themselves to their questioner. Easier to let their imagination go with the flow and give the questioner what they want."

A scenario leaped into Rizzo's mind. He pictured himself out of patience, giving in to a moment of rage and ending with him pounding Cusack. He doubted he could do the questioning without losing his head.

"Doctor Haus, can you be the questioner? I'm afraid I'm too invested. Considering my temper, I would screw up the whole works."

Haus regarded him with understanding. "Well, Agent Fields told me I would be the one to do the questioning, besides administering the drug. I've done a number of them over the years for the bureau. If I take charge, we will get the best results."

"Deal. Now I need to figure out how to grab Cusack." Rizzo stood and faced the doctor. "I'll call you when we have him. It might be late at night when we nail him. You okay with that?"

"Fine with me. I don't sleep much these days," Haus said and handed Rizzo his card.

Chapter Fifteen

U mberto Salazar pushed back from his desk and walked to the window overlooking the boat basin fifteen stories below. He examined the Swan tied up in her berth. The luxury yacht, rising and falling with each wave swell, slammed against the bulkhead. The intensity of the storm increased during the early morning hours. A tropical disturbance, not a hurricane, the report said. It would churn up the coastline and reach the Carolinas by midday before heading out to sea.

"Mr. Salazar, a call on two from San Juan," the voice announced over his intercom.

His secretary, Louisa, refrained from giving the name of the caller. Standing orders with incoming telephone calls from Puerto Rico. "No names," he instructed her, "even if I'm in the office alone."

A smart woman, Salazar thought, smart enough never to question this policy. Also beautiful. A former Miss World beauty contestant from Caracas, Venezuela. The lady had designs on becoming the next Mrs. Salazar, and he found it amusing.

Salazar picked up the phone. "Yes?"

A throaty, heavily accented voice, speaking in English, answered. "Our business is complete at our end. Am I correct you are finished with yours and will be on time?"

The caller's tone sounded sarcastic, the way it did on previous phone calls. The pulse in Salazar's temple quickened. This *Puertorriqueño* scum had the gall to doubt the capability of his organization, that it might not be up to an undertaking of this size and be on schedule.

He pulled the instrument from his ear and glared at it. If instead, he'd been holding the man's neck, he would have choked the life out of him. Salazar took a deep breath and remembered this could be the first of many such deals.

His anger subsided, and he returned the phone to his ear. "I am prepared. Everything is in order and on time."

"Good," the voice replied. "Success will bring us a long association. Failure is not acceptable. Until then—" The call ended.

The Puerto Rico cartel expected his syndicate to prove they were reliable and efficient before there would be more business. Since this was their initial partnering venture, Salazar planned to get personally involved. He would oversee the first transfer of cocaine from the swift boats to the Swan. The transfer, scheduled to take place in the middle of the Caribbean, would happen in less than two weeks.

Salazar swiveled his chair to face the window. Rain pelted the glass like an angry wife beating on the chest of a cheating husband. A feeling of misgiving crept into his body. He would never have become involved in the high-risk world of drug smuggling except for the enormous return on investment it offered. His profit from transferring one shipment of cocaine equaled four months of receipts from his string of whorehouses.

He thought about what might lie ahead and struggled to control his worry about the danger involved. Dealing with the criminal underbelly of the drug trade made him squeamish. He hated it. Eying his reflected image in the glass, he told himself,

"Let's watch how this first one goes. Then I'll decide if continuing is worth putting up with the piece of Puerto Rican *mierda*."

* * *

Luis Fuentes took off his pants and shirt and hung them on the hook at the back of his narrow locker. He reached into the upper shelf and pulled out the folded black turtleneck and black trousers he brought with him to work. He would wear them tonight for his meeting instead of his uniform.

After changing, he closed the locker door. The clang of metal against metal echoed off the walls of the hotel basement.

Fuentes gave a friendly wave to the security man posted at the elevator bank in the lobby. He spun through the revolving doors to Forty-seventh Street and checked his watch. Eleven-thirty-five, an hour before his arranged meeting time. The trip would take him that long to reach the High Bridge Crossing.

He chose the location with forethought. The historic aqueduct-type footbridge spanned the Harlem River, connecting Manhattan with the Bronx, and provided the isolation he wanted.

It was New York's oldest standing bridge, and the most celebrated part of the famed Old Croton Aqueduct. The city recently restored the walkway's brickwork and iron-grille rails. To date, it hadn't completed the installation of the safety-link-fencing over the railing, and the bridge was not yet open to the public. Neighborhood kids all but destroyed flimsy barriers blocking access at both ends, making passage easy.

Eduardo Soto asked why they couldn't meet in a bar when Fuentes insisted on the High Bridge location. He told him what he had to say was too explosive to risk being seen by anyone from the Salazar organization. He explained there would be no one on or near the bridge at that hour. Soto did not argue.

* * *

The walk to the subway and the trip up to Broadway and 168th Street took forty minutes. It was twelve-thirty when Fuentes arrived at the High Bridge station. During the train ride, he mulled over how he would approach Soto. Be direct and accuse him, or hit him with a few telling facts, then wait to see his response? *I swear,* he thought, *I'll break him in two and drop him in the river if he tries to bullshit me.*

He slipped around the destroyed barrier and entered the bridge walkway at the Manhattan end. Twelve-forty and no sign of the man. He directed Soto to meet him in the middle of the span, where he would be waiting. Fuentes figured if they needed to make a fast retreat, they could beat it to either side of the river.

It was well beyond the time for the popular cruises, the cruise boats that circled Manhattan during the day, traveling up the Harlem River, crossing underneath the High Bridge and down the Hudson. Below, the river created a hushed splashing of water. The late hour offered the sound of light traffic motoring on the Harlem River Drive.

Fuentes gazed over the railing and looked down the one hundred and thirty-eight feet to the inky water. The aroma from its floating oil slick filled the air and reached his nostrils. Darkness covered the scene except for the moonlight dancing off the river's surface and the auto headlights lacing the drive. Behind him, the park's cluster of tall, dense trees on the Manhattan side of the bridge blocked any light coming from residential buildings. The wind picked up and created a rustling of tree limbs.

Soto appeared and, drawing near, he called out, "*Oye,* Luis, *qué pasa?*"

Fuentes waited until he came closer before he spoke. "Eduardo. No one knows you came. Right? No one followed you?"

"No one, Luis. Why all the secrecy? *No lo comprendo.*" His voice was charged with concern.

He grasped Soto's hand, held it for a moment, and then gave it a quick shake. "Soon enough, Eduardo. Soon enough."

Resting his forearms on the railing, Fuentes faced down-river. Soto moved to his side. "Eduardo," Fuentes said, lowering his voice. His tone exhibited a slight hint of exasperation. "I heard something a couple of days ago. It angered me a great deal. You know, like tore my guts out."

Soto pushed against the rail and stood shoulder to shoulder with Fuentes. He waited a moment before speaking. "What is it, Luis?"

"Eduardo, didn't you say how Rabbit found out about Rosita was from the guy he met at the bar? Ruby's?"

"That's right, Luis. It was Frankie Cusack. I was there."

Fuentes nodded. His eyes caught a form swooping beneath the bridge. He identified the bat by the shape of its wings, nocturnal creatures nesting among the bridge's infrastructure. He heard, in the distance, the faint rumble of thunder.

"And didn't you say Rabbit told you he was gonna ask the detective for help?"

Soto made a swallowing sound. "Yeah, he told me. He said that to me the next day. Rabbit and me, we were at this diner drinking coffee. The one on East Tremont Avenue."

"No one but you knew he had this meeting set up with the detective. Right? So how do you suppose whoever stabbed him in Grand Central knew he was going there?"

"I got no idea, Luis. I already told you. Maybe somebody from Ruby's was in the diner, overheard us. It's possible."

"You mean, like Frankie Cusack?"

Soto released a self-conscious laugh. "Fuck no. 'Course not. Maybe a guy who knows Cusack tells him."

Fuentes turned his angry face toward Soto. "Like you?"

"What? You gotta be shittin' me. Why would I do that?"

His strong hands grasped Soto by the upper arms and pressed his back against the railing. "You listen to me good,

Eduardo." He paused and waited for Soto's head to stop jerking from side to side trying to see behind him. "A guy we both know," Fuentes continued, "somebody who drinks at Ruby's once in a while, walks in one night, sees you at a table alone with Frankie Cusack. Now, I ain't gonna ask you twice. Okay? Was it you he saw?"

"No, Luis, no. I mean, I didn't know . . . I mean, I was shootin' the shit with the guy over a beer. *Nada mas.*"

Fuentes measured him with growing fury. He tightened his hold to stop Soto from squirming. "So what was it you were doing, Eduardo, while you were shootin' the shit over a beer? Telling him about Rabbit and the detective?"

Moonlight beamed down, illuminating Soto's face. Fuentes could see him turn deathly pale. His forehead squeezed in a panic so that his eyebrows formed one line across. His eyes were blood red, wild with fear. Spittle hung on his quivering lip.

"Luis, I swear on my mother's grave. I never said anything about—"

After relaxing his grip, Fuentes' massive hands flew down to Soto's waist. They locked on each side of him like a vise. With the strength of his powerful arms, he hoisted Soto to the top of the railing into a sitting position. In this perilous balance between life and death, Fuentes nudged his broad forehead against the man's chest. Soto fell backward, out into the black night. His arms flailed in terror. Fuentes held tight to the man's legs with his arms wrapped around the back of Soto's knees. He pressed them to his chest. Soto's head and torso dangled over the river below, his fright-filled screams echoing in the night air.

"Eduardo, you piece of shit. You gave up Rabbit to that rat fuck, didn't you?"

"No, no. Luis. Nooo. Luis, pleeease."

Soto's voice was barely audible. Fuentes guessed the phlegm racing down his throat was choking him.

"I'll let go of you, Eduardo. I swear I will if you don't level with me. They'll think you jumped."

Soto struggled to catch his breath. "Si, *si*, pull me up. I tell you, I tell you."

Slowly, Fuentes edged him back up and over the railing. Once he cleared him, he slammed Soto to the brick walkway on to his back. Then he straddled him and dropped to his knees, landing on his chest. Soto pushed out a loud *oomph!* Coughing and wheezing, Soto struggled to regain his breath.

Fuentes waited. Droplets of rain bounced off the back of his neck. Soto's breathing quieted, and Fuentes bent down and placed his nose inches from the man's face. "Did you tell Cusack about Rabbit's meeting with the detective?"

Soto rolled his head from side to side. "*Si,* I did, I did. I told Cusack. I never believed he would kill Rabbit."

Fuentes pulled away and glared down into Soto's dazed face. He wanted to rip it apart with his fists. Instead, he sucked in a deep breath. In a controlled voice, he said, "Eduardo, you were Rabbit's friend. Why would you betray him? Did you believe Cusack would let it pass without protecting his number one?"

"I don't understand."

"He works for Umberto Salazar, you asshole. You knew that."

Soto nodded, his eyes glazed over.

"Okay, you *hijo de puta*. I'm goin' to spare you for now because when the police bring Cusack to trial, you're gonna be the star witness. *Comprendes, amigo?*"

"*Si,*" Soto whispered. "I promise I will."

Fuentes wiped away the moisture running down his forehead and into his eyes. He looked up. The sky appeared ready to release a downpour of watery fury. With jaw muscles clenched, Fuentes issued his final warning. "Eduardo, you open your yap to Cusack or anyone else, I will kill you. Take that as my promise to you."

Chapter Sixteen

The rain and wind continued all day, slowly morphing into a northeaster and traveling up the eastern coastline from Florida. Cusack pressed the cell phone to his ear, trying to hear Ilya Bodrov over the storm's noise. It was two in the morning. Bodrov returned Cusack's earlier call and message about Soto.

"Frankie, you hear good. Yes? The pig, Soto. He don't know how to keep his mouth shut. Don't trust him. He is bought easy. The story he tell you? Would be funny if he is not a liability. Sorry his friend did not drop him in river."

Their connection, full of static, made it difficult for Cusack to catch every word. The storm was pummeling the South Florida coast and playing havoc with their transmission. He didn't need further instructions. Bodrov was not one to spell out every detail when he wanted action. He expected Cusack to be proactive.

"Do it," the Russian told him. "I come to New York soon. I'll be waiting."

"Not to worry, Ilya, I'll take care of it."

"Ilya never worry. About nothing, Frankie. You know that. Nothing. Not for long. Something worries me, I make it go away. You understand?"

"Yes."

"Signal me when business is done. We talk later. Goodbye."

"Bye, Ilya," Cusack mumbled before the connection broke.

Pressure built in his chest. Another migraine was on the way. He hung up the phone and gaped out the rear window at the twisting tree limbs. How long would it take before one of them snapped? How long before he snapped?

He entered his bedroom, struggling to push the fear from his mind. Cusack pulled up several loose floorboards from the back of the near-empty closet and drew out a metal box. He dialed the combination on the lock, opened the lid and took out the stolen weapon, a 9mm Berretta with the serial numbers filed down. The cold touch of the pistol grip made his hand shake. He needed a drink because he knew sleep would not come.

* * *

By late afternoon, the heavy rain let up. Rizzo arrived at the Hotel Edison's coffee shop after the lunch crowd was long gone. A handful of waiters in black pants and white shirts and several waitresses with sleeves rolled to their elbows and wearing their baseball caps, hustled about setting up tables and booths for the evening dinner business.

Luis Fuentes gestured to a booth against the back wall and headed toward it. Rizzo followed, and at the booth, he removed his raincoat and laid it folded next to him.

Once they settled in, Fuentes said, "I got fifteen minutes for this break, so let me fill you in fast."

"Okay, but you think I could get a cup of coffee?"

Fuentes raised an arm and caught the attention of the nearest waitress. "Maria, *por favor*, can we bother you for coffee? Two, black, no sugar."

Maria delivered the coffee and left.

Fuentes took a quick sip, set down the cup, and launched into the details of his meeting with Soto the night before on the High Bridge walkway. He described in detail how he coaxed the confession from the man.

"I came close to dropping him in the river."

Rizzo looked over the top of his cup. The image of Soto dangling in Fuentes' arms made him laugh. "Who told you Cusack and Soto were together at Ruby's?"

"The bartender tipped me off."

"The bartender? You kidding me?"

Luis broke into a grin.

"I don't understand," Rizzo said. "That guy was in cahoots with the two gorillas who strong-armed me and Jabba the other night."

His stomach pressed into the table, Fuentes lowered his chin. The grin remained. "His name is Tomás Santiago. He's from my hometown in Mexico. I helped get him the bartending job here at the Edison. He worked at the hotel for several years until one night, about a year ago, he put down one of the owners. The owner came in drunk and kept making obnoxious cracks to a woman alone at the bar. Tomás came to her rescue, and the next day they fired him. After that, I helped him find the Ruby's job."

"Wow! Talk about luck."

Fuentes scowled down his long nose, the white orbs of his dark, deep-set eyes raised to the top of the sockets. The barn owl image returned. "Luck?" You don't think we watch out for each other?"

"No, Luis. I meant lucky to have a person on the inside. He can alert us when Cusack is at Ruby's and about to leave. Would he be willing to do that?"

Fuentes bent his head and scratched the back of his neck, his chin almost touching his chest. "Much as I want to grab Cusack, I don't want to put Tomás in any danger."

"No danger. A telephone call is all. To you, Luis, his old friend. A signal spoken in conversation, then you call me."

"What'd you have in mind once you got Cusack?"

"Force him to tell me where they're holding Rosita and her friend. Then set up a rescue operation soon. Christ, it's a matter of time before they decide to get rid of them, so we gotta move on this."

Fuentes stared at him, trying to process the warning. "You're right, and we know what they—"

Rizzo put a finger to his lips. Maria returned with the coffee pot to pour refills. Her baseball cap perched on the back of her head with the bill pointing up. It reminded Rizzo of the way English jockeys wore their caps. Fuentes waved her off, and she refilled Rizzo's cup.

"I gotta go," Fuentes said, looking up at the clock behind the counter. "You stay. Finish your coffee. I'll speak with Tomás, see if he's willing. He says Cusack always comes into Ruby's late on Friday nights." Fuentes stood. "You got any idea how you gonna make him talk?" He tossed a furtive glance toward the door. "There's always the High Bridge, you know," he said with a chuckle.

Rizzo laughed. "I'm not strong enough. I'd probably drop him. No, the plan I have in mind should get us the information and keep him alive. I want him sentenced for Rabbit's murder."

"*Bueno*," Fuentes replied. "Better than killing him." He hurried through the coffee house door and disappeared into the hotel lobby.

* * *

Rizzo and Flo arrived at Joe Allen's Bistro at nine-fifteen. "What would you like to drink?" the trim, young waiter with thick black eyebrows and penetrating eyes asked after they'd been shown to a table. Rizzo saw a resemblance to Marlon Brando and figured him to be another aspiring actor or chorus line dancer. The eateries up and down West Forty-sixth Street in Manhattan's theater district employed many Broadway hopefuls. Joe Allen's was no different.

The early show-going crowd came and left. Those customers who enjoyed the standard, chic New York City dining hour of nine o'clock now filled the establishments on Restaurant Row.

"Have something strong," Rizzo urged. "I need to soften you up a bit."

Flo held a quizzical expression for a moment. "Jack Daniels . . . rocks." She beamed at him. "Darlin', that strong enough for whatever you're thinking about?"

"That'll work."

"And, for you, sir?"

"Virgin Mary. Heavy on Tabasco. Skip the celery. Thanks."

The waiter departed. A low hum of conversation emanated from the bar area. Rizzo glanced around the restaurant. Even though he was AA, Joe Allen's was his favorite watering hole and place to eat, but never between the hours of four-thirty and seven-forty-five. The best time to be at Joe Allen's was between ten and eleven after the shows let out, when the Broadway performers descended on the restaurant for their late-night bites and winding-down nightcaps. Prior to Flo entering his life, he would drop by every now and then for a Virgin Mary.

He looked across at his wife's solemn expression.

"Okay," she said. "What's goin' on?"

Rizzo hesitated. He didn't want to alarm her, yet he knew he needed to take precautions. His eyes narrowed. "The experience at the airport continues to worry me."

"Oh, dear. You think he might come back again?"

The image of Jabba St. James formed in his mind, the Rasta's dreadlocks and hulking body flying through the air to tackle Frankie Cusack.

"No, sweetheart, not to LaGuardia. He's not that dumb. Certainly, not while you have Jamaica's answer to Captain Marvel at your back."

"Well, darlin', what's got you so worried? With the new door lock and alarm system, I assumed we'd be okay."

Rizzo saw no way around it. He wanted her to cooperate. The plan to take Cusack and make him talk would require Rizzo to be away for a night or two, possibly more. The bad guys knew where she worked and where they lived. They were vulnerable. Rizzo clenched his teeth. He hoped Flo would understand and go along with his suggestion.

He took a breath and asked, "What would you say if we have Jabba drive you to and from work for a couple of days?"

"You mean, ask him to come all the way from his Queens apartment to pick me up? And then drive me back here after work? Doesn't make a whole lot of sense, does it?"

The young Brando returned. "Are you ready to order, or do you need more time?" He stood at the table's edge like an obedient soldier.

"A few more minutes, please," Rizzo said without taking his eyes from Flo. He reached across the table for her hands. "No, it doesn't. What I'm suggesting is we ask Jabba to move into the second bedroom for a few days while I'm gone and involved in this investigation." He referred to it like it was just another routine job. In reality, it was more of a journey to retribution. He couldn't tell her that.

"Do you think Jabba would mind?"

Rizzo released Flo's hands and burst out laughing. "Are you kidding? And miss a chance to be with his favorite woman in the whole world? Keep her safe? Eat her great southern cooking? Hell, he'd kill for the opportunity."

"Well, I guess."

"There's my girl. It'll be for a night or two, I promise. I'll be a phone call away." He signaled for Marlon Brando. "Bring us two medium-rare filets," he told him, "your famous Rosemary garlic potatoes, and what're the veggies you're pushing tonight?"

A pleased expression formed on the young man's face. "A sautéed string bean and sliced almonds concoction that's sure to thrill you."

"Hey, thrill us. Oh, and another Jack Daniels, rocks, for the lady. I'll risk another Virgin Mary."

The waiter left, and Rizzo reached over and touched Flo's face with a gentle caress. "Then we'll go home and make mad, passionate love. Okay?"

"You mean like the way Rocky does it?"

"Yeah, you got it."

In the next moment, her upbeat mood changed. Her face squeezed tight with tension. She leaned toward him and whispered, "You believe I'm in danger and need protection, don't you?"

Chapter Seventeen

The two-day storm moved through the city and left puddles scattered about the streets. Sewers clogged at intersections were everywhere. The morning sun helped to dry the wet sidewalks, but crossing at the corners remained a challenge.

Rizzo neared the subway entrance at Forty-seventh and Seventh Avenue to take the N train downtown to his office. His iPhone vibrated in his pocket before he could descend the stairs. He stood on the top step to examine the screen and shook his head. The number was unknown to him. "Hello. Who's this?"

"Frank Duggan from the One-Seven. Catch you at a bad time?"

Rizzo moved to the side of the adjacent building, away from the noisy whooshing air coming up the steps from the subway. "No, it's fine. I'm about to hop a train to my office. What's goin' on?"

"You mind making a detour, like to the precinct? I got a problem I need to go over with you."

"Give me twenty. Okay?" Rizzo assumed the problem related to Rabbit's murder, so he held off asking questions.

"See you in a few."

After trooping north three blocks to Fiftieth Street, Rizzo took his place in the queue at the bus stop. His timing was perfect. The M50 cross-town pulled to the curb at Seventh Avenue loaded with work-bound commuters.

Once aboard the bus, he searched for a seat. Standing room only. He glanced around at those passengers already seated. Most of them boarded at Pier 83, the beginning of the cross-town route. He pictured them all living on houseboats on the Hudson River. It always amazed him how populated the West Side in Manhattan became over the last decade.

The eastbound trip made frequent stops, loading, and unloading, taking him past Radio City, Saks Fifth Avenue, and St. Patrick's, past scurrying workers clogging the streets, heading toward white-collar jobs in the surrounding office buildings. The journey was pleasant enough, but for everyday travel, he much preferred the quick and efficient convenience of the iron horse, New York City's subway system.

* * *

Rizzo hopped off the bus at Lexington and strolled north to Fifty-first Street, to the Seventeenth Precinct located east of the avenue. Entering, he saw Duggan, jacketless with his shirtsleeves rolled up, gazing over the shoulder of the desk officer, studying the sergeant's computer screen. Duggan glanced up, spotted Rizzo in the doorway, and signaled him to the chairs against the wall. Duggan finished his business with the D.O. and joined his visitor.

"For a moment there, I thought you caught the duty," Rizzo said with a laugh.

Duggan snickered, "Yeah, in your dreams." He sat next to Rizzo and said, "Matter of fact, when I came on this morning, the first thing I did catch was a homicide. Looks like a hit.

Guy shot in the back of the head while behind the wheel of his gypsy cab.

"The late tour sector car drove by the spot under the FDR Drive where someone parked the Lincoln. On the third pass, he checked it out. Bingo! Figured the homi happened during the early-morning hours. We're waiting for the medical examiner's report."

"Is that why you wanted to see me? You think I can identify him?"

Duggan shrugged. "Not sure. What we do know is your business card was in his wallet."

Rizzo nodded. He knew who the vic was. He remembered giving Soto his card. The gypsy cab mention cinched it.

Luis Fuentes told him he'd threatened to kill Soto if he spoke to anyone after his adventure on the High Bridge. That was less than forty-eight hours ago. Rizzo doubted Fuentes would go through with it. He said he would kill him to scare him. It was probably Frankie Cusack who pulled the trigger.

"Well, if you found his wallet, you have a name."

"Eduardo Soto. Has a record—minors. A couple of possession charges for smack, one for attempting to sell a small amount of pot. Figured you might connect with him."

"Yeah, I busted him once." Rizzo scanned the station house. "Frank, can't we do this back at your office? I got a good idea who took him out. It relates to the stabbing of my old informant, Rabbit, in Grand Central."

Duggan's head jerked around. He jumped to his feet. "C'mon." Without waiting, he hurried toward the squad room in the rear of the precinct, and, passing the desk sergeant, he said, "Be back, Kelly. Keep searching."

"Take your time, Lou."

Rizzo sat beside Duggan at his desk and explained how Soto connected with Frankie Cusack. He told him that Soto tipped off Cusack about Rabbit's meeting with him in Grand Central.

Since Cusack worked for the Umberto Salazar organization, Rizzo assured the lieutenant that Salazar ordered the hit.

He related the details of his trip to the South Bronx to scout out Ruby's. No doubt word of the visit reached Cusack, and the assault on Flo at the airport was a direct result. He described the attack and explained Cusack's connection with the kidnapped teens from Mexico. Cusack, he said, held the key to finding Rosita and her friend. Rizzo finished his narration without taking a breath.

"The kidnapping? Go talk to Vice," Duggan said—a predictable response.

"They'd dump it onto the Feds," Rizzo replied. "Yeah, in a heartbeat. By that time, the girls could be dead."

Duggan shrugged. "Not my problem."

"Oh, so you know, the plate number of the Lincoln Town Car and the knife Cusack used to threaten my wife, they're in my office safe. The weapon could be the same type he used on Rabbit. You have that one, don't you?"

Duggan's mouth twisted, the corners of his eyes pinched tight. "That was over a week ago. And when the hell were you gonna tell me about this other knife?" His face appeared frozen in a frown. "I can't believe a former NYPD detective would withhold evidence in a murder case."

"Jesus, Frank. Cool down. I wasn't holding back. I was going to call you."

"Yeah? Like when?"

"Christ, it happened only a few days ago. Don't get your shorts all in a knot."

Duggan got to his feet and walked to the water cooler at the wall behind his desk. Rizzo watched him drink. Finished, he crumpled the paper cup and gave it a resigned toss into the trash.

"Alright, listen up. You bring me the switchblade and plate number in the next two hours and I'll do you a favor. I'll forget about you dragging your feet, and the captain stays in the dark about you holding out. Then, I'll go all in with this investigation."

Rizzo rolled his eyes toward the ceiling. "Ah, shit!" Without looking back at Duggan, he added, "See you in two hours," and bolted for the door.

* * *

The taxi dropped off Rizzo at the Flatiron Building. He entered his office and made straight for the safe to retrieve the blade and the scrap of paper with the Lincoln's plate number. At his desk, he grabbed the phone and called Luis Fuentes. After several rings, Carmen Fuentes answered.

"Carmen, Luke Rizzo. Luis is still home, isn't he?"

"Yes, he's here. *Momentito.*"

Rizzo heard the phone hitting a hard surface. He waited while drumming a tattoo on his desk with a pencil.

Fuentes picked up the phone and spoke. "*Oye, qué pasó?*"

"That's what I need to ask you. What happened? Tell me you didn't do Soto last night like you threatened?"

"Fuck ya talkin'?"

"Someone shot Soto while he sat in his Lincoln. Cops found him parked this morning under the FDR Drive in the sixties with the back of his head missing."

"Not me, *amigo*. No, sir."

"Who, then?"

"Maybe this guy, Cusack?"

Fuentes was right. "Luis, the question is why did he shoot Soto?"

"Perhaps the fool told Cusack about our meet on the High Bridge."

"Yeah, but Cusack doesn't make life or death decisions on his own. He's a low-level hitman. He simply follows orders. Which means you might be in danger too."

"So, what do we do?" Fuentes sounded like a man ready for a fight.

"We need to snatch Cusack tomorrow. You said he shows up at Ruby's on Friday nights, gets shitfaced and calls a car service to take him home. Isn't that how Soto came to know him?"

"Yeah. What are you thinking? Jump the guy outside of Ruby's?"

"Christ, no. That would be crazy. We'll follow him home and grab him there. With Soto out of the way, he'll call a new cab service. The driver won't know jack shit so he won't suspect anyone is tailing him."

"Then what?"

"I have a party in mind, and I need your help."

"Of course. Speak."

"Call Tomás Santiago before he goes to work. Make certain he has your cell number on his speed dial. When Cusack gets ready to leave Ruby's tomorrow night, Santiago hits the number, lets it ring once, and then disconnects. That happens, you call me. We'll be outside waiting."

"You want me along? I'll take off from work if you think I can help."

"No, Luis. I'll have enough with Sam and Manny. I shouldn't need anymore to take down Cusack. He'll be too drunk to fight back."

"What next?"

"We take him to a private place, where I've arranged for a doctor to shoot him up with a dose of truth serum. If the injection doesn't get him to give up where they're holding the girls, we head out to the beach."

"The beach?"

"Yeah, I'll explain later. Right now, I got a delivery to make uptown and do a little hardware shopping. Call Santiago right away. Okay?"

"I'm on it."

Chapter Eighteen

Rizzo pointed to a spot, and Sam Hoya pulled the Range Rover to the curb across from Ruby's, fifty yards up from where he and Jabba parked a week ago. He wanted to be sure the Rover wasn't noticed by anyone as they left the bar

The hour was late. The surrounding morgue-like area was void of foot traffic. Except for the occasional passing vehicle along Hunts Point Avenue, Rizzo's ability to keep an eye on Ruby's entrance was not impeded. All the forewarning he would need would be the call from Luis Fuentes and the arrival of the gypsy cab.

It crossed his mind Cusack might use a regular taxi service. Then he remembered Medallion cabbies were notorious for refusing to pick up fares in this part of the city at any hour. And delivering a passenger into the South Bronx? Also a risky proposition. In this drug-infested location, driver-muggings were not uncommon. Cusack had no choice but to use another gypsy cab.

Manny leaned forward from the back seat. "Do we know if he's already in there?"

Rizzo checked his watch. "He should be. If not, your uncle would have called."

"So, tell us, will you? "What are we doing after we take him down?" Hoya said.

"Yeah," Manny added. "How 'bout filling us in?"

Their voices wore a sharp note of anxiety. Neither man had ever been in a position so charged with risk and physical danger. He wished he didn't need to involve them, but they insisted on helping to rescue Rosita and her friend. And he couldn't bring off grabbing Cusack without their muscle.

"Well, after we secure him, we'll toss him in the back. We transport him to a place I prearranged. A doctor is standing by to give him an injection of sodium pentothal. We're gonna see if we can coax some truth from him."

Hoya, his eyes wide with surprise, said, "Isn't that what they call truth serum?"

"Yeah, it's what we're gonna try. I know Manny would prefer to kick the shit out of him, The process takes too long and isn't always effective."

"Does truth serum work?" Manny asked. "I always thought that was something out of Hollywood."

"Depends on the subject, how the questions are put to him, and how much he wants to protect the information. Fear not. If all else fails, we got a backup. A beach party."

Manny laughed. "The bucket back there, and those towels and tape rolls. For the beach?"

"For the beach," Rizzo echoed, "If we get lucky, we won't need them."

The three fell silent while a pair of burly men emerged from Ruby's, exchanged a bit of animated conversation, and then took off in separate directions.

Rizzo bolted upright. "Those are the two goons from the other night. I wonder if—"

The sound of Rizzo's iPhone broke into his words. Luis Fuentes' name appeared on the caller ID readout.

"Go ahead," Rizzo said.

"Luke, I'm sorry. Tomás had to wait 'til Mario and Nelly left before it was safe to call."

Rizzo realized Luis referred to the two men leaving Ruby's. "Okay, why the call?"

"It's Cusack," Fuentes said, sounding out of breath "He's not coming tonight. Not to Ruby's, anyway. Tomás said Cusack planned to meet Mario and Nelly at *La Amistad,* a bar on a hundred and tenth and Lexington in Manhattan. They're heading there now."

"Oh, shit!"

* * *

Sam Hoya steered the Rover toward a vacant parking space on Lexington Avenue between 109th and 110th Streets. "Hold up, Sam. Let's make a circuit around the block, scout out the street activity. Drive slow, so we don't attract attention. We'll grab this spot after we come back around. No problem losing it at this late hour."

Along their route, they passed several local residents sitting outside doorways of tenements, hosting late-night card games and dominoes contests. Street lamps splashed their illumination over the cardboard flats balanced on the knees of the seated players.

In front of one tenement, two NYPD uniforms from the Twenty-fifth Precinct stood next to their parked radio motor patrol, busy chatting with a couple of residents. The policemen, preoccupied with socializing, paid no attention to the Range Rover as it passed. The neighborhood appeared quiet.

Hoya guided the Rover back to the vacant parking space sandwiched between a beat-up Chevy Camaro of undeterminable vintage and a 1970s VW Microbus with covered windows. The bus looked like someone's living quarters. Their position on the avenue provided an unobstructed sightline to the corner and *La Amistad's* door.

Rizzo's original plan was to follow the gypsy cab to Cusack's South Bronx apartment. Once the location changed, the logistics went out the window because he based it on Cusack leaving Ruby's alone.

Now Cusack would likely depart with the two heavies, Mario and Nelly. If one of them drove Cusack home, Rizzo would have a problem. Snatching him without a fight would be impossible. He explained this to Hoya and Manny. The heightened danger didn't appear to scare either man. It did worry Rizzo.

The three men sat in quiet darkness, watching the front of *La Amistad*. Rizzo's mind struggled with the complication created by the addition of the two heavies. There were no options left to him without risking the lives of both of his young helpers. He was about to declare the game over when Manny spoke up.

"There's a chance he'll leave and go home alone, isn't there?"

The hopefulness in his tone rang loud. Rizzo admired Manny's tenacity. He couldn't be certain *Huey, Dewey, and Louie* were even in the bar, but they had nothing to lose except time. "Okay, then. We stay put, wait and watch. If a gypsy cab doesn't come soon, we call it off for tonight and think of another way."

"Couldn't we pull him out of his apartment?" Hoya asked.

"We could if we were the police with a warrant. Since we're not, a home invasion would work against us. No. Grabbing him off the street is the way to go. No witnesses at this hour."

Thirty minutes later, Rizzo spotted the two goons, Mario and Nelly, exiting the bar together without Cusack. One of them crossed over Lexington and walked north to a light-colored BMW. He showed no signs of inebriation, got into his car, and drove off.

The second man disappeared around the southeast corner of 109th Street, apparently heading for his vehicle.

But no Cusack.

Waiting for what seemed like an eternity, Rizzo was losing patience. He raised his watch. Two-twenty. Tomás Santiago told Luis the plan was for Cusack to meet the two friends at *La Amistad*. Did Cusack fail to show up, or did Luis screw up the message?

Rizzo decided to have a look inside the bar. He reached for the Rover's door handle as an old Lincoln Town Car pulled to the curb.

"Damn. That's our gypsy cab."

"Wu . . . what?" Manny mumbled, half asleep. He had been emitting snorts and grunts for the last fifteen minutes. Rizzo let him doze while he and Hoya kept alert.

Wide awake, Hoya leaned forward to get a better view. "Looks like it's showtime. You better drive," he told Rizzo. "I've never tailed anyone before. I'd hate to be the one who loses him."

"Okay, move over here." Rizzo pushed open the door and slid around the front of the Rover, while Hoya dashed to the passenger side.

Cusack appeared in the opened doorway. He stood backlit, swaying and squinting into the shadows.

Rizzo examined the tall, wiry-built man. All he had to go on was Jabba's description and the headshot Fields provided, but Rizzo was convinced the man was Cusack. He wore a leather bomber jacket over an open collar shirt. Struggling to keep his balance, Cusack took a few unsteady steps toward the parked Town Car. He placed his hands on the vehicle's roof and remained motionless.

The driver, a pixie-size Hispanic, bounded out of the car and took hold of Cusack by the arm. He reached back, opened the rear door, and guided his passenger onto the seat like a thoughtful husband.

Rizzo watched the scene unfold. "It appears our guy is shit-faced. Should make bagging him easier."

Neither Manny nor Hoya said anything. Rizzo suspected both were uptight. He couldn't blame them. Edgy himself, he was not convinced they could do this without one of them getting hurt.

They'd gone over the plan and their assignments a number of times in Rizzo's office. He stored all the necessary equipment in the back of the Rover, and he gave each man a supply of restraining ties to use on Cusack once they had him on the ground. Hoya tucked a woolen hood into his pocket. He planned to yank it over Cusack's head when they jumped him. Rizzo didn't want the man to get a visual of either Manny or Hoya. He didn't care about himself. Rabbit's murderer already knew who he was.

"You guys ready?" Rizzo turned on the ignition. "Keep a sharp eye on the Town Car so I don't miss a turn."

The Lincoln pulled out and headed north on Lexington. Rizzo guessed the driver would use the FDR Drive and the Willis Avenue Bridge to enter the South Bronx. He relaxed his grip on the steering wheel. Once over the bridge, he needed to stay close. He had Cusack's address but no idea of its exact location. And the Rover wasn't equipped with GPS.

Rizzo gave Cusack's ride a block head start before he pulled out. With no traffic to contend with on Lexington, keeping the car in sight wasn't a problem.

Rizzo increased his speed when he spotted the vehicle make a right turn on 120th Street heading toward the FDR Drive entrance. Once the Lincoln crossed the Willis Avenue Bridge, he closed the distance between them.

* * *

The Town Car remained on Willis Avenue and traveled north into the Melrose section of the South Bronx. Over the next three miles, the driver caught a few red lights. Each time Rizzo would move to the curb, switch off his headlights, and wait. A short while later the Lincoln reached the intersection of Melrose and 155th Street, slowed, then turned into the street. Rizzo killed the Rover's headlights again and followed.

The Lincoln stopped midway down in front of a two-story commercial building, part of a long series of similar structures—multicolored, graffiti-covered storefronts that took up three-quarters of the block. Rizzo could see many of them were illuminated with night lights. Iron grillwork covered most of their entrances. The street was deserted. None of the windows on the residential second floors showed signs of life.

The pixie-driver had pulled to the curb opposite a doorway squeezed between two stores. Cusack's apartment was on the second floor.

Rizzo slowed the Rover until he saw Cusack emerge. Then he hit the accelerator. He screeched to a stop behind the Lincoln, the Rover's bumper almost touching it. In concert, Manny, Hoya, and Rizzo leaped out. Manny raced to the opened driver-side window of the Town Car and waved Hoya's .38 at the bewildered driver. "Police," he whispered. "Take off. Now!" The driver's wide-eyed reaction needed no further encouragement. The cab peeled away, leaving tire marks behind.

Cusack, oblivious to the taxi's hasty departure, managed a few shaky steps toward his doorway. Rizzo raced to him, grabbed him by one arm and shoved his Glock against his neck. "Police. Down on your knees."

Following their plan, Hoya moved to the front of Cusack to block his path. He stood ready to jam the hood over his head. A confused Cusack hesitated. With a shaky free hand, he rummaged into his jacket pocket.

"Watch out!" Rizzo shouted.

Too late. Hoya took the tip of the switchblade across his raised left forearm and recoiled when the slash cut through his woolen jacket.

Rizzo moved a step back and pounded his heel into the curve behind Cusack's right kneecap. The move sent Cusack face down to the sidewalk. Rizzo jumped on his sprawled body and landed with both knees in the middle of his back. He reached down and grabbed a handful of hair, snapping Cusack's head back. With the Glock jammed against Cusack's ear, Rizzo spit out his warning. "Motherfucker, don't fucking move, or I'll waste you right here."

Cusack's outstretched hand still held the switchblade. Manny rushed over and stomped on the man's wrist. Cusack gave a pain-filled grunt. After easing the knife free, Manny collapsed the blade and stuck it in his pocket. He dropped across Cusack's struggling legs and looked up at the shaken Hoya. "Hey, you okay, bro?"

"Yeah. He got me a little. Not too bad."

Rizzo eyed him with concern. "You bleeding?"

"Yeah, I can feel it soaking my sleeve."

"Let's finish hog-tying this shithead and get the hell out of here. We'll take a look at it on our way."

When they had Cusack secured with wrist and ankle ties, they gagged and hooded him. Rizzo and Manny carried him to the Rover and folded his long body into the cargo area.

Manny climbed behind the wheel and Rizzo got into the back next to Hoya. He rattled off directions to the East Village while Hoya slipped out of his jacket and rolled up his sleeve. Rizzo examined the wound under the glow of a flashlight. The cut didn't go deep. Nothing vital appeared at risk. Rizzo tied a makeshift tourniquet around Hoya's arm to stem the bleeding. He would have Dr. Haus examine him when they arrived at his office.

The lighted face of Rizzo's watch showed three-thirty. He didn't give the doctor a specific time, only that he would call when they were on their way. He entered the doctor's number into his iPhone and waited.

After several rings, a sleepy voice answered "Hello."

"Doc, Luke Rizzo here. We're heading down to you now. Pick you up in a half hour."

Dr. Haus remained silent for a few uncomfortable seconds before he responded. "What's his condition? I hope you didn't rough him up. If you expect his answers to be truthful, he must not feel threatened or intimidated."

"Doc, how the Christ you think we would get him to your office? The man's a hired gun. He's not about to volunteer."

"Is he conscious now?"

"Yeah. Drunk out of his gourd but conscious."

Again, silence.

"Mr. Rizzo, I don't think this is going to work tonight. I would suggest you wait twenty-four hours until he is sober and calmed down."

Rizzo laughed at the absurdity of the doctor's response. "Hey, Doc, I can't check him into a Motel Six while he sleeps it off. I need my information right now. Tonight! Two kids' lives are on the line."

"I'm sorry, Mr. Rizzo, you'd be wasting your time with him under these conditions. Pentothal works only—"

"Fuck it, Doc. We'll go to the beach without you." Rizzo closed the phone and turned to Manny. "Plan B. Pull over when you can. I'll drive."

Manny edged the Range Rover to the curb two blocks before the Willis Avenue Bridge. Rizzo climbed out and beckoned to Manny and Hoya from the sidewalk to join him. Outside the vehicle, he scrutinized the two puzzled faces. Rizzo spoke in a quiet but firm voice.

"Guys, listen to me. What I'm planning is something you might not like. Lots of people are dead set against it. They consider it a form of torture. No guarantee it'll work, although I have a hunch it will.

"What is it?" Manny asked, his eyes full of curiosity.

"Waterboarding."

"You know how they do it?" Hoya wanted to know.

"Yeah. Ten years ago, the NYPD sent me to Fort Benning to attend a two-day FBI seminar on interrogation methods. We sat through demonstrations of how waterboarding worked. They didn't recommend it, but the Feds believed law enforcement should have a working knowledge of this technique."

"Cool," Manny said.

"No, Manny, not cool. Frightening. I know first-hand."

"How?" Hoya asked, his interest peaked.

"Because I stupidly volunteered to be a part of a demonstration, a mistake I would never repeat."

Rizzo noticed both men stared back at him, waiting for him to continue.

"The demonstrators assured me I couldn't drown so long as my head remained on an incline lower than my feet. The position keeps the water level below the lungs. They told me only the mouth, sinus, and trachea would fill with water. Yeah? Well, they did a crappy job of convincing me I wasn't drowning. The experience terrified the shit out of me."

Manny shook his head. "Not gonna bother me none. I'll probably enjoy seeing him go through it."

Hoya hesitated for a second, then nodded. "I'm in."

"Okay, but understand. Should one or both of you want out, say so now. We can put our heads together, try to come up with another idea."

"Hell, no. Let's go," Manny said.

Both men pushed a hand at Rizzo for a high-five.

Slap! Slap!

Chapter Nineteen

R izzo followed Sunrise Highway eastward along the south shore of Long Island. At Clinton Avenue, he cruised toward the sleepy town of Bay Shore. Already familiar with the location, Rizzo found the directions Fields provided easy to follow.

"Where we going, what are we looking for?" Hoya said. His eyes scanned the area.

Rizzo saw the concern on his face and laughed. "Don't worry. It's only a motel. One of the many the Feds have in their basket of helpers."

They followed Clinton Avenue until it dead-ended at the water's edge of the Great South Bay. To the east were the lighted ferry slips off Maple Avenue.

During the long summer season, the busy ferries carried weekenders headed out to different towns on Fire Island. The balance of the year, the boats operated for Fire Island's limited year-round residents, but they did so with less frequency. At this early hour, they were shut down, tied up for the night, and left to bounce gently against their fenders.

Rizzo had spent a few sun-soaked weekends freeloading off several NYPD friends prosperous enough to own a beach house on Fire Island. He remembered his visits here while on the job and married to Terri. They were wild excursions of boozing, dancing and hitting on bikini-clad women in bars until the wee hours of the morning. Those were the antics that helped turn to shit his relationship with Terri.

He recalled his most hilarious weekend at a detective-friend's cottage in the infamous gay community of Cherry Grove. Until that time, he hadn't known the detective was homosexual. He chuckled, remembering that bar hopping in the Grove was a unique experience.

Rizzo passed the turnoff leading to the ferry slips and reached the Seahorse Boat-tel at the base of the long dock. A half dozen boats of various sizes and shapes bobbed in the water.

He pulled into the Seahorse's parking lot, drove to the rear, and checked the time. Daybreak was another hour away. Several cabins lined the road on the opposite side, dark and vacant, their gravel-covered drives void of any vehicles.

"Stay here while I find the owner," Rizzo told Hoya and Manny. He stepped from the Rover and walked around to the motel's front entrance. A figure appeared out of the shadows at the end of the building. Startled, Rizzo reached inside his windbreaker and gripped his holstered Glock.

"Mr. Rizzo. Is that you?"

The greeting seemed a few decibels louder than necessary. Rizzo's tension mushroomed. He scanned the area before he realized the stillness surrounding them amplified all sound. Jackson Bell flipped on the overhead light under the front portico, and Rizzo loosened his grip on the Glock.

Bell stepped into the pool of illumination and faced him. An oversized sweatshirt reached down to his knees and covered his slender frame. A pair of faded jeans and ratty deck shoes completed his wardrobe.

Jackson Bell, a man about fifty, with a receding hairline, and pencil-thin mustache under a long nose, reminded Rizzo of photos he'd seen of John Barrymore, the silent film actor. His eyes sharp and assessing, he appeared wide-awake. Rizzo suspected the man stayed up all night, waiting for them.

"Mr. Bell, I'm sorry to show up so late." Rizzo extended his hand and Bell met it with a solid grasp.

"Not a problem. You parked in the back, I see. Perfect."

Rizzo noticed Bell's voice was tinged with hoarseness symptomatic of a heavy drinker. *Hell, what else is there to do during the long, lonely nights of the off-season on Long Island.*

"Where would you like us to go?"

"Right where you are. Use the end unit. You think you'll need more room, I can move—"

"No. Where we are is fine."

"The door is unlocked," Bell said. "You need anything, I'm in the first unit at this end."

Rizzo gave Bell's shoulder a friendly squeeze. "Thanks for your help." He turned to leave and stopped. "Oh, Mr. Bell. Do any of those boats tied up out there have owners aboard?"

Bell shook his head. "Empty. All of them. This time of year, they rarely come out."

"We'll need to go down to the water. I assume we can reach the shore by going around the back of the building?"

"Yes. There's a brush of pines back there. Plenty of room to go by. About twenty-five yards to the shoreline and the dock. Thinking of doing a little swimming?" The motel's proprietor grinned, undoubtedly aware their visit did not include recreation.

"Not this trip, but our guest enjoys being near water. We're happy to oblige."

Bell nodded, hinting he got the message. He disappeared into the front entrance of the Seahorse, showing no interest in knowing more. It was obvious Fields never told the owner why Rizzo needed the motel room. Bell's arrangement and cooperation with the FBI no doubt stemmed from blind patriotism.

This beach option became Rizzo's last choice, and he regretted it. He needed to squeeze Cusack and without the luxury of time, he could think of no other way. Waterboarding was not an acceptable route with law enforcement or the courts. He would worry about that after he secured the girls' release.

He hurried back to the Rover. "Let's move him inside. We're in this end unit so we can leave the car right here." Before he lifted the Rover's tailgate, Rizzo whispered to Hoya and Manny, "Hey, no last names. First only. *Comprende?"*

Both beds stripped of their bedding, they carried Cusack to one of them. Hoya reached to remove the hood, and Rizzo grabbed his wrist. "Not yet." He turned to Manny. "Get the stuff from the car, will you? Don't forget the First Aid Kit in the sports bag."

Rizzo pulled Hoya into the bathroom and spoke quietly. "How's the arm? Take off your jacket. Let's have a look."

"I'm okay," Hoya insisted. "The bleeding stopped."

"Let's see."

Hoya slipped off his jacket, and Rizzo removed the tourniquet. No seepage. Manny came in with the kit and handed it to Rizzo. After swabbing the wound with alcohol, he covered it with a pad of gauze, taping it securely around the arm. The bleeding under control, he cautioned Hoya, "Don't jolt your arm. We'll make certain a doctor examines you when this business is over."

Manny came back in with a roll of duct tape, a yellow plastic pail, and several towels and set them on the second bed. Rizzo glanced at Cusack and signaled Hoya and Manny to the door. Outside, with the door closed, he said, "Listen to me, here's what we're gonna do. We tape his ankles together, locked, and I mean tight. No movement. Next, we sit him up. Leave on the wrist ties. Tape his forearms to his body so he can't move them an inch. Understand?"

Once they had Cusack trussed to Rizzo's satisfaction, he removed his own jacket, shoes, and socks, and rolled up his pants above his knees. With the pail in his hands and the towels under his arm, Rizzo left the motel room to scout the area along the shoreline. When he returned, he told them, "Looking good."

The beach section they would use, clear of debris and pebbles, inclined about twenty degrees down to the water. The height of the dock on their west side would provide them privacy as the sun came up.

"Let's go," Rizzo said.

Manny struggled to get a grip under Cusack's tightly bound armpits, trying to lift him off the bed. "Maybe I should carry him over my shoulder?"

"You can manage it?"

"Well, if I drop him, I won't worry about it." Manny laughed. "Yeah, I can. He's not that heavy."

They reached the beach area where Rizzo left the pail and towels. The ripple of waves lapping ashore made a rhythmic sound, precisely the ambiance he wanted. Manny stretched out Cusack on the wet sand with the man's head nearest to the water so it was lower than his feet.

Rizzo pulled off the hood and saw that Cusack's tongue forced out the cloth from his mouth. The man squeezed his eyelids like someone afraid of what he'd see if he opened them. His breathing came in deep gasps. Rizzo wet the washcloth and placed it on Cusack's forehead until his puffing evened out.

Across the bay, the sun was minutes from breaking on the horizon. It would be light soon. They needed to start moving.

Rizzo slipped his iPhone from his pocket and switched it to the video recorder. He knelt close to Cusack's head, took Cusack's stubble chin into his fingers, and jerked the man's head toward him. "Frankie Cusack, you with me?" he asked in a soft voice.

Eyelids fluttered, then widened. Cusack's bloodshot eyes squinted, working hard to become oriented. Both the stringy hair plastered to his skull and his breath reeked of booze.

"Frankie, my name is Luke Rizzo. I'm the guy Rabbit was meeting in Grand Central when you stabbed him."

Cusack's eyes jumped.

"I'm telling you who I am 'cause I want you to understand we're not fucking around here."

The man's mouth twitched, and he pressed his lips together as in, *I'm not saying shit.*

Rizzo glanced up at Hoya. "He's gonna be a tough nut,"

He handed the iPhone to Manny. "The setting is on video. I want you to record everything we do, everything he says. We need to have this on record. Don't stop until we're through. And don't put Sam in the picture. Understand?"

Manny nodded.

"Alright, Frankie. I got a few questions. I want the truth. You hold back, you'll be food for the crabs and fish before the sun comes up. That okay with you?"

Cusack's face took on a hard look. He wrenched his head away. "I don't know a fucking thing. Wadda ya want from me?"

It was the first time Rizzo heard Cusack speak. The sound of the man's voice surprised him. Then he remembered Jabba's description of it being soft, like a girl. This morning it was soft but also coarse sounding.

Again, Rizzo took Cusack's chin and wrenched it toward him. "Why don't you start by telling me who put you up to doing Rabbit?"

No response.

"Okay, try these two. Why did you kill Eduardo Soto? And what did you do with the gun?"

"Fuck off!"

"Not the answer I'm looking for. Let's move on to the big one. Where do they have the underage girl you bragged about to Rabbit? The one you said was a great lay? You remember? That's when Rabbit goes ballistic because he believed she was his sister's niece."

Cusack squeezed out his words loud enough for Manny to hear. "She wasn't so great."

Manny stepped toward Cusack and Rizzo raised his hand to stop him. The scrappy Mexican was having a hard time keeping his cool.

Out on the water, the gathering sounds of motor craft broke the stillness. From the shoreline west of them, early morning fishermen headed out to the Atlantic through the Fire Island inlet. Rizzo peered through the mist lifting off the bay, listening to their engines, trying to determine their location. None of the boats sounded within visual distance. The time neared when their presence could become a problem.

Rizzo spoke quickly. "Frankie, my man, those are the four questions I want you to answer. Take these next few minutes to think about them while we prepare to drown you. Meanwhile, if anything pops into your head, give us a shout." His tone remained calm, in control.

Motioning to Hoya, he pointed to the pail and towels. "Hand me those, will you? We need to get this going."

Rizzo waded out a few yards into the water. He soaked the towels, filled the pail, and returned to Cusack. He folded the hand towel lengthwise, and placed it across Cusack's forehead and eyes, leaving his nose clear.

"Pick up his head a few inches," he told Hoya.

Hoya grabbed a hank of hair from the top of Cusack's head and yanked it up. The man emitted a loud groan.

With Cusack's head elevated, Rizzo tucked a rolled bath towel under it. Then he rolled up two more bath towels and stuffed them under each side of the man's head to ensure complete stability. Rizzo pointed to Cusack's legs. "Now, lock them down—no movement," he told Hoya.

Hoya straddled Cusack and sat, placing all his weight on the man's ankles and shins. He leaned forward and pushed down with both hands on his thighs.

"Perfect," Rizzo said. He looked down at Cusack again. "Frankie. Where are we? You ready to answer my little quiz?"

Cusack's mouth parted. For a fleeting moment, Rizzo expected he would respond. Instead, he pressed his lips together again. This time with a nervous tremor.

The worried expression on Cusack's face triggered Rizzo's memory of his own experience with waterboarding. He remembered a conversation with one of the FBI lecturers before he went under. He had asked about the acceptance of the procedure as a form of torture. The agent became defensive and insisted this type of enhanced interrogation did not qualify as torture. According to the manual used by the FBI and the CIA called the White Book, it stated interrogators could do anything to the subject as long as no severe or permanent injury was inflicted. The soft-hearted Washington politicians didn't buy into that. They banned the procedure.

Rizzo had no intention of drowning the man. He merely wanted to make him think he was. Kneeling again, he imagined what Cusack was about to experience. He needed to hurry things along. Every passing hour brought them closer to losing Rosita and her friend.

He leaned close to Cusack's head and spoke to him again, a note of finality in his tone. "Last chance, Frankie. You're not gonna like this, I promise you." The man's mouth opened again. Nothing. "No more bullshit. You're about to go under."

Rizzo reached into the pail, took out a soaked hand towel, stuffed one end into Cusack's mouth and laid the other end over his exposed nose. Raising the pail, he bent over to pour a steady flow of water on Cusack's face. The gag reflex produced a useless struggle against the sensation of suffocating, mirroring that of a drowning man.

After thirty seconds of restricted airflow, Rizzo stopped the pour and removed the towel from Cusack's mouth and away from his nose. Cusack spewed a spray of water from both orifices. His gasping for air was frenetic.

Rizzo paused and waited for Cusack's reaction to settle. "Frankie? Four questions, four answers, and we'll pull you up."

"I can't . . . " he choked, trying to regain control of his breathing. "I can't . . . ." His strained gargled voice was filled with terror.

"You can't, or you won't?"

"He'll kill—"

"Frankie, I don't give a shit about that." Rizzo checked the illuminated sweep hand on his watch. When it reached thirty seconds, he said, "You don't want to talk? Under you go." He shoved the towel back into the man's mouth and covered his nose. Cusack's body stiffened.

The next water pour lasted another thirty seconds. Rizzo set the pail down and waited for Cusack's chest to stop heaving and his desperate struggle to slow. Hoya's eyes met his when he glanced over. The linebacker's face showed serious angst.

"What?"

"Jesus, when you do that, I can feel his body stretch like a piano wire about to snap."

"That's the idea." Rizzo bent toward Hoya and whispered, "A realistic sensation of drowning. Take my word for it. I've been there."

"Is this going to work?"

"Don't know. We're gonna find out soon enough." Rizzo removed the hand towel and ducked the anticipated water spray. He permitted enough time to pass to allow Cusack's breathing to quiet. He spoke again, keeping his tone non-threatening.

"Frankie, let's start with the first question. Who ordered you to take out Rabbit?"

No response.

Rizzo paused before repeating the question. Between deep intakes of air, Cusack mumbled a name, so faint and garbled it was inaudible. "Who?" Rizzo said. "I couldn't understand you."

Cusack's breathing evened out. "Ilya," he mumbled again.

"Ilya? Speak up. Is that what you said?"

"Yeah."

"Does he have a last name?"

Cusack released a long push of breath. "He's gonna kill me. Don't you fuckin' get it?"

The panic in his voice gave Rizzo hope. They were making progress.

"You don't give me what I want, I'll drown you before he can kill you."

Cusack went mute. Finally, with a sigh of resignation, he said, "Bodrov. He works for Salazar."

"He tell you to kill Rabbit, shoot Soto?"

"Yeah."

"Where's the gun you used?"

"My apartment. The bedroom closet, under the floorboards."

"Super. Now here's the last one. Answer it, and you'll run the tables. Where do they have Rabbit's niece?"

He could see Cusack's body go rigid. Rizzo waited, watching. Would Cusack give up the location of the girls? No answer. He bent close to his ear and whispered, "Buddy-boy, you disappoint me. You know where they are, don't you?"

A wave of desperation climbed though Rizzo's chest. He jammed the towel into Cusack's mouth and flipped the end up over his nose.

"Down you go, fucker. This time you may not come back up."

For a third time, he poured a steady stream of water. Manny and Hoya watched, their attention riveted on the man. Rizzo suspected the two empathized with Cusack's incredible sense of panic. He worried Cusack would suffer a heart attack in the next half minute. *If this third pour doesn't break him, well* . . . .

The sweep hand on Rizzo's watch crossed the thirty-second mark. He set down the pail and watched his struggling captive before he removed the towel from his mouth and nose. Cusack responded the same: chest heaves, mouth, and nose spewing water, a frenzied gasping for breath, mouth opening and closing, taking in air, pushing it out like a fireplace bellows. This time, between choking and spewing, Cusack issued a torrent of fitful sounds setting Rizzo back on his heels.

"Oh, God—good God! Please! Please! No more, please! No more!" Cusack's high-pitched, earsplitting voice raced up from his lungs and echoed across the Great South Bay.

Chapter Twenty

"When can you get here?" Duggan said.

"Not right away. I'm still in Bay Shore. Something I need to do first. There's the matter of the two kidnapped teens. I told you about them. Cusack gave up their location. I'm going to pull them out."

"Alone? No backup?"

"None unless you can arrange some," Rizzo said, not really expecting Duggan to offer any cooperation.

"Jesus Christ, Rizzo, you need the Feds in on this. When are you going?"

"I'm heading out now."

"Where's this place? I'll contact the captain of the precinct."

Duggan surprised him. "Corona, Queens," Rizzo said. "A house on 112th, west of Northern Boulevard. A two-story, single-family. Cusack couldn't give me the exact address. He said the fourth house on the left."

"Hold a second. I'll check the precinct map." Duggan returned and said, "The One-Fifteen. I'll make the call. Do nothing until I get back to you."

"Right. Oh, and Frank, I got it all on video." Rizzo gave the iPhone an appreciative tap with his finger.

"And all provided voluntary, right?" the lieutenant said with ringing skepticism.

"Well, yeah. You can't use it as evidence, but it'll get you probable cause for a warrant to search his apartment. The gun he used on Eduardo Soto is under the floorboards of his bedroom closet. When you have the gun, you'll have a case. It corroborates his confession."

"Rizzo, you're off the job too long. You forgot any evidence seized due to an involuntary confession, they throw out the case."

"Not if the perp cops to the killing. Then you got a free ticket."

The detective quieted for a beat. "Jesus, Rizzo, thanks. How the hell did I ever solve a crime these past eighteen years without you?"

He let Duggan's sarcasm slide. "You want I should bring him to you at the precinct or somewhere else?"

"Did you tune him up?"

"Not much. Got him wet, is all."

Duggan paused again. "What the hell does that mean?"

Rizzo knew he stood on shaky ground. He might blow the detective's cooperation before he could convince him Cusack was guilty of a double murder. They were both Duggan's cases and more than a passing interest to him.

"Come on, Rizzo. Don't bullshit me. Will this guy confess voluntarily or not? You didn't coerce him, did you?"

Rizzo figured he couldn't duck the issue. If he stalled Duggan any longer, he'd lose him. "Frank, I'll level with you. I used a little to get him to cooperate."

"How little?"

Rizzo's molars clamped down tight. "Poured water on him."

"What! You outta your God-damn mind? Rizzo, you already face a possible charge of kidnapping. And now torturing a suspect."

"Hell, he wasn't tortured. I didn't harm him."

"You gotta be kidding."

"But Frank, I—"

"Stop right there. I don't want to hear any more."

"Damn, Frank. I know what I got from him is tainted and—"

"Tainted? Rizzo, you shitting me? His confession is God-damn useless."

"Wait. Suppose you question him, and he's willing to cop to both murders?"

"Yeah? How the hell you gonna pull that off?"

"Convince him owning up is in his best interest. Tell him what the alternative is."

"And what's that?"

"Ilya Bodrov and Umberto Salazar."

* * *

They found the house easily, the fourth on the left, single-family, two-story, and similar to all the others along both sides of 112th Street. The building sat on a plot not much bigger than the width of the structure. The narrow broken cement driveway on the right side provided barely enough room for a vehicle to pass to the one-car garage in the rear.

A shoulder-high chain-link fence separated the driveway from the adjacent house. Below the front windows, a stone façade covered the base of the building. Weathered wood shingles clad the rest. Three stone steps led up to an entrance porch, a typical design for this lower-income Queens area.

Rizzo remembered Louis Armstrong once lived in the community until he blew his last note in 1971. Back in the early forties when Satchmo first took up residence, it was a middle-class, black, and Italian section of Queens.

Hoya pulled to the curb about twenty yards beyond the house and shut off the engine. "How we going to handle this if the place is in use?"

"I don't think they service their johns in the house. This neighborhood is too visible. The patrols of the One-Fifteen Precinct would catch on damn quick. This is just where the girls live. A call comes in for a girl, one of the resident pimps drives her to the john. Could be a hotel or his home, wherever. The pimp delivers her and waits in the car."

Manny, hearing the description, frowned. "So you think they could be in the house?"

The anxious tone of his voice was a tell. Rizzo needed to keep a close watch on him, not let him go crazy.

"Well, yeah. That would be my guess. Too early in the day for any action, but you never know."

His eyes scanned the quiet area. The residents of this neighborhood were everyday, blue-collar people. Doubtful they would guess the purpose of the house. They'd notice a man driving away with a woman, they'd assume she was his wife, or at least his girlfriend, and think nothing of it. Everyone minded their own business.

Manny scratched his chest and glared at the house. "What can we expect when we go in?"

"Well, if both girls are inside, at least two pimps will be with them. That's what we have to prepare for."

Hoya looked over his shoulder. "Cusack going in with us?"

"Nah, of course not. We'll leave him on the deck back there. After we pull out the girls, we'll drop him off with Duggan at the One-Seven."

Rizzo spotted a radio motor patrol making the turn from Northern Boulevard and coming into the street. The RMP with two uniforms drew near at a slow speed, the driver scanning the houses, counting, searching. It stopped in front of the fourth one.

"Stay put. Let me talk to these guys about how they want to play this. I know they didn't have time for a search warrant so this could go south."

He got out of the Rover and walked back to the police car. Rizzo caught sight of Manny slipping from the rear door and heading into the driveway of the house next door. Rizzo grimaced. He should have warned him.

He reached the RMP and bent down to the level of the open driver's side window. "Hey, guys, I'm Luke Rizzo, former NYPD narcotics." He handed his P.I. business card to the officer behind the wheel. "You guys from the One-Fifteen?"

"Yeah," the driver replied. "Officer Martell." He nodded to the passenger-seat occupant. "Sergeant Collins."

Collins, a man well into his sixties, leaned over to examine Rizzo's face through the RMP's window. "I think I know you from somewhere. You ever work the South Bronx, the Four-One?"

"Fort Apache? Yeah. In another life."

"I thought so."

Collins was a beanpole of a man with chiseled features and cold blue eyes. He struck Rizzo as a dinosaur, a term the NYPD referred to as a police officer with more than twenty years on the job.

"So what's goin' down here?" Collins asked. "The desk officer said something about a possible kidnapping. Two kids in this house."

"Yeah, two sixteen-year-old girls being held as sex slaves." Rizzo gestured toward the house. "The place belongs to the Salazar syndicate. We believe the girls are inside. The info came from one of the syndicate's lowlifes. It's solid because he gave it up under, shall we say, urgent persuasion."

Martell, a middle-aged man with a port-wine nose, asked, "What do you want from us? Knock on the door? Ask if the kids are in there? Like that?"

Rizzo laughed "If only it could be so easy."

"We couldn't order a warrant. No time," Collins said. He sounded apologetic.

"I figured maybe I go to the door, see what I can do to provoke or say something that makes a warrant unnecessary."

Manny's sudden appearance at Rizzo's side cut short the sergeant's reply. His dark eyes blinked with excitement, his forefinger jabbed at the house. "Up there—up there," he stuttered, struggling to spit out the words. "Inside, I saw her. The window upstairs. She waved to me."

The sergeant stepped out of the passenger side and cast an eye over the top of the RMP at Manny. "Who the hell is he?"

"The brother of one of the teens."

Manny jerked around toward the house. Before he could move, Rizzo grabbed him by the arm and spun him back against the RMP's front fender.

"Hold on, Lone Ranger. You'll screw up this operation if you don't cool down."

"But she's inside. We gotta get her out."

"We will, bro, we will. You just can't go off half-cocked. *Comprende?* We need to do this the right way, or it won't hold up."

Martell pushed open the car door and stepped out. Collins came around from the rear. The two officers stood in front of Rizzo and Manny, their hands on their hips, questioning expressions on both of their faces.

The eyebrows of Sergeant Collins knitted together. "You trust this guy?"

"How do you mean?"

"Well, shit. He really spot his sister in the window?"

"God-damn right I did," Manny shouted, struggling to break free of Rizzo's grip.

Rizzo held him with two hands and brought his face up close to his. "Manny, shut the fuck up." He shook his head. "Sorry, Sarge. He's hopped up right now. Been tough on him and his family since she got snatched. If he says he saw his sister, I believe him."

Collins paused before reaching his decision. He told Rizzo to stand down. He and Martell would go with Manny to the front door, ask whoever answered to produce the sister, tell them her brother spotted her at the window. "They deny she's there," Collins said, "we have a no-hit without a warrant. With luck, they haven't spotted us, and we might catch them off balance."

Hoya joined Rizzo at the curb, watching Manny and the two officers climb the steps to the entry porch. Collins reached to the side and pushed the doorbell. No response. He pushed it again. Out of patience, he rapped his knuckles hard against the face of the door.

The door opened a crack. A voice from inside asked, "Who you?"

"Police. Open up."

"Oh, *lo siento,* officer. *Sí, pronto.*"

The door opened halfway and revealed a short, muscled man in a black tight-fitting mock turtle, and a dark, three-day growth on his jowls. His left hand gripped the edge of the door, his other hand wrapped around the inside knob, poised to slam it closed.

"*Perdóneme,* officer. I think you somebody selling."

"What's your name, sir? Do you live here?"

"Jocqualino, señor."

"That your last name?"

"No, *señor.* Jocqualino Gomez."

"You live here, Jock?"

"*Sí,* I live here."

"Alone?"

"With *mi esposa*—my wife."

Watching the exchange from the street, Rizzo noticed Manny growing impatient with the slow-moving way Collins proceeded.

"Is she here now, in the house?" Collins asked Gomez.

Gomez hesitated, shooting a quick glance behind him. "No, *señor*. She at the *bodega*, she is shop—"

"Maneeee, *ayúdame*! Pleeeze!"

The scream came from the top of the staircase to the right of Gomez. Manny's body tensed before it exploded into motion. He lowered his shoulder, rammed it against the door, and sent it flying. With his left arm, he clothes-lined Gomez and slammed him to the floor. Before anyone could move, Manny climbed halfway up the stairs. Officer Martell followed.

"Sam, back of the house," Rizzo yelled. "The second guy might try to slip out that way. Go!"

Hoya took off, sprinting down the driveway.

Collins jumped on Gomez and rolled him onto his stomach. He straddled him and warned, "Don't move, shithead." He stretched back the man's arms and cuffed his wrists with zip ties. Once the pimp was secured, Collins told him, "You're under arrest, Jocko," and read him his Miranda rights. The sergeant looked up at Rizzo, who stood in the doorway. His mouth formed a half-smile when he said, "After all this, it had better be the sister."

Hoya rounded the corner of the house dragging a stumbling man in a head-lock. "Hey, look what I found," he called to Rizzo. "Tried to jump the back fence."

The second pimp, a swarthy man with a slight build, sported thick side-whiskers, and baggy chinos. Rizzo expected the pimp's eyeballs to pop out of their sockets from the force Hoya's arm exerted around his neck.

The sergeant pulled Gomez to his feet and walked him to the RMP. He opened the rear door and commanded, "Inside." Gomez slipped onto the seat and gawked back while Collins locked him in. The sergeant poked his head into the front seat of the RMP, picked up his radio and called for a backup vehicle for the second pimp.

Officer Martell appeared at the door of the house, holding a sobbing young girl in his hands, her tears trembling on her dark eyelids. She wore faded jeans and an oversized quilted jacket belonging to a larger person. The garment hung open and revealed a blue denim shirt, the tails tied at the waist. Her pale, thin face, screwed tight, showed signs of fear. Martell led her down the steps to the sidewalk, holding on as though he expected her to collapse at any moment.

"The brother has the other girl, "Martell told Collins. "He'll be down with her in a minute. Nobody else in the house. Both kids appear to be okay, with no signs of abuse." He reached out to Hoya. "I'll take him. You hold on to the kid."

Rizzo eyed the occupant of the RMP and the pimp in Hoya's grasp. "Lucky for them," he said to Martell, "or you might have to cuff the brother."

Manny and Rosita hurried out of the house, eager to leave behind all it represented. Rosita Fuentes, a slim-hipped teen with long legs, forced a smile through her pain. She held onto Manny with her arms wrapped around him. Tears glistened on her heart-shaped face, a beauty with short, ebony-black hair, and a young body verging on premature voluptuousness. She wore an Old Navy tee shirt under a light jacket, jeans, and sneakers without socks. If she came to the house with other clothes, she left them upstairs.

Manny held Rosita wrapped in his arms, her face buried against his chest. Rizzo stepped over to them. "Welcome home, sweetheart. You okay?"

The girl pulled away and nodded. Fear filled her wide eyes. She wore a worried expression that said if she spoke, she might awaken from her dream of freedom.

"Upstairs," Manny said, "Rosita told me they forced them to perform sex with a bunch of strangers. The pimps drove them to hotel rooms. Afterward, they took the money from the girls.

Never touched them sexually, thank God, but threatened them when they resisted going on a call."

"They didn't physically abuse them, did they?" Rizzo asked.

"No. According to Rosita, they left them pretty much alone."

"No doubt one of Salazar's policies with the younger ones. A scumbag with a conscience."

"Lucky for them, or I'd have killed those two pieces of shit before . . . ." He let the words trail off, then kissed the top of his sister's head.

The second teenager, under the support of Hoya, continued sobbing, taking deep gulps of air, sniffling her runny nose. Her bloodshot eyes kept darting back to the house.

Rizzo went to her and took her hand. He asked in his best Spanish, *"Cómo te llamas?"*

She swallowed. "Olga Gonzalez."

"You're safe now, Olga. No need to be afraid anymore." Her tense face showed no signs of comprehending. "Manny," Rizzo said, "they understand English, don't they?"

"Rosita does. Olga, some."

The second RMP arrived for the other pimp. Collins read him his rights and loaded him into the back seat. He locked the door and faced Rizzo. "We need to deliver these two mutts to the precinct," he said, "and book 'em. You bring the girls in your vehicle. We'll pick up one of our female officers at the station house to escort them over to Flushing Hospital Medical Center so the doc can check them out. The brother can go along with them."

"Good idea," Rizzo said.

Manny smiled. "See, they're gonna arrange for a doctor to examine you, *pobrecita*. Make sure everything *es buena. Estoy contento.*" Rosita's hold on her brother tightened, her eyes flickered up at his face.

"After that," Collins continued, "they'll come back to the precinct to give their statements."

Rizzo suddenly remembered he couldn't go into the station house with them, leaving Cusack tied up like a sack of potatoes in the back of the Range Rover. Someone in the precinct parking lot might spot him.

Rizzo approached Sergeant Collins. "Okay if just the brother goes in with the two kids? I need to meet with Detective Frank Duggan at the One-Seven in Manhattan before noon. He's expecting me to make an important delivery."

Collins reflected a moment. "Yeah, that'll be all right. Why don't you follow me, drop 'em off, then split?"

"Sounds good." He looked at Manny and said, "Okay, then. You stay with the girls. Sam and me will take off and make the delivery in town. After the doc checks them over, and you're done giving your statements, ask the desk officer to call you a taxi. We'll meet later at your hotel."

* * *

A mile from the Triborough Bridge on the Grand Central Parkway, Rizzo told Hoya, "Pull off at the next exit."

Hoya blinked at Rizzo through the rearview mirror. "You don't want to take the bridge?"

"Not right away. We gonna conduct a short meeting before we hit Manhattan."

Coming up on the turnoff, Hoya asked, "This exit?"

"Yeah, here. At the stop sign, go left, then straight across the avenue under the elevated tracks. This street leads into Astoria Park. When you're close to the river, turn left and pull into one of the parking spots."

Astoria Park, a sixty-acre sprawl of open green spaces maintained by New York City for the benefit of the public, ran parallel to the East River. Nestled between the Triborough Bridge at one end and the Hell Gate Bridge at the other, the park drew huge crowds during the summer months.

Hoya stopped the Rover in a space facing the river. He scanned the area. "This place is deserted."

"This time of the year, nothing. On a summer weekend? Forget it. Crawls with picnicking families." Rizzo glared at the hooded Cusack slouched on the seat next to him. "Right now, we're not here to picnic."

Rizzo reached over and removed the hood, revealing Cusack's stringy, disheveled hair pasted across his forehead with sweat. His bleary eyes flickered in the daylight like a faulty fluorescent tube. Rizzo pulled the washcloth from his mouth, and the man released a sharp puff of air. His wrists remained tied and his ankles bound together with duct tape. His body twitched, and the sour aroma emanating from his dirty clothing was enough to gag even a person with a head cold.

"Listen, my friend, here's how this is gonna go," Rizzo began. "You got three options. The first, we deliver you to the police in Manhattan where you confess to killing Rabbit and Eduardo Soto."

Cusack bolted upright. His voice crackling with exhaustion. "You fuckin' crazy?"

"Wait—wait. You gotta hear the other two options first."

"I don't give a shit what they are, I ain't committin' suicide."

"Not to worry." Rizzo snickered. "For sure, your death won't be by your own doing."

Cusack slammed back against the seat cushion and twisted his head away from Rizzo. He remained immobilized, his eyes staring out the window for several moments, his breathing picking up the pace, all the while making snorting noises through his nose.

"Number two option is this," Rizzo said. "We call your buddies, Salazar, and his frontman, Bodrov. We tell them where they can pick you up."

Cusack's head whipped around.

"But before we tell them, we let them in on how we found the two Mexican kids, and how we shut down the Corona operation. Oh, and the two pimps, Gomez and the other guy? We tell 'em they're in police custody ready to sing like birds about the sex slave operation in New York. How's that one grab you?"

Cusack squeezed his eyes. "Kill me, why don't ya?"

"Don't get ahead of me."

Rizzo's eyes went from Cusack to Hoya's puzzled face. He grinned because he knew Hoya was thinking about the third option. He recalled the linebacker being uncomfortable watching Cusack's panicked reaction during the simulated drowning on the beach. Would he believe this last option, that Rizzo would kill him? It didn't matter. What did matter was, would Frankie Cusack believe him?

"Now for your last choice. Look to your right," Rizzo said, pointing. "See, over there. That bridge. They named it the Hell Gate, and for a good reason. The water below it is a lethal, swirling eddy. Notorious, in case you never heard. Swallowed up everyone who's ever challenged it. So, tonight we come back here around midnight and toss your skinny ass into those waters. You should come up somewhere around Boston."

Chapter Twenty-One

"**F**uck you mean, you can't find Cusack? Where the hell he go?"

"A mystery, Umberto," Bodrov said. His eyelids fluttered. "Doesn't answer phone. I call him early in the morning. Again, one hour ago. Don't have good feeling about this."

"Didn't you tell me we could trust him?"

"Yes, until now."

"Well, you need to get your ass up to New York right away. Check it out."

Bodrov hesitated, staring out the kitchen window of his Miami condominium. There was more. He knew Salazar would freak out when he told him, but he had no chance to hide it from him for long. Sooner than later it would leak from other sources within the organization.

Salazar would blame him. The entire prostitution operation was his responsibility, from New York to Florida. He failed to remain close enough, to stay on top of things. Salazar's demands bounced him back and forth between the sex house operation and their drug smuggling planning with the Ortega cartel in Puerto Rico.

"Something else, Umberto."

"What?"

"Police shut down one house in Queens."

"Which one?"

Bodrov paused before answering. "In Corona, 112ᵗʰ Street. Arrest both guardians, Gomez and his brother. Police take them."

"Okay, okay. Have the lawyer pay their fines. Bail them out, the usual deal. Same with the girls. Pay their bail, then move them to another—"

"Not happen."

"What? Why not?"

"The two girls. Underage ones we get few months ago from Mexico. The brother of one of them there when police come."

Complete silence.

"Umberto?" The snail-like pace of Bodrov's eyelid-flutter picked up speed.

Salazar's voice boomed. "I can't believe it. Didn't I say . . . God-damn it, didn't I warn you about using kids? Oh, sweet Jesus, the shit's gonna come down on us now."

The sound of Salazar grinding his teeth and snorting convinced Bodrov to remain quiet. Wouldn't be smart to intrude on a man going ballistic. He pressed the phone to his ear.

"How'd you find out about this?" Salazar asked between snorts.

"Detective from local precinct—Malone. The one we have in pocket. He call Vinnie Katz. Tip him off. Vinnie call me."

"You mean, had in our pocket. After this, the guy won't come near us, not for any amount of grease. He knows the Feds will become involved now."

"And the private detective, Rizzo. He was there too."

"Well, you handle it. Find him. Figure a way to get rid of him. I'm through with threats. He's a burr on my ass. I want him gone, and I don't want any excuses."

"Okay, Umberto. I take care of it. Call you back when—"

"Wait, wait," Salazar shouted before Bodrov could continue. "How about the brother? How do we know he's not gonna make trouble?"

Bodrov remembered what Katz told him when Vinnie got the call from Malone on the take-down in Corona. The detective said the brother, Manny Fuentes, was registered at a Holiday Inn Express on the West Side. That's what he put on paperwork he completed at the precinct.

"The brother, he stays in hotel in Manhattan," Bodrov said. "I get Zakharchenko twins to work on him, give him scare. Remind him to shut his mouth. Go back to Florida."

"Jesus! Getting' caught fuckin' around with underage kids. We must be out of our minds. Rough him up, you hear?"

"Yes, Umberto." Bodrov clicked off before Salazar said anything else. He squeezed his eyes to quiet them and took a deep breath. He looked out the window at the sky darkened with cloud cover. A tropical storm loomed on the horizon.

The Russian pushed through the bedroom door and looked down at the woman in his bed. Her matted blond hair, splayed across his pillow, was in the same state as when he got up, showered, and dressed. "Mimi, get up. I leave now."

Mimi rolled over on her back and fluffed the pillow behind her head. She glanced at the digital clock on the bedside stand and released a low groan. "But Ilya, it's early. Don't you want to do me again? Make more love?"

"Have to go to airport. Get dressed. Quick!"

"But Ilya, where are you—"

"Mimi, no questions. Get dressed, or I put you outside as you are. No time for games."

"Oh, Ilya, you can be so mean."

"Now! No more talk."

* * *

Rizzo reached into his pocket and pulled out his iPhone. He answered the call without looking at the caller ID readout. "Hello."

"Rizzo. Jack Fields. Where are you?"

"Mid-span on the Fifty-ninth Street Bridge, heading into Manhattan. Why?"

"Damn it, Rizzo, what the hell happened with Haus? You never let me know."

Rizzo realized his dumping the doctor pissed off Fields. He steered the Rover out of the passing lane into the slow lane.

"It wasn't working out," he said, muffling his words. His eyes flashed to the rearview mirror. After Rizzo took over the driving, Hoya replaced the hood over Cusack's head. Rizzo continued. "No condition for what we had in mind. Went to Plan B. We're on the way to the Seventeenth."

The phone went silent.

"Jack? You there?"

"Listen to me, Rizzo. You need to meet with me before you do anything else. It's important."

"Right now?"

"Yeah, right now."

Rizzo glanced again through the mirror at Cusack. He couldn't believe this was happening. He got the guy to cop to the murders of Rabbit and Soto by scaring the shit out of him with waterboarding, then threatened to turn him over to Salazar. Now, this insanity. He worried a delay getting him to Duggan could risk Cusack having second thoughts.

"Jesus, you're not asking me to come to your office, are you?"

"No, not my office. I need you to turn around. Drive to a taxi garage in Sunnyside at the corner of Roosevelt and Forty-first. Take a left off Roosevelt and pull into the alley behind the garage. Call me when you're a couple of blocks away. You follow me?"

Rizzo looked up and rolled his eyes. His attention traveled between the bridge girders on his left and across the stream of eastbound traffic. A helicopter heading uptown over the center of the East River neared the upper span of the bridge.

"I do, but I'm not clear on what's going on. Besides, I'm not alone. Can't this wait 'til I make the delivery?"

"No! You'll understand when you get here. I need you to come to the garage before you go anywhere else. Who's with you? The brother?"

"The other one."

"No problem."

The chopper passed overhead, its noisy rotor churning through the afternoon warm air. Rizzo pictured the helicopter's rotating blades, reminding him of the crazy whirlwind of circumstances he ignited when he initiated his investigation into Rabbit's murder.

"Okay, be there soon. Traffic's a bitch in both directions."

Rizzo slipped the iPhone into his pocket and looked again into the rearview mirror. "A change in plans," he announced. "We're making an unscheduled stop. Keep the hood on him. Don't let him fuss."

"Where we going?" Hoya asked.

"I don't know what's going on, but we'll find out in about a half hour."

Rizzo took the Sixty-first Street turnoff in Manhattan, looped around to Sixtieth Street, cruised back to Second Avenue and onto the ramp to the bridge heading east. The Range Rover, sandwiched between slow-moving, bumper-to-bumper traffic, crawled across to the Queens side of the river. An otherwise seven-minute crossing took twenty minutes.

He reached Queensboro Plaza and followed Roosevelt Avenue, driving under the elevated railroad tracks of the Flushing Line. At Fifty-second Street, Rizzo punched in the agent's cell phone number.

"Fields."

"We're almost there."

"Right. Pull in behind the garage, up close to the door. Wait for me."

Rizzo entered the driveway of the bilious-yellow, concrete-block garage. Several empty cabs awaiting maintenance cluttered the rear area. He nosed the Rover into a space next to the building.

Jack Fields appeared in the doorway. A trio of mechanics in open bays to the side of the door working on taxi cabs ignored them.

"Stay here," Rizzo told Hoya. "Let me find out what the hell this is about. I'll be right back."

Fields held the door. "Follow me."

A short, narrow hallway led to the garage manager's office near the front of the building. Rizzo, pissed off and puzzled, trailed the agent without speaking, his thoughts buzzed with worry Cusack could skate free of his murder charges. He stepped through the doorway and stopped short. His eyes landed on the figure seated at one side of the manager's desk.

"What the fuck—"

A smiling Frank Duggan stood and extended his hand. "Hey, Rizzo. Glad we caught you before you made it to the One-Seven."

* * *

Ilya Bodrov got lucky. He found a seat on the 1:35 p.m., American Airlines flight from Miami International to JFK. He would arrive in New York in three hours and thirteen minutes.

Despite booking late, he landed an aisle seat next to a middle-thirties redhead with long legs. Bodrov stood in the aisle and waited for her to slide over to her window position. She offered him a polite smile, but not before her eyes walked him up and down.

Seated, the woman's knees pressed against the seatback in front while she tested different positions, trying to find a form of comfort. The confines of the inside location defeated her efforts. Her thigh-hugging skirt kept retreating as she struggled to rescue her dignity.

Bodrov turned and spoke in a lowered voice. "Don't give much room, these seats. I exchange with you if you think aisle seat more comfortable."

She considered his suggestion while staring into his eyes. "If you wouldn't mind," she replied. "I always fly first class, but when I called for a reservation, first class was completely booked."

Bodrov unbuckled his seatbelt, stood and stepped into the aisle. His redheaded seat companion got to her feet, sidled past and paused beside him. He found himself looking up into her face and smiled. The woman was taller by two inches. She stepped back, and he slipped past.

Once seated and re-buckled, she said, "I apologize for being such a bother." She patted her knees. "These are the reason I fly first class. A real handicap. Lots more legroom than coach. Really, I'm terribly sorry."

The flight attendant's announcement filled the cabin, drowning any opportunity for him to respond. Bodrov silently waved off the need to apologize.

Announcements completed, he turned toward her again. "Maybe you pardon me, but anyone with attractive legs like you should not call them handicap." He grinned, hoping she hadn't taken offense.

Her smile widened in surprise. "Oh my, what a sweet thing to say. Thank you."

Bodrov nodded graciously.

The Boeing 747 backed from the gate, turned and began its long, bumpy taxi over the tarmac toward their assigned takeoff runway. Bodrov leaned back in his seat and slid up the window cover to view the passing scenery until the plane came to a stop. The rain let up, leaving a light mist on the window.

They were next in line. Soon, the 747 rumbled around into a holding position.

"You are not frightened of takeoffs, no? Because I close cover, so you don't see."

Her laugh made him smile.

"Heavens no. I'm a frequent flier. About sixteen trips a year."

"Forgive me. I thought—"

"I know. It appears as though I've never flown before."

"I not mean to offend you."

"Oh, you haven't, I assure you. By the way, I'm Rita Sands."

"Good to meet you, Rita Sands. I am Boris Alexandrov."

"I create fashion shows for a major women's clothing manufacturer," Sands explained. "My job involves a great deal of travel. I'm quite a seasoned flier," she said with a wink.

The whine of the 747's jet engines signaled takeoff was imminent. Bodrov stole a look at her as she inclined against her headrest with her eyes closed, leaving him to his thoughts.

He admired the woman's self-assurance and recalled his deceased wife exuded the same aura of confidence during their ten years of marriage. He respected this attribute in his wife until she betrayed their wedding vows.

It was unfortunate, for they talked about having children. Not long after their first discussion, Sergei Ivanov, a senior member of the Federal Assembly, turned her head and changed her mind. Bodrov arranged the accident that destroyed them both. Within a week, he fled to Mexico.

The plane bolted forward and sprinted down the runway. The roar of jet engines filled Bodrov's ears. He gripped the armrest while the 747 raced along the stretch of wet concrete. He watched the terminals and parked aircraft zip by his window. The wide-body airliner lifted suddenly, became airborne and bored a path through low-hanging clouds. He exhaled. Takeoffs were not his favorite part of flying.

He examined Rita Sands' pleasant face. With her eyes closed, she appeared relaxed and a trouble-free woman. He liked that. Perhaps, he thought, they might get together in New York.

* * *

Rizzo fought to mask his confusion and anger behind a laugh. "Am I missing something?"

"Sorry about the surprise," Fields said. "The situation developed late this morning." He put an assuring hand on Rizzo's arm. "Grab a seat. I'll explain."

Rizzo glared at Duggan, who walked back to his chair. What the hell were they pulling? Were they about to undo all the time and effort he spent hauling Cusack's ass into custody? He didn't know the detective well, but his gut told him this turn of events would not produce a happy ending. Bureaucratic bullshit. He didn't possess the patience for it during his years on the job.

He took a seat next to Duggan. "So what's this about? I got a double murderer cooling his heels out in the car."

Fields walked behind the desk and dropped into a wobbly chair. A window behind him faced Roosevelt Avenue and the elevated tracks of the Flushing line. Dust mites danced in the patches of sunlight leaking into the room. The agent tilted back and closed the blinds, shutting off the dance.

"I got concerned this morning," Fields began. "When I spoke with Dr. Haus, I learned you dismissed his help. I remembered you mentioned Detective Duggan here," he said, nodding at the lieutenant, "and how the two murders were his cases. I figured you contacted him. So I called. He told me about your phone conversation after you took down Cusack."

"Yeah, and we also rescued the two Mexican kids from the house in Corona," Rizzo added, a note of pride in his voice.

"So I'm told," he said, looking at the seated Duggan. "A nice bit of heroics, even though your method acquiring their location was unorthodox? You claim Cusack is ready to confess on his own? If so, I figured we could convince the detective here to leave the water part out of his report."

"Swell, if delaying him here hasn't cooled off his decision and changed his mind."

Duggan jumped in. "Didn't you say he's scared stiff you would dump him back into Salazar's lap? And it's the reason he's cooperating?"

"Yeah. And back into Ilya Bodrov's clutches, too. Don't forget, the Russian is the one who gave Cusack his orders in both killings."

Fields stood and stepped to the front of the desk. Facing Rizzo and Duggan, he said, "Well, Cusack's my reason for getting you here. Detective Duggan is willing to help out the bureau with my idea. Since you already have a good read on the guy, I figured you'd be in the best position to judge if we have a shot."

"About what?" Rizzo asked.

"A couple of questions first. How scared is Cusack of Umberto Salazar?"

"He shits his pants at the sound of his name. That's how he's sitting in a car outside with a hood over his head." Rizzo laughed.

Fields walked toward the window, paused and turned back to Rizzo. "Do you think Salazar is aware you hijacked his man?"

"I can't imagine how he would know. We took him last night. He hasn't seen or talked to another soul since." Rizzo flashed on the dirty cop in the precinct. He decided to say nothing.

"How informed do you think Cusack is of Salazar's business, about both the sex and drug operations?"

Rizzo grinned. It was as though Fields asked about the Cleveland Browns' chances of winning the Super Bowl. "Christ, I doubt he's up the food chain far enough. Can't imagine he knows much of anything beyond what Bodrov tells him. My guess is they use him to handle the low-level jobs."

"Why don't we find out? Bring him in. Let's see if he can help us out here. Leave the other guy in the car."

"I got him hooded. Do I take—"

"Keep it on."

"You're wasting your time. He's nothing but a gofer-gun for the syndicate. He's not involved in any—"

"Well, let's try him. See what he knows? Maybe more than you give him credit for."

Rizzo returned to the SUV and undid the duct tape from Cusack's ankles. He pulled him out of the Rover and nudged him toward the garage doorway. Taking him by his forearm, he guided him down the narrow hallway and into the manager's office. The man mumbled something from beneath the hood. Rizzo ignored him. The room was silent when they entered. Fields waved to a chair at the side of the desk, and Rizzo led Cusack there.

A smirk formed on Duggan's face. Rizzo paid no attention to him. He took a position to the side of the hooded Cusack and placed his shoulder against the wall. Gesturing to Fields, Rizzo said. "Your show."

Chapter Twenty-Two

Rizzo and Hoya left the taxi garage in Sunnyside to deliver Frankie Cusack to the Seventeenth Precinct in Manhattan. Duggan arrived first and met Rizzo and Hoya in the precinct's foyer, greeting them as though he was seeing the two for the first time.

Cusack opted for door number one, ready to confess, which made Duggan jubilant. Fields, on the other hand, came away empty. The guy couldn't provide the agent with anything significant about Salazar's operation beyond the location of a few sex houses. Rizzo thought Fields should have listened to him.

The booking procedure at the One-fifteen Precinct took an hour. Manny arrived at the Holiday Inn ahead of Rizzo and Hoya and already secured a room for the two girls on the second floor. Both teens, spent from emotion, were asleep when Rizzo and Hoya joined Manny at a table in the hotel's empty breakfast alcove.

Manny whooshed out a lungful of air. "Damn! I'm glad that's over."

"Are they okay?"

"With all they've been through? Yeah. Jesus, how the hell does this shit happen? Those goddamn animals. They should be—"

Rizzo laid his hand on Manny's shoulder. "*Amigo*, sex trafficking has been going on for decades. You haven't been aware because the damn press ignores it. And the women forced into the trade are traumatized and scared shitless for their lives. They're at the mercy of their pimps. If they're not drug users when the pimp first gets them, they soon are. Most tolerate a life of prostitution until they become used up and tossed out."

Rizzo almost added, *or worse.* Giving Manny the real facts would send him into orbit. The truth was the majority of the underage kids abducted or lured by traffickers for the sex trade were routinely raped, beaten into submission, even branded. If they tried to run away, they were tortured and gang-raped. Also murdered.

Shaking his head, Manny gazed back at Rizzo. "Well then, we got lucky. We found Rosita and Olga in time."

Hoya returned to the table from the coffee urn with two cups and slid one across to Manny. "Where do all these kidnapped kids come from?"

"From everywhere," Rizzo said. "Cities, small towns, mostly impoverished areas. I once heard something bizarre from a guy who works for ICE. He told me about this small town near Mexico City, a major source of sex trafficking that feeds the pipeline into New York. And the federales in the Mexican state don't do shit about it."

Manny looked up. "You're talking about *Tenancingo*. It's about eighty miles from Mexico City. Maybe a thousand people. Their local police? Well, damn, they're all in the pockets of the sex ring."

"This may sound naïve," Hoya said, "but I find it hard to believe so many women choose to work as prostitutes. The lucky ones end up in places like the Espinosa brothers."

"Yeah, except operations like the Espinosas' are rare. A lot of the women you're talking about are down-and-outers. No hope of survival except through prostitution. Or they're druggies trying to support their addiction by being in the game. Most houses in the New York area operate like the one in Corona, a place to keep the girls on call. Once they're no longer productive, their dead bodies are dumped in a New Jersey swamp."

"But kids?" Manny said. "Why the Christ do they use—"

"Lots of perverts out there, Manny. Let's thank God we got the girls back."

They became silent for a while. Rizzo could guess the thoughts going through Manny's head. "How'd the booking go at the One-Fifteen?" he asked, attempting to change the subject.

The question returned Manny to the present. He blinked. "Man, I couldn't believe how nice that Hispanic cop was, the one taking the kids' statements. Gentle and kind, I mean, I damn near cried listening to them."

Rizzo grinned. "Nice to hear. Most cops don't deserve the bad rap people lay on them."

"I hope they lock up those two pimps for a long time—the scumbags."

"Don't hold your breath, Manny. Salazar will order his sleazy lawyer to post bail. They'll be out in forty-eight hours." Rizzo shook his head. "Who knows? Maybe not this time. Pimping kids don't sit well in our courts."

Hoya shrugged. "This is one hell of a world."

"Hey, you live long enough, you lose the gloss on your idealism. Guaranteed. Working in law enforcement speeds up the process."

"You think the guy who runs the sex ring," Hoya asked, "what's his name, Salazar? You think he knows what happened at the house?"

"In a nanosecond. The organization keeps a tight watch over all their locations. Gomez doesn't call in when he's supposed to, they check right away. Or—and I hate to admit this—it's likely Salazar has someone at the One-Fifteen on his payroll. If so, the cop made the call right after Manny and the girls left the precinct."

Manny's head jerked up. "So they know about us, Sam, me and you?"

"I'm afraid so. That's why I want the four of you out of here heading back to Florida in the morning. Sooner the better."

"The girls?" Hoya said. "Will they require them to come back for the trial?"

"Unlikely, but you never know. Kidnapping's a federal rap. The Feds might want them to return to testify how they got transported from Mexico, and who brought them to New York."

"Will the two guys from the house go down for it?" Manny asked.

"Nah. Those guys didn't take part in the kidnapping. Probably get ten to life. My bet it will be less. They'll go easier on them if they cooperate, provide information on Salazar's operation. He's the one the Feds want."

"How about Cusack? What happens to him?"

"First-degree murder. He'll face trial. Won't be a long sentence unless he reneges on copping to a plea of guilty. He won't. Duggan and the Feds gave him an offer he couldn't refuse."

Manny turned his eyes toward Rizzo. "What was the deal?"

"Forget it, pal. Better off in the dark. Rest assured though, your uncle—Rabbit, I mean—is smiling."

* * *

On his walk to his apartment, Rizzo remembered this was the one Saturday of the month Flo caught the duty at La Guardia. She should be on her way home about now. He imagined the warm feeling of Flo's embrace. Encouraged by the thought, he quickened his gait. But first a shower, after handling the filthy Cusack for the last sixteen hours.

Rizzo reached the steps of his brownstone apartment building and spotted Flo and Jabba Saint James approaching from the corner at Eighth Avenue.

"Hey, mon, look who is back," the Jamaican said and flashed his gold tooth. Jabba took Rizzo's offered hand into a vigorous shake.

"Easy bro, you'll break the fingers."

Flo studied him with a worried expression. "Darlin', I was so—"

"Baby," he said and entered her upraised arms. "I'm sorry. I'm okay, honest." He pulled her to him and pressed his mouth to hers. A passing delivery truck celebrated the kiss with a horn blast.

Jabba laughed. "Uh oh, I best be going. This could be embarrassing."

Flo pulled back and gave Rizzo a playful slap on his chest. "Why didn't you call, tell me you were okay? I expected to hear from you at least once. I was beside myself." Tears bordered her eyes.

Her upset stabbed at his heart and his face burned with guilt. He forgot to call during the tense two-day chase to grab Cusack. Before Flo came into his life, he answered to no one but himself. After they married, his cases never required him to be away longer than overnight, and a complacent attitude seeped into his mindset. He knew he would need to change his thinking.

Taking her back into his arms, he said, "Damn, Flo, I'm sorry. It won't happen again, I promise."

They embraced until Jabba's voice interrupted. "Hey, mon, I go in, get my stuff, and I be out of your hair."

Rizzo grabbed Jabba's hand and yanked the big man into a chest bump. "You're not going anywhere until I buy you the best damn steak dinner you ever tasted."

"Mon, if I do somethin' to deserve that, I can't remember. But I don't turn it down."

Rizzo gestured toward Flo. "I owe you for watching over my girl."

"You don't owe me, mon." Jabba waved his hands like someone swatting flies. "I be Flo's bodyguard any time. She's my secret pot of gold."

Flo put her arms around the Rastafarian, pressing her head against his chest. "And he's my Lochinvar. Careful I don't ride off into the sunset with him next time you don't call."

"Okay, boss lady. Now, let's go," Rizzo said. "I gotta get out of these clothes. I'll shower, then it's off to The Palm." He folded an arm across Flo's shoulder and guided her toward the brownstone steps with Jabba trailing.

* * *

The Palm, one of Manhattan's oldest and most successful restaurants, was Rizzo's special place. The steakhouse was so much in demand, the management enjoyed a standing joke: To secure a reservation, one required a note from the Pope.

The restaurant's family-ownership maintained a fondness for a particular retired narcotics detective who, eight years ago, saved the restaurant from being fire-bombed by a disgruntled and crazed Cuban drug dealer. The tip on the threat came from the narc's informant, Rabbit.

The narc received a commendation for valor from his NYPD superiors. The more welcomed fallout and far more valuable was something else. From that day forward, Detective Lucas

Rizzo never needed the Pope's help to get a table at The Palm. Nor did he have to worry about a check.

Their booth on the side of the noisy eatery faced the *maître d'* podium at the restaurant's entrance. A white-aproned waiter took their order and returned with two bottles of imported Italian mineral water.

A 16-ounce, prime New York strip arrived on Jabba's platter and caused Flo to gawk. "I don't believe the size of that," she exclaimed. "Looks like they've given you the entire cow. You think you can finish the whole thing?"

"Flo Mae, I'm gonna try," Jabba said, flashing her a toothy grin. "This steak is too good to waste."

Rizzo eyed Flo's dinner and laughed. "What are you talking about?"

"What?"

"Your prime rib. No dainty portion. Did you notice the kitchen had to serve your French fries on a separate plate?" He leaned in close to her ear and whispered, "Watch out. They lace them with parmesan and garlic, so go easy on them."

An hour went by before Rizzo reduced his two-pound Nova Scotia lobster to two remaining enormous claws. The succulent crustacean appendages sat waiting to be cracked. The bowl next to the platter overflowed with shells. With the cracker in his right hand, he held one of the claws in the fingers of his left. Pausing before he attacked the appendage, his eyes landed on a scene at the podium.

A woman and a man standing before Enrico, the *maître'd*, made him smile. They appeared like prisoners waiting to be sentenced. The female companion towered over the man. What amused Rizzo was the man's guarded hand proffered toward Enrico. It palmed a bill of indeterminable value, held in place by his thumb.

Rizzo knew how the system worked. He hoped for the sake of the late-arriving pair without a reservation, the money he offered was not less than a fifty. The man's profile caught Rizzo's eye and produced a flashback to someone familiar. He tried to place him. Nothing came to mind. He returned his attention to the claw in his hand, while Flo and Jabba watched like judges preparing to grade his performance.

He raised the claw, placed it between the cracker's two arms and squeezed. A sharp *CRACK* rang out. Flo and Jabba applauded.

Chapter Twenty-Three

Manny pulled several pairs of skinny jeans from the rolling rack. He stood in the middle of Macy's Junior Department holding them up, smiling like someone who just made a rare discovery. He swiveled his head and searched for Rosita and Olga. The girls, busy flipping through an assortment of light-weight tops hanging from a display against the wall, failed to react when Manny called to them.

This morning, the rescued teens awakened in their hotel room with an intense case of anxiety, still fearing someone would snatch away their newly gained freedom and return them to suffer again through another three months of hell.

Manny hoped to boost their spirits with a little Macy's shopping excursion, have them pick out a few items to wear on their trip to Florida. They owned no more than the clothes they wore. The little extra they brought with them from Mexico was left back in the Corona house.

At eleven-thirty on a Sunday morning, the megastore was not busy and early enough to expect quick service. Manny was eager to be on the road, heading south. He realized they couldn't drive the thirteen-hundred miles straight through the way he and Hoya did traveling north. Their journey would need two days and be at a more relaxed pace, considering the state of mind of his charges.

Hoya stole up behind Manny. "Dude, what the hell you doing?" he asked, punctuating his question with a light slap on the back of Manny's head. "You don't even know their sizes. Let them make their own choices."

"Leave me alone, *amigo*. I'm trying to hurry them. We need to get outta here and back to the hotel to pack up."

Hoya shrugged. "Hey, a few things for the trip. How long could it take? Besides, we're not going anywhere until I have the Rover checked out tomorrow."

"Can't we do that today?"

"No. It's Sunday. I got the name of a mechanic at a local garage from the hotel desk clerk. He told me the guy was good. I'm taking the car to him in the morning. The way the Rover has been overheating, it may need a new water pump."

"Or maybe the cooling fan motor," Manny suggested.

"Whatever. I talked to the mechanic yesterday, and he said he could lay his hands on whatever part he needed and make the installation in a couple of hours. I sure don't want to be caught in the middle of nowhere when the damn engine seizes up."

Manny searched again for the teens. "I hate shopping," he tossed over his shoulder. "Let me find them, see if they like these," and he bounded away with the folded jeans draped over his arm.

Before Manny disappeared behind several racks of merchandise, Hoya shouted after him. "You missed your calling. You'd have made a great salesgirl."

After a half-hour of indecision, Rosita and Olga tried on the jeans Manny picked out. They also selected a few short-sleeved tops in multi-colors and two light-weight sweaters. Their collection of new clothes would carry them for the next few days. When they got to Florida, Manny told them, he and Bella would take them shopping for more.

In line at the register waiting to pay for the purchases, Manny signaled Hoya over and shoved his credit card at him. "Here, take care of this for me, will you?" he whispered. "I gotta go to the john bad. If I wait any longer, I'll shit my pants." He turned to the sales clerk busy ringing up a customer. "Excuse me, miss, which way to the bathrooms?"

The clerk raised her eyes without lifting her head. She pointed with her thumb toward the Seventh Avenue end of the store. "Right before the exit."

"Thanks," Manny said and jogged off.

"Wait for you back here," Hoya called after him.

Manny found the facility and hurried through the door into the empty restroom lined with gleaming white tiled walls. At the first of the four stalls, he pushed through, closed and locked the door. Unbuckling his belt, he lowered his pants and sat in time to avoid his feared embarrassment.

Once his stomach pains subsided, he gave an audible sigh of relief. Relaxed, he studied his feet and reflected on the events of the past two weeks. The incredible accomplishment of rescuing Rosita and Olga made him proud and gratified. "*Dios gracias,*" he mouthed aloud. In a rush of self-consciousness, he added, "*Dios, perdóname.* I meant no disrespect by calling to you in a men's room." He shrugged and silently made a promise to give thanks at his local parish once he returned to Florida.

The toilet's flushing noise echoed in the empty bathroom. Manny buckled up, slid open the stall's locking device and pulled back the door. In the next instant, a flash of white light passed across his brain. The sensation was paired with an indescribable jolt of pain. He took delivery of a blow to his temple that had the force of a sledgehammer. He fell to his knees, and a split second later, a hand shoved his face into the toilet bowl water and held it there. Manny had no idea how long he'd been submerged. But when he surfaced, he opened his eyes, choked and gasped for breath.

Still bent over the bowl, Manny spewed water from his mouth and nose. He struggled to breathe, as he turned his head and gawked into the blurry face of a complete stranger. The giant-size man lifted him by the armpits, held him inches off the floor. Stepping out of the stall with him, the ape whirled and flung Manny against the wall like a rag doll. His back and shoulders slammed into the tile squares with a savage force, and his head bounced like the recoil of a pinball.

Manny dropped to the floor and lay motionless, face down. The sturdy shoe of his attacker landed, toe first, between two of his ribs, and then against his temple. Slowly, a black curtain fell on Manny's shopping excursion.

* * *

Hoya checked his watch. *What the hell's taking him so long?* Out of patience, he considered running down to the men's room to check it out. The girls, seated a few feet away, chatted about their new clothes. He couldn't leave them alone. Hoya glanced up and spotted one of Macy's roving uniformed security guards walking in his direction.

He approached her and said, "Excuse me, miss. I wonder if I can ask you a question."

She stopped and stared hard at him.

"I need help."

"What's the problem?" she asked with a noticeable distance in her tone. She was a heavyset Hispanic-appearing lady who, he assumed, dealt with a variety of off-the-wall bullshit all day long.

Hoya explained the situation. The girls were from Mexico, didn't speak English, and would be frightened to death if he left them alone while he checked on Manny. "Would you mind waiting here with them while I run down to the bathroom to find what's taking so long?"

The security guard listened patiently while scrutinizing Hoya. Pointing to the seated teens, she said, "This Manny, he's the brother of one of them?"

"Yes. Rosita Fuentes, the one on the left."

The guard stepped over to the two girls. "Es *Rosita?*"

Rosita looked up, startled. "*Si.*"

"*Cuál es el nombre de su hermano?*"

Hoya grinned. The guard was thorough, verifying her brother's name.

Rosita hesitated. "*Manny Fuentes. Por qué?*"

"*Y quién es este hombre?*" the security guard asked, motioning to Hoya.

"*Amigo de mi hermano.*"

Satisfied, she turned to Hoya. "Okay, I needed to be sure you didn't kidnap these kids."

Tempted to say, they've been there, done that, Hoya swallowed the words and stifled a smile.

"So, you'll hang in with them?"

"Yeah, go ahead. I'll stay and chat with my new *amigas* until you come back."

Hoya spoke to Rosita and Olga in Spanish. "Wait here," he told them. "I'll go find out what's keeping Manny. I won't be long. This nice-lady-security guard will stay with you until we come back. Okay?"

The girls examined the guard's uniform. Two heads bobbed in unison.

Hoya sprinted off in the direction Manny took.

The giant cue ball blocking Hoya when he reached the entrance of the men's room grunted, "Closed. They clean. Use one on second floor."

The man reminded Hoya of Hulk Hogan, minus the coifed blond hair and bandana. The behemoth staring him down with blue ball-bearing eyes had an enormous bald head on top of shoulders capable of supporting a house. Hoya went up against a few oversized linemen in his playing days at FSU, but nothing the size of this Goliath. A black mock turtle under a shiny black suit jacket covered his massive chest. Two short strings of gold chains hung from his tree-trunk-size neck and provided a touch of bling to his imposing figure.

Before Hoya reacted, the door to the men's room burst open. A second giant emerged, a duplicate of the one standing in front of him. Same physical dimensions, same hairless globe sitting on a huge body, even the same black mock turtle and shiny suit. Missing was the bling of gold.

The two oversized bookends raced by Hoya like Brahma bulls released into the ring. Hoya's quick juke to one side saved him from being knocked to the floor. The black suits disappeared through the exit door and out onto Seventh Avenue.

Stunned, Hoya sucked in a deep breath and forced himself to push through the bathroom door. Inside, he reined up over Manny's sprawled body. He detected no movement, but he noticed two gold chains looped around the fingers of Manny's one hand.

Hoya's heart squeezed itself like a fist. His friend lay beneath the line of washbasins, the side of his head turned away, his body curled into an unnatural shape. Nothing Hoya saw reassured him Manny was, in fact, alive.

After his call to 9-1-1, Hoya raced back to the security guard and the girls. By the time the guard radioed the situation to the Macy's Security Office, the Mount Sinai Beth Israel Hospital at East Sixteenth Street dispatched an EMS ambulance to the store.

With the two girls at his side, Hoya watched the medics secure Manny inside the ambulance. The vehicle sped off, its siren shattering Manhattan's Sunday morning tranquility, and disappeared around the corner going east. Hoya stepped off the curb and whistled to a cruising taxi. During the cab ride back to their hotel, he did his best to calm the two hysterical teenagers.

At the Holiday Inn, Hoya ushered the teens to their room. "Stay here," he told them. "Keep the door locked. Don't be scared. I'll be back soon." Without pausing for a response, he raced down the stairs to the ground level and darted out of the hotel entrance. Back into the waiting taxi, he told the driver, "Beth Israel Hospital, fast!"

* * *

The receptionist in the hospital lobby pointed to the two electronically controlled doors. Behind them was the corridor leading to the emergency room. Hoya stepped toward the doors and stopped when his cell phone chirped in his pocket. The caller ID displayed Luke Rizzo's name. He retreated to a chair in the reception area and in a voice filled with stress, he said, "Luke, my God, I'm glad you called."

"What's your status, Sam? Are you on the road yet?"

"Shit! No!" he replied, louder than he intended. His eyes scanned the lobby.

"You don't sound good. What the hell is going on? You alright?"

"I am but Manny's not. He's at Beth Israel Hospital. I'm here too." Hoya went silent while he tried catching a breath.

"Sam, what happened? Is he okay?"

"I'll know when I can speak with someone here. Manny looked bad when they loaded him into the EMS ambulance."

Hoya explained the shopping trip to Macy's and how he found Manny on the floor of the men's room. He described the two goons who used his friend as a punching bag and put a serious hurt on him. He couldn't finish. His voice faltered. The cell phone at his ear shook, and he stopped talking.

"I can't believe this," Luke said. "I need you to hold it together, Sam. I'm in my office. I'll grab a cab. Be there in ten minutes. Wait for me in the lobby."

"I'm here."

* * *

Rizzo phoned Flo at home and explained the situation. He exited the Flatiron building on the Fifth Avenue side and spotted a taxi pulling to the curb. The door opened, and the passenger got out. He jumped in before the man could close the door. "Sixteenth and First Avenue," he shouted to the cabbie.

Rizzo entered the hospital lobby, panned around and spotted Hoya leaping to his feet. A tense expression painted the face of the former linebacker.

"What floor?"

"This one. Emergency room."

"Was he breathing when you found him?"

"Yeah, I think so. I couldn't tell. Seeing Manny lying on the floor, it shocked the hell out of me. I called 9-1-1 for medical help, and I rushed back to the security guard."

Rizzo glanced around the room. A stab of panic came over him. "Where the fuck are the girls?"

"They're okay. I took them back to the hotel. Told them to keep the door locked. Don't open up for anyone."

Rizzo shook his head. "You comfortable leaving them alone? You want me to call my wife, send her over to watch them?"

"No, they'll be safe enough locked in the room."

"Alright, let's go inside," Rizzo said, pointing to the ER doors."

The two men stopped in front, and Hoya signaled to the woman behind the reception desk. The locking device clicked. He pressed the pad on the wall, and the doors opened. They walked in silence along a long corridor and headed for the nurse's station.

As they walked, Rizzo glanced at Hoya. Guilt surged through him. *I should never have gotten them involved. What the hell was I thinking?*

They reached the station and approached the duty nurse. Rizzo exchanged looks with Hoya when the nurse raised her head. Hoya failed to speak up, so Rizzo told her, "Manny Fuentes," and he produced his NYPD shield. "How is he? Any condition report yet?"

She looked down at the chart on her desk. "The doctor is examining him," and pointing to an alcove on the far side of the corridor, she said, "If you'll take a seat over there, I'll let you know when we have any information."

The TV set mounted on the opposite wall flickered with soundless images dancing across the screen." Hoya bent forward in his chair, arms on his knees, studying the floor. Rizzo sat across from him, his eyes alternating between Hoya's anguished expression and the television.

"Anyone notify the police?" Rizzo asked.

Hoya lifted his head without raising his torso. "Huh?"

"The police. Did someone call them?"

"Oh, yeah. Macy's security. Two officers from the local precinct. They were here a while ago. Gave them what they needed to make a report." He lowered his head again.

"Tell me about the two gorillas. What did they look like?"

Hoya sat up, his eyes coming to rest on Rizzo's face. "I told you about them on the phone."

"You didn't finish. Tell me again. Describe them."

Hoya got to his feet and paced the floor like an expectant father. "Well the most obvious thing," he began, "they were mirror images of each other."

"You mean, like twins?"

"Yeah, like identical. Both bald, with fat round heads, huge bodies, and dressed exactly alike. Black was their favorite color." Hoya reached into his jacket pocket and pulled out the lengths of gold chains he found curled around Manny's fingers. He handed them to Rizzo. "Manny probably grabbed these from the neck of the one who came out of the men's room. He wasn't wearing them like the twin outside the door."

Rizzo examined the chains, closed his eyes for perhaps ten seconds, inhaled audibly, and said, "These two giant-sized bowling balls are the same ones in the headshots my FBI friend gave me in my office, along with the photos of Salazar and Cusack." He looked up at Hoya. "The guy . . . the one outside the men's room . . . he spoke to you. Right?"

"Yeah."

"He have an accent like a foreigner?'

Hoya stopped pacing and glanced up at the TV as though he noticed the screen for the first time. He scratched the back of his neck. "What I heard was, 'Closed. **They clean. Use one on second floor.**' He said nothing else." Hoya's expression suddenly came alive. "Yeah, that's it. Now that you mention it, he spoke like someone from Eastern Europe. Not a guttural sound like German, still with a hard edge."

"Maybe Russian?"

"Could be. I'm not sure."

Rizzo glanced toward the nurse's station. The nurse was on the phone. "Yeah, it was them. Believe it or not, Manny got lucky. These bozos rarely leave you alive when they're ordered to beat down someone. They're former Russian Mafia. Twin brothers. Ilya Bodrov recruited them. They work for Umberto Salazar."

Chapter Twenty-Four

The Holiday Inn's breakfast alcove was empty. The hour was long past the time when guests would show up. Rizzo strolled back from the coffee machine carrying two cups. He sat at the table and pushed one of the cups to Hoya.

Earlier at Beth Israel, the attending doctor went over Manny's injuries with them. The CT scan revealed damage to his nose. He suffered no serious facial injuries to his jaw or cheeks. The blow he received fractured his nasal cartilage. It caused considerable bruising and swelling around the nose and eyes.

The doctor assured them both effects would ease up in two or three days. His nose didn't need a reset, a procedure he called rhinoplasty. The bone would heal on its own.

X-rays of his chest area revealed two cracked ribs. Luckily the fractures did not interfere with his breathing. Lots of pain though. He was taped up and sedated. He would remain in Beth Israel overnight for observation. They could pick him up after one o'clock tomorrow.

Taking a sip of coffee, Rizzo asked, "Did you reach her—his sister—what's her name?"

"Isabella . . . Bella. Yeah, and she really lost it when I described what happened. Manny called her yesterday after we got the kids and told her we'd be heading back today or tomorrow. Now, this."

"The kids okay? Calmed down?"

"Yeah. Promised them I'd bring them lunch. They asked for Big Macs, so they're back to normal. Now I need to find a McDonald's somewhere."

Rizzo laughed. "There's one on Fifty-first, corner of Ninth, close to here. You can walk faster than trying to find a parking spot on the street."

"Stay for lunch. My treat."

"No, thanks. I should go home. My wife gets antsy when I'm gone too long." Rizzo gazed off for a moment. "You know, you need to stick close to those kids until you pick up Manny and you're on the road. I worry those brothers know you're here in this hotel."

"I worried about that, myself. How the hell did they find out?"

"Easy. The dirty cop at the precinct in Corona. He probably read Manny's report where it showed an address where he could be reached. So, this morning, the twin shitheads followed you to Macy's."

Hoya raised the cup and paused. He narrowed his eyes. "What about this idea? I put the kids on the first flight I can book out of here today to South Florida. I move to another hotel for the night and in the morning have the Rover serviced. Then I pick up Manny, and the two of us can be on our way by early afternoon."

"What's it need? Oil change? You can always get one on your route south, can't you?"

"Might be the water pump. If so, I'll need to replace it."

"You can get it done in the morning?"

"Yeah. I've lined up a mechanic at a garage close by. He can order a new pump in the morning and finish the installation in less than two hours."

Rizzo looked at his watch. "One-thirty. I'll call my wife. She can check Delta's schedule, see if we can find a flight out of La Guardia."

Hoya pulled out his wallet. "Here's my credit card. She finds one they can make, tell her to book it. I'll drive them to La Guardia. When we know the arrival time, I'll call Bella. She can meet them at the Ft. Myers Airport."

"Okay, but forget about moving to another hotel. You spend the night with us. We got room. No point in risking another visit from the brothers."

Rizzo made the call to Flo and gave her the girls' names and their destination in Florida. He hung up and walked over for a coffee refill.

Halfway into his coffee, Rizzo's phone rang. "Hi, Flo. What do you have, sweetheart?"

"I booked them on a seven-twenty-five non-stop out of LaGuardia," Flo said. "There was an earlier one. It required changing planes in Atlanta."

"No, no, the later one's perfect. Having to change planes wouldn't be a good idea. Too much exposure. Sam will call Bella with the information."

"Arrives 10:55."

"Great. Thanks. Be home soon." Rizzo slipped the iPhone into his pocket.

"That's a load off my mind," Hoya said. "Now, about those Big Macs."

"Tell you what. You head out to Mickey D's. I'll wait here until you come back."

Hoya jumped to his feet. "I'm gone," and he disappeared past the front desk and out the door.

Rizzo finished his coffee and flashed on a problem. The girls were without any form of identification and wouldn't pass airport security. He pulled out his iPhone and tapped the private number of Jack Fields. He guessed the agent wouldn't be in his office on a Sunday. He was right.

Fields answered. "Must be important if you're calling me at home. What's up?"

Rizzo described Manny's situation at Macy's and the airport ID dilemma. Fields told him he'd have his office fax a boarding authorization to the Delta ticket counter at La Guardia. Rizzo gave him the names and flight number and Fields said, "I'll call you back if there's a problem."

He left the breakfast nook and strolled to the seating area of the lobby. He dropped into a cushioned chair facing the hotel's front door. A *Sports Illustrated* on the coffee table caught his eye.

While paging through the magazine, Rizzo glanced out the door and his attention went on tiptoe. A black Chevy Suburban pulled to the curb on the opposite side of the street. No one got out. He could make out the figure seated on the passenger side, a shiny head on massive shoulders. No need to guess his identity.

He hurried to the front desk. "Does this hotel have a rear door?"

The clerk paused to think about the question. "Why, yes sir, we do. Straight down the corridor to the back. Opens onto our parking lot."

"Thanks," Rizzo said and returned to the breakfast nook. Out of sight, he reached for his iPhone. Hoya answered, and Rizzo told him, "There are two huge visitors out in front of the hotel. They're anxious to recoup their losses. You got the burgers yet?"

"They're bagging them now."

"Hustle back, but when you arrive, don't come in the front door. Go through the parking lot and use the rear door with your room key. Don't let anyone see you. I'll wait for you in the breakfast area." Rizzo shot a look at the desk clerk. "Sam, get your ass back here, pronto."

"Got it. Bye."

Hoya arrived and Rizzo explained what he did with Fields regarding the identification problem. "Be sure to flag the Delta Agent at the ticket counter when you check in the girls. They'll have the temporary authorization the kids will need to show security."

"Glad you thought of it."

"Give me your credit card again. I'll settle up for you at the desk while you grab your stuff from your room. I'll meet you upstairs."

He completed the check-out process and took the stairs to the second floor. Hoya waited outside the girls' room with his and Manny's bags lined against the wall.

"Okay, go in and get the girls ready. The less said to them about what's happening, the better."

Hoya slid the key card into the slot and paused without pushing down on the handle. He turned his head and spoke softly over his shoulder. "What the hell are they after?"

"The girls," Rizzo whispered. "Salazar wants them dead."

Hoya twisted around. "Christ, why don't we call the police?"

"And what do you think they'll do without proof? Arrest them for parking?"

"Well, at least—"

"Forget it. We don't want more face time with those animals. The car's in the lot, right?"

"Yeah."

"Drivable."

"Oh, yeah. But I wouldn't trust it for a long haul."

"I'm going down to the lobby. Text me when you're in the car, about thirty seconds before you're ready to leave. I'll come up with a distraction for the brothers so they won't notice you pulling out. Go right to La Guardia. You'll be about four and a half hours early for the flight. They'll be safer there than they are here. You can buy them dinner."

"Where do I go after they've taken off?"

"Call me. I'll direct you to an Avis garage near my apartment. I'll meet you there. We'll arrange for parking the Rover overnight."

Rizzo stood outside the doorway of the hotel. He surveyed the street, looking like he was waiting for someone. Thinking back to the morning in his office when he agreed to allow Hoya and Manny to help him, he rocked his head in disbelief. How the hell could he expect that they wouldn't be in harm's way? They were going up against the Salazar mob. What a damn fool.

He recalled Manny's funny quip about his athletic ability—running. "From the *Federales.*" Rizzo chuckled as his cell vibrated, signaling a text message. The display read, *On the way.*

With purpose and an air of authority, Rizzo stepped to the curb. He crossed the street to the parked Suburban and positioned himself at the passenger-side windshield to block the man's forward view. Holding out his NYPD shield case, he gestured to the twin to lower the window. The big head swiveled toward Rizzo. Eyes raised in an icy stare, he shot Rizzo an expression that said, fuck-off. Rizzo tapped the windshield with his ID case and waited.

The window lowered, and the twin's voice growled, "Fuck you want?"

"Are you waiting for someone?" Rizzo asked in his best authoritative voice.

"Yesss," the brother hissed through his teeth.

Rizzo smiled. "Well, I'm afraid you need to move. This spot's reserved for the Chief of Police. We have an investigation going on, and he'll be here in the next—" Rizzo spotted the driver-twin reaching for the door handle. "Thanks a lot," he said without finishing, and fast-stepped back into the hotel, through the lobby, and out the rear door.

After breezing across the hotel's parking lot, Rizzo made off the several blocks toward his apartment, checking over his shoulder to ensure the twins hadn't followed. He climbed the steps of the brownstone and snickered, wondering if they were still sitting there.

Chapter Twenty-Five

J ack Fields pushed aside the report and pressed the intercom button. "Yes, Rachel."

"Agent Ralph Brancuso on two."

"Thanks." Fields switched to speakerphone and connected to the call. "Ralph, how the hell are you?"

"Good news. I'm coming back to Federal Plaza. Transfer approved last week."

Fields held back a laugh. He had made the recommendation to the new boss, Carter Brooke, a month ago. A week later, the official request landed at the home office in Washington D.C.

Fields initiated the return of Brancuso after his number two man, Tony Condon, transferred to the Los Angeles office. He was left with a problem. No one among his current stable of agents was experienced enough to replace Tony. He wanted an agent he could work with, someone he trusted to be *Robin* to his *Batman*. Getting Brancuso back to the New York office gave him the special partnership again.

"Back to the city, Ralph? How come? Weren't you sitting pretty up in Albany, top dog of the office and all that?"

Brancuso laughed. "Been up here too long. Almost died of boredom. Besides, with Stevenson gone, the enticement was too good not to jump on the offer."

Karl Stevenson was in charge of the FBI's New York City Field Office for more than a decade. Six months ago he reached mandatory retirement age and put in his papers. Brancuso had endured a term of service under him at Federal Plaza.

"Christ, I never believed the old fart would go out on his own. I was positive somebody would poison his morning coffee before he retired."

Fields laughed. "He was lucky you left for upstate. It might have happened under your watch. Right?"

"Maybe."

Stevenson's arrogant, autocratic personality didn't mix well with Brancuso's tough, bulldog-like persona. Their frequent conflicts over procedure and policy became Brancuso's undoing. The stocky, balding Italian-American with the broad forehead was an outstanding lawman, but he was given to uttering expletives that would make a dockworker blush, particularly when Stevenson's bureaucratic restrictions frustrated him. This practice, all too often, offended Karl Stevenson's sensibilities, and away went Ralph Brancuso to the Albany office.

"Well, I'm glad we'll have your charming soft-spoken self with our family again. When do you leave?"

"Today. I'm driving the wife down to the Jersey shore to drop her off for five days, you know, visiting her family. I'll be in the office in the morning." He raised his voice an octave. "Holy shit, Jack, you have no idea how much I'm looking forward to being back in the Apple. I hope you're gonna be comfortable having me underfoot again."

"Couldn't be more relieved," Fields replied.

Fields was high on Brancuso's experience working in the drug enforcement arena. He expected him to be an essential addition to his team now that the FBI had Salazar and the Ortega cartel in their sights.

"By the way, how's the new boss?" Brancuso wanted to know.

"Brooke is a great fit. You'll get along fine. He's out of the Washington D.C. area, but he never knew J. Edgar Hoover." Fields chuckled at the not-so-subtle reference to Karl Stevenson's inclination to speak of the old FBI director like they were asshole buddies. Stevenson, frequently prone to hyperbole, became the subject of office jokes. Everyone knew he didn't join the FBI until the year before Hoover died.

Brancuso emitted a throaty laugh. "Well now, that's a fucking blessing."

* * *

Flo departed for work leaving behind a quiet morning in the apartment. Rizzo said nothing to her about the twins' visit to the Holiday Inn last evening. It infuriated him that Salazar and Ilya Bodrov knew so much about him and Flo, where they lived, where they worked. They were vulnerable, and he would have to be vigilant until the FBI could take them down.

Jack Fields was currently involved in a scheme to do exactly that. With the rescue of the teens accomplished, Rizzo waited to hear from the agent as to what role he had in mind for him.

Hoya was in the bathroom shaving, while Rizzo sat at the kitchen window, sipping his morning coffee and watching the streaks of sunlight dancing between the bare limbs of trees on the street. His thoughts wandered to a fantasy he often played with whenever life became too complicated: retirement to a rustic mountain setting upstate, hunting and fishing in the daytime, writing detective novels at night. This romantic dream would float above his head like one of those cartoon balloons, and eventually, the picture would pop like the soapy shape from a kid's bubble pipe.

Rizzo accepted who he was and where he anchored his roots. He was a product of the Big Apple, born in Queens and educated in that borough's public schools. He bled New York City, he liked to say.

The livelihood he chose kept him in New York. His destiny might have changed had he opted for a different career path, one that beckoned to him upon graduating high school. As a starter on his school's varsity squad, Rizzo's performance on the baseball diamonds around the five boroughs landed him on the scope of the New York Yankees. And at the end of his senior year, he turned down an offer of a baseball scholarship to Fordham University. Instead, he joined the NYPD.

Not unlike many of his blue brethren who made a similar compromise, the question of *what if* always nagged him. That morning while he waited for the elevator in the lobby of the Flatiron Building visualizing Sam Hoya roaming the outfield of a baseball stadium, Rizzo was, in fact, imagining himself.

Hoya exited the second bedroom and Rizzo looked up. "How'd you sleep? Bed comfortable enough?"

The linebacker poured himself a cup of coffee and pulled out a chair. "Great. I can't thank you enough for the accommodation. Mrs. Rizzo off to work?"

"Yeah, somebody's gotta earn a living." Rizzo laughed. He studied Hoya's face. The man possessed a strong sense of self-worth. Rizzo had grown fond of him. He thought about Hoya's job in Florida. Was it his first career choice? He couldn't resist asking, "You ever consider playing pro ball?"

The man's grimace telegraphed his response. "The Bucs drafted me. Didn't take. Too light for a linebacker. A no-brainer when you think about the size of those guys in the game today. Might have made it as a wide receiver. Instead, I decided enough with the headbanging. Besides, I was engaged at the time, and she didn't want me playing football for a living."

Rizzo couldn't recall Hoya mentioning a wife or family. He figured the wedding plans, along with his Bucs tryout, also didn't take.

"Then you're not married?"

"Not anymore. Married for seven, divorced for eight."

He was on the verge of getting too personal with his probing, but Rizzo asked the next question anyway. "Think you'll marry again?"

This time Hoya flushed, then laughed. "Well, I got my eye on someone. It's still early. Manny's sister, Bella."

"Aha! So that's how you became involved with all this shit? The sister's your connection, right?"

Hoya drank his coffee and remained silent.

"Okay. You ready for breakfast?"

"I booked the mechanic for eight-thirty. Maybe I better skip eating and be on my way. I can always grab a bite in the area while he's working on the car. In fact, the McDonald's I went to yesterday is nearby."

"What time you picking up Manny?"

"Any time after one."

"Come back here when they finish the car repairs. We can go down to the hospital together."

"Right. Oh, and Manny wanted to know how much we owe you?"

"For what?"

"For helping us find the kids and getting them back. We want to pay you for all the time you spent—"

"I'll send you a bill when you return to Florida." Rizzo stood. "Don't forget, part of the time was for Rabbit."

"I'll tell Manny."

* * *

Rizzo and Hoya walked into the hospital room at twelve-forty-five and found Manny sitting on the edge of his bed. Luis Fuentes rested on the second one. If Manny had croaked from his inflicted injuries, his uncle's solemn face couldn't have conveyed a sadder expression.

Fuentes got to his feet and approached Rizzo. *"Amigo mio,"* he squeezed out, sounding like a family member welcoming a close friend to his nephew's wake. After a long embrace, he clasped Rizzo's hand with both of his and pumped vigorously like trying to draw water from a well. *"Gracias amigo, muchisimo gracias.* Finding my niece, rescuing her, a miracle, *verdad?"*

"I had help," Rizzo said, motioning to Manny and Hoya. "Sadly, Manny was the one on the receiving end of their payback—those twin gorillas from Salazar's assortment of thugs."

Manny, dressed and looking anxious, peered out over the top of the bandage across his nose. His two blackened eyes gave him the appearance of a pug with a losing record. He perched on the edge of the bed, his rigid posture indicative of a patient with taped ribs. Rizzo knew Manny would not fare well sitting for long stretches during their drive to Florida.

"The girls get off alright?" Manny asked Hoya.

"Yeah. Like I told you, we got them on a non-stop into Ft. Myers. Bella called me last night after they arrived."

"Dios gracias. The Rover fixed?"

"Parked downstairs, ready when you are."

Manny turned toward the doorway. "What the hell's taking them so long? Been ready for a fuckin' hour."

As he finished speaking, a tall, regal, white-capped nurse appeared at the door and rolled a wheelchair into the room—a Nicole Kidman look-alike.

"Your ride is here, Mr. Dirty Mouth. We had to wait for the doctor to sign your release. Perhaps I should go back and tell him you don't wish to leave. You like it here too much."

Manny gaped at her for an instant, then leaned back and exploded with laughter. The shock of pain delivered by his outburst made him wince. His eyes scanned the three men in the room. "Nurse Ratchet here has the hots for me. Tried kissing me all night."

"Alright, funny guy, hop on. Time to shove off."

* * *

Their attention followed as the Rover disappeared around the corner of Fifteenth Street and headed west. Rizzo had given Hoya the route to the Holland Tunnel entrance on West Spring Street, and once he went through the long tube, the directions to The New Jersey Turnpike. Manny wouldn't be doing any of the driving. Hoya planned to handle the twelve hundred miles by himself with one overnight rest stop.

"Damn glad to see them on their way," Fuentes said. He and Rizzo walked to the corner.

"I've been worried," Rizzo said, "Salazar would pull shit like what happened at Macy's. The truth is, they could've killed Manny if Salazar had a mind to. The kid was lucky."

The two walked shoulder to shoulder, going west on Fifteenth Street. Rizzo quickened his pace to keep up with the long strides of Fuentes. He was a big man, and despite his middle age, he appeared solid and in good physical shape. After listening to the account of the High Bridge episode, Rizzo assumed Luis Fuentes, given the right provocation, could show the same feistiness and temper of his nephew.

They approached the corner of Fifteenth and Third and waited for the light to turn green. "You working today, Luis?"

"Yeah, I go in at three."

"What are you doing until then?" Rizzo held up his watch. "You got an hour and a half to kill. Time for a beer? I'm buying."

"Okay. I'm in for one, but that's all. They smell booze on me when I check in, the puritanical pricks at the desk go ape."

"Good. I know a friendly joint on Fourteenth and Union Square. Haven't been there for a while. Later, you can hop an uptown subway at Union Square."

Rizzo, out of breath by the time they reached Aiden's Irish Pub, shook his head in amazement. Fuentes breathed easily.

They entered the near-vacant tavern where a lone customer occupied a stool at the end of the bar. Aiden's Pub offered the warm, quiet atmosphere of a neighborhood saloon. Empty tabletops lined the window side, set up for the predictable two-for-one crowd piling in around five o'clock.

The tubby owner, hands submerged in a basin of soap suds, raised his head, and with a tone of joyful recognition, shouted, "Luke, me boy, is that you?"

"Aiden, the little fire. How in the hell is the pride of Sligo Bay these days?"

Rizzo and Fuentes pulled out two stools in the middle of the long bar and sat opposite the smiling Irishman. Aiden wiped his wet hands on his apron and reached his right across to Rizzo.

"Good Jaysus, man, where you been hiding?"

Rizzo took the hand and gave it an energetic shake. "Aiden, say hello to my good friend, Luis Fuentes. He needs a Corona, or he'll never make it to work."

Aiden extended his hand. Fuentes folded it into both of his own and rocked it twice. "Nice to meet you, Aiden."

The Irishman set the Corona Light in front of Fuentes, "So Luke, what will you have?"

"Ginger ale."

Aiden's quizzical look settled on Rizzo.

"Yeah, I'm still AA."

"Sure you are, Boyo," he said and did an eye roll.

"No, I'm serious. Off the stuff. Been close to three years. Damn, has it been that long since I was here?"

Aiden's face glowed with an impish grin as he placed the glass of ginger ale in front of Rizzo. "Must be. That's how long the mirror over the sink in the men's bog has been cracked. Boyo, you were hammered that night, you were."

"Don't remind me," Rizzo said, raising his glass of ginger ale.

"Well, it's always nice when a friend comes home." Nodding to Luke's soft drink, he added, "Plenty more where that came from, so don't be a stranger."

"Thanks, Aiden. Hey, you don't mind if we move over to that table, do you?"

"No, go ahead," Aiden said, and hurried off to the end of the bar to refill the lone patron's glass.

"Come on," Rizzo said and slid down from his stool. "I want to fill you in on something."

When they were seated, Rizzo said, "You understand why they roughed up Manny?"

Fuentes lowered his eyes down the length of his beak-like nose and answered in a whisper as though afraid Salazar himself might overhear. "Because Manny rescued the girls."

"Those twin brothers, each the size of a miniature tank, they did the deed on Manny. They work for Salazar. They're from a section of Brooklyn called Brighton Beach. Full of the Russian mafia."

"I heard about that group. Bad guys."

"The worst."

"Think they'll come after you?"

Rizzo looked across to the park at Union Square. He pictured his encounter with the twins in their Suburban. "They came close yesterday."

Fuentes took a pull on his beer. "What happened?"

Rizzo explained about the brothers showing up at the Holiday Inn. He described how he distracted them while Hoya ducked off unseen with the two girls and drove them to the airport.

"Yeah, Luis, these are bad guys. You need to be on your guard until this blows over. It might take a while before they lose interest. Until then, you and me, we're on their list."

Fuentes took another swallow of beer. "For Christ's sake, how do I protect myself? I can't hide forever. I gotta work. Should I go to the cops, ask for protection?"

"Without evidence Salazar threatened you, that your life is in danger, no court would issue an order. Luis, you own a gun?"

Fuentes bit his lip, then glanced over his shoulder. "Yeah. At home . . . a .38. I bought the gun off a guy years ago. I ain't licensed, so I never carry it. Carmen doesn't know. She finds out, she'd kill me."

"Why'd you buy it?"

"Well, you know, the neighborhood, the break-ins and all the crap that goes down nowadays. Figured I better have a weapon. Be ready anything happens."

"Think you would use it?"

"Yeah, I guess. If someone was threatening me or Carmen. Sure I would. I have it mostly for scaring anybody tryin' to break in. Shit like that."

"Listen to me, my friend. Leave the damn gun home. Don't get caught carrying it. They come down on you hard. You need to protect yourself in the house. Then you have no choice. That's considered self-defense, licensed or not. You'd be in trouble, but not like you'd be if they nailed you for carrying."

Fuentes shrugged, picked up his Corona and took a long pull. When he set down the emptied bottle, he looked up at Rizzo. "Truth is, I never fired a gun in my life. With my bad eyesight, I probably couldn't hit a bull's ass with a spade."

Rizzo smiled. "You ever arrested for anything?"

"Shit, no."

"Well, maybe I can help you apply for a license after you take a course at a small arms range. Meanwhile, be cool. Watch yourself when you go anywhere. Besides, there's less chance they're interested in you. It's me they want."

"What am I supposed to say? I hope so." Fuentes' expression was brittle with fear.

"Not to worry about me, *amigo*. I'm experienced. From now on I carry my 9mm with me everywhere."

Rizzo saw Fuentes flinch.

"You ready to jump on the subway to work? You got a half an hour."

Fuentes stared out the window.

"Hey, man, I didn't mean to scare you. All I'm saying is you need to be alert, stick to the subway, be around people. The Edison uses ex-cops as their hotel security, so you're in safe hands at work."

Rizzo waved to Aiden behind the bar on their way out to the street. They crossed over the avenue and shook hands at the subway entrance. A few steps down, Fuentes stopped. "Hey, you and your wife. You come up to the house. Carmen will cook you a Mexican meal like you never had."

"That would be great. Let's stay in touch."

Fuentes disappeared, and Rizzo took a path through Union Square Park and headed north on Broadway. At the Flatiron Building, he rode the elevator to his floor.

His ringing telephone filtered through the door of his office. The sound stopped before he could open the door. A blinking light on the console indicated the machine was in a recording mode. He suspected the caller was Matt. His son called him either at the office or on the home phone, rarely on his cell.

Rizzo reached over to interrupt the message, but the light stopped blinking. *Hmm, short message.* He pressed the *play* button. The voice was not Matt's.

"Mr. Rizzo, I am sorry you not there."

The speaker's voice had a flat, firm tone.

"I call to caution . . . no, to warn you. Stop meddling my client's business. It is bad. You stop now. You don't wish harm come to your family. Please, you listen to warning. Yes?"

The call ended, leaving Rizzo steeped in anger.

"Fucking Ilya Bodrov?" he screamed.

His body tensed, his neck muscles knotted, Rizzo stood and scowled for several moments at the recorder. His eyes traveled to the closet in the corner. He walked to it, knelt before the SentrySafe positioned against the back wall and punched in six numbers. He opened the door, reached in, and took hold of his holstered 9mm Glock. "Okay, sweetheart, from here on out, you and me are going steady."

Chapter Twenty-Six

I lya Bodrov didn't want to use his cell phone. That would have left his number in the detective's *calls-received* file. Instead, he made the call using Rita Sands' home landline. He ended the message and hung up. Hopeful the detective would heed his warning, he sat back and searched for the TV remote. It was then he became conscious of the woman's presence and looked up.

Rita stood in the doorway with her shoulder resting against the bedroom door jamb, barefoot, silent, her face painted with a bemused expression. A bath towel encased her torso and wild ringlets of wet, red hair tumbled over her brow and ears.

Unable to disguise his surprise, Bodrov bolted to his feet. "Your shower, it was good?" he said, grinning, and drew her damp body into his arms. "Very quick, I think. American women take long showers. No water shortage in America."

Rita jerked back her head and squinted, trying to bring his face into focus. "Boris, what was that about?"

"What?"

"The phone call you just made. It sounded like something from *The Godfather* movie."

"No, no, no, you mistake." Bodrov released his embrace. "I only tell one of my employees his behavior not acceptable. How you say—to shape up. Nothing more."

She searched his face with a quizzical expression. Bodrov shrugged, returned to the sofa and fell into it. Rita disappeared into the bedroom without speaking.

They had spent the latter part of the afternoon in her Murray Hill apartment making love. Two days ago when they first met on the flight from Miami, Rita Sands asked what he did for a living. He told her he was an international bond trader for a Moscow financial conglomerate. His business often required travel from his Miami headquarters to New York City. She admitted the world of finance was beyond her understanding, so she didn't ask more questions. Relieved, Bodrov proposed having dinner, and she suggested they go to one of her favorite New York restaurants, The Palm. Since he neglected to call ahead for reservations, he needed a fifty dollar bribe to secure a table. The night had ended in Rita's bed.

The drone of the blow-dryer coming from the bathroom annoyed Bodrov. He turned up the TV volume to block the noise and gazed at the screen, at the program host interviewing a man in a military uniform. Bodrov's thoughts were elsewhere, his mind caught up in his awkward blunder.

He'd been convinced Rita was in the shower, out of earshot, when he called the detective. No question she heard what he said. Regrettable, for now he needed to address the complication.

It hadn't occurred to him her landline telephone could also be recorded in the detective's *calls-received* file, enabling a trace back to her. He realized his mistake after he hung up. What a shame. He thoroughly enjoyed their time in bed.

The blow-dryer quieted and Bodrov switched off the TV. He stepped to the bedroom door and leaned in. "Rita, I leave now. I go to my hotel to change. I return at seven, pick you up. Reservation at *Le Cirque* is eight o'clock."

"Okay, Boris, I'll be ready." Rita couldn't hide the tension in her voice.

* * *

Silence cloaked her living room and jangled her nerves. Boris Alexandrov was not who he said he was. Rita was confident of that. But who was he? Trembling, she approaced the front door and put her eye to the peephole. The corridor appeared empty. Did he leave for his hotel? She hoped so.

She moved to the antique brass bar cart against the wall, opened the bottle of Johnny Walker Black and filled a highball glass halfway. Her mind in a fog, she added several cubes from the ice maker in the kitchen. Back in the living room, she dropped into the sofa. The alcohol ran down her parched throat with a soothing effect.

On edge, she sipped the scotch, questioning in her mind who Alexandrov's frightening call was meant for? Could it have been one of his employees like he claimed? Was his explanation of the message true? Did she mishear it? Her eyes fell on the phone next to her elbow. Boris was the last to use it.

She picked up the telephone and pressed *redial*. The phone program called back the number he had dialed. She hoped the machine would respond with the owner's identification. On the third ring, a man's voice answered.

"Hello, Luke Rizzo."

Surprised by the live voice, Rita considered disconnecting. Instead, she drew in a breath and waited.

"Hello, who is this?" The voice sounded annoyed.

"Er—ah, Mr. Rizzo, please don't take this as a weird call and hang up. I need to ask you a question. I need a yes or no."

"Ask away," came a friendlier response.

"Ah, do you—do you work for a man named Boris Alexandrov?"

Silence on the other end.

Rita sensed the tension.

The man said again, "Who is this?"

She lowered the phone, inches away from hanging up. Her hand shook. She lifted it again to her ear and replied in a softer voice, "Mr. Rizzo, who I am doesn't matter. A short while ago a man—Boris Alexandrov—made a call to your number on my phone. He left a message. An angry message. A threatening one. Was the message meant for you?"

The sound of his breathing told Rita he hadn't hung up. Certain she made a big mistake calling back the number, she thought about breaking off the connection.

The man finally spoke. "Look, whoever you are," he said with a tinge of anger. "I'm a private investigator. When did he make the call?"

Rita hesitated. "Not ten minutes ago."

Another pause. "This Boris guy, he spoke with an accent?"

"Yes."

"Okay then, the message was for me. I checked my file earlier for the telephone number and it appears it's the same as this call. The man who made the call, if you don't already know, is not Boris Alexandrov. His real name is Ilya Bodrov, a Russian mafia thug. And he prefers to see me dead. So now, you tell me why he made the call from your phone?"

Rita's heart raced. She released a wheeze. "He's someone," she began, "who sat next to me on a flight from Miami two days ago. We became—ah, um—friendly." Her hand shook. She pressed the phone to her ear. "He told me his name was Boris Alexandrov. We were here in my apartment when he made the call. I was in the shower. He didn't notice when I came out of the bathroom. That's how I overheard most of the conversation." She gulped and swallowed the saliva collecting in her throat. "And when I asked him about it, he said he was talking to his employee, berating him for something he did. I didn't believe—"

"Miss, listen to me. This person, Ilya Bodrov, is dangerous and you need to protect yourself. Where do you live? Here in the city?"

She drew in a breath. "Manhattan . . . Murray Hill."

"Okay, that's the Seventeenth's jurisdiction. Give me your address. I'll call a Detective Duggan, have him send over a couple of uniform policemen."

"But he's coming back at seven to pick me up. We're supposed to go out to dinner."

"Miss, you have to trust me. What's your name and address? The police can be there in no time."

Rita felt a tightening in her neck muscles. *Can I believe this man? How can I verify who he is?* An idea came to her. "Mr. Rizzo, is your office in the city?"

"Yes, in the Flatiron Building on 23rd Street. I'm there now."

"Are you listed in information?"

"Under Lucas Rizzo, Investigations."

"Hold on." She put down the landline phone, removed the mobile from her purse, called information, and gave the operator Rizzo's business name. The operator confirmed his address and phone number. *He's telling the truth, thank God.* Picking up her home phone, she said, "Mr. Rizzo, you there?"

"Yes."

"Okay, my name is Rita Sands. I'm at 201 East Thirty-seventh Street, northeast corner of Third Avenue, apartment 17B."

"Got it. Lock your door, Miss Sands, and don't open it for anyone except the police. I'll call Detective Duggan now, and we'll be over in fifteen minutes."

* * *

At a quarter after five, rush hour, the traffic backed up the streets east and west at all the avenue crossings. Rizzo's taxi ride took longer than his fifteen-minute estimate.

Duggan stood at the front entrance of the Sands apartment building with his arms folded across his chest. Rizzo's call to the lieutenant was not well-received. It took heavy convincing to bring him around.

As Rizzo approached, Duggan bitched, "Jesus, Rizzo, what the hell you think, I got nothing better to do but chase down every crank call?"

"That was not a crank call, Frank. Neither was the earlier phone message to my office. I'm telling you, the crazy Russian, Bodrov, is here in the city, and the woman's life is on the line."

They rode the elevator to the seventeenth floor and found the B apartment tucked around the corner at the southwest end of the building. At the turn, Rizzo spotted the partially opened door. He didn't have a good feeling.

Duggan pushed the buzzer positioned under the peephole. In doing so, the door swung open, revealing an empty living room.

"Hello, Miss Sands?" the detective called out.

No reply.

"Miss Sands. Luke Rizzo here."

The two exchanged wide-eyed looks.

"What do you think?" Rizzo said.

"We go in."

Duggan led the way. He crossed the living room with a quick glance into the kitchen. They paused in front of the doorway of what appeared to be the main bedroom. Empty. The closed second bedroom door was a worrisome tell. Duggan pulled his service weapon from under his jacket and, rising on his toes, approached the closed door. Cutting his eyes to Rizzo, he motioned him to stand to one side. Duggan reached over, twisted the knob, and flicked open the door.

Rizzo saw her first. "Ah, Christ almighty." She lay flat on her back between the twin beds, the hole in the middle of her forehead clearly visible.

"Not a crank call, after all," Duggan said.

"Fucking Russian."

"Rizzo, don't touch anything," Duggan cautioned like Rizzo didn't know any better. He pulled a pair of surgical gloves from his jacket pocket and slipped them on. "Wait out there while I call this into the precinct."

Rizzo walked back into the living room and crossed to the wraparound window. He stood gazing out at a panorama of city views, both west and southwest. Framed in the span of glass, the majestic Empire State Building loomed high above the lower neighboring structures. He noticed the lights on a number of the upper floors. It was still too early for the decorative colored display that tinted the iconic landmark each evening. Rizzo imagined how much Rita Sands must have enjoyed that inspiring sight—while she lived.

Duggan's call came from the bedroom. "Rizzo, don't leave."

"I'm here."

The detective appeared in the doorway. "I'm gonna need your statement on the phone call you received from the woman."

"Okay."

"The crime scene unit is on the way. I'd ask you to hang around until the M.E. investigator arrives, but that could take hours."

"I can stay as long as you need me."

Duggan walked over to Rizzo and stood beside him. "I need to speak with you anyway about Frankie Cusack."

"Yeah? I've been meaning to ask. What's his status?" Rizzo said without turning his head.

"Well, when we first sat him down on Saturday, I assumed it would be a waste of time. He surprised me when he admitted to the Rodrigo Vega knifing in Grand Central even before we started the interview. We read him his Miranda fast before he changed his story."

"He say who ordered him to do Rabbit?"

"His boss, Ilya Bodrov. Cusack insisted he didn't shoot Soto. His prints were all over the Town Car, including the front seat. He claimed he used Soto's gypsy cab service several times these past months."

"That's true. And he drove the same Lincoln the day he threatened my wife at La Guardia. I verified it was Soto's car by the license plate."

"Well, he hasn't been arraigned yet, so a court-appointed defense attorney hasn't been named. And that's good since he signed the confession to the knifing of your snitch. For certain, he'll go down for that one. The other one . . . well, depends on what comes back from ballistics on the weapon we took from his apartment. He wouldn't consent to the search, so we got a warrant. If there's no match, he might not go down for the Soto one."

"The snake. He told me Bodrov ordered that one too."

"Yeah, but he told you under coerced conditions. Right? How would that hold up in court?"

Rizzo turned to face Duggan. "Why the hell would he cop to Rabbit's murder and not Soto's?"

"Figures he'd get a lighter sentence that way. Hell, I don't know. He might skate on both if his appointed attorney can convince a jury you poured water on him."

"Shit! Maybe he needs to be reminded of the alternative. He dodges these two murders, Bodrov and Salazar will not allow him to breathe free air for long."

"And maybe why he took the stabbing charge. We told him we had a witness to the knifing. Someone saw him do it and caught a look at his face before he slipped through the mob of people and left the terminal. The wit came to the precinct the same night to report it."

"True, or are you hustling him?"

"It's true, but we have your little water party to worry about."

"Has he said anything about it?"

"Not yet. We'll see what happens when his lawyer sits down with him."

"You think you could subtly remind Frankie that Salazar and Bodrov are eagerly awaiting his release?"

"Yeah, I'll drop it in when I can." Duggan pulled out a spiral notepad from his inside pocket. "Okay, now tell me about the woman's phone call."

Chapter Twenty-Seven

The ringing telephone woke Rizzo early the next morning. Luis Fuentes' voice surprised him. Seated on the edge of the bed, he shook the fog from his brain while Fuentes explained the strange phone call Carmen received last evening while he was at work.

"She said his name was Lieutenant Collins, a detective from the One-Hundred and Fifteenth Precinct. He told her he was calling about the arrest they made. Those two pimps."

"At the house in Queens?"

"Yeah, that's what she remembers him saying."

"What did he want?"

"He said he needed me to come into the station house in the morning . . . eleven-thirty. Something about signing a form. You know Carmen. She wasn't too clear. She had trouble understanding him."

"Seems odd. Did he say why you?"

"He said it had to do with Manny. He claimed Manny named me as Rosita's next of kin in the New York area. At least, it's what Carmen thought she heard."

"I'm confused, Luis. They already have the girls' sworn statements. I can't think of anything other than those requiring signatures."

"What's your guess?"

"Well, the Collins involved in the arrest is a sergeant. It's possible she got it wrong. But the signing of a form? I don't know."

Fuentes said nothing, his breathing the only sound for several seconds.

"Tell you what," Rizzo said. "You don't have a car, so why don't I drive you? We'll find out what this is about. Make sure it isn't a bunch of bullshit Salazar drummed up to get his guys off the hook. I could call this Sergeant Collins, but if there's a police officer pulling something fishy, it'll scare him off. Best we take care of this in person."

"Man, I hate bothering you."

"Not to worry, Luis. Can you make it to the Avis garage at Fiftieth and Ninth Avenue around ten-thirty? I'll pick up a rental there, and we'll drive out to the One-Fifteen, find out if anyone's playing games."

"Yeah, I'll be there."

Rizzo ended the call and saw Flo in the doorway of the bathroom, staring at him. A towel wrapped around her wet hair, her shower-dampened, naked body glistened within the shaft of morning sunlight sneaking through the bedroom window. A raised eyebrow signaled concern.

"Well, that sounded ominous."

Rizzo gazed on her nakedness, and he felt himself jumping to attention. The sight of her standing before him caused a warm rush of desire.

Flo posed with folded arms across her damp breasts, and grinned. "Luke, honey?"

He reached out for her. "Come here a minute. I want to tell you something."

She hesitated, then eased over. Rizzo reached up and rested his hands on her hips, smiling up into her flirtatious eyes. He paused, remembering Flo needed to leave for work in thirty-five minutes. *I wonder how quick—Nah.* He lifted his chin, stretched his neck and kissed each of her breasts like a parent sending the twins off to school.

"Damn, you are the sexiest woman in the world."

Flo giggled. "Hon, you ever think otherwise, I'll whup your ass." She stepped away before he could pull her back. "Tell me about the phone call. You're not getting yourself into anything dangerous, are you?"

Rizzo explained what Fuentes told him. "I'm suspicious someone is pulling a stunt to get the two pimps off. I'm going out to Queens, to the precinct, check it out. Nothing to worry about."

"You promise?"

"I promise."

* * *

The One-Fifteen Precinct, on Northern Boulevard at Ninety-second Street, was located ten blocks from the house where they rescued the teens. Rizzo considered the closeness of the two locations gave further weight to the possibility of a dirty cop.

At eleven-twenty, he and Fuentes entered the station house, walked to the sergeant at the desk and announced they were there to meet with Sergeant Collins.

"Is he expecting you this morning?" the desk officer asked. She sounded doubtful.

"Yes. We're a bit early."

"You're really early. He's not on duty today. You sure you got the right day?"

Rizzo eyeballed Fuentes.

Fuentes shrugged. "I don't know, man. She was certain he said, 'in the morning.' Maybe everything else he told her is on the fuzzy side, but she's sure about that. He said in the morning at eleven-thirty."

Rizzo turned to the sergeant. "My name is Luke Rizzo. NYPD retired. I'm a private investigator now."

"That's nice," she said, forcing a smile.

"Anyway, this man's wife received a phone call last night from a person who identified himself as Lieutenant Collins of the One-Fifteen."

"We have no Lieutenant Collins here," the DO said, her tone edged with impatience. "Our Collins is a sergeant."

"I know that. The guy who called Mrs. Fuentes told her Mr. Fuentes here needed to come in to sign a form relating to the collar of a couple of pimps four days ago."

The sergeant nodded, signaling she knew about the arrest.

Rizzo continued. "I figured she got the rank wrong. That's all. I was with Sergeant Collins and Officer Martell during the take-down . . . the house on 102nd Street where they held the two kidnapped sixteen-year-old Mexican kids."

"What kind of form was this gentleman supposed to sign?"

"That's what stumps me. One of the two girls, Rosita Fuentes, is Mr. Fuentes' niece. The girl's brother, Manny Fuentes, came to the precinct with the girls when you booked the pimps. He left to go back to Florida yesterday, so I don't have the foggiest—"

"You think maybe somebody's playing a joke?"

"I hope not."

"Hold on, let me ask our captain to speak with you." The sergeant disappeared and after a few minutes, she returned with the precinct boss.

Rizzo introduced himself and Luis Fuentes to Captain Briggs. The CO came across as a well-groomed lawman with an intelligent face and soft eyes.

Briggs shook Rizzo's hand. Instead of letting go, he held on while he studied him. When the cloud lifted, he said, "Four-One, the Bronx? Narcotics, right?"

"That's me, Captain. Fort Apache. My last posting. Do I know you from there?"

"You no doubt wouldn't remember me. Platoon commander for about two years. I heard of your hot-shot reputation in narcotics. They said you were a good cop."

"Thanks, Captain. I appreciate that. Your Sergeant Collins also remembered me from the Four-One."

"That's right. Collins did a tour there too. Fill me in. What brings you here?"

Rizzo repeated the same scenario he'd given the DO. He mentioned the pimps and the Corona house were part of the Salazar syndicate.

Briggs gave him a polite listen, nodding throughout. He allowed Rizzo to finish without interrupting.

"Sounds like they went out of their way to mislead you." Briggs produced a telling grin. "Someone wanted to drag you out here. Why? I couldn't say. The fact the caller knows we have a Collins working here is an important piece of information for us."

Briggs didn't elaborate. He didn't have to. The unspoken inference said there's a cop on the take in the precinct, someone in Salazar's pocket. And he's on their radar.

Rizzo thanked Captain Briggs and the desk officer, and he and Fuentes left the station house, heading for the parking lot at the rear of the building. A light drizzle fell by the time they reached the rented Ford.

"Well, that was curious." Rizzo turned on the ignition and stared out the windshield through the streaks forming on the glass.

Fuentes faced him. "Why the hell would anyone want me to come all the way out here? For nothing? Beats me."

A cold emptiness rolled down Rizzo's throat into his stomach. "I can guess why."

Fuentes stared.

"I'm the one they wanted to lure out here. Not you."

"So why call me . . . I mean, Carmen?"

"Whoever called figured you were at work, and Carmen wouldn't question him. He couldn't call me because I would have seen through the ruse. He made an educated guess you'd tell me, and I'd want to go with you. They seem to have me down pretty well. Scary."

"Why here in Queens?"

Rizzo shrugged. "Could have been anywhere. They needed to lure me out into the open with my guard down. What's a less threatening place than a police station?" His neck warmed as he pressed his arm against his left side and elbowed the holstered Glock through the thickness of his leather jacket.

Out on Northern Boulevard, Rizzo turned east. They went past the Louis Armstrong School, one street beyond the station house. He pictured Satchmo blowing his horn, but the image faded fast. It wasn't Louie who blew smoke at Carmen Fuentes. He felt his grip tighten on the steering wheel.

He headed the Ford south onto Junction Boulevard, the road that would lead them to the Long Island Expressway and back into the city. The Ford's wipers beat a slow rhythm while Rizzo mulled over the morning's event. Midday traffic moved along the boulevard at a guarded pace, headlights on, drivers cautious on the wet roadway.

They reached Thirty-seventh Avenue, the first stoplight. Rizzo glanced through his rearview mirror at the surrounding vehicles. The signal changed, and the pickup on his left pulled away fast, spinning wheels until the tires grabbed. The VW behind the truck moved forward and came abreast of the Ford. Both vehicles entered the intersection at the same time. Rizzo's eyes traveled to his side-view mirror. A black Chevy Suburban appeared in the left lane hanging back at a safe distance.

"Those mother sons a—"

"What?"

"The twin bowling balls, they're behind us. A black Chevy Suburban."

"Holy shit, where did they come from?" Fuentes twisted around. "Where, I don't see them. You sure?"

"I'm sure. On the left, three cars back."

Rizzo kept pace with the traffic ahead. Now's not the time to panic, he thought. He needed to find a way to lose them.

He was familiar with the area. Both sides of Junction Boulevard were dense residential neighborhoods, made up of a hatched maze of avenues and one-way streets with parked cars on one side. If he ducked into one of those streets, he couldn't speed. Not with stop signs at every corner. On the plus side, the street's narrowness would leave no room for the Chevy to pull alongside.

He considered doubling back to the One-Fifteen. What for? Short of providing a police escort to the city, the captain could do nothing. Rizzo needed to shake the tail and do it soon.

"Shouldn't we move the hell off this boulevard?" Fuentes said, a note of panic in his voice. He swiveled his head from side to side like a spectator to a Ping-Pong match.

"Yeah," Rizzo answered. "I'm looking for the right spot to turn without them seeing us."

At Elmhurst Avenue, the next traffic light, Rizzo slowed and prepared to stop. In his peripheral vision, he noticed to his left an Allied Van Lines truck moving straight ahead into the crossing. Rizzo made a guess the driver would not turn south onto Junction Boulevard but would continue west, following Elmhurst Avenue.

Before the moving van reached the middle of the intersection, Rizzo pulled out. He whipped a hard right ahead of the truck and sped down Elmhurst Avenue, leaving the stymied Chevy SUV on the boulevard. The Allied van rode the Ford's tail, blocking the twin's view. If there was any chance of losing them, it was now.

Rizzo zigzagged through streets and avenues until he assumed he'd lost the twins. Being extra cautious, he backed the Ford into a resident's driveway. Their position between two clapboard houses protected the car from view of passing vehicles. Rizzo pressed back in his seat and waited. His breathing returned to normal. He rubbed his sweaty hands on his pant legs and watched for a time until he determined it was safe to head out toward the expressway.

He backed the Ford out onto Elmhurst Avenue, looped around the block and continued to Junction Boulevard. There, he turned south again.

"Keep an eye out for the SUV."

"Okay," Fuentes said with a shaky voice.

The rain let up before they reached the intersection of Woodhaven and Queens Boulevards, but the road surface remained wet. Rizzo took the access ramp up to the elevated Long Island Expressway and merged into the heavy flow of traffic going west toward the city.

"Looks like we're clear," Rizzo said, settling the Ford in the center lane doing fifty-five. "At least for now," he added with an uneasy laugh.

Fuentes undid the toggles on his coat and opened it. He removed his golf cap and used it to wipe his sweaty brow. "Jesus, those guys, they must have a fucking sixth sense. They're everywhere, like dogshit. I can't believe it."

"Yeah, they're determined bastards. They were laying for us outside the police station."

They remained quiet. Rizzo's eyes darted to the vehicles in front, then to those appearing in the rear and side-view mirrors. He scrutinized the traffic, his mind preoccupied with the image of the dangerous twins. He knew escaping them today would not make them disappear for very long.

Movement in the rearview mirror captured Rizzo's attention. It held his eyes for a long moment. He turned to Fuentes. "Seems I spoke too soon, Luis."

Fuentes broke from his thoughts. "What?"

"The bowling balls. They're behind us. My guess is they were sitting back there at the expressway access ramp. I missed seeing them."

Fuentes' eyebrows jumped. He twisted around. "Where?"

The black SUV barreled up in the outside lane, tailgating a Mini Cooper. The Cooper's right directional flashed as the driver looked for an opportunity to move out of the way. The Ford's speedometer steadied on fifty-five. Rizzo felt helpless. He couldn't increase his speed without running up the rear end of the vehicle in front of him. The car to the left of him, ahead by three-quarters of a length, kept pace. The slow lane on the right was bumper-to-bumper.

"He's gaining," Fuentes shouted when he spied the Suburban.

"Christ, I can't go any faster. I'm blocked."

Once the slowed Cooper moved out of the lane, the twins' Suburban had fifty yards of clearance ahead of them. They were closing fast on the Ford. A giant arm, bent at the elbow, hung out the SUV's open passenger side window. The meaty hand at the end of the arm gripped a gun. Rizzo expected the Suburban to pull within shooting distance in less than a minute. A wave of desperation came over him.

Van Dam Street, the last exit in Queens before the Midtown Tunnel into Manhattan, appeared off in the distance. Rizzo knew once they were beyond this turn-off, they faced no chance to escape until they reached the toll booths at the tunnel entrance.

Rizzo looked to his right and eyed an opening in the slow lane. Frantic, he sliced across between cars in time to turn off at the Van Dam exit and onto the long, sloping exit ramp that ended at a stop sign a hundred yards ahead.

Caught by surprise, the Suburban darted across two lanes of traffic to the exit, narrowly escaping a collision with a slow-moving Buick.

Twenty yards ahead to the left of the Ford on the expressway side, a waist-high steel guard rail flanked the ramp. It traveled the full distance to the stop sign. With the SUV tight on his tail, Rizzo made an instant decision. Before he reached the beginning of the guardrail, he turned the Ford to the left. The car bounced over a low curb and back out onto the expressway. It cut in front of a slow moving vehicle and just missed being rear-ended.

The Suburban's driver, unable to duplicate Rizzo's maneuver in time, flew by the start of the guardrail, and beyond a point of no return.

Rizzo sped west toward the Midtown Tunnel when the sound of a horrendous explosion reached him. He hoped whatever caused it involved the twins. For the moment, he was home free, and that was his primary concern.

* * *

Rizzo dropped off Fuentes at the Edison Hotel entrance on Forty-seventh Street.

"I'm an hour early," Fuentes said, "I gotta come down a little. My nerves are shot. I'll grab lunch in the coffee shop if I can get the food down."

"Call Carmen, tell her you're okay!" Rizzo shouted. He pulled from the curb and continued west to Ninth Avenue toward the Avis garage.

On the walk to his brownstone, Rizzo replayed the wild chase on the Long Island Expressway. He and Fuentes came close to losing their lives. He felt his anger rising. He decided to skip the office today. And for certain he wouldn't mention anything to Flo.

In the apartment, he threw himself onto the sofa and closed his eyes. His heartbeat regulated for the first time since he left the Corona precinct. He thought about Fuentes' reaction during the chase. The poor guy never faced anything like that in his life.

With his stocking feet up on the coffee table and sipping a Hires Root Beer, Rizzo watched the local news channel. He sat up when the newscaster went into a story about an accident on the Long Island Expressway.

"A bystander who witnessed the crash reported the Suburban's driver applied his brakes and skidded on the wet pavement into the rear end of a mammoth-sized cement truck, which was stopped at the end of the ramp."

Rizzo assumed when he turned to go back onto the expressway, the eyes of the twin driving the SUV had remained on the disappearing Ford and failed to spot the cement truck until it was too late. The TV reporter said the cement truck driver was not injured, but no one in the Suburban survived the explosion. Rizzo chuckled, recalling something his father taught him many years ago. The first rule of safe driving is *Keep your eyes on the road.*

He snapped off the TV and stretched out. Exhausted, he allowed the collection of close calls and threats during his years on the job to rumble through his memory. Rizzo couldn't count the number of times a drug dealer attempted to slip a toe tag on him. At this point in his life, and struggling with middle age, he was not eager to revisit another experience like today's brush with death. The vulnerability he faced during the insane pursuit would haunt him for a long time.

He wanted payback, big time. The twins' demise was not enough. Nothing short of destroying Ilya Bodrov and the Salazar organization would satisfy him. And he wanted to settle the score for Rabbit's murder. He thought of Jack Fields and his talk of having a role for him. He was anxious to hear what the agent and the FBI had up their sleeve.

Chapter Twenty-Eight

Jack Fields examined Ralph Brancuso, seated on the sofa opposite him. Brancuso, his new number two agent, had a coffee mug in his hand and a Ronald McDonald smile on his face.

The agent had reported to the FBI's Manhattan office Tuesday morning and spent the first two hours getting settled. He passed the latter part of the morning in a meeting with Fields and Carter Brooke. By early afternoon, Fields completed his briefing on all the active cases in which he wanted Brancuso involved, including the upcoming operation in San Juan.

Brancuso set his mug on the coffee table and looked up. "Rizzo's the private investigator up to his ears with that mess upstate a few years ago. Right? Him and that English dame?"

Fields nodded. "Same guy. He's married now."

"To her?"

"No, someone else."

"And you want to use him as an undercover for this take-down operation?"

"He's perfect for it."

"Why? He speak Spanish?"

"Street expressions. The stuff he picked up working in narcotics in Spanish Harlem. His value is his anonymity."

Brancuso's broad brow furrowed, aiming toward his nose.

Fields chuckled. In the past, the expression always reminded him of Telly Savalas, the actor, but with more hair. He turned to face Brancuso. "Here's the situation in San Juan. The cartel is familiar with the entire Puerto Rico police force, local and state. If they don't already have someone in their pocket, at the least, they know their faces. Goes for our assigned federal agents, too."

"They don't know me."

"True, you haven't been down there in many years, but I wouldn't bet on it. Their agent-picture-file runs deep."

"No shit!"

"I've talked with Puerto Rico's Police Superintendent, Emilio Sanchez, over these past several months, planning for this operation. The lack of anonymity among those in law enforcement ranks as one of the superintendent's biggest issues. That, along with his uncertainty of who within the departments is clean and who isn't. Makes his job near impossible."

"But why Rizzo?"

Fields raised his shoulders and gestured with open palms. "Rizzo is a blank page. He's beyond the eyes and ears of the cartel and the Puerto Rico Police. He has zero chance of having his cover blown, especially if he brings his wife along. You know, Mr. and Mrs. Tourist, like thousands of others."

"You think he'll go for it?"

"We haven't discussed it yet. Rizzo did commit to helping us. He has no idea of the job, what it is, where it is, and what's involved. And, for certain, he hasn't a clue about including his wife."

"I don't know. This guy—I mean, he didn't impress . . . ." Brancuso let his words trail off.

"What? Finish your thought."

"Christ, Jack. I don't intend to sound so fucking negative this early in—"

"Cut the bullshit, Ralph. You never hesitated to voice your opinion before, so don't start now. What's bothering you about this? Tell me."

Brancuso rose to his feet. He gazed down at his coffee cup, reached to pick it up, changed his mind and sat down again.

Fields waited.

"It's Rizzo," Brancuso said, shaking his head.

"What about him?"

"That situation a few years ago. He never struck me as the sharpest private eye out there, the way he let the old man disappear. I mean, how responsible—how dependable is this guy?"

Fields remained quiet, thinking about the agent's agitation. Ralph Brancuso was an all-in personality with an equal, uncontestable dedication to whatever side of an issue he was on. Luke Rizzo was much the same animal, unafraid to go up against anything standing in his way. Like Brancuso, Rizzo possessed enormous respect for justice. Fields needed to convince his new sidekick Rizzo was right for this job. Then, he had to persuade Rizzo—a greater challenge.

"I don't believe you have a complete reading on what happened back then," Fields said.

"Well, you already told me—"

"Wait. Hold it a second."

Brancuso folded his arms, crushing his tie against his chest.

Fields repositioned himself on the sofa, trying to find a more comfortable pose. "There's no reason to blame Rizzo for what happened upstate. He never underestimated or shirked his responsibility toward his client. In fact, when he tracked down the German, he went after him with a vengeance. Chased him to a rooftop in Brooklyn, where the man took a header three stories to his death." Fields grinned at the memory.

Brancuso leaned over the coffee table. Lifting his mug, he took several sips.

Fields worried his new team member would continue to resist him. If he did, he couldn't ignore it.

"Okay, Jack. I'm with you. Maybe I was quick to judge. From what you say, he sounds like he deserves the benefit of the doubt."

"Good, because if Rizzo accepts his role in our operation, I'll need you to go down to San Juan to watch his back. You'll be wallpaper, of course, to everyone. Rizzo, in particular. After all, I did promise him the best protection the bureau had to offer."

Brancuso leaned back into the sofa's cushion. The Ronald McDonald smile returned.

* * *

Ilya Bodrov's eyelids flickered wildly when a blue and white RMP drew to the side of their parked SUV on West Forty-eighth Street. The police officer lowered his passenger-side window, motioned to the driver to lower his, and waited.

The SUV's driver was a short, muscular man with a scarred face ornamented by a shaggy, black mustache protruding from under the tip of a hard nose. He turned toward Bodrov with a deadpan expression.

Bodrov's nervous tic continued. "Open, Ivan. We don't want trouble."

Ivan rolled down the window.

"You're in a no-parking zone," the officer said. "You need to move it."

"Officer, we wait for someone. Won't be long."

"Sorry. Find a legal spot. I'm gonna circle the block once. I want you gone by the time I come back here. Understood?"

Bodrov reached across and poked Ivan's shoulder. "Tell him, yes."

"Yes, officer."

The officer acknowledged the response with a raised chin and drove off.

Ivan switched on the ignition. In a raspy voice, he asked, "Where we go?"

"Find parking garage near. We walk back. Important you see detective, what he looks like. He leave for work soon."

They turned north on Eighth Avenue. Within a few blocks, Ivan located a parking garage at the corner of Fiftieth Street. He pulled the SUV into the entrance and the two men exited the vehicle. Ivan took the ticket from the uniformed attendant and they fast-paced it south on foot.

At Forty-eighth Street, Bodrov took a position in a doorway across from Rizzo's brownstone. Ivan walked twenty-five yards down the street on the brownstone's side and stopped in front of a building two up from Rizzo's. He propped his shoulder against the railing to the side of the building entrance and took out his iPhone.

Bodrov checked his watch nervously.

At eight-thirty-five Rizzo came out the door of his brownstone, hopped down the four steps to the sidewalk, and turned east toward Eighth Avenue. Bodrov signaled to Ivan with a head bob. The Russian raised the iPhone to his face and pretended to be on a call. From fifty feet away, the approaching detective appeared on the phone's screen, and Ivan clicked off several shots.

Rizzo passed unaware, reached the corner and disappeared. Ivan crossed the street to rejoin Bodrov.

"You get picture?"

"Yes, four. I get good ones of his face. I will memorize, not make mistake when I aim."

"Excellent. You should not be stupid like Zakharchenko twins and become dead. We would not like that."

"I agree," Ivan said.

Chapter Twenty-Nine

Rizzo retrieved his mail from the box in the lobby and rode the elevator to his fourth-floor office. Inside, at the base of the door, he found a three-fold menu from one of the local deli takeout joints. The distributor of the flyer slipped it through the narrow opening under the door. Rizzo tossed it on the desk next to the packet of mail and pressed the *play messages* button on his lighted answering machine.

The recorder clicked alive. "Rizzo, get back to me when you can." It was the voice of Jack Fields.

Rizzo rotated his chair to face the window. Gathering his thoughts, he allowed his eyes to scan the buildings across Fifth Avenue. He gazed at their facades, something he often did when he couldn't put his finger on whatever was bugging him. After several moments of chewing on the mystery, an image of the deli's menu flashed in his mind.

The Flatiron Building posted signs warning against unauthorized solicitations. They appeared on the wall near every elevator on every floor. This posting was standard practice in buildings throughout the city, particularly those without lobby security. The Flatiron had a guard. Despite the security, violators hawking their wares or services often managed to slip past unchallenged. Rizzo would find handbills or flyers under his door. Not an everyday occurrence, but happening enough to become a nuisance to most tenants.

With yesterday's chase on the Long Island Expressway fresh in his mind, Rizzo's heightened sense of exposure put him on edge. He hated playing defense. The brush with death elevated the annoying ease of building access to more than a nuisance level. His shoulders tightened.

The morning sun bounced off several windows of the taller buildings on the opposite side of the avenue. The glare pulled Rizzo's thoughts to another track of concern: a shooter with a long-range weapon. A bead of moisture formed on his forehead. He pushed the worry from his mind while he fought the anger welling up from his gut. *Son of a bitch, stewing over this shit will paralyze me. I can't let this happen.*

Rizzo reached for the phone, hit the speaker button, and punched in Fields's number.

"Jack Fields's office," Rachel answered.

"Hi, this is Luke Rizzo, returning his call."

"Hold on a minute, Mr. Rizzo."

Fields picked up. "Hey, Luke."

"I got your message. What's up?" Rizzo's voice was laced with anger.

Fields paused. "Rizzo, something wrong?"

"Ah, no. Nothing important, Jack. What's going on?"

"How about meeting for lunch? I'm buying."

Rizzo's eyes landed on the flyer. He reached over and swatted the paper off the desk like a pesky mosquito. Time to be proactive, go on the offense.

"You buying? In that case, I'm in. What happened? You pull the short straw?"

"Yeah, ain't that the pits? No, wiseass, I need to discuss your future."

"What? In a Burger King over a Triple Whopper with onion rings? That's where you want to discuss my future?"

"No, not there. Later. Back here in my office. The Triple Whopper is to soften you up."

"Okay. I'm free. J.Lo never called to confirm our lunch date at the Four Seasons. Where do we meet?"

"How about Angelo's, north end of Madison Square Park on Broadway? Twelve-Thirty. You like Italian, don't you?"

"Jack, I like anything when you're buying. See you there. Oh, and hey, so you know, I'm carrying these days. I never leave home without it."

"That's fine. Try not to shoot me before I pay the check."

"I'll keep the safety on."

* * *

After checking his weapon at the front desk lock-box, Rizzo followed Jack Fields into his office and dropped onto the sofa "Thanks for lunch. I forgot how good that restaurant was."

Fields pressed the intercom button. "Rachel, ask Ralph to come in. We're ready to begin the briefing." He looked up. "You want anything? Coffee, soft drink?"

"No thanks, I'm good for about a week."

Fields pulled out the center drawer and took out a green folder. He laid it on the desk and glanced at Rizzo. "Ralph Brancuso will join us in a minute. You met him a few years ago when he was the FBI's lead agent in the Albany office."

"At the schoolhouse upstate, right?"

Fields nodded. "The bureau transferred him here to replace Tony Condon."

Rizzo remembered the short, stocky agent—balding, clean-shaven with a gruff demeanor and a salty vocabulary. Brancuso didn't impress him as the prototype FBI agent. The man had to have something going for him, Rizzo acknowledged. He was a lead agent, and if Jack Fields accepted him in place of Tony Condon, well . . . .

What stiffened Rizzo's back about the man was the way Brancuso dismissed the FBI's effort to help find the old man three years ago. "Leave the problem to the local cops," he said and bailed out of the upstate schoolhouse.

As Fields searched through the contents of the folder, Rizzo reflected on what the bureau might have in mind for him. Fields admitted it involved an element of danger without elaborating. In any event, if it were a big enough operation to take down Salazar, he wouldn't turn away any involvement the agent offered.

At lunch, Rizzo had related the story about the questionable telephone call Carmen Fuentes received, and how it lured him and Luis Fuentes out to Queens. He described the chase through the streets, then onto the Long Island Expressway. Fields laughed at Rizzo's account of the twins' relentless pursuit and the fatal result at the Van Dam Avenue exit.

"Go ahead and laugh," Rizzo said. "Wasn't so God damned funny when I was running for my life."

Ralph Brancuso entered the office. The pieces of physical description Rizzo recalled fell into place. He waited for Fields to make the intro.

"Ralph," Fields said, coming around to the front of his desk "You remember Luke Rizzo from a couple of years back? We're going to explore how he can help the bureau with our project."

Brancuso extended his hand. "Yeah. Nice seeing you again."

Rizzo took the agent's stubby fingers into his grasp. "Same here, Agent Brancuso."

"Name's Ralph," Brancuso corrected. "Let's not get too damned formal."

Fields motioned to the sofa. "Have a seat, Ralph. He turned to Rizzo. "Before we start, you sure you don't want something—coffee, a soft drink?"

"Positive. Thanks."

Fields dragged a side chair up to the coffee table and placed the folder in front of him. "Okay, let's begin by providing a bit of background for Luke."

Rizzo stretched an arm across the top of the sofa and leaned back. He recalled Jack Fields conducted a similar briefing several years ago in this same office. Rizzo and his English client sat through a long-winded history lesson presenting the background of those eight saboteurs who, in 1942, landed on US shores. Rizzo figured this would be another long one.

"I told you about Umberto Salazar getting involved in drug smuggling, didn't I?"

"You mentioned it."

"He's hooked up with the Ortega cartel in Puerto Rico. The federal and local authorities down there have been fighting these monkeys for over a decade. They failed to stop the smuggling from Puerto Rico primarily due to the corruption on the island among the politicians, especially within all branches of law enforcement."

"Makes it a tad difficult to keep things under control."

"Ralph, here, would agree with you. He had a long and frustrating posting there in the FBI's drug enforcement area several years ago."

"Yeah," Brancuso snorted. "We didn't accomplish all that much, except we put a dent in the cigarette boat manufacturing business. We believed we were making progress and then the runners pulled an ol' switch-a-roo. They began using submersible vessels and fishing boats to transport drugs. These days they're back to the go-fast boats. At full throttle, those powerful two-engine fuckers reach speeds up to sixty miles an hour."

Fields continued. "Puerto Rico remains the number one transfer point for drugs to the States. The island is a US territory, so no customs to clear. Interdiction is stymied despite the use of Customs Border Protection aircraft and Coast Guard patrols."

Rizzo was aware of this trafficking problem from his years on the job.

"Cocaine is the leading drug smuggled from Puerto Rico," Fields said. "It's trafficked into the island from source countries like Colombia, Venezuela, and Peru. At night, the CBP pilots fly at about 3,500 feet, monitoring the waters between the Dominican Republic and the US Virgin Islands. They're equipped with infrared cameras, and yet the smugglers slip through."

"And with all those resources, we can't stop them?" Rizzo said.

Fields flipped open the folder. Picking up the top page, he read. *"To a great degree, the lack of success stopping this huge, profitable drug trade is the under-funding of this effort by the United States. Federal offices in charge of monitoring illegal trade and commerce are occupied with maintaining the heavily patrolled border between the US and Mexico."* The agent paused. "Here's the grabber. *The fallout is an estimated 90,000 plus kilos of cocaine circulated every year through Puerto Rico and into the United States".*

"I guess it's a serious problem for you guys," Rizzo said, smiling.

"You asked about our resources to stop them? The figures show our interdiction efforts are catching a mere twenty percent of the total."

This time Rizzo laughed. "Jesus, how about we put a blockade around the island?"

"Oh, that we could," Brancuso said.

Fields shook his head. "Yeah, and that would do it for tourism. As it is, Puerto Rico has a murder rate of six times the US national average. You can imagine how this affects tourism. Gang violence boosts the level of homicides. Drug wars between clans of dealers discourage law enforcement to crack down. Adds up to an insane and dangerous environment."

Leaning forward, Rizzo raised his eyes and squinted at Fields. "Am I to assume all this background you're feeding me is necessary to know in order to do whatever the bureau expects of me?"

"The answer is yes," Fields said and closed the folder. "We'd like you to go down to San Juan for about five days. To be fair, we want you to know the not-so-fun parts before we tell you about the fun parts. So why don't you take a day to think about it?"

"Don't you want to tell me what's involved before I give you an answer?"

"No, that's not possible. There's a need for absolute secrecy. Lives are at stake. We can't have anything leak. You're a former undercover so you can appreciate the precautions. Think about the assignment. Call me no later than Friday morning."

Rizzo eyed the folder on the coffee table. "How important would my role in this be?"

"The role is critical, but if not you, we have a backup. Another person with the same qualifications."

"You want to tell me what my qualifications are?"

Fields hesitated.

Rizzo grinned. "Admit it. You like my sense of humor."

"For now, this is the only thing I'll say, so no more questions until you decide. Your qualifications? You mean besides being a funny guy?" Fields held Rizzo's eyes. "It's your anonymity."

* * *

Rizzo exited the elevator on the fourth floor and headed toward his office, his mind lost in thought about his meeting with Fields. The metallic clang of the closing fire exit door at the end of the corridor caught his attention.

He looked toward the sound and remembered the times he would lose patience waiting for the elevator and use the emergency stairway to walk down the four flights. Was it another impatient tenant opting for the stairs?

His answer came in a flash. The *thump* made by pushing the bar on the inside of the door made Rizzo rein up. A form stepped through into the corridor. A short man with a bushy growth under his nose, he wore a Navy-blue ski parka and light tan khakis. The overhead neon fixture bounced off his slicked black hair. The man stood outside the doorway, his right hand behind him, his mouth spread in a thin-lipped sneer, his squinty eyes fixed on Rizzo's face.

Rizzo reached under his opened jacket and gripped the butt of his holstered Glock. He stared down the figure and waited.

"You Luke Rizzo?" the stranger's scratchy voice asked. The question was rhetorical. The man knew who he was.

"Who the hell are you?"

The stranger's right arm moved from behind. Rizzo spotted the weapon. In one quick motion, he dropped to his knees, raised the Glock in both hands, and fired, hitting the man in the right shoulder. The force spun the gunman around, his trigger-finger reflex sending a round from his weapon into the wall. The man struggled to regain his balance, steadied, then bolted through the fire exit door. His gun slipped from his weakened grasp before the door closed. Rizzo pursued, pushing his Glock out front.

The wounded man reached the landing between floors as Rizzo came through the door. "Freeeeeeeze, you piece of shit," Rizzo roared

For a split second, the man halted. He glared back at Rizzo while holding his injured right shoulder, then he let go. He turned on the landing to continue his descent to the next floor, and in his rush, he reached out for the left side handrail for support and missed. Rizzo watched him take two stumbling steps. His torso twisted, trying to grab at the handrail again. He fell backward, bouncing down the stairs like a rubber ball, his head careening off the sharp metal edges of each step, his crumpled form coming to rest on the third-floor landing.

No movement or signs of breathing. Rizzo approached the body with caution. He bent over the man and put two fingers to the carotid artery. The absence of a pulse and the pooling of blood forming under the attacker's head lent support to Rizzo's suspicion. The man was very dead.

Rizzo returned to his office and telephoned 9-1-1. The two uniformed patrol officers from the Thirteenth Precinct on West Twenty-first Street were first to arrive. Officer Lopez, young, in his early twenties, closed off the stairwell entrances on both floors with yellow crime scene tape. Officer Grimes, the senior of the two, radioed for backup to help secure the scene and for assistance from his supervisor. Tenant chaos on the two affected floors took time to clear. Once the patrol supervisor and support arrived, the officers secured both levels.

Rizzo stayed in his office out-of-the-way and waited for the investigators from the Thirteenth's Detective Squad to arrive. Rizzo knew Vince Christopher, one of the two detectives, as someone he often swapped war stories with at a local cop hangout in the Chelsea area. Rizzo described the way the shooting went down and how the man's fall happened. Satisfied, Christopher reminded him he needed to appear at the precinct to make a formal statement then left to return to the crime scene.

It took almost four hours for the technicians to finish their work. The investigators completed their examination, made sketches, and photographed the scene. Detective Christopher found the man's wallet and driver's license and called in his identity to the desk officer at the Thirteenth. A quick criminal background check revealed he was a Russian hired gun named

Ivan Kozlov, thirty-eight years old, and in the country illegally. No surprise.

The crime scene unit inventoried the dead man's weapon and his wallet. The medical examiner investigator supervised the hefting of the body bag down three flights of stairs to a waiting transport vehicle. Rizzo stood watching in the stairwell, mindful of the fact he might have been the one in the bag had he not shot first.

Grimes informed Detective Christopher what he'd learned from Rizzo, and after completing his initial report, he and Officer Lopez left the building. Rizzo returned again to his office and fell into his chair. Elbows on his desk, he braced his head with his hands, squeezed his eyes shut, and reflected on how close he came again to taking a bullet.

Images of the past two and a half weeks flickered through his mind like a miniature movie: The *Guayabera* shirt Rabbit wore when he arrived at Grand Central Station; the faces of the two Mexican teens coming out of the Corona house; the appearance of Rita Sands with the bullet hole in her forehead; the weapon in the twin's hand hanging out the SUV's window. Now, this inept hitman trying to take him out. *Jesus, how much longer do I have to put up with this shit?*

Rizzo rotated his chair, leaned back and faced the window. He gazed off into the past, rolling over images of all the take-downs and arrests he'd made during his time on the job. These were accomplishments that provided meaningful satisfaction, the reason he joined the NYPD.

His thoughts turned to the many occasions he stared death in the face. Oddly enough, those experiences never fazed him. His indifference came from the feeling of pride he enjoyed while wearing the blue uniform of New York's Finest. In later years, he accepted without question the inherent dangers described by his job as a narcotics detective. He served at the behest of the city he loved, protecting its population.

It was something else now. Working in the private sector lacked the noble purpose offered by his former NYPD career. And for that reason threats to his life became more personal. He spun around in his chair and smirked. "Fuck you, Salazar," he said in a loud voice.

He bounced forward, reached for the phone and called Jack Fields.

"Jack, it's Rizzo. I don't need to wait until Friday. I'm in."

Chapter Thirty

Rizzo followed Jack Fields down the Berber carpeted corridor. The wall along the way was decorated with several Leroy Neiman lithographs of famous sports celebrities. They moved past a series of doors before entering the outer office of Carter Brooke. A Miss Moneypenny look-alike seated at her desk shot them a warm smile and gestured with a raised hand toward Brooke's closed door. Fields acknowledged her with a thumbs up, pushed open the door, and allowed Rizzo to enter first.

Brooke rose from his desk and came around to shake Rizzo's hand. "Mr. Rizzo, welcome. So glad you came." He pointed toward the leather sofa at the windowless corner of the room and told him, "Please, take a seat."

Ralph Brancuso, already seated on the sofa, lifted and greeted Rizzo with a halfhearted wave. "Hey, Rizzo, nice to see you again."

"Same here, Agent—ah, Ralph." Rizzo laughed and dropped into the sofa at the opposite end.

Brooke and Fields chose the Barcelona chairs at the corners of the slate-top coffee table.

Rizzo noticed the three agents, attired similarly in traditional FBI uniforms, wore dark blue, single-breasted suits with soft-padded shoulders. White shirts served as backdrops to the single varying element of their appearance, their ties; sailboat images on Fields, blue and white stripes on Brancuso, and solid red silk fabric on Brooke.

Rizzo, out-of-place in his informal Harris tweed sports jacket and open-collar shirt, let it pass with a lack of concern.

A full coffee carafe, cups, and saucers sat on a buffet against the back wall. "Anyone for coffee?" Brooke asked.

No one responded, and Brooke signaled to Fields to start.

Fields turned to face Rizzo. "You asked me yesterday about your qualifications. I told you it was your anonymity . . . aside from your sense of humor."

Rizzo snickered.

The agent continued. "Did I mention that many in Puerto Rico's law enforcement are in the pocket of the Ortega cartel? At a minimum, the cartel is familiar with anyone on the island with a badge. An impossible situation, at the very least, for Police Superintendent Emilio Sanchez. His efforts to have his investigators conduct undercover operations?" Fields chuckled. "Forget it. They're exposed before they begin."

"Even federal agents?" Rizzo said in a skeptical tone as if it were a mathematical impossibility for an FBI agent to be corrupt.

Fields glared at him. "We believe our agents assigned to San Juan are clean. The problem is they're well known to every waiter, taxi driver, and uniformed police officer. Nothing remains a secret in Puerto Rico for long."

"And you're confident no one knows me?"

"Ever been to the island on assignment for the NYPD? Or on a job for a client? Even on vacation?"

"Nope. But I've had the pleasure of arresting quite a few Puerto Rican drug dealers during my years on the job."

"Well, there's no reason to think anyone would recognize you. You're simply an American couple enjoying vacation time in the sun."

Rizzo jerked back into the sofa's cushion like a boxer ducking a right cross. He narrowed his eyes and said with a disbelieving edge, "Couple?"

"Yes. It's something we'd like you to consider." Fields bobbed his head like he was trying to short-circuit a rebuttal. "The assignment doesn't hang on it. You could go solo. We reasoned if you were with your wife, it would enhance your believability—a tourist couple on the island."

"Wait—wait. Hold on. You told me back when we first talked about a job for me, there'd be some danger involved. I remember you said I'd have the bureau's resources. A backup. From what you tell me now, your resources seem pretty lame."

Fields looked to Carter Brooke, received a nod from the man, and turned back to Rizzo. "When we first talked about this, we hadn't firmed up what role you could play. Since then, our plan has taken shape. Your involvement would be minimal. You would function as a conduit of information. Nothing more."

"Explain that, please."

Fields glanced at Brooke again. "Here's a summary. The FBI has a source embedded in the Ortega cartel. The organization controls most of Puerto Rico's drug trade. Our undercover works at night. He's a blackjack dealer in a luxury hotel-casino in San Juan. The hotel is where you'd be staying." Fields paused. "A five-star facility, I might add." He said it as though Rizzo's decision rested on this perk.

Fields continued. "Not long ago our asset got word to us of a major shipment of cocaine about to launch off the coast soon. Two thirty-five-foot go-fast boats, each loaded with 1,000 pounds of cocaine in twenty waterproof bales. That forty-bale-shipment has a street value of about $37 million."

Rizzo's eyes widened. "You can't interdict the launch, bust it before it gets underway?"

"Let me finish. We could, but we're not. That would allow the big fish on our scope to escape. Listen a minute. You'll enjoy the rest of the story."

"Go ahead," Rizzo said and leaned forward, resting his elbows on his knees.

"Okay. Here's how the plan goes. The boats launch after midnight. No date yet, and we're uncertain from where, but about seventy-five percent of the time it's Fajardo, a coastal fishing town about thirty miles east of San Juan. They cast off under darkness for La Romana, a secluded port in the Dominican Republic. They toss a blue tarp over each boat and lie low throughout the daylight hours. At sundown, they refuel and set out again. Here's the part that should light your fire."

Rizzo picked up his chin. "I'm ready."

"Late at night, they're scheduled to meet up with—" Fields let a beat go by— "Umberto Salazar's yacht, the Swan. He'll be returning from a cruise to Aruba."

The room became silent. Rizzo's pulse quickened. His attention shot sky-high. He raised his eyes. "You mean, he's taking on the shipment?" he said with a quick, breathy laugh.

"You got it."

"I can't believe he's opening the door to—"

"Wait. Here's the rest of it. Two CBP aircraft track the yacht's journey from Aruba. They follow the yacht to the rendezvous point in the Caribbean. The pilots are in constant contact with two Coast Guard fast-response cutters along the route. The two cutters, ported in San Juan, are out in the dark, waiting. Also, the Coast Guard Air Station in Borinquen dispatches two well-armed Pave Hawk helicopters." Fields waited, and settled his gaze on Rizzo's amused face.

"What's the location where all this takes place?" Rizzo asked.

"Their plan, as our undercover explained, is for the go-fast boats to rendezvous with Salazar's yacht at a point west of Jamaica. We wait until they load on the shipment and secure it in the yacht's hold. We don't want to give them a chance to dump the bales overboard. After they're loaded and stored below, the two Coast Guard cutters move in. If the go-fast boats break for La Romana, no problem. One of the CPB planes follows. The Dominican Republic police will be waiting."

"Where is the yacht supposed to deliver the cocaine?"

"To a port in Cancún, Mexico. Members of the Sinaloa cartel are waiting to offload it."

"Jesus, your guy is good. What fantastic info."

"Yeah, and that's why we go to great lengths to protect him. About a month ago he came close to being compromised. The threat was temporarily squelched. A case of mistaken identity. Regardless, we're pulling him out after this operation. We believe they're watching him."

"Can he become a liability to the operation?"

"That's where you come in."

Rizzo glanced up at Fields, meeting his eyes before he turned away. "And whatever part I play can't happen unless my wife is with me?"

"No, no. Not what I said. We're suggesting she go along to add credibility to your cover. You're a vacationing couple. That's all. Better than a single guy hanging around at the hotel pool ogling the bikinis."

Rizzo laughed. "And what role do you intend for me in this fantastic takedown of Salazar?"

"You would be the conduit between the undercover and me. Simple as that."

"Simple how?"

"You would need to spend time each night in the hotel-casino. Once you spot his signal, you relay it to me by telephone at a secured number. The signal indicates the shipment is leaving the following night."

"The rest of the time I do what?"

"You're on vacation, for Christ's sake. You do everything vacationers do." Fields glanced at Brooke again. "At the bureau's expense, of course. There's not much that should concern you. No communication with the undercover, no direct contact whatsoever. Getting the sign from him requires nothing more than your two eyes."

Rizzo sat back and pressed his head against the leather pillow. *This sounds too easy. Something always screws up and things get hairy.* He attempted to shut out everything around him. His concentration settled on the ceiling fixture while taking in several breaths through his nose and then expelling them from his mouth—a breathing technique he used to slow his heart rate while working out at the gym or taking down a drug dealer.

"When do I leave?"

"We believe the launch will happen toward the end of next week. You should go down there right after this weekend in the event the cartel pushes it up. The timing work for you?"

"For me, yes. For my wife, well, I don't know. I'll talk with her tonight, see what she thinks about joining the party."

"Okay, but we need to know about her one way or the other by mid-day tomorrow. There are arrangements to be made, plane tickets, hotel reservation, coordination with Police Superintendent Sanchez."

"No one else? He's your backup for me in San Juan?"

"Hey, Sanchez won first prize in the island's Police Academy's marksman contest three years in a row." Fields laughed.

"Oh, well, now that puts me at ease. Do I go armed? I'll need authorization for that."

"You won't need a weapon. Anyway, how do you conceal it in a bathing suit, or in shorts and a golf shirt? Too hot this time of year to be wearing a jacket. More important, you'd raise unwanted attention and concern with casino security if you showed up armed."

"Then I'm on my own, no protection?"

"No, we'll have your back."

"I'd be happier with my own weapon. My Sig Sauer nine fits nicely under a shirt in my belly band holster. Daytime, I can leave it in the hotel room safe. At night when I'm dressed up cruising the town, I'll carry it. Except when I'm in the casino. Or skinny-dipping in the pool."

Rizzo scrutinized him. He saw equal parts amusement and concern in his expression. Fields grinned and Rizzo knew he won the point.

"Okay. I'll prepare the proper documentation for you before you leave. Don't forget to inform the agent at the Delta check-in you've got an unloaded weapon in your suitcase." Fields turned to Carter Brooke. "I'm taking Mr. Rizzo down to my office, fill him in on the nitty-gritty details now that he's committed to helping us."

Brooke and Brancuso stood and shook hands with Rizzo.

"Welcome aboard," Brooke said. "So glad you agreed to join us."

"Yeah, and don't forget your Speedo and sunscreen," Brancuso added with a smile as warm as a December afternoon.

On his way out the office door, Rizzo looked back at Brancuso. "I'll send you photos."

Brancuso laughed and shot him with his index finger. "You do that."

* * *

At sea in the Caribbean, immersed up to his belly in the swirling water of the Jacuzzi on the upper aft deck of the *Swan*, Umberto Salazar held a *piña colada* in one hand and a thirty-four dollar Cuban cigar in his other. The radio on a tray and clipped to the tub's ledge was on speaker.

"You make sure you're there a day or two before the shipment leaves Fajardo."

"They know I come?" Bodrov asked.

"Of course they do. Listen, you think Ortega would let us sign off without making a physical count of the shipment? He knows we're not stupid. The Sinaloa people in Mexico are expecting a ton of cocaine . . . forty bales. We need to count them before they load them on the go-fast boats. It would be our asses if the Mexicans were shortchanged. We'd be dead meat."

"Understand," Bodrov said. "I book flight for Wednesday. Is quick enough?"

"Should be. The launch is set for this Saturday night. Gives me plenty of time to get the Swan up the Caribbean to the rendezvous spot for the loading."

"Oh, Umberto. I send Ivan Kozlov to take care of detective."

"Christ, I hope so. I'm tired of your Russian guns botching their assignments. Maybe you should hire a hitman from the Italian Mafia for a change." Salazar chortled and drew in on his *Cohiba Esplendido*.

"I look into that, Umberto."

"Good. "Call me when you get to San Juan. We'll still be in Aruba."

"Okay, Umberto. Bye."

* * *

Rizzo settled on the sofa in Fields's office and didn't wait to be asked. "Jack, I could use a coffee now."

Fields made the call to Rachel, who quickly delivered two mugs.

The glass and steel office towers framed in the window behind Fields's desk captured Rizzo's gaze. How would he break the news to Flo when he arrived home? Despite what Fields said about her adding credibility to his cover, he was not going to force the issue. If she said she didn't want to go, that was it. He'd settle for ogling bikinis.

Fields came to the sofa with the green folder in his hand and sat. His taut face and eyes took on a conspiratorial look. Rizzo wondered: is he about to drop another unexpected twist?

The agent laid the folder on the coffee table. "I'm going to share with you a major confidence because I want you to understand and appreciate how important your part is to this operation."

Rizzo set his mug down and lowered his eyes, resisting a quip that crossed his mind. Not the time to make light of the situation. "Since it involves Salazar," he said, "I get the drift."

"I'm glad because the asset you will be observing . . . I repeat, observing, has been especially valuable to the bureau for the last several years. Also, he's turned around his personal life at great risk to atone for his past mistakes."

"Former druggie?"

"Good guess."

"An easy one. Where'd you find him?"

"He's the son of a high-ranking Puerto Rico police officer killed in a drug-bust operation ten years ago. The kid went off the rails after that. A few years later, they busted him in a drug scam. That's when we learned about his father."

"How'd you turn him?"

"The bureau offered to send him stateside to a rehabilitation program after he served his time—eighteen months. Then we would give him a chance to work undercover for us when he completed his rehabilitation. He agreed. Before he entered the Guaynabo Federal Detention Center, we provided him with a complete set of false identification. We didn't want anyone connecting him to his deceased father."

"Wait a moment. You saying they imprisoned him under a phony name?"

"Right. Prison officials never knew about it."

"Jesus, how the hell you pull that off?"

"By limiting the knowledge to Sanchez and me."

"It had to include those in the bureau who produced his identity documents, right?"

"No chance. We never revealed the real person the false documents were meant for. We hid his existence from the bureau's San Juan field office, and all of Puerto Rico's law enforcement. Except for Sanchez. All with the approval of Washington, of course."

"How'd he come to be working for the cartel?"

"Five years ago, he infiltrated the Ortega organization through contacts he made in prison. They used him initially in low-level smuggling operations. Gradually, he gained the trust of a person higher up. He became exposed to their planning. Over time, he provided useful information to Sanchez through a pre-arranged coded system. The chief would pass the info on to our head agent in the San Juan field office. The agent knew enough never to question the source. Minor stuff. Nothing significant like this drug shipment about to go down."

Fields turned over a page from the folder and picked it up. "This from Sanchez back a month ago," and he read: '*I received information a member of the Ortega cartel claimed he saw our undercover speaking to a known FBI agent in a restaurant in Bayamon. Later, the man admitted he made a mistake. The person he saw was someone else.*'" He shoved the page back into the folder. "The original claim was a phony. We knew that. Then again, we had no way of telling if it was a ploy to lower his guard."

"Maybe," Rizzo said. "I wouldn't be surprised if this was an attempt to discredit him by some low-level grunt jealous of his status in the cartel."

"That too; nevertheless we can't risk it. We're pulling him out after this operation."

"Who knows about him?"

"The three of us here and Sanchez in San Juan. You're the fifth. While we trust you, we won't give you his name. We'll show you his photo. You'll etch it in your memory so you'll recognize him. He won't know you, but he'll be aware someone in the casino is watching for his signal. So, should he run into trouble, you can't be connected to him."

Rizzo picked up his mug of coffee. Cold. He'd left it untouched while Fields gripped his attention with the undercover's story. He set it down and wrinkled his nose.

"How about a fresh one?" Fields asked.

Rizzo squinted. "You got much more to tell me? For example, how this is gonna work?"

"Oh, yeah. That's next." Fields got to his feet and opened the office door. "Rachel, think we can have two refills before Mr. Rizzo develops withdrawal pains?"

Rachel delivered two new mugs, picked up the old ones, and left.

Rizzo rocked his shoulders. "It's not the coffee giving me the shakes, it's the complexity of this operation. I'm a small town narc, used to nothing more sophisticated than a shootout in Harlem."

Fields laughed. "I'm convinced you can handle this. Which brings me to what we expect of you."

"Do I take notes?"

Fields held his eyes for a moment. "Only if you suspect you're getting senile."

Rizzo squirmed back into the sofa. "Okay, give."

258 - CROSSING INTO DARKNESS

"Very simple. Each night you visit the hotel's casino. You vary the times. Should you elect to take your wife, you can go in together or go in alone. Your call. Stay as long as you like. Play the slots, or try your luck at poker. You're a vacationing couple behaving like tourists. The undercover will be at one of the three blackjack tables. If you play, avoid playing at his. When you arrive on the first day, stroll around the casino like any newcomer would do, trying to get the lay of the land."

"Can I keep my winnings?"

Fields ignored him. "Each night, make certain to walk by his table. Not right away. Anytime between your gambling activities. You're looking for the 'go' sign." He paused and locked on to Rizzo's face. "Do you know the difference between a full Windsor knot and a four-in-hand?"

"You mean, like the way one knots a tie?"

"Exactly."

"Yeah, although I haven't worn a tie since my First Holy Communion."

"However, you can distinguish the difference from a distance, moving at speeds slower than the Road Runner?"

Rizzo nodded. "My eyesight is still 20/20."

"Wonderful, because the sign you're looking for is based on the way the dealer knotted his tie—normally a four-in-hand but changed to a full Windsor—if the launch is set to go the following night."

"Wow! Who in the hell would notice the way anyone knotted his tie? It's far out-ingenious."

The agent laughed again.

"You mean if I spot it when I arrive, I shouldn't race to a phone to call you?"

"You do, and we'll shoot you before you reach the door."

Fields jumped to his feet. He walked to his desk with the green folder in his hand. Rizzo watched him. Had he pissed him off with his wiseass comment?

"I'm kidding, Jack. Relax, I know the drill. I'll hang in, play the slots, a few hands of poker, then wander up to my room."

Fields turned to him, his collegial expression back in place. "Yep, and you make a call on a pre-paid cell phone we give you to a private number in the US. You ask to speak with a fictitious name. You'll hear, 'Sorry, wrong number.' The phone will go dead. The next day you lose the cell phone in the Caribbean. We'll give you the phone, the number, and the phony name before you leave for San Juan."

"That's all? I won't have to shoot my way out of the hotel?"

"Uh-uh. For all your heavy lifting, you're treated to an all-expense vacation in sunny San Juan. And I mean all-expense, including your lost gambling money, so keep track of it. And yes, you keep your winnings. Whatever pleasure strikes your fancy while you're there, big or small, the bureau is picking up the tab."

"Man, you can't beat that."

"Oh, I almost forgot. You'll receive double your normal daily rate for the days you're there, including your travel time. Any questions?"

"Damn, I don't see how my wife can turn down this deal."

"As to the reason you give her for this vacation trip, we'll leave the invention up to you."

"Thanks. My wife's a savvy woman, but don't worry. I'll schmooze her about why we got so lucky."

"Which brings up a major concern. We hope your wife agrees to go with you for the reason we stated earlier. If she does, you can't share with her any information about the operation. You're not to reveal the real purpose of the trip. No reference to the undercover or—"

"I understand."

"It's vital you do."

"I get it, Jack, for Christ's sake."

Chapter Thirty-One

R izzo waited until after dinner to drop the bomb. The dishwasher loaded, and the leftover fried chicken stored in the refrigerator, they moved into the living room. Flo sat in her favorite chair and reached for the TV remote. He stopped her before she turned on the set.

Her eyes remained on his face as Rizzo spelled out the FBI's unusual vacation offer. He wrestled with a variety of plausible reasons for being offered this assignment and settled on a scenario in the neighborhood of the real thing without giving away the store.

He hated lying to her, but it was critical to keep her in the dark, for her sake, and to safeguard the integrity of the plan. Sounding credible was important to minimize the questions she would ask. Rizzo couldn't judge to what degree of success he was having. If pressed to describe the expression on her face, he'd use the term befuddled.

She listened with her eyes squeezed closed, and her head bobbing like one of those plastic dolls on the dashboard of a pickup. When she opened them and ceased bobbing, she said, "I'm sorry, hon. Tell me again what they expect you to do?" The expression on her face sailed from suspicion to resentment to tenderness, all within a half second.

Jesus, I should have told them I'd go alone. "I'm there to pick up an important message at the front desk of our hotel. It's supposed to arrive between Wednesday and Sunday. They don't know which of the five days. Then I call it into the FBI's New York office. Simple."

"That's why they're giving us a paid vacation in San Juan?"

He tried not to look at her when he added, "Plus, they're willing to pay me double my daily rate for the time we're there."

"And they don't want to use an agent on their staff because . . . .?"

"I told you." His voice cracked, and he swallowed hard. The guilt was fast becoming a mountain. "Because they suspect one of their two agents in their San Juan field office is on the take. They can't risk using the wrong agent."

Flo held his eyes. "I don't know, hon. Will it be dangerous?"

He broke from her stare. "Sweetheart. You don't have to go with me if—"

"Of course I want to go with you. You want me to, don't you?"

"Certainly. But if you're worried, I'm not pressuring you."

"It's not that . . . aah . . . well . . . I just worry you'll leave me alone in the hotel for long periods of time."

"Not gonna happen. I'll be with you every minute, day and night."

"You understand, Jabba, my Lochinvar, won't be there to watch over me."

"I know," he said, feeling a heaviness in his chest.

Flo took a deep breath through her nose, held it for a moment and let it out very slowly through her mouth. Her eyes found his face, and she gave a resigned shrug.

* * *

Rizzo raised his head from the pillow. The lighted digital clock displayed one-fifteen. Awake for the past two hours, he struggled with sleep refusing to come.

Next to him, Flo's breathing steadied. Given the fact they'd climbed into bed a few minutes after eleven, he judged she was not yet into a deep sleep pattern. He watched her for a while, wondering if he should wake her now or wait until the morning to tell her.

Flo made the decision for him. She rolled up on her elbow and rested her chin in her hand. "What's the matter, hon? Can't you sleep?"

"I thought you were asleep."

"I was until I felt you bouncing around like a rodeo rider."

"I'm sorry. This San Juan trip is making me restless." He pushed upright against the headboard and reached for the night table light. "Flo, since you're awake, I need to say something to you."

She remained propped on her elbow and gazed up at him with a sleepy smile. "I kinda suspected that." She plumped her pillow with two deliberate punches and placed it behind her head. "Okay, what's bothering you?"

"Maybe we should forget about you going with me to Puerto Rico." His tone was firm. He didn't expect she would resist.

Flo sat up, folded her arms and turned to look at him. "Why? Didn't you say it could be fun? I'm up for a little fun in the sun."

"Yeah, I'm—"

"You said you'd be with me every minute of the time, didn't you?"

"Yes, I said—"

"So I'll always be safe?"

"Well, yeah, but there's always—"

"And this assignment is important to you, right? And to the FBI?"

"Very. But I can do it alone, sweetheart. You don't have to come with me."

"Then how come they wanted you to take me?"

Rizzo hesitated. *Damn! Did I tell her that?* He glanced at Flo. The vein in his right temple throbbed. "Okay, I'll level with you. They told me, with you along, it would enhance my cover. You know, just one of many vacationing couples. We wouldn't appear suspicious to anyone." Rizzo laughed. "Me? Suspicious?"

Her brow rippled with lines, "Hon, tell me again. Is what they expect you to do dangerous?"

"Don't be silly. The FBI wouldn't suggest you come with me if they believed I would be in danger. But in this type of work, there's always some risk."

"And with me along, the chances are reduced?"

"Well, yeah, but there's no guarantee—"

"Turn off the light, sweet pea, and go to sleep. I'm packing my sexiest bathing suit."

Chapter Thirty-Two

Rizzo pushed back into the headrest after the plane reached cruising altitude, and his gaze followed the mountains of puffy cumulus clouds sailing by the window. He might have dozed off if not for the image of a murdered Rita Sands rummaging around in his thoughts. The bullet hole in the center of her forehead became vivid as the day he found her in her apartment. It saddened him that the woman's involvement with the Russian, Ilya Bodrov, became a fatal failure in judgment.

The case would be no easy ground ball for Duggan and the Detective Squad of the One-Seven. Doubtful they would bring a quick resolution to the murder. He knew if this FBI operation took down the Salazar organization, Bodrov would go with it. Then he would burn his ass for killing Rita Sands.

Their 11:59 a.m. Delta flight had taken off from JFK on time. They were scheduled to arrive at San Juan's *Luis Muñoz Marín* International Airport in under four hours. He smiled at Flo, who was smart enough to pack a book, a John le Carré thriller. She started the novel while they waited at their departure gate for their boarding call and was well into her read. Rizzo occupied himself during this time by scanning faces of the surrounding travelers in the area, studying their behavior. Everyone appeared suspicious to Rizzo, including the Delta agent.

He was happy Flo decided to come with him, despite her initial reluctance. Her final decision to jump aboard was a welcomed surprise. He loved her even more for it. Now, to keep her safe. To keep them both safe.

Raising her eyes from her book, Flo asked, "What's the name of our hotel?"

"*La Concha.*"

"Aha, the shell. Near the beach?"

"A few steps from the rear of the hotel. Googled the place last night. Looks great. Five stars."

Flo smiled and went back to her le Carré thriller.

An hour and a half into the flight, the service cart came rolling down the aisle. The flight attendant paused at each row, taking drink orders. She came abreast of them, and Rizzo tapped Flo's arm.

"You want something, sweetheart?"

Flo bookmarked the novel and rested it on her drop-down tray. "Yes, that would nice." Smiling up at the attendant, she asked, "Do you have a Cabernet or a Merlot?"

"We have both," she said. "Which would you prefer?"

"A Merlot, please."

"And sir, anything for you?"

"A Sprite would be fine." Turning to Flo, he said, "Glad you didn't ask for a Jack Daniels. I would be so embarrassed. We'd have to join the Mile High Club." The flight attendant giggled.

Flo elbowed him. "Hush, you silly goose."

Rizzo credit-carded for the wine, and once the cart moved off to the next row, he whispered, "I miss the days of full meals and free drinks."

"As my old Dad used to say, 'Dem days are gone forever.'"

"Ain't that the truth?"

* * *

At three-fifty, the plane touched down on the San Juan airport runway and taxied to the arrival gate. The moment the seat belt light turned off, passengers unbuckled, and a symphony of clicking sounds filled the cabin. Before Rizzo loosened his, a host of people with their carry-on bags in their arms crammed the aisle and waited for the ground crew to complete the docking procedure.

The mild weather of seventy-nine degrees, according to the digital readout on the wall in the baggage claim area, welcomed them to their tropical adventure. At the carousel, Rizzo examined those passengers crowding around the moving belt. The two uniformed police officers standing near the exit paid them no notice. They retrieved their bags and headed to the taxi stand. Within minutes, they boarded a mini-van.

"*La Concha* Hotel," Rizzo told the driver.

* * *

Flo crossed the room to the window and drew open the curtains, exposing a narrow balcony and a sun-sparkled vista of the Caribbean shoreline. "Oh, my," she exclaimed. "This view is spectacular."

Rizzo closed the doors to the wardrobe after hanging up his new blue blazer and slacks, and he came up behind Flo. He rested his hands on her shoulders and looked out at the scene eight floors below that captured her attention. A postcard view of beige-tinted sand and rows of blue reclining lounges dotted the expanse of beach. The lounges, occupied by a handful of sunbathers, stopped twenty yards short of the waterline. Two young couples splashed about in the rolling waves. Off to the left, a rocky jetty reached out to serve as a breaker between the *La Concha* and the hotel next door."

"Not many people on the beach or in the water. You suppose sharks are lurking about?"

Rizzo squeezed. "You mean, besides me?"

"You're not a shark, are you?" Flo reached back to pat his hand.

"Not to worry," he said, nuzzling her neck. "There are sharks, yeah, much farther out. It's rare they would come in close to the shore. At least that's what I read in the guidebook I bought over the weekend."

"Tell me, why so few people in the water?"

"It's late in the afternoon. Besides, didn't you notice all those sun worshipers by the pool as we came through the lobby? I suspect that's where the late-day action takes place."

Her face blossomed with a smile. "Action? Is that where you'd go if you wanted action?"

"Don't be crazy." Rizzo turned her into his arms. "I got all the action I need here."

"You got that right, sweet pea." Flo took him behind his neck and pulled him down for a long kiss.

They came up for air, and Rizzo said, "Suppose we finish the unpacking later? Let's jump out of these clothes and shower off the plane ride. Then get into real action."

Flo giggled. "I'll race you."

* * *

Fields looked at his watch and then at the speakerphone. "Yes, Emilio. He arrived this afternoon. Checked into the hotel around five. He's there now."

"Alone?"

Fields considered the question. Was he guilty of not telling Sanchez about Rizzo's wife? He couldn't imagine how he'd overlooked that. Then again, Rizzo didn't confirm she was going until late Friday.

"Jack, you there?"

"Oh, sorry, Emilio. I was trying to remember if I'd told you about the wife. Yes, she decided to go with him."

"The last we spoke, you said it wasn't one-hundred percent."

"I apologize. I never got back. Yeah, she's with him."

"*Bueno.* Makes his presence in the hotel so much more credible."

Seated across from him on the sofa, Ralph Brancuso, his elbows on his thighs, whispered, "Jack, ask him if the undercover reported any more signs of being watched."

Fields raised his eyes, looking uncertain he heard the question. A moment later, he acknowledged Brancuso's query with a headshake and repeated the question to Sanchez.

"Nothing worrisome, but it doesn't mean we can lighten up."

"You're right. The longer he stays in place, the greater the risk. Someone in the cartel doesn't like him, doesn't like his access to top-level people. Luke Rizzo suggested one of the lower grunts might be envious and trying to discredit him."

"That may be so. In any event, we can't do anything without chancing full exposure."

"We're close to the end of this operation," Fields said. "When it's over, we bring him to the states. Meanwhile, let's stay informed. I'll speak to you tomorrow."

"*Esta bien. Adios.*"

"Bye, Emilio."

"Doesn't sound too worried," Brancuso said. "The jealous-punk idea? Probably closer to the truth than anything else."

"Yeah. Let's hope that's all it is. You set to leave?"

"Bags packed and booked on an eight-thirty Delta flight tonight. I arrive in San Juan around midnight." Brancuso stood and turned for the door.

"Got your disguises ready?"

The agent stopped and laughed. "Yeah. Fake mustache and dark glasses. You think I'll need any more than that?"

Fields grinned. "I hope it doesn't become impossible to keep tabs on them. Around the hotel, on the beach, and in the restaurants . . . shouldn't be a problem. It's when they're walking around out in public, watching them becomes sticky. Stay close."

Brancuso peeled off his words in a measured tone. "Okay, Jack. It's not my first rodeo. I'll handle it."

"Sorry, Ralph. I know you will."

* * *

Rizzo admitted the beauty of the hotel's *Perla* Restaurant was at the top of all his dining experiences. He grinned, watching Flo's head swivel from side to side, her eyes flashing around at the luxurious setting. She was a child on Christmas morning.

Her gaze traveled up to the hotel's signature image, the underside of a contoured, white shell-shaped ceiling. Flo's concentration stayed suspended until she lowered her attention, and her eyes landed on Rizzo's smiling face.

"Oh, darlin', this is dreamy. I feel like I'm sitting in the middle of a seashell. It's *Alice in Wonderland*."

Rizzo, delighted in her pure childlike enthusiasm, hoisted his glass of sparkling water. "Let's toast the shell's newest pearl, Florence Mae Rizzo. Lucky for me, I found my precious nugget before anyone else."

Flo raised her wineglass, and they clinked. Meeting Rizzo's gaze, she said, "Darlin', you are the most romantic man in the entire universe. Thank you. And you're so handsome in your new blazer."

"Well, this has to be the world's most romantic setting. I have to rise to the occasion."

She scanned the restaurant again. "This table—it's so perfect. Even though you fibbed to get it. You're a sly devil."

Earlier, Rizzo called the Perla from their room to make a dinner reservation. He told the hostess it was their anniversary without defining the notable event. The woman responded with what sounded like a long *aah* and a promise of a good table. To his surprise, *a good table* turned out to be a two-top situated against the beach-side glass window. The shell-canopied restaurant sat on a lighted infinity pool elevated above the beach, and their table's location treated them to a breathtaking panoramic view of the Caribbean.

Their waiter, attired in a red velour vest over a white dress shirt, arrived to take their order. His nametag read Sebastian.

Rizzo peeked at Flo, who was studying the menu the way a law graduate crams for the bar exam. "You ready, sweetheart?" She smiled and recited her selections.

For starters, Flo ordered the grilled prawns in coconut sauce, while Rizzo settled for the seafood chowder in lobster broth. Then, changing her mind several times, Flo opted for the grilled swordfish steak with green papaya slaw as her main course. Rizzo chose the snapper with octopus creole sauce.

Sebastian placed their appetizers in front of them, and the aroma of prawns and lobster broth cast a hypnotizing effect over the table. Flo sipped her white wine, and Rizzo his sparkling water, their attention fastened on their starters. Neither attempted to eat. A quiet moment passed before Rizzo reached for his spoon. "Let's see if it tastes as yummy as it smells."

They savored a leisure hour of dining before Sebastian returned to take dessert orders. They both declined, confessing, "No room."

Later, Sebastian dropped off the check and removed their empty plates while his eyes flitted to and from Rizzo's face.

Aware he was being studied, Rizzo became slightly self-conscious. He gazed around at the other diners. "I may never leave this place," he said. "The presentation of our food—beautiful. It's what a five-star restaurant is all about. This could turn me into a snob."

"Hon, you're already that," Flo said. She smiled at the young waiter and turned back to Rizzo. "The Palm in Manhattan. Remember? They've spoiled you beyond belief."

"Yeah, except that's an atmosphere of a testosterone-laden steakhouse. This restaurant's classy ambiance is worlds apart."

The waiter's face broke into a broad grin as he stepped closer to Rizzo. "Pardon me, sir. I thought you looked familiar when you came in. When your missus referred to The Palm, I knew it was you."

Rizzo went on alert. He looked up and narrowed his eyes in disbelief. "You know me?"

"You're that detective, the one who stopped the crazy Cuban from blowing up The Palm several years back. Right?"

A red flag went up. *Should I be flattered or should I be concerned? Seems I'm not as anonymous as Jack Fields believes.*

"Jesus," Rizzo said, "I can't imagine how you remembered me after all this time. Were you working there?"

Sebastian laughed. "Not when it happened. A year later. I heard about your heroics like every other employee did. We all came to spot you whenever you came in."

"You live in San Juan now, do you?"

"I was born and raised here, in Santurce. I dropped out of college to go to New York for a few years to make real money. I got hired at the Palm."

Flo reached out to shake his hand. "Well, Sebastian, I'm sure my husband is pleased by your recognition. Thanks for sharing it."

"Yeah," Rizzo said, taking his hand. "Here for a vacation, and I'm outed by a fan."

"I wish you much enjoyment during your stay in San Juan." Sebastian motioned to the check folder. "I'll take that whenever you're ready," and walked off.

"Well, that was nice," Flo said.

"Not if I'm outed too often."

"You're being modest."

"Not really. Anxious? Yes." Rizzo glanced at his watch. "Nine-thirty. Let's cruise the hotel-casino for a while, scope out the action. After, we can stop off at the lobby bar for a nightcap? I hear they're having a special on—"

"Wait, wait. Let me guess. Jack Daniels?"

"Damn! You ruin all my fun."

* * *

The youthful, dark-suited security man at the *Casino del Mar* entrance came off more like a college senior posted at the doorway to the Junior Prom, checking students for hidden bottles of booze. Rizzo expected to find the person in the role to be the size of an NFL lineman. So much for hotel security.

Flo took Rizzo's arm and he guided her past the dark suit. The room opened into a blaze of lights, noise, and movement. They kept to a leisurely pace, passing the blackjack and poker tables in the middle of the long room. He took an inconspicuous peek at the three blackjack dealers and picked out his man with no difficulty. Players of both sexes crowded the craps tables, and the din of chatter and laughter convinced Rizzo everyone was having a happy time losing their vacation money.

Mid-way into the room, a tall man with silver hair, wearing a gray suit, blue button-down shirt, and striped tie, stepped from a cluster of people. He stopped in front of them, and with a smile, he reached out to Rizzo. "Good evening. I'm Hector Ruiz, one of the casino's floor managers. "Your first visit to Casino del Mar?"

Rizzo shook his hand. "Uh-huh."

He suspected the floor manager possessed a photographic memory if he recognized everyone new entering the casino. Or, perhaps Rizzo and Flo came off like small-town rubes lost in the big city.

"Welcome. If you have questions or need help with anything, we're here for you. Are you staying here at the hotel?"

Rizzo hesitated. *Too many questions.*

"We are," Flo answered, gifting him with her most gracious smile.

"Well, that's swell. So have fun, you two." He waved and disappeared into the crowd.

"My, they're very friendly here," Flo said.

"Yeah, friendly like a loan shark."

They strolled through the maze of slot machines and paused in front of one blinking its display of multicolored lights like a desperate street hooker. The ambient noise and the chattering players surrounding the bank of machines produced a carnival-like atmosphere.

"Want to try your luck?"

She studied the machine for a moment. "Where's the lever? What do you pull?"

"No levers. You're thinking of those old-fashioned One-armed Bandits. Today, all you do is press a button. Computers power them. Works the same as the old ones. If you line up certain combinations of symbols, you win. The less likely it is to line up a particular set, the higher the payout."

"Don't we need coins?"

Rizzo checked the instructions on the face of the machine. "Nope. Takes paper money. Ones, fives, tens, twenties. I got a hunch this one's a winner." He slipped a five-dollar bill into the slot. "Take a seat. You can wager as little as a quarter or any amount up to five dollars. If you hit, you're rewarded according to the amount you bet."

Flo exhausted the investment in no time. She'd gambled in conservative fifty-cent increments and received a modest payoff after three rolls. She was in the red when Rizzo took out another five-dollar bill.

Flo waved it away. "No more. I don't have the patience for this. Let's go get my Jack Daniels." The corners of her mouth shaped a grin. "At least I know it'll return a better dividend."

Chapter Thirty-Three

Rizzo tossed the guidebook onto the bed. "I've read enough ancient history for today. "Let's head into the old city. Do a walking tour. Later we can have lunch down there. I found an interesting restaurant in the guide."

"Give me a second to put on lipstick."

"Wear your sneakers," Rizzo called to her. "You'll be more comfortable in them than in shoes."

The uniformed doorman at the hotel's entrance signaled for a taxi. They piled in and Rizzo told the driver, "Drop us where the old city starts."

"*Si, señor.* In front of *Castillo de San Cristóbal.*"

"That's the old fortress, *El Moro*, right?"

"No, no. *San Cristóbal* is a different fort. *El Morro* is behind the city."

The scenic ride from *La Concha* followed Ashford Avenue past the many hotels of the *Condado* district. Once over the bridge spanning the lagoon, the taxi hugged the northern ridge of *Avenida Muñoz Rivera,* running parallel to the Caribbean, passing a series of commercial structures and modern government buildings, all flaunting tropical colors. They exited the taxi in front of *San Cristóbal,* the fortress, and Rizzo said to the driver, *"Muchas gracias."*

Flo looked at him and smiled. "My goodness, darlin', you speak such wonderful Spanish."

"Learned from a drug dealer I busted several times back in New York. He always thanked me that way."

They crossed the cobbled surface of *Plaza de Colón* and arrived at *Calle San Francisco,* the beginning of San Juan's historic quarter. Centuries-old art déco buildings flanked the ascending cobblestone streets leading up to the sprawling expanse fronting El Morro Castle. The sidewalks were narrow, wide enough to allow a single-file passage, and the uphill climb became a test of stamina.

Halfway, Rizzo noticed Flo's pace slowing.

"Can we rest a moment?" she asked. "I'm out of breath."

"Okay. We'll take a break here. The café I read about is around the next corner."

Rizzo stood with his back to an ornate wooden doorway. He checked up and down for anything suspicious. He saw nothing but other tourists and multi-colored, three and four-story structures bordering either side. Many buildings were in disrepair, commercial establishments gone belly up. Several appeared in a state of renovation.

Those with completed renovations stood out in their elegant restored appearance. Their stucco facades painted shades of pale blue, green, yellow or white, and the balconies on the upper floors framed with latticed ironwork railings caught the attention of tourists snapping photos. The structures reminded Rizzo of those in the French Quarter of New Orleans.

"Ready?"

"Ready," and Flo stepped off with a refreshed bounce.

They arrived at the next cross street, *Calle del Cristo,* and turned the corner. Rizzo examined the building number and realized the café was farther up three more streets. They continued the hike, passing open doorways to restaurant kitchens, inhaling odors of tantalizing Spanish cooking, hearing indiscernible shouts of waiters to cooks busy at their ovens and ranges. Rizzo's hunger grew with each step.

The Bookstore Café across from the *Plaza de San José* was a combination lunch place, library and performance studio. A hostess escorted them past the front counter, through a line of tables bordering both sides of the narrow aisle, toward a table at the rear of the restaurant. Antiqued brick covered the left wall from floor-to-ceiling, making an interesting backdrop for several funky photos hanging on carpenter nails. Along the right side, a glass-windowed wall separated diners from a room of bookshelves, upholstered sofas and chairs, and a tiny raised stage with a microphone stand.

Rizzo's guidebook described this as *a performance area where one could enjoy listening to readings presented by San Juan's literary set – Unique and popular with the locals.* Their server informed them the readings took place in the evenings. Maybe, he thought, he'd suggest returning tonight after dinner and take in the performances.

Both ordered the same light lunch: a salad with avocados, tomatoes, walnuts, and feta cheese, washed down with a glass of strawberry iced tea.

Flo commented, "It's not exactly what you'd call an authentic Spanish meal."

"Just as well," he told her as he handed the server the check with his credit card. "We need to save our appetites for what I've planned for tonight."

"Oh, are you going to share it with me?"

"Not yet. But according to what I've read, you shouldn't be disappointed."

"Another Rizzo plum, plucked from your handy-dandy tourist guidebook?"

"Yep."

Upon leaving the café, Rizzo suggested they walk the two streets north to visit *Casa Blanca*. "It's the home of Ponce de Leon, the island's first governor. "Historic, and almost five hundred years old."

"Hey, I once toured the historic Hemingway House in Key West. It turned out to be a rundown shack. So what shape do you expect this *Casa Blanca* to be in? It's way older than Hemingway's house."

"Woman, it's a museum, now," he said, ignoring her comparison. "Have you no sense of history? Gardens, fountains in the courtyard, and . . . ." His voice trailed off when he saw Flo laughing. "Okay, smarty, you got me. Let's get outta here, go back to the hotel and jump in the pool. I'd prefer seeing you in a bikini, anyway."

* * *

Ralph Brancuso stood mid-plaza behind the full oak tree that occupied the forward area of the square. He watched the couple from his position, entering the café. Behind him, on a white pedestal base, a bronze statue of Juan Ponce de Leon dominated the rest of the plaza. Both of the old markers, oak tree or statute, provided adequate cover should Rizzo and his wife stroll in his direction after leaving the restaurant.

He wore a white Guayabera shirt hanging out over his baggy Levi denim pants. The shirt covered the 9mm Glock tucked into the belly holster. His wide-brim Panama straw hat pulled down over his eyes gave him the appearance of a native gentleman out for an afternoon constitutional.

The agent walked to one of the paint-flaked benches scattered about the plaza and sat. He leaned back, ankles crossed, and examined his surroundings.

He pondered the enormous infrastructure changes he'd witnessed around San Juan since his last visit. The progress astonished him. As a Navy lieutenant serving in intelligence, he recalled how much he enjoyed the city during his three-month TDY assignment attached to the Naval Air Station at Roosevelt Roads. He'd been sent there to take part in a military mission, charged to help Puerto Rico deal with drug trafficking, illegal immigration, and other problems. That was twenty years ago.

Thinking of the FBI's current joint operation about to go down, he wagged his head in wonder. He turned and looked back at the statue of Ponce de Leon and laughed. "Yeah, the more things change, the more they remain the same. Ain't that so, Juan?" The statue failed to answer.

* * *

The night cooled by the time they exited the Bookstore Café. It was close to ten o'clock. The nighttime clientele noticeably changed from what it was earlier over lunch, consisted of fewer tourists and more locals.

"This was a fun way to cap off our romantic dinner," Flo said. "I'm glad you suggested coming here for the readings."

"Something different."

"I loved my dinner at El Convento. You were kidding, weren't you, about the restaurant being a house of prostitution before it became a convent?"

"That's what I read in the guidebook. And now it's a first-class hotel and restaurant. See, it goes to prove, all sinners are redeemable, including me."

The area around the plaza was deserted and dark, leaving them with little chance of finding a cruising taxi. Rizzo remembered seeing a taxi stand at the bottom of Calle San Francisco. He took Flo by the arm. "Come on. It's all downhill from here," he said with a chuckle. "Walking down should be easier than the climb up this morning." They went single file over the narrow sidewalk of del Cristo, passing the few open stores still hoping to catch the late shopping tourist.

"I liked the second poet, the guy with the beret. He was the best of the four presenters," Flo said over her shoulder "At least, I understood the poem. Perhaps it was the way he read it. Did you enjoy the readings?"

"Not the poems. I've never been hot for poetry. I liked the long-haired hippy, though. The scene he read from his journal made me think of Ken Kesey's *On the Road.*"

"That was Jack Kerouac. Kesey wrote *One Flew Over the Cuckoo's Nest.*"

"Never read it, but I saw the movie. I do remember reading *On the Road.*"

They neared the corner of *Calle San Francisco* and prepared to turn south. Twenty yards ahead on the opposite side of *del Cristo*, a dark figure peered out of a doorway. Rizzo caught the movement in the low-level streetlight. He didn't process the threat until it was too late.

A short, youngish male, dressed in dark jeans and a black tee shirt, rushed into the street. He crossed over and stopped in front of Flo and Rizzo. He was a kid in his early twenties. But the stiletto in the young punk's hand, catching a flicker of moonlight, said he intended to cause harm. He pushed Flo against the building. Holding her, he flourished the long blade at her neck.

"You give me your wallet," he demanded, ignoring Rizzo.

Taken by surprise, Rizzo stepped back. Before the kid could utter another word, Rizzo lunged toward him. He shot a right fist to his temple, the blow sending the punk to his knees.

"Luke, watch out," Flo shouted.

Rizzo turned his head in time to see another kid rush from the same doorway. He came at him with a two-foot-long pipe. The Sig Sauer 9mm was out of Rizzo's holster in a flash. He pointed it at the second attacker. "You better understand English because I'm not saying this in Spanish. One step closer, and I'll blow your fucking head off." The kid stopped and lowered the pipe. No translation necessary.

The first attacker struggled to get to his feet. Rizzo dropkicked him in the chest and sent him face down to the curb and the knife flying from his hand. "I suggest you stay there," Rizzo said and picked up the weapon.

With both kids at bay, Rizzo couldn't decide what to do. He couldn't hold them for the police without compromising his cover. Besides, turning them in would be a waste of time. He remembered the statistics offered by Fields of the rampant crime that permeated the island. Arresting these two would do zilch to affect those numbers. They'd be out on the street in the morning.

"Okay, here's what we're gonna do," Rizzo said, leveling the 9mm at the one standing. "First thing, lay the pipe on the ground." The kid complied immediately. Rizzo looked at the one stretched out at the curb. "Get up. Take your buddy by the arm and waltz your asses up the street. Don't stop until you reach *La Fortaleza*. Then find a church to thank God I didn't shoot you or turn you in."

Rizzo held the pipe and stiletto and watched the kids slog their way up toward the Governor's Mansion at the top of the street until they were out of sight. He pocketed the knife and tossed the pipe into a dumpster at the base of a building under renovation.

Looking back to Flo, he said, "You okay?"

"Yes, but God that was scary. What's with my strange magnetic attraction to people with knives? Lucky I had my personal action hero with me."

"And he's taller than Tom Cruise. Now, let's go find a taxi."

* * *

Ralph Brancuso, tucked away in a doorway at the darkened southwest corner of *Calle del Cristo*, laughed as the two young punks passed him on their hike up to *La Fortaleza*, their heads lowered like an army in retreat. He admired the swiftness of

Rizzo's handling of the two attackers, and glad the man hadn't needed him to step in. Rizzo was fun to watch. Brancuso followed down *Calle San Francisco,* quietly tailing Rizzo and his wife, thinking of how much Jack Fields was going to enjoy hearing about the incident.

* * *

Rizzo and Flo entered the hotel and headed toward the lobby bar already populated with guests.

"We'll have a couple of pops here," he said. "Calm us down a bit." He edged her toward two stools at one end of the bar that a young couple just vacated. "And later we can wander through the casino, test our luck again. Okay?"

They climbed up on the stools, and Rizzo caught the barman's eye. "The lady will have a Jack Daniels . . . rocks. I'll have—ah—you carry a non-alcoholic beer, don't you?"

"Yes, sir. Becks, Coors or Bucklers."

Rizzo hesitated. "Never heard of Bucklers."

"Dutch, a tasty brew with a wheaty flavor. Only 150 calories."

"What the hell. I'll try it."

While they waited for their drinks, Flo said, "That's funny."

"What?"

"Something you said. It seems funny, that's all. Even though you no longer drink liquor or beer, you continue to use that old-fashioned word."

"What? You mean, pop? Hey, old habits die hard."

"You miss it?"

"Oh, yeah. Beer, not the hard stuff. I learned back in my AA days, there's no halfway when it comes to alcohol."

Flo's wistful eyes scanned his face. Rizzo leaned over and kissed her. "It's not that bad."

"I know." Then casting him an impish grin, she added, "And don't forget all the fun you're having from Big Jack without having to drink it."

The barman arrived in time to overhear Flo. He held up their drinks in front of them as though he was trying to remember who gets what. A knowing smile crept into the corners of his mouth. When he set the drinks on the bar, getting his delivery right, Flo applauded.

Off to one side, through the wall of glass, Rizzo could see the pool, hear the swooshing sound of the waterfall behind it, and inhale the lemon and mint aromas of the surrounding tropical vegetation. He considered this assignment the cushiest in all his years in law enforcement. It was the honeymoon trip he and Flo never had. Thanks to Fields and the FBI, they were floating in luxury.

His attention wandered around the lobby, taking in the hotel's beauty. A warm glow of contentment enveloped him. Across the floor, his gaze landed on a man who looked familiar. A short person wearing a Panama hat tugged down over his eyes who entered the hotel from the street. Rizzo was too far away to get a good read on his face before the man vanished into a waiting elevator.

At ten-forty, Rizzo finished a second Bucklers, and Flo still had some left of her Jack Daniels. He slid down from the bar stool and said, "Wait here a minute while I go up to the room and drop off my friend in the safe." Without waiting for her reply, he dashed off toward the bank of elevators.

"You ready?" he asked when he returned and signaled to sign the check.

"Yep. And I'm feeling lucky."

"Hold that thought. What should it be? The slots or a couple of hands of blackjack?"

"I'm not great at cards. Let's stay with the slow-witted game."

Hector Ruiz, the floor manager, gave them a smile of recognition as they made their way into the casino. This time, Rizzo smiled back. They passed the blackjack, poker, and craps tables, strolling arm in arm, and headed toward the armada of slot machines. On this pass, Rizzo didn't glance at the undercover. He'd check him on the way out.

The casino was crowded, more so than on Monday night. They found a vacant machine seductively blinking its bright, multicolored lights.

"Isn't this the same one we used last night? Flo asked.

Rizzo scanned the line of bandits. "They all look alike. I think this was the one."

Flo sat and rubbed the side of the machine with her open palm.

"What are you doing?"

"I'm warming him up. See if I can tease him into a more giving mood."

"Why not? Works on me," he said with a chuckle. Rizzo slipped a crisp ten-dollar bill into the slot. "There, this should light his fire."

After forty-five minutes of Flo oohing, aahing, moaning and giggling, plus an additional ten-dollar contribution, she punched the "cash-out button" and took the ticket to the cashier's window to collect her fifteen dollars.

At the elevators, Rizzo said, "Not bad. At least you didn't lose the whole twenty."

"And think of all the fun I had."

"I saw that. Those noises you were making turned me on."

"So?"

"You're right. It was worth the investment. We'll cash in again when we get upstairs."

Chapter Thirty-Four

R ising early, Rizzo went down to the Avis desk in the hotel lobby to order a car. He requested a mid-size vehicle. The clerk, upon learning Flo was a member of the family—an Avis supervisor at New York's La Guardia Airport—upgraded them to a new lipstick-red Ford Mustang, no extra charge. Rizzo thought the agent would comp him. He thanked him anyway and accepted the upgrade. The FBI was paying the tab, so why should he worry?

* * *

A twenty-dollar bribe didn't cut it. Brancuso failed to learn from the Avis agent in the hotel where the renter of the red Mustang headed. The eastern end of the island was all the information the clerk could give him.

After Rizzo left the Avis parking lot, Brancuso started up his rented plain vanilla Chevy Cruze and pulled away from the curb. He dropped back to a safe distance and followed. The red Mustang stood out on the highway, making it easy to tail. He knew sooner or later slower traffic would get between them and become a problem. He wished he knew their destination.

* * *

The road trip to the *El Yunque* rainforest was not the scenic one Rizzo expected. A dense range of high-rise apartment houses and office buildings crowded both sides of a modern highway until they were beyond the city limits. Farther out, they connected with Route 3, a two-lane road in poor condition, and they traveled over miles of potholes and broken pavement until they arrived at the rainforest.

* * *

Brancuso noticed once the Mustang reached the secondary road of Route 3, it dropped down to a manageable speed and navigated the rough surface. He stayed safely behind, always keeping them in view. He saw Rizzo make a right at an intersection with a billboard on one side of the road marked *El Yunque*. The turn led to the rainforest, and he knew following them was going to be hard work, if not impossible.

* * *

After a morning of meandering around a mere fraction of the rain-sodden wilderness covering forty-four-square miles of fantastic forest and spectacular waterfalls, Rizzo presented Flo with his next surprise idea.

"It's twelve-thirty. How about we drive to the *El Conquistador* Hotel over on the coast? We can lunch at their cliff-top restaurant and enjoy what the guidebook called one of the most glorious views on the island?"

"Is it far?"

"Not according to the Avis guy. He marked the route for me on this map. Said it would take about a half hour. Want to do it?"

"Well, I'll admit this moisture does wonders for my complexion, but I'm soggy down to my sneakers. Yes, let's go."

Rizzo put the Mustang's top down to allow the sun's rays to bathe them in welcoming warmth. He drove northeast toward the tip of the island, and once back onto Route 3, Rizzo followed the signs to Fajardo, the fishing town the hotel overlooked.

At the *El Conquistador* signboard, he took a left off Route 3 and navigated local roads for the next five miles. Rizzo guided the Mustang over the rising roadbed, taking the bending and twisting turns like a race car driver. At one intersection, Rizzo missed the signpost pointing in the hotel's direction and had to backtrack.

"Are you practicing for the next Indy 500?" Flo asked.

"Sorry, hon, am I going too fast?"

Flo nodded and Rizzo slowed down.

Soon, the road leveled. "We're getting close," he said, indicating the steep sloping swath of green ahead. A section of the hotel's golf links bordered each side of the road. Twin fairways broadened on the horizon. One spilled down from an incredible height on the left, a second on the right appeared as if someone painted it on the sidewall of the mountain. Neither fairway afforded the poor duffer a flat lie.

Rizzo parked the Mustang in the lower parking area. A four-seater golf cart awaited and shuttled them up to the *El Conquistador's* grand entrance. On their walk through the hotel lobby to the outside restaurant, Rizzo inspected the elegant interior and décor.

"The description in the guidebook said they'd completed construction of this place fifty-eight years ago. Obviously, they've done much upgrading, but I'm amazed. So much of what appears to be the original elegance and beauty of the hotel has survived. Usually hotels this old become dog-eared after a time."

Around the tiered terraces of the restaurant, fluted columns supported trestles of colorful flowers. Beige sandstone, multi-storied wings of the hotel flanked both ends of the terraces.

Rooms with windows and balconies facing the Caribbean side provided guests with spectacular views.

A hostess showed them to a table on the second terrace. Rizzo picked up the menu, but his attention detoured to the stunning vista before them. From high atop their mountain perch, he squinted at the island of Vieques and its national wildlife refuge. Farther out at twelve o'clock, the smaller island of Culebra appeared beneath wispy bands of low hanging clouds. The blue of the sky and the water matched. He hoped Flo was enjoying the scene.

Rizzo's attention returned to the menu, and a disturbing visual popped into his head. Prior to leaving the hotel, he made a careful study of the map. With the briefing in Jack Fields's office a fresh memory, he grasped the reality of what lay below all of this ethereal beauty. Somewhere, 250 feet down at the water's edge, in a hidden inlet or structure, the Ortega cartel was probably preparing go-fast boats to smuggle a ton of cocaine into the US.

How many of the hotel's employees, or for that matter, the residents of the town of Fajardo, were aware this tropical paradise served as the launching spot for most of the drug trafficking from Puerto Rico into the States? And what would Jack Fields say if he found out he and Flo were eating lunch so close to the FBI's golden prize? He wouldn't tell.

* * *

It was ten-fifteen when they entered the casino. They had dined in Serafina, the hotel's Italian restaurant, where neither enjoyed their dinners. "Hey, you want good Italian, you gotta be in New York City," Rizzo told Flo.

He passed the blackjack section and spotted the knot in the dealer's tie. Still a four-in-hand. They reached the rows of slot machines, and a worrying feeling struck him. Was he checking out the wrong guy these past three nights? He'd spent hours in his office studying the man's photo, committing it to memory, and he was confident he would have no trouble recognizing the dealer and identifying the knot. Could he have missed seeing the Windsor knot? No, he was sure he hadn't missed it. He would take a second look on the way out just to be certain.

Rizzo slipped onto the seat of a slot machine at the end of one line. "Let me try out this bad boy. Maybe he'll be more generous."

Flo sat at a vacant machine next to him. "Good luck, Beauregard."

Forty-five minutes and twenty dollars later, he cashed his ticket at the window for a one-hundred and seventy-five dollar payout. "Well, that covers dinner. Let's hurry upstairs for dessert."

On their way to the casino's exit, Rizzo paused at one of the blackjack tables. Floor manager Hector Ruiz stood nearby, talking with an overdressed woman who looked like she could have been a hooker. Rizzo took a position behind a seated player, affecting the pose of a curious onlooker. He scanned the card action in front of him and stole a peek at the undercover two tables away. Satisfied he'd been looking at the right man, he examined his tie. No Windsor knot.

Rizzo breathed a sigh of relief. He caught Ruiz's stare when he turned away. He smiled and shot him a friendly wave. Overcome with euphoria, he hurried to catch up with Flo. Why wouldn't he feel a high? He'd beaten the slots for a hundred and seventy-five bucks, plus received visual confirmation his eyesight was still 20/20. And he wasn't suffering dementia.

Chapter Thirty-Five

Rizzo sat on the edge of the bed while Flo coated his back and shoulders with a spray of Solarcaine Aloe. The result was like an ice-cold blast hitting a wall of burning flesh.

"Hon, I wish you listened to me this morning. I told you twice to put on your shirt."

"Yeah, I know, I know. I didn't think I'd burn so quick."

"This tropical sun is strong and works fast. You were on the beach chair for quite a time. I should have covered you with the towel."

"It's not blistering, is it?"

"No. Not yet, Mr. Red Lobster." Flo carried the Solarcaine into the bathroom. "At least there's no medicinal smell. You need another spritz, it's in here."

"Hey, it appears I'm not the first person to underestimate Puerto Rico's sun. The store in the lobby is loaded with the stuff."

Flo stood next to him. "Did the cool shower help? They say you should do that when you burn like you did."

"Yeah. It took the sting away. Soon as this stuff dries, I'll put on a shirt, and we can go down for dinner."

"Should we order from room service? Stay in tonight?"

Rizzo broke into a grin. "What an interesting idea."

"Stop smiling. You're in no shape for that."

"I'm fine. Should I call down to Perla, find if we can book a table? Unless you prefer going Italian again?"

"I'd rather not."

"Good, and after dinner, we can hit the lucky bandit in the casino. Maybe coax a few more bucks out of him."

* * *

Hector Ruiz was nowhere in sight. His night off, Rizzo thought.

It was nine-twenty and his shoulders itched from the burn.

"We won't stay long," he said.

Rizzo led the way along the right side of the casino at a leisure pace, avoiding the blackjack tables. Going by the crowded roulette area, excited bettors shouting encouragement at the twirling wheels caught their attention. They continued to the clusters of slots in the rear. Rizzo lingered for a moment to glance across to the blackjack tables. He recognized the dealer from the back of his head.

Zeroing in like a heat-seeking missile, Flo dashed ahead for the unoccupied machine from Rizzo's prior night's success.

"He's been waiting for you," Flo said when Rizzo arrived. She gave the machine an affectionate pat as he sat down. Peering over his shoulder, she recited in his ear, "Round and round they go. Where they stop, nobody knows."

Rizzo turned his head and grinned. "You're getting into this, aren't you?"

"Just trying to add a bit of color to the game, that's all."

Without warning, he cupped his mouth with his hands and shouted. "Innkeeper, drinks for my men. We ride tonight," and slid a ten-dollar bill into the slot.

Thirty minutes and thirty dollars in the hole, Rizzo decided it was not his night. He directed Flo to sit. Another twenty went into the machine. On her third roll, Flo scored big time with five matching icons. Lights flashing and whistles blowing, she hit for three hundred and twenty-five dollars. Mesmerized, she sat gawking at the noisy display of her triumph while Rizzo whooped and hollered behind her.

A man in a suit jacket and tie came over. "Yippee, we got a winner. Congratulations."

Rizzo gave him a wary once-over before he realized the man was one of the other floor managers. He relaxed and said, "Thanks. Beginner's luck. Gets us even for the year."

"Beats losing," the man said with a smile. "Good job," he told Flo as he moved off toward the noisy roulette tables.

"Let's quit," Rizzo said, "while we're playing with house money. We'll have a nightcap before we head up to the room. Okay?"

She sat frozen, her eyes glued to the display screen.

"You alright?"

"I think so. I'm . . . well, I never won this much money in my life . . . at anything."

"Yeah, you have. You won me, and I'm worth a buck three-eighty."

Flo gave him a dreamy smile. "Yes, you are." She rose to her feet and kissed his cheek.

"Hey, the ticket. Push the cash-out button."

"Oh, my, I almost forgot." She pressed the button and retrieved the ticket. "Let's go get my money and a Big Jack. Drinks are on me."

They glided past the blackjack tables. Rizzo glanced at the undercover dealer and stopped dead. The Windsor knot—he was certain. His system ignited with an adrenaline rush. He came close to tripping when he hurried to catch up with Flo.

With painful impatience, he waited at the casino window for Flo to cash out, struggling to keep his excitement in check. His work in narcotics involved him in many successful drug busts. None with the enormity and importance of what his next phone call would initiate. The throwaway cell phone, the note with the telephone number and fictitious name awaited him upstairs in the room safe. His heartbeat increased. *Don't rush. Don't be obvious.*

In an effort to keep with the routine he established over the prior four days, they stopped for a drink in the lobby before going to their room. He sat at the bar fidgeting with his coaster and drinking a Coke. Flo was well into her Jack Daniels. She held the barman's attention as he smiled, indulging her while she chatted on about her success in bringing the one-armed bandit to its knees. Rizzo was certain it would be the highlight of her trip.

She drained the last of her Jack Daniels, and Rizzo said, "Let's go, I got a call to make."

"My, aren't you the impatient one?"

"That, too."

* * *

Ilya Bodrov had landed in San Juan the day before. He found the envelope left for him at *La Concha's* front desk. The envelope contained a hand-written note in Spanish. In his hotel room, he pieced together the message using the Spanish-to-Russian pocket dictionary purchased earlier in Miami.

The note instructed him to meet a contact in the *Plaza de Colón* in Old San Juan the next night at ten-thirty. *Wait at the base of the statue of Christopher Columbus*, it read. The message failed to identify the person Bodrov was meeting and gave him no clue how to verify the contact's authenticity.

"Assholes," he scoffed. "Incompetent amateurs." Nothing compared to the many operations he conducted for the Russian FSB.

To be on the safe side, Bodrov arrived at the plaza an hour early to await the contact. He assumed whoever they sent could identify him. At least, he hoped so. The contact would then take him to a location where he would count and confirm the forty bales of cocaine.

With an hour to kill, Bodrov spent the time in a café across from the square, eating a light meal and sipping strong, black Puerto Rican coffee. At ten-fifteen, he ambled over to the statue.

The night air was sticky but cool. Bodrov wore a pair of cargo trousers and a lightweight safari jacket over a short sleeve cotton shirt. He had insisted on being armed in Puerto Rico, and in spite of Umberto Salazar's initial reluctance, the boss man arranged for one of his contacts in San Juan to deliver a weapon to Bodrov's hotel room late last evening. The safari jacket he wore hid a 9mm Beretta in a shoulder holster under his left arm. A silencer sat deep in his cargo pants pocket.

The Russian stood at the base of the Christopher Columbus statue, taking in the surroundings, smoking his French cigarette and checking his watch. The light-stanchions around the perimeter of the plaza flickered through tree branches shifting in the occasional cool breeze. To his left, a queue of taxi vans appeared on the side of the square. He looked at his watch again. Ten-thirty-five. A wave of concern flowed over him.

The plaza, populated with fun-seeking tourists, was active at the late hour. Two pre-teen girls darted past him, giggling like champagne bubbles at their own humor, with a pair of concerned parents in pursuit. "Don't go too far ahead," the mother called out.

In a moment of nostalgia, the children incited thoughts of Bodrov's now-deceased wife and their frequent discussions about raising a family. How different their lives might be today, he thought, if she hadn't been unfaithful.

At ten-forty-five, he spotted a man nearing him from between the stand of trees ahead. Bodrov's attention went on alert. His hand slipped under his safari jacket, waiting, fingering the grip of his holstered Beretta, tasting something bitter in his throat.

The stranger wore torn khaki pants, a striped Guayabera shirt hanging over his waist, and a dark blue New York Yankees cap turned sideways on his head. He stopped a few feet from Bodrov.

"Taxi, *señor?*"

Bodrov measured him for a moment, trying to determine if he wasn't merely a driver from the taxi stand hustling for a fare.

"No, *gracias*. I wait for someone."

"I think not," the man countered in a forceful voice. He gestured to the queue of taxis. "You come with Pedro. *Si?*"

Bodrov remained with his hand under his jacket, his fingers resting lightly on the Beretta. *Is he my contact from the cartel? What idiots. If their instructions contained a password, I would not have to second guess.* Bodrov scanned the plaza. No one noticed them.

"Where do you take me?"

"To count. *Es verdad?*"

Bodrov inhaled through his nose and exhaled out his mouth.

"You come," Pedro said, gesturing again to the taxi stand.

His reluctance aside, Bodrov accompanied him through the trees and out to the street. Vans lined up in the queue reached to the corner. Pedro led him to the last vehicle and slid open the side door. Bodrov got in and caught his breath. It was like entering the locker room at the Luzhniki Sports Stadium in Moscow where, in his youth, he played football. The van's interior smelled of sweaty socks and unfinished takeout dinners.

Nearby, the drivers of the other vans chatted and smoked, ignoring Pedro and his fare. Bodrov suspected they were aware of his business. They were careful not to show him any unwanted attention. Pedro backed up the van and pulled out on the street. Bodrov spotted one of the drivers raise his head to look and snap it back down.

* * *

The van turned the corner at *Avenida Ponce de Leon* and headed east toward Bodrov's hotel. Instead of going over the bridge into the Condado district, Pedro continued straight. He followed *Avenida de la Constitucion* for several miles before connecting with Route 26E. Bodrov remembered his taxi driver used this same route yesterday from the airport. They passed the airport exit, and Bodrov wondered how much farther they needed to travel.

He leaned forward and spoke to Pedro. "How long we go?"

"*Treinta minutos, más o menos.*"

Bodrov sat back and watched the scenery change. The landscape devolved from luxury high rises to low commercial structures. Once outside the city limits, it became miles of dense vegetation. Lights were visible from an occasional patch of seamy-appearing houses and storefronts. The road surface became rougher the farther they traveled from Old San Juan.

After thirty minutes of driving, Pedro slowed and pulled off the road, stopping on a gravel surface at what was once a gas station. Two corroded pumps stood in front of the tumbledown structure. Bodrov looked at his watch. The time was close to midnight. He looked around and saw no signs of life.

Pedro opened his door, causing the van's interior light to go on. The driver stayed in his seat and reached his arm back toward Bodrov. "You wear this," he said. A black sleep mask dangled from his fingers.

Bodrov's eyebrows jumped. "Fuck is that?"

"You wear to counting place. Location is secret." Pedro gave him a flinty glare.

"Bullshit!"

"You no wear, you no go."

The Russian clenched his teeth. He slumped back into his seat and beat his fist against his thigh several times, then bent forward. "Damn! Give me."

Once Bodrov masked his face, Pedro closed his door and drove onto the highway. He took a sharp left turn on a secondary road and navigated through a series of turns while the terrain rose and fell under the vehicle.

Even if I could see, I would not know where I was. What fools, these people.

The long, undulating descent ended when the road leveled out and the van moved along a sandy surface. The sound of lapping waves hinted they were close to their destination. Bodrov could taste the moist air coming through Pedro's opened window. He needed to leave the smelly vehicle and stretch his legs.

Gravel pelted the under chassis of the van before it turned right and stopped. Bodrov reached to remove the mask and hesitated when Pedro cautioned, "No touch. *Momentito.*" Pedro got out and crunched around the gravel to the other side. He slid open the door. Taking Bodrov by the elbow, he tugged him from his seat into a standing position.

"Welcome," a voice in perfect English said. "He can remove the mask now, Pedro."

Bodrov pulled off the mask, and Pedro took it from him. He blinked in the darkness, waiting for his eyes to bring his greeter's face into focus.

A tall, middle-age man with silver hair and a pale complexion stood before him. His business-like attire—a dark suit, white shirt, and a solid tie—surprised Bodrov. He couldn't help being amused by the man's appearance. It was polar-opposite to the ratty pants, sweaters, and hats worn by the underworld characters of his Russian past during these kinds of covert operations.

The man greeted Bodrov with a handshake and a smile. "I'm Hector Ruiz. Forgive our method of delivering you to this place. Not too disagreeable, I hope, but I'm sure you can appreciate the need for absolute secrecy and tight security. I trust Pedro was a courteous escort."

Bodrov imagined he'd entered a James Bond movie. No Russian black marketer, drug-dealer or hired assassin he knew ever behaved in the polite manner of Hector Ruiz.

"Yes, yes. Everything fine. Long ride, no problems."

"Well, why don't we go inside?"

Behind them, tucked between clusters of mangroves, a weathered boathouse with a peaked roofline appeared at the edge of the shore. Ruiz guided him across the sandy surface to the rear of the wooden structure.

Positioned at the entrance, several men with AK-47s slung over their shoulders smoked and spoke in low voices.

Bodrov trailed Ruiz into the lighted boathouse and surveyed the interior. A raised platform ran along each side and across the back of the structure, forming a U. The platform supported the boathouse over water and rested on cement pilings sunk deep in the mud. A narrow wood deck extended out from the center, dividing the interior in half and creating separate berths for two boats. Both berths were vacant.

Bodrov said to Ruiz, "The boats?"

"We bring them in tomorrow night. Then we load the bales and prepare the go-fast boats for launch at midnight."

Ruiz pointed to the two rust encrusted tarps covering a pair of waist-high mounds. They sat on wood pallets at the rear corners of the building. A folding chair and a table with a writing pad and pencil were placed inside the doorway.

Moving toward the doorway, Ruiz poked his head out and called, "Chichi, Armando, *ven aquí, por favor.*" He turned to

Bodrov. "They're stacked in a way to provide easy visibility for your count."

Chichi and Armando peeled back the tarps and revealed the cocaine bales. After folding the covers, they carried them outside. Before leaving, they hefted both pallets away from the wall to allow 360-degree access.

"Is there anything else you might need?" Ruiz asked.

"Nothing, I think."

"When you finish, and if you're satisfied the tally is correct, we will need you to sign a release. Pedro will drive you back to your hotel. I'll be outside if you require anything else," Ruiz said and stepped through the door.

Bodrov nodded and wrinkled his brow. *And I count less than forty, maybe Pedro loses me in the ocean.*

Chapter Thirty-Six

The young waiter placed the espresso in front of him. "Would you like juice with your eggs Benedict?"

"Orange," Bodrov said. "How long it takes?"

"Not long. Ten minutes."

He reached for the free copy of *USA Today* he picked up entering the breakfast café on the mezzanine level. His stomach rumbled to remind him he should have come down earlier. The late-night return journey got him to bed close to three in the morning. The result was he slept longer than was his habit and, despite the extra hours, woke up exhausted.

The newspaper flattened in front of him, he read the headlines on page one. Nothing interested him. He pushed the paper aside. Bodrov's glazed eyes stared out over the mezzanine's railing while he thought about his journey to the boathouse. He never worked a clandestine operation like last night's without other FSB agents to back him up. The tension he experienced throughout the trip hadn't yet passed through his nervous system.

The waiter arrived with his food. "Would you like something else?" he asked, and he set the plate in front of Bodrov.

The aroma from his breakfast order floated to his nostrils, intensifying his hunger. He shook his head, waved off the server and dove into the eggs Benedict.

Breakfast finished, he sat back, waiting for the check, drumming his fingers on the table with growing impatience. He knew Salazar would be anxious to hear from him. The man, always uptight, would be eager to learn how the inventory went. The Swan was to set sail in twenty-four hours from Aruba for the rendezvous point in the Caribbean.

Bodrov gazed around the lobby. The mezzanine-level café gave him an unobstructed view of the front desk. In his groggy state, he almost missed seeing the couple turn from the concierge podium and walk toward the elevators.

He studied them and an image formed. The photos Ivan, his bungling shooter, took of the detective with his cell phone. Incredible, Bodrov thought. Not twenty feet away the same man stood at the bank of elevators. He was sure it was him.

The waiter arrived with his check and Bodrov signed it. He hustled from the mezzanine café down to the concierge podium, where he waved with impatience to the young woman at the desk.

"Excuse me," he said when she came to the counter. "That man just here. I find his watch in beach chair this morning. I don't know name. I wish to return."

The clerk smiled. "Oh, you mean Mr.Rizzo. I suggest you leave the watch at the front desk, and they will contact—"

"No, no, I want to give to him myself. Where they go now?"

"I don't know," she said. "I saw them walk toward the elevators. They might have gone back up to their room."

"What is number their room?

"Oh, sir, we're not permitted to give out the room number of our guests. If you leave the watch—"

302 - CROSSING INTO DARKNESS

"No!" he said, raising his voice, unable to control his frustration. He realized he had frightened the young lady and apologized. "I am sorry, Miss, I scare you."

The clerk smiled. "That's alright, sir. No problem. Why don't you try waiting by the elevator bank? I believe they'll be down soon. They planned to taxi to Old San Juan to visit *Castillo de San Cristóbal.* At least, that's what they were inquiring about."

"Oh, Miss, thank you. And again, I say sorry." Without waiting for a response, Bodrov hurried back to his room and placed the call to the Swan.

"Yes, forty bales," he told Salazar. "They load boats tonight."

"They weren't on the go-fast boats when you counted them?"

"No boats in boathouse. Only two stacks. Twenty each. Boats come tonight."

A long pause. "I hope all forty make it aboard. No way to verify they do. Maybe you should be there tonight when they load." Another pause. "On second thought, forget it. I don't want to raise a question of distrust. It's too early to start that."

"It's okay, Umberto. I sign release form say I count forty. I have a copy. Boss guy, Ruiz, also sign copy."

"Well, shit! If they did shortchange the shipment, who the fuck you think the Sinaloa people gonna blame? Form or no form." Another long pause. "You got anything else?"

"One more thing, Umberto. You remember that detective, Rizzo?"

"What about him?"

"I see him this morning . . . here in hotel. On vacation with a woman."

The phone went silent.

"You gotta be wrong."

"No, Umberto. I am sure."

"I can't believe it. You suppose there's something to it or just a coincidence?"

"Don't know. You want me get rid of him?"

"Jesus, are you fucking nuts? Don't do a goddamn thing. They catch you, you fuck up the whole operation down there."

"Okay, Umberto."

"When do you leave for Miami?"

"Flight tomorrow night."

"Good. Phone me after I return on the Swan next week."

Bodrov disconnected the call and unlocked the room safe. He took out his holstered Beretta, strapped on the weapon under his cotton safari jacket, dropped the silencer into his pocket and turned for the door.

* * *

The taxi dropped off Rizzo and Flo at the bottom of the ramp. A slow one hundred-yard climb brought them to the visitor's entrance of *Castillo de San Cristóbal*, the enormous cliff-top fortress that repelled the British invasion of 1797.

"I love this kind of history," he said when she asked him why he wanted to visit an old castle. "The guidebook's description got my juices flowing. I can imagine me as one of those colonial soldiers loading cannons and firing shots across the bow of a British ship."

"Ah, ha! A regular Walter Mitty."

Rizzo laughed. "My secret life."

Entrance fee paid, Rizzo looked around and asked at the counter why the castle appeared to be light on visitors. The attendant explained the school year was back in session, and they were into the slow season. "Try being here in August," she said with a laugh.

Rizzo picked up an illustrated brochure and led the way through the museum rooms filled with various historical photographs and memorabilia. They followed the route suggested in the brochure, touring the castle's multi-layered expanse where thick inner and outer walls fortified each level.

Battery placements with pyramid-stacked cannonballs dotted the perimeter, creating great backdrops for tourist photos.

Rizzo found the Spanish Musketeers' meager barracks interesting. He confessed he'd go AWOL if he had to live there. Next, Flo insisted on visiting the Santa Barbara chapel in the main plaza to offer a few words to the Musketeers' favorite saint.

They climbed to the second level and came upon the two massive wooden doors protecting the original formal entrance to the fortress. Lined up across the front, five life-size fiberboard cutouts of Musketeers stood at attention.

The Musketeers, dressed in the colonial blue and white uniforms and bicorn hats of the late 1700s, guarded the castle's historic portal. Flo snapped a photo of a grinning Rizzo posing with his arm around the shoulder of a soldier.

"Do I look like I could be a member of this regiment?" Rizzo asked.

"Did they have lackeys in their ranks back then?"

"Hey, just because my uniform is at the cleaners—"

"Enough, soldier! Let's move on."

They crossed the grassy parade grounds toward the entrance of a darkened underpass constructed by the Spanish to link the fort to various defensive positions around the perimeter.

Flo hesitated at the opening. "I'm scared. It's dark in there."

"Not to worry, sweetheart. I'll protect you," Rizzo said, giving it his best Bogart imitation. She held tight to Rizzo's arm and let him pull her into the passageway.

They traveled through the semi-dark underpass, over the rising and falling cobbled surfaces, stopping once to catch their breath. Despite the eighty-degree temperatures outside, the air inside cooled them like an efficient air conditioner.

Rizzo paused under a dim overhead light, holding the brochure up to his face. *The tunnels were built to provide protected movement of troops and artillery.* A sudden knotting in the back of his neck brought him up short. *Shit! We're in the wrong place if someone is stalking us.*

He jerked his head around when he caught the echo of footsteps approaching from the shadowy passageway ahead. Rizzo brushed his arm across his middle, over the 9mm Sig Sauer tucked in the belly holster. When the footsteps took on a human form, Rizzo's hand slipped under his shirt. A dumpy man dressed in walking shorts and wearing a backpack appeared, and with a polite smile, continued past.

Rizzo glanced at Flo, wondering if she'd picked up on his sudden concern. "Come on," he said and took her by the arm.

He guided her to one of the many exits and out in the bright tropical sunshine on the fort's empty upper battlements. Rizzo tossed a glance back at the exit opening. Was the man who passed them in the underpass another tourist? Rizzo wasn't letting his guard down. He watched the exit for a moment with his hand back under his shirt. No one emerged.

At the western-most corner of the castle, they lingered in front of the three-foot-wide, waist-high perimeter wall overlooking the Caribbean. A circular stone sentry box with a domed roof was tucked into the crook of the wall. The box showed battle scars from over two hundred years of enemy attacks.

Rizzo surveyed the empty battlement area again. A six-person tour group and their guide went by without stopping and disappeared behind an inner wall.

He pointed west toward another historic fortress a half mile away. "The *Fortaleza San Felipe del Morro*," he announced. "The Spanish built the fort to guard San Juan's harbor. Took them two hundred years to complete."

"Oh, my. Are we planning to visit that one too?"

Before he could reply, a loud voice came from behind.

"Mr. Rizzo."

He turned toward the sound. The speaker stood at the tunnel exit they just came through. Rizzo looked hard at him and then stiffened. Not the walking-shorts man. Someone else, someone taller and with a weapon in his hand.

Who the hell is he?

His first notion was an undercover agent from the local San Juan police providing security for the landmark castle. It wasn't until the stranger stepped forward and raised the gun that Rizzo saw trouble.

"Now we find how clever you be," the man called out.

The voice rang with familiarity, and his identity flashed alive. The Russian, Ilya Bodrov.

Rizzo exploded, grabbed Flo by the shoulders and spun her around. She took a sharp breathy intake of air. "In there. Stay down on the ground," he shouted and he pushed her into the safety of the narrow sentry box interior.

With the 9mm Sig Sauer in his hand, Rizzo leaped onto the perimeter wall and ducked behind the sentry box. A muffled round ricocheted off the crown of the box. He crouched, not moving, and waited. The one hundred and fifty-foot drop to the waters of the Caribbean loomed behind him. The parapet's three-foot-wide surface provided him no wiggle room.

Another muffled shot pinged off the dome, scattering stone fragments out into the water. *He's waiting for me to stand, the bastard.* The sentry box shielded Rizzo's left flank. His unprotected right side concerned him. The Russian had him pinned. He couldn't see Rizzo and Rizzo couldn't see him. Unless Bodrov moved to the right of the wall, neither of them would have a clear shot. He concentrated the Sig Sauer in that direction.

Edging to the right, he peered around the top half of the dome. Bodrov hid somewhere out of his line of sight. A third bullet ricocheted off the stone box close to his head. Rizzo pulled back in a hurry. He was at a disadvantage, having no idea of the man's position on the battlement.

The Russian didn't fire again. The silence worried Rizzo. Out of patience, he stepped off the wall and flattened against the right side. He leaned out and spotted the Russian on the left, creeping along the low wall toward the sentry box doorway.

Panic raced up Rizzo's spine. *He's going after Flo.*

Desperate, Rizzo moved out into the clear. He raised the Sig Sauer to eye level and paused. A booming shout reached him from beyond the Russian. The shout came from behind the pyramid of stacked cannonballs fifteen yards away and sounded to him like the voice of God.

"Ilya Bodrov, put down your weapon. This is the FBI."

The Russian whirled and fired three rapid shots at the voice. Bullets ricocheted off the cannonballs with a series of high pitched pings. Bodrov turned and saw Rizzo.

Rizzo, out in the open, with the Sig Sauer clasped in both hands, squeezed off two rounds before Bodrov could fire. One of the shots missed wide. The second caught Bodrov on the right side of the chest. The impact spun the Russian's body and sent him falling back across the top of the stone wall.

The FBI agent raced out from behind his cannonball protection and sprinted toward Bodrov. "Rizzo, hold your fire. Jesus, hold up, will you?"

Rizzo gaped at the lawman in full stride. *What the hell is Ralph Brancuso doing here?*

The Russian's legs were about to follow his torso over the wall when the agent, covering the last three yards in large strides, dove, catching Bodrov by one ankle before he could disappear into the blue waters of the Caribbean.

After dragging the body away from the wall, Brancuso let the Russian's wrist thump to the ground. "Fucking dead." He looked up at Rizzo and saw Flo standing beside her husband, his arm draped over her shoulder. "Oh, sorry about that, Mrs. Rizzo. I didn't see you."

Flo forced a grin but remained silent. Her eyes were glazed with tension.

Brancuso rose to his feet and faced Rizzo. "That was good shooting."

"Luck."

"Yeah, timely luck," Brancuso said with a nod. He cast a look at Flo. "He might have reached your missus."

Flo shook, and Rizzo tightened his arm around her. "No way was I gonna let that happen." His eyes carried down to Bodrov's inert body, and he fought off the urge to slam his heel into the Russian's head.

Brancuso scanned the area, squinting into the shadowed corners of the battlement. "We got a few problems here."

"I guess we do," Rizzo said, exhaling a sigh.

"Number one, we need to move him fast, out of sight and into that sentry box before a tourist group comes strolling through and freaks out."

Rizzo hefted Bodrov under the arms while Brancuso caught him under the knees. They slow-walked the body inside the box and laid him at the back end of the interior.

The agent stepped outside. "Our next problem," he said, taking in Flo's panicked expression, "is the local police. We call them now, how do we explain what went down here, why he was stalking you?"

"How about we finish the dive over the wall? Leave him for the fishes? No one would—"

Flo reeled around. "Luke Rizzo, you wouldn't."

"I'm only kidding, sweetheart. Besides, the noble Federal Bureau of Investigations would never do something like that."

"You got that right," Brancuso said, "much to my chagrin."

"Can't you get Sanchez on the horn—ask him to handle it with the locals? I'm sure he can come up with something."

"That's what I'm about to do. Another problem though is Umberto Salazar. Why was Bodrov here in San Juan? What role did he play in the cocaine shipment? And would being missing set off alarms?"

"Maybe Sanchez comes up with a plausible explanation?"

"Let's hope so. No point in you two hanging around. Go back to your hotel. I'll call you after we clean up this mess."

"You alright with that?" Rizzo said.

"Yeah. Without you here, me and the bureau can take the rap for shooting Bodrov. He was a sex trafficker, down here to recruit. I tailed him from Miami. Cornered him here, and he fired at me. That's what I'll tell the police. Sanchez will back me up. Leave me your weapon. I'll return it later."

"Sure, but I owe you at least a dinner. Where are you staying?"

"Same hotel as you."

"No shit? You been following me all this while?"

Brancuso grinned. "Not so's you'd notice."

"Were you aware Bodrov was also on my tail?"

"I didn't know he was in San Juan until I spotted him coming out of the underpass."

"Damn glad you did. We'll look for you at the *La Concha* bar." Rizzo turned to leave and discovered Flo was already on her way toward the exit.

Rizzo reached her on the sloping walkway leading down to the street. He took her arm and stopped her. "Are you okay?"

Flo spun around. "I have never been so scared in my life. I can't stop shaking." Her face drained of color, and when he pressed her to his chest, she vibrated with fear.

"I never . . . I mean, this is the last thing I expected. I'm so sorry, sweetheart."

"Stop. It's not your fault." Flo swallowed hard. "I'm upset because . . . I mean, God, I never witnessed anyone killed."

The weight of guilt shook Rizzo. "This damn job. I should have followed my first instincts and not taken you with me."

Flo pulled back. "Stop it! You couldn't have known this would happen." She wiped the trickling tear from her cheek. "I'm over it. Look at me. I'm over it." A weak smile formed. She palmed away another tear.

"You're gonna be okay?"

"Yes, but I need a Big Jack now."

"We'll take care of that when we get back to the *La Concha*." Rizzo smiled. "Did you enjoy our little historical adventure?"

"I could have done without the experience, but I'm sorry you didn't have time to fire a cannon."

"It was too late, anyway. The Spanish already sunk all the British ships."

"Foiled again, *El Capitan*."

* * *

The multi-story office building in Hato Rey, home to San Juan's eleven police precincts, housed a myriad of specialized units. The building also served as Headquarters for the Puerto Rico Police Department. Ralph Brancuso found the well-known location with no problem.

Police Superintendent Emilio Sanchez leaned forward over his desk, trying to keep his voice low even though he'd closed his office door. Brancuso sat facing him, his eyes on the superintendent's lips, his ears primed, so he wouldn't miss a word.

"I requested Colonel Mendez, the commanding officer of the San Juan region, to accompany the investigating officers to *San Cristóbal*. I wanted to stress confidentiality in handling the situation. I hope he accomplished that?"

"He did, keeping questions of the officers to a minimum. Your uniforms were effective detouring tourists out of the area until they bagged the body and hauled it off. The two investigating officers with him were polite, more so when they heard the shooter . . . me, was FBI and on a case."

"I gave Colonel Mendez that story," Sanchez said.

"Does it end there?"

"Yes, if no one inquires of Bodrov's whereabouts. In light of his real purpose for coming to Puerto Rico, I doubt that would happen."

"Then you know why he was here?"

"Yes. We spotted Bodrov when he landed on Wednesday and followed him to the *La Concha,* where he checked in. We've had him under surveillance these past few days. I would have alerted you if I knew you were in San Juan."

"Fields never mentioned I was here?"

"No. I assume Jack had his reasons. Did you know the Russian made a trip to Fajardo last night to inventory the shipment?"

The info piqued Brancuso's attention. It confirmed the launch would be from that area, making the task of tracking the go-fast boats easier for the Coast Guard's two CBP aircraft.

Sanchez explained, "One of the cartel's taxi drivers we have in our confidence took him there. We didn't follow him because we knew why Bodrov was making the trip."

"Jesus, you guys are thorough."

Sanchez laughed. "We try. Sometimes the job is like salmon swimming upstream."

"Been around drug trafficking long enough to appreciate the feeling."

"Did I mention," Sanchez said, "we checked with the airlines? The Russian booked a flight to Miami on Sunday?"

"Aha, so he must have spotted Rizzo and his wife in the hotel this morning and followed them. With the inventory done, he had time to try to take them out before leaving."

"That's the way I read it."

"I doubt anyone will miss him," Brancuso said. "At least not for the next few days, if ever."

Chapter Thirty-Seven

Fields leaned over the speakerphone on his desk. "And you never spotted Bodrov around the hotel?" A note of frustration laced his tone.

"No, Jack. Too busy keeping tabs on Rizzo and his wife. They didn't spend much time in the hotel, where I might have run into the Russian. Christ, next time let's contract someone who's not into tourist traps."

Fields turned to Carter Brooke and shrugged. "Well, I screwed up. I never figured Salazar to send someone down to take inventory of the shipment. I shouldn't be surprised since Salazar wouldn't trust his own mother. So he sent the Russian."

Brooke rose from the sofa and walked to the desk. "Taking him out that way, I assume was necessary?"

"Yes, sir. The Russian shot at Rizzo and me several times. But when he went for Rizzo's wife, the guy gave him no choice. It was the one time he returned fire. Incredible. Two shots, one of them a lethal body shot."

Brooke laughed. "He doesn't fool around, does he?"

"Hell of a marksman," Fields said. "We knew that from having seen his NYPD service dossier."

Fields thought about a question his former sidekick Tony Condon once asked about Luke Rizzo. *Do you think he would make a good agent with the bureau?* Fields remembered saying Rizzo was a tough son of a bitch; still, he didn't believe his M.O. would sit well with the top brass. Fields figured Carter Brooke might feel the same. But the agent would argue this time around, Rizzo was an excellent resource for the FBI.

"The Superintendent effectively finessed the shooting with the locals," Brancuso said. "Now, I'm the shooter. Rizzo wasn't there. He says he now owes me a dinner."

Fields chuckled. "Yeah, just remember, if he pays off, it'll be at our expense."

"I'll find a cheap Taco Bell."

"How about the arrangements with our undercover? Everything set for his extraction?"

"Got me a charter lined up to take us to St. Thomas early Sunday morning. He doesn't work Sunday nights so no one will miss him at the casino until Monday night. We'll lie low in Charlotte Amalie for a day at a guest hotel, the Galleon House. The owner's a friend. I've booked us on a Delta flight to JFK for Monday afternoon."

"When do the Rizzos leave?" Carter Brooke asked.

"He hasn't said. Don't they have an open return?"

"Yes," Fields said. "That's the way we set up their travel because we were uncertain when the launch would happen. He can stay a day or two more if he likes. Make sure he doesn't think he's on an extended vacation. Oh, and find out if he wants me to call him when we board and seize Salazar's yacht tomorrow morning? So he can celebrate."

Brancuso laughed. "Hell, I'm sure he won't mind being rousted out of bed in the wee hours of the morning."

* * *

"Come on, Rizzo, it's only two-thirty."

Raising his head off the pillow, Rizzo peeked at the bedside clock's digital readout. "Yeah, but in the morning, Jack." He rolled over to check to see if the cell phone's ringtone, *Take Five,* woke Flo. It did.

"Who is it?" she asked, her voice full of sleep.

"Jack Fields."

"Rizzo, Rizzo," the agent's impatient voice blasted. "Put your phone on speaker so you both can listen. Curtain time is minutes away."

Still groggy with sleep, Rizzo reacted robotically. He sat up, pressed the speaker-on button, and placed the iPhone on the nightstand. "What the hell is going on?"

"Since you and Mrs. Rizzo did such an outstanding job for the bureau, it's only fair you have a front-row seat to the destruction of Umberto Salazar."

Flo threw off the sheet and sat up on the edge of the bed. Her sleepy expression disappeared, replaced by a look of shock. "Good God, not another death!"

"No, no, Mrs. Rizzo," the agent's voice said. "I apologize. We're not killing him. What I'm talking about is the destruction of the Salazar syndicate, the lawful removal of a vile piece of garbage along with his despicable operation."

"Okay, I'm awake," Rizzo said. "How's this gonna go?" He planted his feet on the floor and sat erect.

"I'm in my office connected by radio to Elias Janner, Special Agent in Charge of the DEA's Caribbean division. He's aboard one of the Coast Guard Cutters approaching Salazar's yacht about two miles off and closing fast. I wanted to put you on the scene by listening to me relay his narration of the operation as it goes down. You interested?"

Rizzo looked to Flo for her reaction. She nodded.

"You got our undivided attention," he said. "This should be worth losing sleep over."

"Roger that. You're gonna love it," and Fields began his narration. "At this point, the pilots of the two CBP aircraft tracked the yacht's journey from Aruba . . . in constant contact with two Coast Guard fast-response cutters along the route. Oh, yeah, here we go. Now the cutters are steaming toward the yacht . . . closing in . . . preparing to intercept."

In the background, Rizzo could make out the crackle of the radio transmission from Janner, the DEA agent. Much like a translator for a foreign speaker, Jack Fields repeated the information the agent fed him with a lag of a few seconds.

Fields continued with his feed. "Two heavily armed Pave Hawk helicopters are hanging back out of sight and hearing. They are watching on their infra-red video. The Swan's crew is now on-loading the bales of cocaine."

The transmission went silent for a minute, then jumped alive with Fields's voice. ". . . aaand . . . the last few bales have now reached the Swan's deck. Crew members are hustling them below into the hold. Everything's secured. Too bad we can't give you a live video feed. Rizzo, you with me?"

"Yeah. I haven't gone anywhere."

"Are you smiling, because I am?"

"Ear to ear."

"Oh, wait. The Pave Hawks are moving in . . . about to swoop down on the yacht. Yeah, there they go. One put a warning shot over the bow of the Swan . . . required by international law. Now the Hawk's speakers are ordering the yacht to freeze. Uh-oh, the two fast boats took off, heading for La Romana. No problem. One of the CBP planes is following them. The Dominican Republic police are ready to take them if they come ashore."

"Is Salazar aboard the yacht?"

"Yes. The helicopter got him on their infra-red video earlier."

The rest of the narration went on for another hour. A Coast Guard crew from one of the cutters boarded the Swan, secured the boat and took over control. By five-thirty Sunday morning, Salazar was in custody. That was all Rizzo needed to hear before he and Flo crawled back under the covers.

Chapter Thirty-Eight

Manny Fuentes, out of character in a blue pencil-stripe, summer-weight suit, and a solid tomato-red tie over a white button-down, strolled up to Rizzo and Flo. They were standing outside the crowded tent in Naples, Florida. If it weren't for the occasion of Bella and Sam's wedding, Rizzo would not have recognized Manny. His hair cut short, his face razor-shaven, his weight ten pounds lighter, the handsome Latino cut an impressive image.

"*Mi amigos*, I'm so glad you guys came down." He grabbed Rizzo's hand and shook it for the fourth time in two hours. The iced daiquiri in his other hand tipped and splashed onto the grass.

Rizzo stepped back and laughed. "Hey, bro, careful. You're wasting the good stuff."

"No worries, I made friends with the bartender. Told him to cut me off after ten. I'm only halfway."

"Your sister, Bella, she's so beautiful," Flo said. "I can see why Sam fell for her."

"Yeah, she smiles a lot these days. I don't have to worry about her no more. That's Sam's job, now."

"Ah, but you still have Rosita to mother-hen," Flo said. "How's she doing?"

"Great. She's in high school. She dropped back a half year to catch up. The other kid, Olga? Returned to Mexico. She's in school there too."

"Your folks here?" Flo asked.

"Yeah. They're sitting inside at their table."

Luis and Carmen Fuentes exited the tent, arm in arm, cut between a trio of chatting guests and approached. Carmen headed straight for Rizzo. She halted in front of him, reached around his neck, pulled him down into a wet kiss on his cheek, leaving her lipstick imprint.

"Wow, what's that for?" Rizzo said when Carmen released him.

"Because you make this happen," Carmen said with a sweeping hand gesture. "No find Rosita, no Bella wedding."

"Not exactly. I suspect Sam had a head-start on the idea."

Luis Fuentes pulled Carmen to him and wrapped his arms around her waist. "I think what she means is the family owes you for all this happiness. Not only for Bella and Sam's but for what the rescue of Rosita meant to all of us. And don't forget Cusack's conviction. Rabbit is smiling, I'm sure."

Hoisting his Root Beer, Rizzo said, "*Tu alegria es mi alegria.* Your joy is my joy."

"Hear, hear," Manny shouted.

Flo smiled. A tear clouded one eye.

Jabba joined the group. "What's all you cheerin' about?"

"A toast," Rizzo said, "to the new couple."

The Rasta smiled like a lottery winner and raised his Bud Lite. "Cheers." He turned to Rizzo and asked, "Hey, Sam told me they conerferskated the big boat, Salazar's yacht. True?"

"That's confiscated, bro. Yeah. The DEA has it up for auction. You interested?"

"Naah, too big for my bathtub."

"That's what they do with the stuff they grab in drug busts?" Manny asked.

"Depends. If the seized boat, car or whatever, isn't in good condition, they trash it. They burn or sink most boats. Yachts the size of Salazar's in mint condition are sold at auction for half their original cost."

"Wow, what a bargain."

Jabba slapped Manny's back. "Yeah, but you need a bathtub big enough. You got one?"

Rizzo gazed around at the guests exiting the tent. He took Flo by the hand and said, "Let's go find the bride and groom. We haven't talked to them since the reception began." They excused themselves and headed in the direction of the tent.

"Nice affair and setting, don't you think? Flo said as they strolled.

Rizzo lowered his head and said in a quiet voice, "This country club owed the boss of Sam's construction company a sizeable debt. The club paid half. His boss picked up the rest."

"How wonderful."

"When Sam told me, I said, 'See, nice guys don't always finish last,' and he laughed."

Flo stopped before the entrance of the tent and drew Rizzo to her. "That was a beautiful toast you made back there, and in Spanish, no less."

"Something else I picked up from a grateful drug dealer I once busted."

Flo grinned. "Come on. The truth."

"Oh, okay. I made a guess Hoya would ask me to give a toast, so before we left, I looked it up. I found it in a Spanish-to-English phrase book."

With a smile, Flo replied, "Hon, I'm sure glad I married you," and she kissed him.

Acknowledgments

I need to thank a few people for their encouragement and help in writing this book. I begin by acknowledging the members of my critique group, Jean, Karna, Jeff and especially author John Wayne Falbey, who was with me from start to finish, providing valuable feedback. I owe a large debt to retired Plantation, Florida, Police Sergeant Richard Vincent and retired NYPD Narcotics Detective Bob Machado for keeping me authentic with references and terms in police work. And where would I be without the sharp eye and patience of my alpha reader, Linda Rennick, a treasured friend and voracious reader of suspense/thrillers? I also need to thank my patient wife, Rita, for her indulgence to serve as my oft used sounding board during the writing process. Lastly, my great appreciation goes to Carole Greene, my agent, and Joe Clark of Blue Water Press for their continued support and belief in me as a writer.

Author's Note

Sex trafficking is a form of modern-day slavery. This crime occurs when a trafficker uses force, fraud or coercion to control another person for the purpose of engaging in commercial sex acts or soliciting labor or services against his/her will. Force, fraud, or coercion need not be present if the individual engaging in commercial sex is under 18 years of age. If you know of any sex trafficking violations or suspect anyone of being a victim of human trafficking, call 24/7 the National Human Trafficking Hotline: 1-888-373-7888.

We hope you have enjoyed Howard Giardono's *Crossing Into Darkness.* Be sure to check out his other titles, *The Second Target* and *Tracking Terror.*

His works can be found with others on the BluewaterPress LLC website at bluewaterpress.com, along with other interesting and intriguing titles from an eclectic mix of subjects.